10:59

N R Baker

Burning Chair Limited, Trading as Burning Chair Publishing
61 Bridge Street, Kington, HR5 3DJ

www.burningchairpublishing.com

By N R Baker
Edited by Simon Finnie and Peter Oxley
Book cover design by Martin Webb and N R Baker

ISBN: 978-1-912946-11-2

This book is dedicated to the millions of people
who make the world a better place

And especially to Connor
who deserves the best world I can give him

'When the last tree is cut, the last fish is caught, and the last river is polluted; when to breathe the air is sickening, you will realise, too late, that wealth is not in bank accounts and that you can't eat money.'

A version of a Native American saying

10:59:01

Tick, Tock, Tick, Tock

Research Vessel Phoenix, *Arctic Circle*

They could quite easily have been killed that morning. The *Phoenix* had been pushing steadily through the slushy pancakes of ice covering the surface of the ocean off the coast of Greenland, and then Mother Nature had decided it might be fun to put on a little display of power. There were a couple of loud cracks like gunfire and the forbidding frozen cliffs suddenly started to deform and shift before their eyes.

'Oh my God, it's calving!' the research assistant had yelled, pointing unnecessarily.

Don 'Mac' McIntyre, the skipper, was already urgently adjusting the ship's controls. While he fought to put a safe distance between their small boat and the collapsing shoreline, the other three members of the crew watched in horrified fascination as an iceberg the height of a skyscraper tore away from the face of the glacier with a primeval groan and began to roll towards them. The thunderous protests of the ancient ice were deafening, and the ocean's usually languid surface exploded into mountainous waves.

It was only Mac's quick reactions and skill that kept the tiny craft afloat; even then, by the time they'd retreated to calmer waters, two of the crew members had been injured. One had been thrown against a rail and was sedated in his bunk with a broken wrist and ribs, awaiting transfer to a hospital the next day, and the other was in her cabin nursing a nasty concussion.

A few hours later, Mac appeared without warning at the researcher's side. 'Time for a dram, Creepy?'

Steve Crawley visibly jumped. 'God, Mac, don't *do* that! After what happened earlier, I'm down to the last of my clean underwear.' He'd been completely absorbed in his work, studying the complex data displayed on the three computer screens in front of him.

'Och, come on, mate. Let's call it a day and have a drink. The ice'll still be melting tomorrow.'

'That's a safe bet,' Steve said, stretching his back. 'How about one of those hot toddies of yours?'

Mac grinned. 'Sure. I'll go and put the kettle on.'

The two men blew steam from the potent drinks cradled in their gloved hands, watching the spectacle of the Northern Lights dance in the darkening sky.

'So, are we still in trouble, then?' Mac asked.

'Yup. The sea ice albedo feedback—'

'Creepy, you know I don't speak scientist. I just drive the boat. Spell it out for me in plain English.'

Steve laughed. 'Sorry Mac. Okay, sea ice is melting at an accelerating rate. We expect a melt every summer, of course, but the sea ice up here in the Arctic never disappears entirely. Previous estimates indicated that we could be looking at an unprecedented complete melt by the end of the century, but some people reckon it could be as early as 2050. Worryingly, my latest data supports that view.'

'And then sea levels rise, right?' Mac took an appreciative sip of his hot whisky.

'Actually, no. Sea ice is already floating and displacing its own weight,' Steve said.

'Ah, okay. Like ice cubes in a drink.'

'Exactly. When the ice melts, the level of the drink stays the same.'

'Not in my glass, it doesn't. So I'm okay to buy myself a wee place on the coast, after all?'

'I wouldn't, if I were you.' The humour faded from Steve's eyes. 'Problem is, the thick ice sheet covering Greenland is melting, too. That's about three million cubic kilometres of ice that's *not* already floating in the ocean. And within the last few years we've been seeing completely new phenomena, like changes in the characteristics of the ice. It's terrifying, actually.'

Mac frowned. 'When you science types start using words like "terrifying", it's time to worry. So what happens if it all melts?'

'All the ice on Greenland?'

'Aye.'

Steve sipped his drink and then said grimly, 'Global sea levels would rise by more than six metres.'

Mac considered the implications of this. 'So your professional advice would be to base my retirement plans on a mountain retreat, then?'

'Definitely. Although, if sea levels rose that much, it would also mean major changes in weather patterns, food chains, habitats...' Steve looked troubled. 'Let's just say it wouldn't be a good idea for a polar bear to start reading a long novel.'

Mac was silent, staring warily at the massive glaciers that loomed off their port bow.

*

A classified location in North Korea

'Do you think he'll ever actually press the button?'

Ri Joo-Won's colleague glanced nervously around the empty corridor before answering quietly. 'I hope not. But who knows?'

'I don't think he will. I reckon it gives him a rush just knowing that he *could*.'

'Shh! Don't talk like that. You know they listen to us.'

Ri Joo-Won made a rude hand gesture, but he held his clipboard up so that the surveillance cameras wouldn't see it. 'This isn't what

I wanted to do when I was studying. I'd have chosen a different path if I'd known I'd end up babysitting a load of nuclear missiles that will probably rust in their silos without ever being used.'

The second man, Mun Chong-Hae, used his pass to let them out of the restricted area and waited until they'd turned a corner in the next corridor before responding in hushed tones. 'You talk like you *want* him to launch them.'

'Maybe it wouldn't be the worst thing. The West is always posturing and threatening, poking their noses into the rest of the world's business, while their wasteful consumer lifestyles are bleeding the planet dry. Maybe it's time the balance of power swung our way.'

'But they'd retaliate.'

'Not if we take out their missile sites first.'

*

London, England

The Houses of Parliament may look impressive from the outside, but inside most of the offices are as mundane as any others. Jayne Fletcher-Harris had lofty ambitions, proud parents, and a first class degree in law and politics, but she spent most of her waking hours traipsing up and down on threadbare carpets and cracked linoleum tiles, running errands for the Secretary of State for the Environment, and questioning her life choices.

Her current boss, The Right Honourable Philip Deakins MP, had only been in the post for four weeks and was struggling. Jayne might have been more inclined to help him if he spent less time staring at her chest. She fastened the top button of her shirt before knocking on his office door and entering.

'Ah, Jayne,' he said. 'You're a sight for sore eyes, as always. Is that a new blouse?'

She ignored the question and his leering smile. 'Sir, here are the latest bulletins on the climate change protests. They're ramping up again, with more civil disobedience planned for this Friday. The

PM has sent a reminder that your report and proposals are needed ahead of questions in the House.'

The Environment Secretary took the file from her with a loud sigh. 'Bunch of hippies,' he muttered.

'Sir?'

'It's Greenham Common all over again. I suppose you're too young to remember that nonsense.'

'We read about it at uni. Weren't they protesting about nuclear weapons, not climate change?'

'Oh, they're all the same, these people. Misguided do-gooders with their banners and their dungarees, thinking they're saving the world when in fact all they're doing is stopping decent law-abiding citizens from getting on with their jobs. It's a phase, that's all. Main thing we need to do is minimise disruption until it blows over.'

'Didn't the Greenham Common protests go on for nearly twenty years? And actually, sir, a lot of the climate change protesters' concerns are fully supported by scientific evid—'

'Good lord, Jayne! Anybody'd think you were on their side. Besides, this is politics, my dear girl. Give it a few more years and you'll realise that facts have precious little to do with anything. Now, if you wouldn't mind rustling up a cup of Earl Grey and one of those nice pastries with the almonds, that would be splendid.'

Jayne was glad to leave his office. No wonder the country was in trouble: run by patronising, hypocritical, lecherous old sods like him. He'd been Secretary of State for Transport until the cabinet re-shuffle a month ago; he knew precious little about transport and even less about environmental issues. She thought about taking him to a tribunal for being ageist and sexist. Instead, she got him normal tea instead of Earl Grey and one of the apricot pastries she knew he hated, and then emailed her CV to an employment agency.

*

Deonar Dumping Ground, Mumbai, India

Kamya woke up before dawn on her seventh birthday and put on her bright yellow dress.

Early mornings were the best time. Beams of hazy sunlight reached out to touch the towering dunes of rubbish as if they were something beautiful, and you could even pretend they were real mountains. Later though, the heat would become vicious and the choking fumes made you feel dizzy.

Kamya was a clever girl. She knew which items were worth the most money and, with her small fingers and sharp eyes, she was good at sifting through the treacherous waste piles. She had never known a world without flies and the stink of dirty nappies and rotting food, so these things didn't bother her; but she was careful around syringes and broken glass.

When she had filled the first sack with plastic bottles, she dragged it back to where her mother was working with some of the other adults from the slum. Kamya knew that her mother was ill, but the traders who paid a few rupees for the bags of recyclable materials at the end of each day showed no compassion towards those who did the dirty work. There was no sick pay or health insurance for ragpickers, so you worked or you starved.

When Kamya had filled the second sack, the sun was high, and it was getting hard to breathe at the dumping ground. She hauled her burden over to the adults. Her mother was lying on the ground like a bundle of dusty rags among the other rubbish. Kamya knew a dead body when she saw one. Her mother was thirty-two years old. It wasn't a bad age for a ragpicker.

As she tenderly placed an old newspaper over her mother's head to shade her face, Kamya's huge brown eyes filled with tears. She couldn't read, so she had no idea that the headline announced 'India Bans Imports of Waste Plastic'.

*

Long Island, New York

Roger Vee did the usual sum in his head to check the time difference, before picking up his phone and selecting a London number from his contacts list. He sighed heavily and looked out of his window, feeling the full weight of this dreaded moment. The moon was bright above the trees at the end of the garden, casting long shadows and silver light across the lawn, and his office in Manhattan seemed a million miles away.

'Roger? It must be the early hours of the morning there. Is everything all right?' The soft female voice was full of genuine concern.

'Hi, Eve. Yeah, I wanted to catch you first thing. Are you free to talk?'

'Yes, you picked a good time. I'm on my own in my office, just going through some emails. What's up?'

'I've just been reading the latest report from the Arctic research vessel we sponsored.' He paused.

'Oh dear. Bad enough to give you a sleepless night, huh?'

'Absolutely, but it's not just that. It's all of it. Everything's escalating. It's happening, Eve. We have to—' Roger broke off, and Eve waited while the man she knew so well drew an unsteady breath on the other end of the line. 'I'm not sure we can afford to wait any longer. Please tell me I'm wrong, but I think we have to set Plan B in motion.'

The gravity and regret behind Roger's words were tangible on the opposite side of the Atlantic. The woman in London closed her eyes for a long moment.

'Eve? You still there?'

'I'm here. It's just… I hoped this day would never come.'

'We all did, Eve. We all did.'

10:59:02

Screaming

Dad's favourite t-shirt says, 'I don't need Google. My teenager knows everything.'

It's not true. We don't know everything.

I think it's just... Well, we're discovering that nobody else knows everything either. The people we believed were the founts of all wisdom — our parents, our teachers — aren't as smart as we thought they were. Suddenly there's stuff we know that they don't, and we realise everybody's basically blagging it. It's kind of exciting and kind of terrifying, all at once.

And when our hormones aren't confusing the hell out of us, the things teenagers know are clear and certain. Our edges haven't yet been worn down by relentless propaganda and worrying about whether we can afford the rent this month. Our potential hasn't yet been tamed by the mundane reality of having to think about what to cook for dinner every single night. Our dreams haven't yet been dulled by wondering if the car's going to get through its next MOT. We're sharp and sure, and we don't yet believe the people who tell us it can't be done. Of course, having the confidence to do anything useful with all that is a different matter—

A scream stabbed my daydream. Such a shrill and unnecessary sound, demanding attention. I'd always thought people only screamed like that in films, but this was a proper real-life one. It was quite impressive, actually. I leaned over to look past my dangling feet, down into Cuthbert Street nine storeys below me, wondering what the drama was.

Another hideous shriek. Blood-curdling, some would say. My blood seemed okay, but the noise did sort of set my teeth on edge. Someone must be getting murdered at the very least.

I looked around. There was the usual bunch of six or seven lads hanging out by the steps that led into the flats: Flaky Ollie and his cronies, messing about on skateboards. They were a couple of years below me in school and fancied themselves as hard cases. Flaky Ollie had really bad eczema, poor kid. He was a total prat though. Apart from them and a couple of women nattering in the doorway of the chippy over the road, all I could see were the tops of people's heads as they walked quickly past. It wasn't the kind of neighbourhood you really wanted to hang around in. But no murders in progress, no flashing blue lights. Another non-event in Mareton. Big surprise.

I'd been sitting on the concrete for quite a while and my backside was starting to go numb, so I stood up from my favourite perch on the edge of the flat roof. There was an Oscar-worthy scream this time and I finally spotted its source: one of the chippy doorway natterers. I knew it was her, because now she was in the middle of the pavement, pointing up at me. The other woman was standing behind her, talking animatedly into a mobile phone.

I sighed. Why couldn't people just mind their own business? I was so tempted to wind them up, give them something to really squeal about. I could balance along the edge — I'd done it a hundred times before — and pretend to wobble a bit, wave my arms around. But then the cops would arrive and there'd be a huge fuss, and I couldn't be bothered with all that, to be honest.

I backed away from the parapet so that the women couldn't see me. They meant well, but I hated busybodies. Just because someone was sitting on the edge of a roof didn't mean they were contemplating suicide; I'd been perfectly happy until that stupid

9

woman interrupted me with her irritating nonsense. I bet she didn't scream at people waiting for trains just in case any of them were thinking of launching themselves onto the tracks. Or maybe she did. When she wasn't too busy spoiling people's fun on Cuthbert Street, maybe she hung around in supermarkets screaming at people buying paracetamol, on the off chance that they were considering necking the whole packet.

I picked up my rucksack, knowing I'd have to go downstairs in case the police turned up. I heard sirens in the distance, right on cue.

I came up onto the roof of the flats most days, if it wasn't raining. Heights had never bothered me, and it was difficult to find somewhere to be alone in a town like this.

Mareton used to be small, apparently. I'd seen photos in the town museum taken in eighteen-oh-something, when it wasn't much more than a fishing village. I couldn't get my head around that. Now it was a big sullen coastal town, dominated by industrial buildings and loads of copy-and-paste nine-storey blocks like ours. It wasn't a seaside resort by any stretch of the imagination: Mareton straddled a muddy grey estuary and had no beach. It was the kind of place that had probably never looked clean and new, even when it was clean and new. The perpetual breeze did a better job than those pathetic little street-sweeping machines, tidying all the cigarette ends and discarded wrappers — idiot droppings, Mum used to call them — into litter-drifts that were a permanent feature of every doorway and corner. The few trees in the town, brave splashes of dusty green, had the melancholy air of zoo animals, as if they yearned for the dense forests that had once existed there before the tide of concrete swept in. And noise cluttered the atmosphere: droning traffic, shouting people, moaning sirens, yapping dogs, wailing alarms, thumping music; even at night the town was never silent, and the snoring of freight trains was added to its repertoire.

So yeah, just about the only way to find anything resembling peace around here was to get up on the roof.

I reluctantly headed inside and started down the stairs,

having closed the door carefully behind me. Needless to say, you weren't *supposed* to go onto the roof, so there were big red dangerous-looking signs on the inside of the door as a deterrent, saying 'EMERGENCY ACCESS ONLY' and 'THIS DOOR IS ALARMED'. The door hadn't been alarmed in all the years I'd lived in the Cuthbert Street flats. Mildly perturbed perhaps, in a high wind, but never alarmed.

You could see a lot from the roof. Lots of houses, lots of streets, lots of shops, lots of cars, lots of rubbish, lots of people.

Too many people.

*

'That you, Louis?'

'Yeah Dad.' I aimed my reply at the lounge door, loud enough to penetrate the monotonous chanting and commentary of a football match which filled the room.

The soundtrack of my childhood. Despite Dad's encouragement, I'd never understood the fascination. His unspoken disappointment that I didn't share his passion for the sport suddenly weighed on me. I slumped down the corridor and dropped my bag onto my bed. I had a ton of homework to do but I wasn't in the mood. I really hoped they weren't right when they said your schooldays were the best time of your life. I was glad I was nearing the end of my sentence at Mareton School and couldn't wait to turn eighteen. Not that I had even the faintest idea what I was going to do after that.

I kicked off my shoes, turned on my games console, grabbed the controller and sat on the bed to annihilate a few undead nasties before dinner.

Killing virtual zombies did me good, actually. When I checked my watch after what seemed like ten minutes, an hour had somehow whizzed by. By the time Dad called me to the kitchen I was feeling much less grumpy and had nearly started work on a maths past paper. Nearly.

11

'So how's it going, kiddo?' He had his back to me, dishing up bangers and mash.

'Oh, you know, same old same old,' I said, extracting knives and forks from the container on the draining rack. I poured us each a glass of juice from the carton in the fridge and sat down. It was a well-practised ritual. Dad slid a steaming plate onto the table in front of me and then ruffled my hair, his way of showing affection. He could only really do it if I was sitting down these days, as I was taller than him now.

'How's that presentation thing of yours coming along?'

I pulled a face. 'Slowly. I need to do a bit more work on it after dinner. Can't wait for next Thursday to be over.' He, of all people, knew how much I was dreading it.

'You'll be fine, Lou. You'll get through it.' Realistically, that was about the most either of us was hoping for. There wasn't much else he could say.

'Yeah. Thanks Dad. Anyway, how was work last night?'

While we ate, he told me the latest antics of his mates at the factory. I'd never met any of them, but I felt like I knew them from his colourful descriptions. Dad had been promoted to supervisor three or four years ago; it had meant changing to the night shift, but the money was a lot better. Evening meals were the only time we saw each other during the week, and it was nice to chat. I liked listening to his stories.

'So then I hear 'em all chuckling over by the canteen. Steve's got a laugh like a bloomin' drain. Infectious, it is. You can't help yourself. So I wander over there to see what's so funny and as I get nearer, I can hear the new lad's voice coming from inside the kitchen and he's saying, "Turn me on. That's not doing it for me. Come on, turn me on. TURN ME ON!" Apparently Bob G had told the poor kid the new kettle was voice-activated and that's what he needed to say to get it to work. You'd think he'd know by now. It was only last week they sent him to the wholesaler's to buy a new bubble for Steve's spirit level and a set of left-handed screwdrivers.'

After dinner, I washed the dishes and then went back to my

room to tackle the maths paper and do some more on the dreaded presentation. It was the fact I was going to have to stand up and talk in front of everyone that was the big problem. The thought of doing that was literally giving me nightmares. I didn't mind the project itself and doing the research. I knew a lot of my classmates had struggled to come up with their ideas but, for me, that bit had been dead easy. I already knew how to change the world.

What I *didn't* know was how soon the world as everyone knew it would come to an end. I didn't know that the countdown to disaster had begun long before I was even born. I didn't know I'd find myself in the middle of it all.

Dad's t-shirt was wrong. If I really had known everything, I'd have stayed well away from Phoenix. And I'd probably be dead now.

10:59:03

Lambs

The project was where it all started, really. It was set for us by a substitute teacher who we were saddled with after our form tutor went off on maternity leave. Mrs Dench wasn't supposed to finish until the end of term, but she had a problem with her blood pressure or something and she had to leave early. The sub, Mr Jones, was a thin spotty guy with seriously bad taste in clothes and a nervous habit of pushing his glasses up on his nose all the time. He didn't look much older than us and had zero chance of maintaining any kind of discipline in the classroom. We guessed the school had had to take what they could get at such short notice. I felt sorry for Mr Jones — everybody's got to start somewhere — but he looked such a wimp.

'Sit down, please, everyone! I need to do the register.' His voice went high-pitched when he tried to shout. When he opened his mouth on that first day, I thought he didn't stand a chance. Only four people sat at their desks. 'Now, please!' Louder and squeakier. He pushed his glasses up, looking panicky. 'Right, I'm going to call the register and anyone who isn't sitting at their desk when I call their name will be missing break.' The threat worked, despite being delivered in Mr Jones's by now near-soprano voice, and the rest of us slowly took our seats.

'Sunila Afzal?'

'Here, sir.' Mr Jones looked up at Sunila as she answered, wanting to start learning who was who. Sizing up the enemy.

'Peter Bailey?'

Pete gave a casual wave. 'Here, sir.'

'Ewan Booth?'

'Here, sir.'

'Jay Butler?'

'Yup.'

Mr Jones raised his head, frowning, and pushed his glasses up. He hadn't been quick enough to spot the source of the monosyllable. 'Where are you, Jay?'

Jay, at the back of the room, didn't say anything but lazily half-raised his hand. His slouched posture spoke volumes. Mr Jones took one look at Jay's belligerent expression and physical bulk and returned his attention to the register, giving his glasses another push on the way.

'Louis Crawford?'

Everyone laughed. I'd been waiting for it, and had my usual correction primed and ready. Raising my hand, I said, 'It's Louis with a wiss, not a wee, sir.'

I glanced at Jay further along the row, waiting for the inevitable comment. He didn't disappoint.

'Lou*ise*, more like.'

I rolled my eyes.

Mr Jones either didn't hear him or chose to ignore him. 'Ah, right. Okay. Lou-*wiss*. Right.'

I'd asked my dad more than once why my name couldn't have been spelled Lewis, to avoid confusion. Apparently, names had been Mum's department.

Mrs Dench used to be able to do the register in under a minute, but in Mr Jones's inexperienced and visibly shaky hands it seemed to take half the morning. Towards the end he'd abandoned all attempts to stop us talking and was squeaking the last few names through the din like a determined hamster. It was a relief for everyone when he finally finished.

He picked up a trembling piece of A4 paper from his desk and stood, pressing his glasses repeatedly against the bridge of his nose.

'This is a letter from the company, Phoenix. They're sponsoring a—' Mr Jones realised he was wasting his breath. No one was listening. I looked around at everyone chattering away, ignoring him, and I felt kind of embarrassed that we were being so rude. Mr Jones looked flustered. Then he turned around and wrote on the whiteboard in big letters:

'£200 CASH PRIZE'

They say money talks, and it certainly talks much louder than a nervous substitute teacher. The classroom gradually became quiet and Mr Jones allowed himself a half-smile at his small victory. He spoke quickly while he had the chance.

'I'm sure you've all heard of Phoenix. They're sponsoring a project for Year Thirteen students and there's a cash prize of two hundred pounds on offer to the winning entrant from each school. The headmaster has chosen this class to represent Mareton.' There was a chorus of groans but, by mentioning the money again, Mr Jones held the flimsy attention of our unruly group. The silence of the insubordinate lambs. 'It'll be ongoing throughout this half-term, but you all need to get your ideas to me by the end of this week. The—'

At that moment, the bell went for first lessons, a Pavlovian trigger for chaos. Mr Jones looked comically startled. He lunged for a pile of paper on the corner of his desk and raced to station himself in the doorway, where he could thrust a printed sheet at each of us as we left the tutor room.

Why anyone would choose to be a secondary school teacher, I couldn't imagine.

So that was how it all started, for me. I've often wondered if I'd have done anything differently if I'd known then what was to come. Probably not. And at least I survived.

There've been times since then when life seemed a fragile, throw-away thing. But when it comes to it, I guess we're all programmed to want to live. For me, it's mostly just curiosity. I want to know what happens. If I walk out of my own personal movie a quarter of the way through, I might miss all kinds of cool stuff.

10:59:04

Superlogic

I'd always had a problem with school, and school had always had a problem with me.

I reckoned I was basically just the wrong shape. They kept trying to fit me into their neat little pigeonholes but none of their labels would quite stick to me. Between the ages of five and ten I was assessed and tested for everything from dyslexia to ADHD to autism. I can remember wondering why it mattered to them so much and what real difference it would make to me or to them if they did manage to find a label they were happy with. All the grown-ups seemed to think it was important though, so I jumped through their hoops for the sake of a quiet life and just carried on being me.

Since nothing quite fitted, the experts whose job it was to apply the labels ended up hedging their bets by saying I was 'possibly' this (autistic) and 'mildly' that (dyslexic) and 'borderline' the other (ADHD). For a while I thought that was what people meant when they talked about living on the edge. That was me. I was always on the outside, looking in. Not that I can ever remember having any desire whatsoever to be in there with all the 'normal' kids. I was perfectly content to stand back and observe. You learn a lot that way.

I looked up all the terms online when I got a bit older. Attention Deficit Hyperactivity Disorder didn't sound like me at all. Being hyperactive sounded too much like hard work, and I had no problem focusing for hours on stuff that interested me. Autism and Asperger's seemed to be mostly about difficulty with social interaction and abstract concepts; I didn't think I had difficulty with either of those. Okay, so I was no extrovert, but I was perfectly capable of interacting when I needed to or wanted to. Most of the time, I didn't particularly see the point. The kids in my class were muppets, generally speaking, and I knew from personal experience that interacting with them beyond sharing a classroom wasn't an especially rewarding pastime.

I tried to explain it to one of the specialists once, in terms that might make it easy for her to understand. I told her that I chose not to eat gherkins because I thought they tasted disgusting but that didn't mean I had *difficulty* with eating gherkins. She nodded slowly, glanced at my dad, and then carried on as if I hadn't said anything at all. So I didn't bother after that. People are idiots. And if using gherkins to make a point isn't an abstract concept, I don't know what is.

Then when I was ten, of course, any mild or borderline issues I may or may not have had were totally eclipsed by what happened to Mum, and I saw a counsellor once a fortnight for a while. I didn't want to at first, but she was cool. She wasn't bothered about labels or pigeonholes and it was nice to be able to talk about it. Well, maybe not nice, exactly. But I could say the words that Dad and other people couldn't bear to hear.

When I got to secondary school I was suddenly an insignificant fish in a much bigger pond and, from then on, I was pretty much left to fend for myself without the help of any experts, which suited me fine.

I was never a troublemaker. I wished I could be, sometimes, but I was always the kid who bagged a spot at the back of the room and hoped people would just forget I was there. You have to enjoy being the centre of attention to be a troublemaker and that definitely wasn't me.

It didn't dawn on me until I was about fourteen that I must have a sort of superpower. I didn't even know it was a superpower at first. I mean, when something comes naturally to you and always has, you kind of assume that everyone can do it until enough people comment on how unusual it is.

It was a curse rather than a blessing. I'd have rather been born with the ability to spell and read better, if I'm honest. That would've been more useful, and I wouldn't have had to spend an hour a week with Mrs Adams all the way through primary school. She was meant to help me with words and stuff, but she never did, much. She was always kind of angry at me. Not on the surface, but underneath. On the surface she used to say friendly things like, 'Right then, Louis, let's get to grips with some of these tricky old spellings once and for all, shall we?' But there was impatience and irritation oozing out between all of her words and it was totally obvious to me that she was thinking, 'Right then, Louis, these spellings aren't tricky at all for clever people like me. It's just that you're thick, so I'm probably wasting my precious time.'

Anyway, my superpower wasn't one of the cool ones that superheroes have in comics and movies. I couldn't fly and I wasn't super-fast or super-strong or anything like that. Of course not. You have to be from another planet or be in a freak accident involving radioactivity or mutant insects or something for the cool ones.

My superpower was that I could see things that were apparently invisible to everybody else.

I'm not really sure how to explain it. It was as if I was immune to all the irrelevant noise and confusion that other people seemed to get bogged down in. I came to think of it as 'superlogic'. I'd get frustrated when other people ignored facts that were staring them in the face and got their knickers in a knot over trivial stuff. Where was the logic in that? It made no sense to me when they stressed about the results of a problem without tackling the problem itself.

I may have been shy, but I had arguments with my teachers about history and religion. They flatly refused to accept that the books on which they were basing their lessons didn't contain much in the way of facts and were full of biased perspectives and people's personal interpretations of events. We could have had some interesting conversations about it all if the teachers hadn't been so defensive. It wasn't as if they'd written the books themselves. I guess I must have come across as an arrogant little git. I'm sure those teachers were as delighted as I was when I dropped their subjects at the earliest possible opportunity.

When things are blatantly obvious to you, it's not that tricky to predict the future. I don't mean the lottery numbers or anything, but general trends, big picture stuff. I may not have been great at writing stories or spelling, but a lot of maths and science came easily because patterns jumped out at me and I found it simple to predict logical outcomes once I knew the facts. I could look at the world around me and see it in stark clarity as if I had some kind of filter that blocked all the trivia and nonsense that seemed to blind everybody else.

People are fond of telling teenagers that we have our whole lives ahead of us, that anything is possible, that our stories are yet to be written… But I looked at the way my classmates behaved and it wasn't hard to see which ones would have interesting lives, which ones would end up bored to death trapped in a well-paid job because of a huge mortgage and a couple of kids, and which ones would always be bullies.

10:59:05

The Phoenix Project

I remember sitting on my bed reading the paper that Mr Jones had given us about the project and wondering if fate was giving me a chance to use my superlogic to save the world. It seemed a ridiculous thought at the time. I had no idea then how close it would be to the truth.

The photocopied sheet was double-sided. On one side there was the letter from Phoenix and on the back were guidelines for the project and a bit of small print.

I read the letter first. It opened with a paragraph summarising the numerous fields in which Phoenix was involved, from sustainable forestry and water conservation to alternative energy sources and Arctic surveys, and everything in between. It might have been easier to list what they *weren't* involved in. Phoenix was one of those really massive faceless global organisations that everybody'd heard of because they'd been around forever and were always getting mentioned on TV for having their fingers in just about every eco-pie on the planet. Their familiar logo was on the letterhead: a stylised representation of Earth as seen from space, cradled in two hands whose fingers became flames.

I skimmed ahead to the part about the project. It was described as 'a ground-breaking international initiative offering a new generation of world citizens' — I guessed that was us — 'an opportunity to play an active role in creating a more viable future'. Maybe they were running out of ideas. Phoenix had picked schools all over the world — presumably at random rather than on merit, since Mareton School was included — and they were indeed offering a prize of two hundred pounds for the best idea from each school. The letter was signed by someone called Eve Gyer, whose title was given as Regional Coordinator, Southern England, and she would personally be judging some of the shortlisted projects.

It was decent loot for a seventeen-year-old. I paused to consider what I'd do with two hundred pounds and realised I honestly hadn't got a clue. Not that it was likely to be an issue, as I'd never won anything in my life. Actually, that wasn't entirely true. At a school fair a few years back, I'd recklessly decided to gamble some of my spending money at the tombola stall. The table was groaning under the weight of all kinds of goodies and I had my eye on a huge box of chocolates at the back. I picked my tickets from the tub and felt the tension mount as I unfolded them. One of them was a winner and I waited eagerly while the woman behind the stall looked to find the prize that matched it. I could see that it wasn't the number for the chocolates and was hoping I wouldn't get something lame like bubble-bath or notepaper. The woman finally turned around with an unreadable expression on her face and handed me a tin of kidney beans.

I returned my attention to the page about the Phoenix Project and flicked it over. The guidelines were pretty straightforward. Basically, we each had to come up with something that would change the world. We had about a month to develop our ideas and get to a point where we could present them. It was suggested that we should do some research, focusing on the needs or problems that would be addressed. There were no limits on the nature or scope of the ideas, but they would have to have a significant impact and be reasonably feasible. The small print went into specifics about eligibility criteria for the project, things like entrants having to be aged seventeen or eighteen on the judging date, and not being allowed to work in pairs or groups. Participating schools needed at least twenty individual entries, three of which were to be selected by a school judging panel. The woman from Phoenix would be doing the rounds in about six weeks' time to pick a winner from those three.

Like I said, I didn't have to think about an idea to change the world. I already knew exactly what I would do. I'd known for years. It was that time at Auntie Cheryl's that really kicked it off.

I'd always gone to stay with Auntie Cheryl for the Easter holidays. She was cool. She lived about thirty miles away from Mareton but there was a train that went there. Mum used to take me. Dad didn't often come with us because it was difficult for him to get the time off work. I guess we mostly went because it was a cheap option for a holiday, but I loved it there and we always had a great time. I carried on spending my Easter holidays there, even after Mum died. Dad used to put me on the train in Mareton and Auntie Cheryl would meet me at the other end. It helped, afterwards, being there at her place. Remembering. Continuing. It had always been a happy place for me.

Auntie Cheryl lived in the countryside, in a village called Much Wheadle. It was the sort of place they took photos of for the lids of biscuit tins: lots of thatched cottages with white walls and neat little blue doors and flowers everywhere. There was a small church and a village shop and a duck pond and a green, all sort of snuggled up together, and loads of huge trees. If you got anybody to imagine a perfect English country village, they'd basically imagine Much Wheadle.

Auntie Cheryl's house wasn't one of the biscuit tin ones. She lived on the edge of the village in a plain-looking cottage that was joined onto another one. Semi-detached, I suppose you'd call it, although that sounded too urban. The best thing about her house was that it backed straight onto the woods. God, I loved those woods. When I was little, we'd go for walks there and I could run and climb and get muddy. All the things I couldn't do in Mareton. As I got older, the woods were my playground. They were whatever

I wanted them to be in my childish adventures: a tangled jungle where I was stalking tigers and wolves, a magical land of wizards and giants, an alien planet where I had to dart between shadows to avoid death-ray sunbeams. In spring and summer, when we spent the most time at Much Wheadle, the trees were green with promise and the whole place was pulsing with life and begging to be explored. Those woods were my escape from the dead concrete and the traffic noises of Mareton. My sanctuary.

I think I was eight or nine years old when the diggers arrived and kicked off my ideas about how the world needed to change. Mum was already dying by then. She knew it, but I didn't. Not yet. We'd just arrived at Auntie Cheryl's and I couldn't wait to go and explore my woods. I left her and Mum drinking tea and talking, and went through the little gate at the end of the back garden that led into the trees.

I walked until I couldn't see a single house, then stood there with my eyes closed and my head tipped back, taking deep breaths. The air was soft and damp and brown. I wandered around for a while, checking out some of my favourite spots and noticing the changes: the old rotten stump got smaller every year and had a galaxy of tiny mushrooms growing on it, sudden saplings and clumps of bluebells and new animal burrows had appeared, the rope was frayed on the makeshift swing that dangled patiently from the best climbing tree.

Then I went a bit further and in between the trunks there were rumbling and clanking sounds, and the light wasn't as green as it should have been. I stood at the ugly wire mesh fence that now dissected that precious wild place and watched bulldozers biting into the living earth, tearing up the roots of trees that had been friends to a solitary eight-year-old boy. I couldn't bear to see any more and ran, bereft, back to Auntie Cheryl's not-biscuit-tin house.

She stood up as I burst into the lounge, took one look at my face and knew immediately why I was upset.

'Oh Louis, honey! I'm sorry. I should've said, should've warned you. I never thought. Here, don't cry.'

25

'What's wrong? What's happened?' Mum looked worried.

I hadn't even realised I was crying but my words came out as sobs. 'My trees! Why are they doing that? Why are they digging up all the trees?' Mum pulled me onto her lap and mopped my hot tears with a tissue from her pocket. She still didn't understand what was going on.

'It's not all of them. Only up to that damn fence. They're building more houses.' Auntie Cheryl was explaining to Mum as much as to me. 'Twenty-three, apparently, although God knows how they're going to fit that many in there. More identical little boxes, I suppose. Starter homes, mostly. And a few three-bedroom "executive townhouses" if you please.'

'But how can they?' I protested. 'Who let them? How could you let them?'

'Oh, Lou. Poor sweetheart.' Auntie Cheryl crouched down and stroked my damp cheek. 'We tried to stop them; we really did. There were protest signs up all over the place and meetings in the village hall until I was sick of hearing about it.' She sighed and stood up.

'People've got to live somewhere, I suppose,' Mum said, sounding sad and tired.

'I tell you what, I made you some chocolate cake, the way you like it with the soft icing. I bet a piece of that will cheer you up, huh?' Auntie Cheryl beetled off to the kitchen without waiting for an answer.

Mum gave up wiping tears and just hugged me.

It turned out that the neighbouring village kept expanding because that was where the railway station was, and people could travel to work in the big towns and cities but still live in the countryside. They didn't seem to notice that they were slowly turning their nice rural village into a big ugly town. A commuter hub, they called it. And the inhabitants of Much Wheadle with their signs and petitions were no match for the politicians and developers who stood to make lots of money from the starter homes and the executive townhouses and the twenty-three families who would live in them. And so somebody in an office who'd probably never even seen the woods at Much Wheadle had drawn a neat line on a plan and signed the death warrant for nearly half of my trees without a second thought.

My world was suddenly smaller and less magical.

10:59:06

Tick, Tock...

Four-star General William Barrett had been both expecting and dreading this moment for a number of years, and he knew it couldn't be put off any longer. He poured himself a refill of black coffee and settled back on one of the Oval Office couches. As head of America's Central Intelligence Agency, Bill Barrett was effectively one of the most powerful men in the world and now he looked across at the familiar faces of two of the others: Mike Hughes, the Director of the National Security Agency, and Charles Wentworth, the current President of the United States.

There was a fourth person in attendance at this high-level, top secret meeting: an inconspicuous man by the name of Ken Burford, who had worked for Barrett for almost two decades. Barrett trusted him to lead a small, covert division of the CIA that didn't officially exist, and the two of them had put a lot of careful planning into this meeting.

'With all due respect, Mr President, we're going around in circles,' said Barrett. 'And everything we've discussed so far would merely be papering over the cracks.'

'Well come on then, Bill, you called this little confab. Let's cut to the chase. Given the present company, I kinda guessed there was more to all this.'

They'd been talking for nearly half an hour about the critical resource shortages that were affecting several major US cities.

Barrett took a breath and gave a curt nod to Ken Burford, who hadn't so far participated in the conversation very much but had apparently been waiting for this cue. Burford seemed at ease, despite the prestigious company and venue. The truth was that he viewed politicians as a necessary evil and generally had little respect for them.

'Gentlemen, the fact is that these shortages of drinking water, foodstuffs, fuel and so forth — as hard-hitting as they may already be — are merely the tip of the biggest iceberg the world has ever seen. We can no longer ignore the elephant in the room. Fact is, the elephant has run out of room. Our planet can no longer sustain the current human population.'

The President gave a hollow laugh. 'Jeez, that old chestnut. Can't this wait another couple years until the end of my term? Make it the next guy's problem?'

Burford didn't smile. 'I don't mean to be rude, sir, but it's largely because all your predecessors basically said the same thing that we're in this mess.'

Barrett cut in quickly. 'We can't wait. According to our scientists we're already well beyond what they call the STP: the Sustainability Tipping Point. We need to act. And we need to do it now.'

'But there are all kinds of initiatives on the go,' Wentworth protested. 'There are international summits discussing better ways to manage resources—'

'Far too little, way too late,' Burford said bluntly. 'Besides, it's a vicious circle. Governments put pressure on businesses to develop sustainable practices and reduce the drain on the Earth's resources, but there's little real incentive when raw materials are going up in price and those businesses are facing squeezed profit margins and ever-increasing demand from consumers who have their heads stuck firmly in the sand. Let's face it, most people's idea of doing their bit to save the planet is buying free range eggs and recycling their junk mail.'

'So what exactly are we talking about, then?' asked Mike Hughes. 'Population control? One child families and that sorta thing?'

'This is the Land of the Free!' exclaimed Wentworth. 'Damned if I'll go down in history as the President who tried to dictate how many kids people are allowed to have.'

'Sir, if the human population remains unchecked, we're looking at an imminent scenario where people won't have enough food to eat, water to drink, room to live and clean air to breathe.' Burford stated.

'Even here in North America? Really?' Hughes was sceptical. 'I can't believe things are that bad. My local food store always has plenty of stock. At worst, surely it's just a question of redistribution so that everyone has enough?'

'I only wish that was the case,' said Barrett. 'I'm afraid the situation is every bit as serious as Ken's described.'

'But… air to breathe? Isn't that a little melodramatic?'

Burford looked unruffled and about as far from melodramatic as it was possible to be. 'Los Angeles is choking to death. The air in Bakersfield is full of pesticide and fertilizer particulates. I could go on and on. The whole of California has gotten so polluted that people are already dying as a result. And that's only the beginning.'

'Population control, then.' Charles Wentworth rubbed his temples, imagining the headlines. He had four children of his own. 'Some kind of incentive for smaller families, or… what are we looking at here?'

Barrett gave Burford another subtle nod. The conversation was going exactly as they'd anticipated.

'Actually, sir, it's rather too late for that.'

'What do you mean?'

'No matter how effective any population control measures were, and how quickly and successfully they were implemented, they wouldn't make a meaningful difference for several generations.'

'So what are you suggesting?'

'Direct intervention, sir.'

'What? What does that even mean?' Wentworth was massaging his temples again. 'We can't go around culling *people*, for Christ's sake!'

'We're not talking about Americans. After all, this is a global problem, not just a US one,' Barrett said in placatory tones. 'We have a duty to the entire human race.'

'Goddamnit Bill, now this is sounding like a movie script.'

Barrett rubbed his nose. It was the pre-agreed signal for Burford to drop the bombshell.

'Sir, we have four teams of covert operatives ready to trigger catastrophic events that would wipe out millions in four of the most populous foreign countries.' Burford's matter-of-fact voice was at odds with the words he'd just spoken. Mike Hughes had his eyes closed.

The President looked stunned.

'Forget it. No way I'm sanctioning mass murder. Jesus H. Christ. And don't you think these foreign countries might have something to say to us about these "catastrophic events"? We'd be no better than terrorists! Look at the outcry when just a few people are killed by a car bomb. No. It's unthinkable.'

Barrett sat forward on the couch. 'Mr President, *somebody* has to think the unthinkable. We need to buy the world some time. There are outcries over acts of terrorism because they're known to be deliberate.' He saw Wentworth move to interrupt and carried on quickly. 'The events we're talking about have been meticulously planned so that they'll look like natural disasters or major industrial accidents, and they'd be triggered over a period of several months. In those circumstances, people tend to just get on with picking up the pieces, even though the death toll is of a much higher magnitude than any terrorist attack.'

Wentworth shook his head. 'Let's assume for one second that I was even considering saying yes to this "direct intervention" of yours. It's too risky. The slightest leak… The smallest clue leading back to this Administration…'

'Sir, in order to maintain your position of plausible deniability,

I can't give you more details. Suffice it to say, we've gone to great lengths to make absolutely certain there'd be no traceable links back to the US.'

The President turned to Burford. 'What about your teams? They must know what their objectives are?'

'The teams have been kept as small as possible and each of them knows nothing about the others. No one outside this room knows there are four potential targets. The few operatives involved have been selected with immense care, they know they're acting for the greater good, and as soon as they've achieved their objectives they'll be… taken care of.'

'Jesus. I wish I hadn't asked. I wish I didn't know about any of it. Honest to God.' Charles Wentworth had hoped to leave his mark on world history, but not like this. Despite the cold logic behind the arguments, it was a monstrous proposal.

Burford hid his distaste at the President's squeamishness. It was a luxury he couldn't afford in his line of work. 'Sir, America would be poised to step in and offer humanitarian aid to the countries affected. We'd look like heroes. And in truth that's exactly what we'd be. Ultimately, we're doing this to save the rest of the human race.'

Wentworth stood up and paced as a different set of headlines flashed through his mind. He wondered if he could pull it off, looking grief-stricken at press conferences and promising to help mop up a hideous mess that he'd secretly sanctioned; an atrocity that he'd personally allowed to happen. His companions were silent, recognising that he needed some thinking time. How was he supposed to get his head around this?

Then again, anything was better than having to tell hundreds of millions of American voters that they weren't allowed to have any more babies.

He sighed. 'Look, you guys are my most trusted advisers. I don't need to tell you that this is pretty damned hard to stomach but I have to believe you've already done all the thinking and legwork and soul-searching ahead of this meeting. And what I'm hearing from you is that we don't really have a choice. Have I got that right?'

Barrett had kept his trump card for this moment. He held eye contact with the President and said, 'Sir, if we don't act now, someone else will. And chances are, they won't have our scruples. Not long before you were elected, we exposed a plot to unleash a bioweapon on a major US city. It was dealt with by our anti-terrorism guys but some of the evidence pointed to foreign government—'

'Who?' Wentworth was outraged. 'Why wasn't I told about that?'

'The threat was neutralised,' Barrett said enigmatically. 'And the details of that particular incident don't matter now.' Only he and Burford knew that it was entirely fictional. He continued. 'The point is that, like I said, this is a global problem. Other countries know as well as we do that something needs to happen. Something big. And from the intelligence Mike's people have gathered, we have every reason to believe that if we don't do it to them, they're sure as hell gonna do it to us.'

'Mike?' Wentworth looked to the Director of the NSA for his opinion.

Hughes gave a deep sigh. 'I think Bill's right, we've got to be pro-active. Not that I like it. Not one little bit. Perhaps we should consider triggering the first event and see what happens before deciding whether we go ahead with any of the others.'

There was a weighty silence before the President softly said, 'Agreed.' He closed his eyes for a moment. 'Jeez, I need a Scotch.' He walked over to a polished walnut cabinet, then returned to the table carrying a crystal whisky decanter and four glasses. 'Ken, does this goddamned operation have a name?'

'Sir, this operation doesn't exist.' Burford reminded him. 'But, strictly between these walls, we call it the Four Horsemen.'

*

In the People's Republic of China, the seven members of the Politburo's inner circle were attending a clandestine meeting. These men were no strangers to secrecy, or to tough decisions that they knew were often regarded as ruthless by weak Western civilisations.

'Once again, China has led the way. We have proved that social engineering works, yet in forty years the rest of the world has failed to follow our excellent example.' Bi Jiao Hui was referring to China's family planning policies. 'They call our methods controversial and whine about civil liberties while their profligate lifestyles accelerate the exhaustion of the planet's dwindling resources,' he said angrily. 'Since 1979 we have successfully prevented over four hundred million births. Four hundred million! We have done our part.'

Chairing the meeting, Wang Xiao dipped his head respectfully towards his colleague. 'You are absolutely right, of course, comrade. But Western countries look at headline statistics and see only that sixty percent of the world's population lives in Asia. We cannot be complacent, my friend. We must recognise that we will be an obvious target when things get worse — which they soon will — and the West seeks to apportion blame for the Earth's problems. Because one thing is certain: no matter how negligent they have been, the last place they will ever lay the fault is on their own doorstep.'

Other heads around the table were nodding in agreement.

'I am not suggesting that we should take military action,' Wang Xiao continued. 'Not yet. However, I believe it would be wise to ensure that we are fully ready to do so.'

The heads continued nodding.

10:59:07

Plagues

After that day at Much Wheadle I was more aware that there were too many people in the world. I started taking an interest in news stories and nature programmes on TV. And the more I looked, the more I saw. One day I was flicking through channels and I watched a few minutes of a documentary about grasshoppers swarming. Farmers were spraying them with insecticide to try and save their crops, but there were so many of these bugs that you couldn't even see the ground. I flicked to the next channel and there was a clip of a load of people jostling to get on to an underground train in rush hour. You couldn't even see the ground.

Dad used to laugh at me when I talked about it. He'd say things like, 'Blimey Lou, you're much too young to be worrying about stuff like that.'

But the thing was, nobody *else* seemed to be worrying about it. With my superlogic, it seemed so obvious. I could see that we couldn't just keep filling the world with more and more people. Eventually there wouldn't be enough food or water for all of them, or space for houses and roads. I couldn't understand why there weren't TV programmes and signs and petitions and protests about the plague of humans. And I knew that sooner or later they'd bring their chainsaws and their bulldozers to what was left of my woodland at Much Wheadle.

Dad wasn't the only one who didn't take me seriously, either. It seemed everyone regarded it as a problem for other people, and for another day. I tried talking to a few of my teachers about it. In Year Six there was Miss Smith. She seemed interested at first but then she said she was late for a staff meeting and would talk to me about it later in the week. She never did. In Year Eight I broached the subject with Mrs Ryan, our geography teacher. She was one of those nervy people who seem like they're constantly fighting the urge to run away. Maybe she'd been teaching at Mareton School for too long. When I spoke to her she looked panicky and then abruptly said she would nominate me for the school council. I had my doubts that the school council would be able to do much to tackle global overpopulation, but I thanked her anyway. And then in the sixth form it didn't seem very tactful to try and talk to Mrs Dench about there being too many humans on the planet when she was busy incubating another one.

Nobody was interested. It was too big an issue, so it seemed that automatically made it somebody else's problem. Perhaps there were experts working on it out there somewhere, although as far as I could tell they weren't doing a very good job. At least people were starting to take climate change more seriously, but nobody wanted to mention overpopulation as the root cause. It was something that needed to be tackled by world leaders, not by ordinary people. Not by the voracious plague of ordinary people. We were just grasshoppers.

The only person who was prepared to listen to me ranting about it was Auntie Cheryl, actually. Not that she had much choice, as she was a captive audience. I went to stay with her for the Easter holidays as usual and the weather was awful, so we spent most of the time indoors watching movies, eating chocolate cake and talking. I can't remember how the subject came up — probably after one of those hateful TV adverts about accident claims — but, once it had, all the thoughts I'd been storing up for years just came flowing out and poor Auntie Cheryl was on the receiving end.

'People never want to take responsibility for themselves, for their own actions. They never want to be accountable. If something goes wrong, the very first thing they do is look for who else they can blame, and they act like that's way more important than putting the wrong right. If they eat too many burgers and get fat, it's the fast food companies' fault they can't see their own toes anymore. Honestly, people like that are the reason they have to print stupid labels on everything, like "Caution: contains nuts" on packs of peanuts and "Warning: contents may be hot" on take-away coffees. Ugh.'

Good grief. I was going to need a ladder to get down from my high horse, at this rate.

'Oh you're so right, Lou. D'you know, at work a couple of months back, the new girl in marketing — she can't be more than a couple of years older than you, mind — was asked to help sort out the storeroom where we keep all the leaflets and brochures and whatnot. Well, somebody'd put a couple of spare polystyrene ceiling tiles up on top of a cupboard in there and one of them fell down and hit this girl on the head. I mean, those things are light as a feather. Next thing we hear, she's been signed off with whiplash. Whiplash!' I shook my head, looking suitably gobsmacked. 'Anne in accounts knows the mother, and apparently she managed to claim a few grand off the council a couple of years ago when she tripped over an uneven bit of pavement. Only bruised her knee but hasn't done a day's work since. Runs in the family, that kind of attitude to life, I reckon.

'Shall we have another cuppa?'

I smiled and followed her into the kitchen. She refilled the kettle and then I rinsed our mugs.

'I have to say I'm not especially proud to be a human, Auntie Cheryl. As a species, we do so much stupid stuff. Talk about failing to achieve our potential.'

'Lou, honey, I've told you before that this "Auntie" business is making me feel old. I'm not sure I can be dealing with anyone taller than me calling me Auntie. Okay? Just Cheryl will do fine.'

'Okay, Aun— Sorry. Cheryl.' It didn't feel right. Old habits die hard. She laughed as I pulled a face. 'I just need to get used to it.'

She plopped fresh teabags into the cups. 'I'm not sure I agree with you about humans failing to achieve their potential. A lot of them are a right royal pain in the backside, I grant you, but what about all the amazing things people have achieved? Look at technology and medicine and things like that. Could you grab the milk out of the fridge for me, please?'

'Yeah, but look what we're *doing* with our amazing achievements.' I passed the milk carton and waited to put it back when she was done. 'Take technology. We find better ways to blow each other up. And people would rather put themselves in debt to have the latest widescreen TV than buy decent food for their kids.'

Cheryl frowned, stirring tea. 'Mobile phones, then. And all the clever things you can do on the internet these days. I can video chat online to my friend in Spain. And it's free, too. Lucky really, the way she talks.'

I smiled. 'True, that's cool. But people also waste hours and hours on end looking at mindless nonsense and taking selfies and posting pictures of what they had for dinner and making snarky comments on forums. And then they don't spend time with family and friends because they say they're too busy. I reckon we're getting *worse* at communicating with each other, even though it's easier now than it's ever been.'

'Hey, I'm supposed to be the cynical adult, remember? You're absolutely right, though. My elderly neighbour was saying — only last week, I think it was... yes, it must've been Tuesday because I'd just got back from the optician's — anyway, she was saying that she misses the days when people used to write letters to each other. I mean, you had to find some nice paper, sit and write it all out by hand, pay for a stamp and walk to the post-box, but people did it all the time. They cared enough to make the effort, I suppose.'

I nodded. 'I honestly don't know what's going to happen, Aun— I mean, Cheryl.'

'How d'you mean?'

'Well, you must've seen those graphs about population growth. The ones where the line gets nearly vertical at the end.' I drew in the air with my finger. 'It can't keep going like that. I mean, it just can't. Something's got to give. But nobody's even talking about it.'

'*We* are,' she said.

She was easy to chat to. She knew I didn't expect her to have the answers, but it felt so good to finally have a proper conversation about it all. We hadn't even made it back to the lounge, we were so busy talking. We were leaning against the kitchen counters and the tea was nearly gone.

I was only just getting started. 'I can picture the future, you know? Easily. And it's scary. In all the Hollywood movies, when something's threatening Earth or mankind, people pull out all the stops to save the day. I know that's not real life, but you sort of grow up believing that if humanity's collective back's against the wall, there'll be a concerted effort to fight for survival. Or at least a few heroes. You know? But it looks like — even though we've seen this coming for centuries — we're all just going to march miserably to our deaths like a bunch of brainless lemmings without even trying to do something. It's depressing. I can just picture the last few humans saying, "I told you so," or "Why didn't anybody warn us?" as they curl up and die.'

I paused, but Cheryl could see that the floodgates were well and truly open now. 'Go on,' she said.

'Well… I know it sounds ridiculous… I mean, I'm nobody. But because there don't seem to be many people who can see how bad the future's going to be if we don't do something about it, I feel like I should… I don't know… maybe try and help fix it somehow, while there's still time. But I have no idea where to even start. And I just think it would be like… like yelling at cows. You know?' Cheryl raised an eyebrow as I explained. 'Well, maybe you've never done it, but it's pretty pointless. When you yell at cows, there are basically three reactions you get. Most of them ignore you completely. They pretend you're not there and just carry right on munching grass like they haven't even heard you at all. Some of them look up and stare at you like you're some kind of weirdo for a few seconds before they put their heads back down and carry on. And a few of them act startled, skitter away a little bit, and then stand there chewing, keeping a wary eye on you like you're definitely not to be trusted and probably dangerous. But before long they go right back to munching grass, like nothing ever happened. And none of them listen to what you actually said or make any effort to understand what it is you're yelling about. I reckon trying to tell humans that everything's going to go completely pear-shaped unless we do something would be exactly like yelling at cows. So I don't know if there'd be any point at all.'

It was the longest speech I'd ever made.

'D'you know something, Louis Crawford? I've never heard you talk like this before.'

'Nor have I,' I said.

She smiled, shaking her head. 'It's been such a privilege watching you grow up, you know. I always knew you had a wise head on those young shoulders of yours. Just don't try to take the weight of all the world's problems on them, okay?' She came over and put her hand on my arm. 'I absolutely cannot wait to see what you do with your life,' she said, pulling me into a tight hug. 'I only wish your mum could've been here to see it, too.'

10:59:08

How to Change the World

Mr Jones had made a painted papier-mâché globe with a slot in the top for our Phoenix Project ideas, presumably in his own time. He clearly needed to get out more. I'm sure he regretted it as soon as people started arriving in the tutor room and sniggering, but by then it would have been an act of weakness to remove it. Poor guy. He was wasted in the sixth form; a few years ago we'd probably have thought it was pretty cool. Probably.

'Sunila Afzal,' Mr Jones said loudly, staring straight at her. She looked startled, wondering what she'd done wrong, then realised he was beginning to call the register. He pushed his glasses up with an air of quiet determination. He'd clearly decided on a new tactic for day two.

The register got done in less than half the time it had taken the previous day. I reckoned that teaching teenagers must be a bit like being a prison guard. It was a silent war of wills, with both sides aware that the balance of power was fragile and could tip into anarchy at any second. Unfortunately, any credibility Mr Jones might have gained with his no-nonsense approach to the register was wiped out by the papier-mâché creation sitting on the front of his desk.

Taking advantage of a brief lull in the tutor room chatter,

Mr Jones said, 'Remember, each of you needs to get your world-changing idea to me by Friday.' He held up a little stack of paper slips. 'Date, name and idea on one of these, please, and drop them in here.' He gestured at the home-made globe, pushing his glasses into place. The papier-mâché ideas box was a mickey-take waiting to happen. We knew it. He knew it. This was a crucial moment in the unspoken war. An uncharacteristic silence fell as we waited to see how the rookie would play it.

Mr Jones looked down at the globe. Then he looked up at us, removed his glasses and gave us a lopsided smile. 'It was going to be the Phoenix symbol. You know, with the hands? You should've seen it when it had two inflated pink rubber gloves stuck to the sides.'

We were all in hysterics when the bell went for first lessons.

At break, I went back to the tutor room, filled in one of the slips and posted it into the globe. Mr Jones had said he'd be emptying it at the end of each day and logging the ideas, and he would let us know if there were any duplications. I was suddenly paranoid that somebody else might have got in first with the same idea — it was so obvious, after all — and that would be a disaster for me.

On Friday, we had our first extended tutor group session with Mr Jones. 'Ex-tut', as it was known at Mareton School, was a weekly lesson slot that got used for miscellaneous stuff like health education, which was basically when the kids brought the teachers up to date with the latest information about drugs and smoking and sex. To be fair, we'd also had a couple of useful sessions about exam and revision tips, applying for university places and so on.

Mr Jones's weedy frame sagged in a blue checked shirt and brown cords. The guy looked like a complete numpty and dressed like a colour-blind pensioner, yet he'd somehow managed to earn our respect over the course of the week and the tension associated with imminent anarchy had evaporated completely. We were almost attentive when he stood up after doing the register.

'Okay, we've got just under an hour to have a look at how you lot are going to change the world. He patted the much-ridiculed papier-mâché globe affectionately. 'Peter, could you come up here, please?'

Pete went to the front of the room and stood beside Mr Jones, looking apprehensive.

'I've written everyone's ideas onto sticky notes,' said Mr Jones. 'I'm going to call each of you up to tell the rest of the class what your idea is, and I'd like you to say a short sentence or two about why you chose it. Okay?' He handed a yellow sticky note to Peter, who cleared his throat self-consciously.

'Um, well… Mine's to build monorail systems and hover-cars.' Everyone laughed. No one was sure why; it just seemed the appropriate response.

'And why did you choose that idea?'

Pete was fiddling with his sticky note. 'Um, well… Because traffic jams are getting worse all the time and congestion and pollution are big problems in loads of places, and petrol's expensive and… well, it's running out, I think. And monorails and hover-cars could maybe help with all that and use magnets or electricity instead.'

Nobody laughed.

'Excellent,' said Mr Jones. He'd obviously chosen his first non-volunteer carefully. Pete was a pretty safe bet. 'Futuristic but definitely worth exploring. Well done, Peter. Could you stick your idea on the whiteboard, please?'

Pete pressed his sticky note onto the blank board. Mr Jones thanked him and told him he could return to his seat, then took a black marker pen and drew a large circle around Pete's idea. He wrote 'Transport' above the circle. He turned back to face us, pushing his glasses up on his nose. I realised that he was doing that less often these days.

'Okay.' He checked his notes on the desk. 'Beatrice, your turn.'

Bea's idea was to ban cigarettes. 'Because they cause all kinds of health problems and fires and litter and they smell disgusting. The world would be nicer without them,' she announced. She was doing well until she stuck her idea on the board right beside Pete's.

43

'Transport?' Mr Jones challenged.

Bea looked at him. 'People smoke when they're driving and it causes accidents,' she offered.

Mr Jones acknowledged her quick thinking with an ironic little bow, but repositioned her idea in the centre of the board. He drew a huge ring around Bea's idea, overlapping the Transport circle, and wrote 'Health' above it.

Ewan was next. 'I'm doing the "pay it forward" thing, where you do something nice for three people and, instead of paying you back, they have to pay it forward to three more people,' he said.

'Hey, I saw that movie,' Bea piped up.

A couple of other people said, 'Me too.'

'And?' said Mr Jones. 'None of these ideas are completely original and that's fine. And actually the concept of paying forward dates back at least as far as ancient Greece and has appeared in various writings over the centuries.' That shut us up. 'I Googled it,' he confessed. 'There you go, Ewan, I've done a bit of your research for you.'

Mr Jones put Ewan's sticky note in the Health circle and added '& Happiness' to its title. 'Right, where are we? Ah yes, Anna and Hannah, could both of you come up?'

Best friends since primary school, Anna and Hannah sounded — and behaved — like characters in a cheesy sitcom. Everyone knew the two of them shared a brain cell and were utterly incapable of independent thought. Mr Jones put their curiously similar ideas side by side in the Health & Happiness circle on the board. Hannah wanted to make pocket money compulsory 'so that kids are happier and learn to manage money'. Anna wanted to make pets compulsory 'so that kids are happier and learn to look after animals'. Mr Jones did a commendable job of ignoring Jay's loud false cough which barely masked the word 'barf' —with accompanying actions, in case anyone missed it — and reminded the girls that their presentations next month shouldn't be too alike.

The next two ideas went into the overlap between Transport and Health: crash-proof cars and more bike lanes.

Mr Jones added a new circle entitled 'Energy/Resources' and, where it overlapped the central Health & Happiness ring, James placed his idea to link gym equipment to power generators. There were two other Energy/Resources ideas: desalination of sea water and using wave power to generate electricity. Other people had obviously considered the fact that about seventy percent of the Earth's surface is covered by oceans, too. Michaela suggested building floating towns and farms (her idea went into the overlap between Energy/Resources and a new circle labelled 'Housing') and Jay's idea was to dump waste out at sea. The initial outcry was quickly hushed by Mr Jones, who asked us to let Jay explain himself.

'Not floating waste,' Jay began.

Somebody said, 'Eeewww!' and the rest of us laughed.

Mr Jones looked exasperated. 'Guys, come on, we're going to run out of time.'

Jay continued, 'I mean stuff that'll sink, like metal and concrete. The metal'd rust quicker in the sea. And I saw a thing on telly where these sunken ships and stuff had made, you know, like, habitats for stuff.' It wasn't often we heard Jay exert himself with three-syllable words like 'habitats'. We were impressed.

Mr Jones drew a new 'Waste' circle for Jay's sticky note. Sunila's idea to eliminate plastic bottles and packaging was added to it, and Martin's clever suggestion to compact rubbish into building blocks went into the overlap between Waste and Housing.

There were two other ideas that ended up in the Housing circle. Qamar said there were lots of dilapidated buildings standing empty that could be refurbished to create new homes, and he suggested criminals could provide the labour and learn new skills as part of their rehabilitation. Dariusz's idea was to build more high-rises instead of taking land that was needed for farming. I had mixed feelings about that one. What was left of the woods at Much Wheadle might be safe for a while longer if people built upwards instead of outwards, but growing up in the Cuthbert Street flats hadn't made me a fan of multi-storey living.

We had less than twenty minutes of the session left. I was dreading my name being called. The prospect of standing up and speaking at the front of the class was bringing me out in a cold sweat. My heart thumped every time Mr Jones announced another name, but the next few belonged to other people and I felt a flare of hope that the bell might go for break before it was my turn. I watched the clock while ideas were added to the big Health & Happiness circle: cutting footballers' crazy salaries and giving the money to charities, splitting lottery jackpots to benefit more recipients, world peace… I wasn't really listening anymore. Six minutes. The Venn diagram on the whiteboard was full of sticky notes.

Mr Jones checked his watch, pushed his glasses up and glanced at his notes.

'Louis.'

My heart seemed to relocate itself to my throat and it stayed there while I stood up and walked to the front of the room.

Mr Jones was still talking, addressing the whole class. 'Actually, there's a slight problem with Louis's idea. It's too big to fit on a sticky note.'

Various people, including me, looked confused. Jay put his hand against his forehead in an L-shape and mouthed 'loser' at me.

Mr Jones saw this and smiled. 'Actually Jay, you couldn't be more wrong.' Jay's ears went a satisfying shade of bright pink. 'Because Louis's idea would address every single issue that's represented on this diagram, and then some. All the health, housing, transport, resourcing, and waste problems. So I'd need a sticky note large enough to cover the whole whiteboard.'

There was a lot of frowning and whispering and shrugging among my classmates. Mr Jones bent down and picked up one end of a roll of yellow paper that was on the floor below the whiteboard and gestured to me to grab the other end. There were two chairs against the wall either side of the board and I followed his lead as he stood on one and I stood on the other. There were already blobs of sticky putty on the top edge of the paper and we pressed them to the top of the whiteboard, keeping the roll wound up. The whispers behind us were getting louder.

Mr Jones looked across at me conspiratorially and winked. I realised I was actually enjoying myself. 'Shall we?' he said.

We let go of the weighted roll and it unfurled to cover the bristling Venn diagram, revealing three words: 'Reduce human population'.

'Speaks for itself, I think. You can sit down again, thanks Louis.'

I hadn't uttered a single word.

Mr Jones checked his watch. 'Okay. Great work, everybody. You've got three weeks to research some facts. Your presentations can be in any format but remember they'll be five minutes, maximum, and—'

His last words were drowned by the bell. Nothing stands between schoolkids and break time.

10:59:09

Justification

President Wentworth was suddenly seeing evidence of overpopulation everywhere, or so it seemed. Were there really more signs? Or was he just noticing them now because he was more aware of the issues, thanks to that awful meeting with Bill Barrett? Mrs Wentworth had said it was called the *Baader-Meinhof Phenomenon*, or something like that, when you saw things because you were looking out for them… But wasn't that the name of some terrorist group? Maybe she'd got it wrong, although that would be unusual.

The President hadn't been sleeping well since the meeting with Barrett, and kept having nightmares where that creepy CIA guy, Ken Burford, was hovering in the shadows. Wentworth had come close to calling the whole thing off, several times, but — however unpalatable it may be — he knew deep down that something had to be done. Whether this was the right solution remained to be seen. Who was he kidding? This terrible secret plot involving Burford's 'Four Horsemen' sure as hell wasn't right, and it wasn't even a solution. However, it would make a dent in the world population, without denting any Americans, and it would hopefully keep a few other countries too busy to target the United States for a while. And if he played it right, he might even scrape through the next couple of years looking like a statesman and a humanitarian, even if it was all a big fat lie. Wasn't that what politics was all about?

Charles Wentworth sighed and massaged his temples. He'd already decided that he wouldn't run for re-election when the time came. Although he was proud of his achievements, he'd come to realise that the presidency was something of a poisoned chalice and he'd be only too glad to hand it on to the next person, especially now that the whole planet was really beginning to show signs of strain.

An aide tapped on the office door and brought in a tray bearing a pot of coffee, the President's favourite mug, a plateful of choc-chip cookies and a sheet of paper summarising the day's business.

Wentworth flicked on the TV to watch the morning news. While he waited for the commercials to finish, he glanced over his schedule. In an hour's time, he had a meeting to discuss immigration policy because the number of people entering the US — both legally and illegally — was increasing pressure on systems and resources that were already overburdened by the existing population. The afternoon's appointments included a crisis meeting about potentially widespread crop failures caused by an unfortunate combination of climate anomalies and a plague of beetles whose main natural predator was almost extinct due to habitat loss.

On the TV, the adverts finished with an excitable family extolling the virtues of disposable baby wipes, and then the news bulletin led with a story about toxic air in California following another spate of wildfires.

The President dunked a cookie and wasn't at all surprised when a soggy chunk dropped into his coffee. His wife had been right about the *Brahms-Heimlich Phenomenon*, or whatever the hell it was called. Although there really did seem to be signs of human overpopulation just about everywhere you cared to look, now that he came to think about it.

He would let the first of Burford's Four Horsemen do their thing, and take it from there.

*

In China, Wang Xiao had called another special meeting of the Politburo's inner circle. The seven men had already discussed various reports confirming what they already knew: that the country's armed forces, missile sites and other military resources were at full strength and on standby.

There was a lengthy pause, during which Wang Xiao's colleagues sat in silence, patiently waiting for their leader to speak. Their faces were sombre.

'My friends, we have a difficult decision to make. Perhaps one of the most difficult decisions in the history of mankind.' Wang Xiao spread his hands on the table in front of him. 'We in this room are all aware that the world's resources are running out, much faster than most people realise. In the West, where they fail to control their media, there are increasing signs of societal breakdown. You need only look at a handful of international news headlines to recognise that the weak governments in America and Europe are in turmoil and under growing pressure to address the environmental concerns of their citizens. It will not be long before we are reading reports of mounting civil unrest.'

Bi Jiao Hui — always one of the most outspoken members of the group — made a conscious effort not to interrupt while the Chairman finished his speech.

'Western citizens are starting to demand answers and their leaders have no answers to give. As we have said before, that is when their politicians will look for somewhere to lay the blame. And they will look to Asia,' Wang Xiao continued gravely.

Bi Jiao Hui was literally biting his tongue now. The arrogance of the West defied belief, when they had done nothing at all to control either their population or their consumption, but he was worried by talk of possible military action.

'Gentlemen, we live in dangerous times,' said Wang Xiao. 'And it falls to us to decide whether to wait until the West finds an excuse to make the first aggressive move against the People's Republic, or whether we should seize our destiny in our own hands. Knowing that we would have the full support of our allies in North Korea and Pakistan, we must decide whether we should strike first.'

As the Chairman sat back, Bi Jiao Hui could contain himself no longer.

'Honourable comrades, we would be starting a third world war!'

Wang Xiao looked across at Bi Jiao Hui with a sad expression in his eyes.

'You may be right, my friend.' Wang Xiao's gaze hardened. 'But the next war will be fought for the world itself, and we will be failing in our duty to every Chinese citizen on Earth if we do not fight to win.'

10:59:10

Judgement Day

Thursday the twentieth had arrived frighteningly fast. This was the day our tutor group was due to present the Phoenix Project ideas to the in-school judging panel. I'd hoped Mr Jones would be one of the judges, but he said he'd been too close to the whole thing and the decision ought to be impartial. The three best ideas would be chosen by the headmaster, two other heads of department and the chair of governors. The project had generated quite a bit of interest and we'd been warned that there would be a small audience of other governors and teachers who were free on Thursday afternoon and wanted to see what it was all about. And as if the prospect of standing up in front of that little lot wasn't daunting enough, Mr Jones had told us that a reporter from the *Mareton Herald* would also be coming along. So, no pressure then.

I woke up before my alarm was due to go off, got dressed and shuffled through to the kitchen, yawning. Dad had left the cereal box out ready for me on the counter with a clean bowl, which contained a spoon and the torn off corner of an envelope on which he'd written 'Good luck!'. I tucked the wish into my shirt pocket.

Most of Year Thirteen had a free study period on Thursday afternoons and any other lessons had been reshuffled to create a two-hour window for our presentations. Mr Jones had repeatedly reminded us that we'd each be limited to five minutes and should only plan to talk for about three, otherwise we wouldn't get through everyone. There were twenty-two of us, so even then it was going to be fairly tight. We had a running order this time so that we could be ready for our allocated five-minute slots and I was due to go last again. At least I wouldn't have that horrible Russian roulette feeling, wondering when it would be my turn. It occurred to me that we might run out of time for my presentation and I was surprised to find that I didn't want that to happen. Despite my nerves, I really wanted to have my say. Who'd have thunk it?

A laptop computer had been set up for those who wanted to project pictures or videos and Mr Jones had suggested we could also use props to make our presentations more interesting and help us illustrate key points, but he'd warned us not to get too ambitious. A few of my classmates had ignored this advice. James needed help to lift an exercise bike into the middle of the hall and then used two minutes of his presentation time connecting it to a screen that would show how much power he was generating when he pedalled it while he was talking. The output wasn't that impressive and the display was very distracting. The same could be said for James's rather tight-fitting Lycra gym shorts.

There were two other notable prop disasters. One was Michaela's model of a floating town in a fish tank, which had suffered a miniature tsunami on the way to the hall and sunk. The other was Mrs Pinkles. Anna was using her fluffy white cat to illustrate her presentation about making pets compulsory, so her mother had brought the unfortunate animal into school at lunchtime in a small wire cage. It was an unnecessary gimmick anyway, as we all knew what a pet was. Mrs Pinkles started meowing loudly during Hannah's presentation about pocket money, but Anna was up next so she couldn't leave the hall. Hannah was visibly displeased with her best friend. Anna hoisted Mrs Pinkles's cage — not without some difficulty, as there was a lot of over-fed feline under all the white fluff — and plonked it on the presentation table. Anna talked loudly over the insistent meowing for all of thirty seconds before

Mrs Pinkles turned her backside towards the judges, raised her tail and deposited a very neat but incredibly stinky turd in the corner of her cage. It didn't seem possible that such an evil, pervasive stench could have been produced by such an innocent-looking animal. No wonder she'd been distressed. Everyone in the hall was, too. Mr Jones and several other audience members rushed to open windows, and Anna burst into tears. Hannah didn't comfort her. I held my sweater over my nose and checked my watch.

I thought the best presentation of the afternoon was Sunila's. She'd found out a lot of very sobering facts about plastic waste and she presented them really well.

'Up until about fifty years ago, if you bought a drink it used to come in one of these.' She reached into a simple cloth bag she was carrying over her shoulder and held up a glass bottle. 'These are made from sand and they can be refilled and recycled endlessly.' She placed it on the table in front of her. 'Nowadays, of course, most drinks come in *these*,' she said, producing an empty plastic water bottle, 'and the world is full of them.' She pressed a button on the laptop and a picture appeared of a huge mountain of plastic bottles. 'Plastics are made from oil, which we're running out of.' The picture changed to one of an Asian boy collecting plastic bottles, standing waist-deep in a polluted river whose surface was completely covered with rubbish. 'Some plastics *can* be recycled. However, we only recycle a very small percentage and it takes a lot of fuel and other resources to do it.

'Nobody's lived long enough yet to know how long it takes for plastic to break down. It doesn't biodegrade — in other words, it doesn't get eaten by bacteria. So basically, all the plastic we've ever manufactured is still in the world. Some plastics can *photo*degrade but it takes a long time and the particles that break down in light still exist as tiny polluting fragments. And since we bury a lot of our plastic waste in landfills, it won't photodegrade anyway.' While Sunila was saying this, the screen behind her showed a landfill site with big rubbish trucks dwarfed by piles of plastic waste.

She pressed the button again to bring up a photograph of an

enormous berg of rubbish floating in the sea. 'Around eight million tons of plastic ends up in our oceans each year, and that rate could easily double in the next ten years.'

Sunila held up the plastic bottle she still had in her hand. 'We can't keep chucking these away without worrying about where they're going to end up. But we don't seem to care. We're willing to sacrifice our environment for the sake of convenience. I couldn't find any proper figures for the UK, but Americans use something like two and a half million plastic bottles every *hour*. That's enough plastic bottles to fill this school hall from floor to ceiling about twenty times over. In America alone. Every single hour.'

The last picture had several Indian people in the foreground — one of them a pretty little girl in a bright yellow dress — picking through giant heaps of rubbish that stretched away as far as the eye could see in every direction. I wondered what had been there before the rubbish.

Sunila finished by saying, 'It wouldn't be too big a deal to go back to the more environmentally-friendly and recyclable packaging materials we used before, like paper, glass and metal. Plastic has its place in the modern world. But if we at least stopped using plastic bottles and carrier bags it would drastically reduce the amount of waste we generate. Glass bottles, cardboard cartons and paper or cloth bags are easy alternatives.' She put the plastic bottle down on the presentation table and pushed it to one side in a gesture of rejection, replaced the glass bottle in her cloth bag, and walked back to her seat as the dismayed audience gave her a well-deserved round of applause. I was glad I didn't have to do my presentation straight after Sunila's.

Ewan went immediately before me, talking about the idea of paying it forward. He showed a clip from the movie where the characters started drawing a simple diagram to show that, if each person pays good deeds forward to three more people, 'It gets big really fast'. This had emphasised the power of exponential growth and I suspected Mr Jones had realised that might be helpful to me.

We were running late but suddenly Ewan was coming back to

his seat and it was my turn. The long-dreaded moment had arrived. According to my watch there were eleven minutes left until the end of the school day. Mr Jones, a blur of busy corduroy, darted over to speak to the judges and they whispered and nodded among themselves while I willed my legs to carry me to the centre of the school hall. My palms were sweating, my heart was pounding, breathing seemed a conscious effort, and I felt horribly ill. I was literally about to die from nervousness.

I knew my face was glowing red while my fumbling fingers clipped a rigid metre ruler to the top of each of the presentation table's front legs, but Mr Jones was providing a distraction by telling everyone that this was the final idea and the judges would have to announce their decision the following morning, as there would be no time for their deliberations today before school ended at 3:30pm. As he finished speaking, I unfurled a big roll of white paper across the front of the table and taped its edges to the sides. The paper was about one and a half metres high and I sank gratefully into a chair behind it, completely screened from view, and put my notes in front of me with shaking hands. I took a deep breath and gave the audience a few seconds to look at the giant graph I'd drawn on the roll of paper, with its exponential curve illustrating the growth in human population from the year 1200 to the present day.

I didn't trust my voice, but I remembered what Mr Jones had told us about trying to speak loudly and slowly. I swallowed, and began.

'My idea to change the world is to reduce human population,' I was surprised that my words didn't sound anywhere near as shaky as I felt. Being invisible behind the huge graph helped enormously. 'If we could do that, then almost every other idea you've heard today would be completely unnecessary because the problems they address wouldn't exist.' I paused to let that sink in and took another steadying breath, and my concerns about my imminent demise ebbed. 'The graph you're looking at should speak to you more clearly than I ever could. I was shocked when I first saw it a couple of years ago. I remember thinking that surely something would have to change, and I couldn't understand why everyone wasn't worrying about that. I still don't understand. This rate of growth is so obviously unsustainable, yet we're doing very little — far *too* little — about it.' I glanced at my watch. It was 3:23pm. Talk about cutting it fine.

'It took the whole of human history until 1804 for our numbers to reach one billion. But by 1927, the human population had doubled to two billion, just one hundred and twenty-three years later. Then it only took another forty-seven years for the number to double again, to four billion in 1974. That brought things into perspective for me because 1974 happens to be the year my dad was born. He's not that old — hopefully only about halfway through his life — and in the years since he was born the world's population has nearly doubled again. There are now seven and a half billion of us.'

The words I'd rehearsed so many times at home sounded clear and confident, even to my ears. Finally, I'd been given a chance to get people thinking about this stuff. The issue was so much more important than my nerves. I owed it to the world to do my little presentation as well as I possibly could.

'The net population increase is currently running at about 240,000 per day. That's the entire population of Mareton being added to the planet every single day. So with every month or so that passes we're adding the entire population of London. Every year that's an extra eighty-four million new human beings, which is more than everyone in the UK: it's the entire population of Germany.

'If any other species was increasing its numbers at such a runaway rate, we'd have done something about it long ago. We wouldn't let other creatures threaten the future of the planet and yet that's exactly what humans are doing. We have to stop reproducing so irresponsibly. The problems it's causing aren't in the future anymore. We're already facing them and they're going to get much worse, very quickly.'

I wasn't checking my watch. I was just the vehicle through which this important message was being relayed and I had to make it count.

'Even if the Earth had unlimited resources, we're already borrowing from future generations. Seven and a half billion people is too many when we're using stuff up faster than we can replace it. Right now, it takes a year and a half to regenerate what we use in one year. And Earth's resources *aren't* unlimited. We're going to run out of things that people need to survive, not to mention all the other species on the planet that we seem to think are less important than us. We're tipping the whole global ecosystem completely out of balance and stripping the planet of every usable resource, like a plague. We reckon we're so much cleverer than any other lifeform on Earth, but making our own environment uninhabitable is pretty stupid. And taking everything else down with us is downright selfish.' It felt like I'd been talking for ages, but time seemed to have stood still and I ploughed on. 'More than a hundred other species of living things become extinct every day. That's nearly a thousand times the rate that would die out naturally if humans weren't around.'

There was only one paragraph of my notes left. I hadn't heard a sound from the audience for ages and it crossed my mind that I might emerge from behind my paper screen to find that they'd all gone home. I was too chicken to take a look.

'Failing to control our own behaviour so spectacularly is basically mindless vandalism on a global scale. We're condemning future generations to starve and kill each other in the polluted husk of what was once a beautiful, thriving, diverse planet. We're committing mass suicide because if we don't reduce our numbers, our own stupidity will eventually do it for us.'

I'd been worried that the last bit sounded over-dramatic, but I was yelling at cows here and I needed to get them to listen. Besides, dramatic or not, it was all true.

The hall was silent. I was shaking like a leaf. It was all I could do to gather my notes and get to my feet. I walked out from behind the graph, half expecting to see empty chairs. Everyone was still there and a smattering of applause started, sounding like a rain shower, but before I could get back to my seat at the side of the room the final bell went and the thunder of people getting to where they needed to be rumbled throughout the school. I sat down anyway, feeling wobbly. It was over. I'd done it. I wondered if what I'd said would change anything. Meanwhile, after the weeks of build-up and dread, suddenly everyone was draining from the hall and the adrenaline was draining from my body, and all I was left with was my well-creased notes and a sense of anticlimax.

10:59:11

Headlines

I went home and opened the door of the flat really quietly as always, just in case Dad was still sleeping after his night shift. Half the time he was already up, but sometimes he slept until about 4:30pm, which was another reason why I often went straight up to the roof for a while. That Thursday afternoon I was still feeling unsteady — the after-effects of venturing so far outside my comfort zone — and sitting on the edge of a parapet nine storeys up didn't seem like the best idea.

'That you, Lou?'

He always asked, although it was more a greeting than a real question. There was no one else who would let themselves into our flat with a key.

'Yeah, Dad.'

'I'm in the kitchen. Cuppa tea?'

'Uh, yeah, cool. Thanks Dad. Be there in a sec.'

By the time I'd dumped my stuff in my room and gone through to the kitchen, there was a welcoming mug of strong tea waiting for me, and an open packet of my favourite biscuits. Dad was sitting at the table. I looked down at him with his tousled bed hair and got a weird flash of role reversal.

'So? How'd it go? You survived, I see,' he said, smiling up at me anxiously.

He'd never been demonstrative. Even when Mum died, he'd done his utmost to hold his emotions in check. God knows why. It was just something men were supposed to do. There'd been times when I wanted Dad to show his feelings and it had made me angry that he didn't. I suppose I saw it as a form of dishonesty. When I noticed the tears on his face at Mum's funeral, I realised it was the first time in my life I'd ever seen him cry. Now I could see that he was genuinely keen to hear about my day, knowing how scared I'd been about doing the presentation, and I felt a rush of affection for him.

'I did survive.' I grinned, taking a seat. 'Although it was touch and go at one point.'

I told him all about the afternoon and he listened avidly while we drank our tea and dunked biscuits. It was nice.

'I'm proud of you, Lou. Really. Well done, kiddo.' He gently punched my arm, which was about as effusive as Dad ever got.

I could tell how sincere he was. 'Thanks Dad.'

'So you'll find out tomorrow if you're in the running?'

'Yeah. I doubt it, though. Some of the other ideas were really good. I'm not bothered about winning. Besides, if I'm shortlisted, I'll have to do my presentation all over again next week.' I pulled a face.

'Ah, you've done it once. Next time'll be a doddle.'

'I dunno about that. Anyway, if what I said got a few people thinking, that's all that matters, really.'

*

Every Friday morning, the whole school crammed into the hall for weekly assembly. It was the only time all the pupils were together in one place, a fidgeting, whispering sea of bottle green sweatshirts. The class tutors prowled the shoreline wearing frowns and issuing sharp 'Sshh!' noises every few seconds until the headmaster, Mr Sanders, stepped to the front of the room.

'Good morning everyone,' he said in his usual strident tones.

'Good morning Mr Sanders. Good morning everyone,' we chanted flatly.

'Mr Jones's class, could you stand up please? Just where you are.'

It was surprising how much noise was involved in twenty-two teenagers straightening their knees. Mr Sanders waited for the scraping of chairs to subside. We were in our usual place at the back of the hall with the rest of the Year Thirteen kids, and remained standing while he continued.

'Thank you. Now, for those of you who don't already know, these students,' he gestured in our direction, addressing the whole room, 'have been involved in a project about changing the world. Yesterday afternoon, they all presented their ideas to a panel of judges comprising myself, Mrs Prior, Mr Ahmed and our chair of governors, Mrs Long. Our task was to select the best three ideas—' He paused until another susurrating wave of whispering ebbed. 'As I was saying, we had to choose the three ideas that we felt were the best of all those presented to us yesterday. Now, we had a pretty tough job on our hands, let me tell you. I can genuinely say that the four of us were very impressed with the range of ideas, the amount of research that had obviously been done in most cases, and the way these students presented their thoughts.

'The project sponsors, Phoenix, had given us some judging guidelines, so we weren't just focusing on the slickest or most confident presentations; we were looking for the ideas that would have the most significant impact; those that would address some of the major problems facing the world today, and those that would be reasonably feasible. Hands up if you can tell me what "feasible" means.'

A few hands were raised and there was a soft collective sigh from our class. Our legs were collectively starting to ache from standing up and we collectively wished that Mr Sanders would cut to the chase. He scanned the room. His attention was drawn to a girl in Year Eight; her arm was enthusiastically vertical beside her ear and her hand was flapping like a small, irritating pink flag in a blustery wind.

'Yes?' Mr Sanders pointed at her obligingly.

'Able to be done,' the girl stated in a small but assertive voice.

'Perfect.' Mr Sanders smiled at her. The nobody-likes-a-smart-arse vibes from the rest of the school were almost tangible. 'Able to be done, indeed.' He pulled a folded sheet of paper from the inside pocket of his jacket. Our class collectively shifted from foot to aching foot.

'Right, then. As I said, we had a tough job choosing from the many excellent ideas; in fact, I'll include a list of them in next week's school newsletter, since they all deserve recognition. But in the end we agreed unanimously on the best three.'

We collectively held our breath, partly awaiting the result and partly in anticipation of Mr Sanders asking for a definition of unanimously. Thankfully, he didn't.

'We hesitated over selecting two ideas that were to do with managing waste, but the presentations were especially good and it was felt that waste management is certainly one of the most pressing issues currently facing mankind.'

There was much head-turning and whispering as we worked out who had presented waste-related ideas. Sunila, Jay and Martin blushed.

Mr Sanders switched to the voice he used for special announcements. 'The three shortlisted students are…' He paused for dramatic effect, then added, 'Please don't applaud until I've announced all three names. And would the following three students please come up to the front. Then the rest of you may sit.' Talk about dragging it out. 'Sunila Afzal, Martin Hart, and Louis Crawford.'

I was stunned, buffeted by applause and by anonymous hands patting my back and shoulders. My legs, glad of an opportunity to move, had conveyed me to the front of the hall before my brain caught up with what was happening.

Mr Sanders summarised each of the three winning ideas: Sunila's ban on plastic bottles, Martin's building blocks made from compressed rubbish, and my reduction of human population. I felt a thousand pairs of eyes on me and was simultaneously pleased and horrified. The three of us stood there self-consciously while Mr Sanders announced that Sunila's idea would be applied with immediate effect in the school and a message was being sent to parents asking them to avoid using non-refillable plastic drinking bottles, carrier bags and other single-use plastics wherever possible.

It was a shame my idea wouldn't also be applied with immediate effect, but I supposed it wasn't really the done thing to ask parents to avoid providing students with any more siblings.

*

Dad bought the *Mareton Herald* on Saturday morning and we scanned it together in search of the article about the Phoenix Project. The reporter they'd sent to cover the story had been a bored young guy who'd given the impression that he'd have rather been anywhere other than Mareton School. Much as I could sympathise with that sentiment, I wasn't overly optimistic about his journalistic prowess.

I'd dared to entertain the notion that the newspaper might feature global overpopulation on the front page, now that I'd drawn their attention to the crisis. I'd imagined the excited junior reporter rushing back to tell his editor about the shocking statistics I'd included in my presentation. After all, I reckoned they'd be hard pressed to find a bigger or more important story. However, the main headline was "MUSEUM IS HISTORY!" and Dad and I skimmed through the article. Apparently, the Mareton museum had been threatened with closure eighteen months ago due to falling attendance figures, but local historians had stepped in to staff it on a voluntary basis and raise the funds needed to keep it going. It seemed they'd only managed to delay the inevitable, since the museum occupied a piece of prime real estate in the town centre and the volunteers had lost their battle against the rising costs of maintenance, insurance, etcetera. I'd only been to the Mareton museum once on a primary school outing and it had seemed comprehensively dull. Nevertheless, I was sad to read that a fast food chain would soon be opening a new restaurant on the site. The other piece of front-page news was "Pensioner Hits Lamp-Post" accompanied by a large colour photograph of the dented pole. The eighty-year-old had hit it with his car, which made the story less impressive. All of which was far more important than the end of the world.

Eventually we found the item we were looking for at the bottom of page twelve, under the witty headline "What a CATastrophe!" There was a black-and-white picture of Mrs Pinkles in her wire cage and most of the text was devoted to a pun-laden description of the turd incident. At the end, a short paragraph mentioned what the project had been about and listed the names of the three students shortlisted to win the cash prize. The reporter had managed to misspell all three.

Dad was proud, regardless, and sent me on an errand to the corner shop to buy another copy of the newspaper for Auntie Cheryl and a celebratory packet of biscuits.

10:59:12

The First Horseman

Lieutenant Kyle Dempsey had no idea what he'd done to get selected for this mission. Whatever it was, he wished he hadn't done it.

Delhi was hellish on this searing hot day and by mid-afternoon the pollution in the air was tangible, like trying to breathe soup. He briefly removed his safety helmet so that he could use the dirty sleeve of his overalls to wipe the sweat from his face. He checked he wasn't being watched, finished discreetly placing another pack of explosive and then carefully added a wireless detonator.

Kyle used to joke to his friends that he'd only joined the military so he'd get to travel on the American taxpayer's dollar. Well, he'd travelled, all right. To rock-strewn deserts and poisonous jungles and bombed-out towns in the back end of nowhere. And now this: India's seething capital. At least it wasn't an active war zone and he wasn't dodging bullets, so that made a refreshing change.

Lieutenant Dempsey knew exactly why he'd been picked for this job, actually. He could thank his mother: or would, if the mission wasn't top secret. Jaz Dempsey's parents had emigrated to Washington from Rajasthan and she'd been born in America as Jaasritha Singh. Kyle had inherited her Indian good looks and charm, and had learned to speak fluent Hindi from his maternal grandparents. It was these things which, unfortunately for him, made him ideal for this mission.

'Hey! You there!'

Kyle jumped, quickly closing the canvas tool bag in which the one remaining pack of explosive was nestled. He peered down over the gantry to see the factory supervisor waving up at him from ground level, trying to attract his attention. Kyle waved his clipboard at the man in response. The supervisor gestured at his watch and Kyle put the clipboard down so that he could hold up ten spread fingers in reply.

Ten minutes should be plenty, and the sooner he was finished, the better. He pulled a complicated diagram of the pipe network from inside his overalls, consulted it briefly, and then set off to place the last of his bombs.

A career soldier, he'd been trained to follow orders without question, but there was no denying that this particular operation had him seriously rattled. There were going to be a lot of civilian casualties and that didn't sit right with him at all. But what was he supposed to do? It was hardly his place to demand explanations from his superiors. He'd been assured that the target — a huge chemicals factory on the outskirts of New Delhi — was of strategic military importance and, as always, his task was not to think or to question; it was to trust the powers that be, carry out his assignment to the best of his ability, and keep quiet.

Twelve minutes later, he was signing out at the factory's security office.

'Ministry, eh?' said the burly guard, casting a cursory glance at Kyle's excellent fake ID. 'Did we pass the inspection, then?'

Kyle replied in colloquial Hindi, 'Oh, yes. Just routine, really.'

'You based in the Delhi office, then?'

Kyle nodded.

'In that case, you must know my brother-in-law, Runjit Patel!'

The guard didn't notice the flicker of unease that flashed briefly in the ministry inspector's eyes.

Kyle shrugged. 'Sorry, no. Not yet. I only transferred up from

Mumbai three weeks ago and they've been running me ragged ever since.'

The guard looked disappointed. 'Oh. Well, you'll know him when you meet him. People say we look like twins. Then you can tell him Ramesh says hello, okay?'

Kyle feigned an easy smile. 'Sure, I'll do that.'

He picked up the tool bag and clipboard, and walked gratefully to the car. He'd be glad when this mission was over. He was due some leave soon and was planning to propose to his long-term girlfriend. Deliberately turning his mind to happier thoughts, he drove through the hectic Delhi streets, weaving slowly between traffic and stray dogs and the ubiquitous green-and-yellow tuk-tuks.

The high-rise hotel was a complete dive, but the chemicals factory was visible from the window of Kyle's room, about half a mile away, and it had been chosen for this reason. He stared down through the haze at the countless people and vehicles in the streets below. Yes sir, he'd sure as hell be glad to put this one behind him and get home. He checked his watch and raised the small aerial on the long-range remote detonator. Then Lieutenant Dempsey transmitted the code that would kill almost eight thousand people in the initial blast when the chemicals factory exploded, and at least four million more when the cloud of highly toxic gases engulfed the teeming city.

Kyle watched in horrified fascination as the ball of flame blossomed in the distance.

'Jesus H. Christ. I hope you guys know what you're doing,' he whispered to the empty hotel room.

At that moment, a bullet from a silenced revolver entered the back of Kyle's head at point-blank range.

'Oh, we do, son,' said Ken Burford, calmly stowing the gun in a hidden shoulder holster. 'We know exactly what we're doing.'

Burford could have sent someone else to finish things off, but there was nothing like the personal touch. He took the transmitter from Kyle Dempsey's dead fingers, threw it into the tool bag, and left the room, placing a "Do Not Disturb" sign on the door handle on his way out.

10:59:13

Eve

Dad wasn't exactly right when he said that doing the presentation would be a doddle the second time around, but I was certainly less nervous. It helped that the audience was so tiny this time that we were using our tutor room instead of the school hall. Besides the three shortlisted students — myself, Sunila and Martin — there was only Mr Jones and the lady from Phoenix. I wasn't even shaking very much.

I'd vaguely expected Phoenix's Regional Coordinator for Southern England to be some self-important, officious old frump, so Eve Gyer was a bit of a surprise. Mr Jones fussed and held the door open for her. From her well-cut grey hair to her well-cut slate blue skirt suit, she subtly radiated class and looked completely out of place in the visibly unloved surroundings of Mareton School.

She came straight over to the three of us, lit by one of the warmest smiles I'd ever seen. She said, 'You must be Sunila,' shaking hands. Sunila was the only girl in the room, so this was hardly a feat of brilliance, but I was impressed that the woman cared enough to have memorised our names. 'And which one's Martin?' Martin awkwardly held out his hand. Lastly, Mrs Gyer turned to me. 'Then that makes you Louis, right?' She pronounced it correctly with a wiss not a wee, and her handshake was firm and cool. I liked her immediately. I would learn later that Eve had that effect on almost everyone she met, and always checked her facts.

Sunila did her presentation first and Mrs Gyer asked her a couple of questions afterwards.

'That was really impressive, Sunila. A strong idea, very well researched and presented. Tell me, what made you think of it?'

'Um, well, I got a lift in someone's car. My sister's boyfriend's. Anyway, the back seat and the footwells were *full* of empty plastic bottles. I was gobsm— um, I couldn't believe how many there were. He apologised for the mess and said he needed to get around to clearing them out, but… well, he just buys another drink or two every day and chucks the bottles in the back. It made me realise how quickly they mount up. And that's just one person.'

'Mm, scary, isn't it? Somebody needs to buy your sister's boyfriend a refillable drinks bottle.'

'Oh, he's already got a few. But he can't be bothered to make his own drinks. He's a lazy… um… person.' Mr Jones looked relieved that Sunila hadn't used a more colourful noun. It was obvious that she didn't approve of her sister's taste in men.

Mrs Gyer gave Sunila another of her warm smiles, conveying sympathy more than humour. 'And that's precisely the problem. As you said in your presentation, we're willing to sacrifice our environment for the sake of convenience. You mentioned recycling. What did you find out about that?'

'Well, I know that some plastics can be recycled, but not all of them,' Sunila answered.

'So, if we can't change your sister's boyfriend's lazy habits, how about getting better at recycling all the rubbish he generates?' asked Mrs Gyer.

Sunila thought about it for a moment, then said, 'I don't think it's very easy. It sounded like quite a faff when I read about it online. It all has to be sorted before it can be recycled. That's what those poor people were doing in those pictures. And it's not just sorting the plastic from all the other rubbish; the plastic has to be sorted into different types, too. And then when they've got a bunch

71

of the same type of plastic, they can chop it up or melt it down or whatever. But I reckon it takes quite a lot of work and fuel and stuff to do all that.'

'You're absolutely right. Far better, then, to try and reduce the amount of plastic we produce and use. And I understand that Mareton School has already banned carrier bags and disposable bottles in school, so your idea has already started changing the world, Sunila. That's pretty cool. Well done.' Mrs Gyer twinkled at Sunila, who beamed back.

Martin was up next, presenting his idea to use compressed rubbish to make building blocks. Again, Mrs Gyer asked what had inspired him.

'I was overtaking a truck that was carrying blocks of scrap metal.' Martin was one of a few kids in our year who'd already passed his driving test and he referred to it at every possible opportunity. 'They'd been cars once — you could see recognisable parts — but they'd been squished into these perfect cubes, like big building blocks. Then I looked online and found out that people are starting to use that idea for real with other types of rubbish.'

'They are indeed, and it's a brilliant initiative that solves a few problems at once. Phoenix is involved in at least one project that I'm aware of in the States along those lines. The results are very promising and the range of waste products that can be used is incredible. You mentioned something in your presentation about Heineken making glass bottles that could be used as bricks. I'd never heard of that. Fascinating. Do you know any more about it?' Mrs Gyer wasn't just making polite chit-chat, she seemed genuinely interested.

'Yeah, so the Heineken thing was absolutely *ages* ago. Back in the early sixties, I think.' It hadn't occurred to Martin that Mrs Gyer might have been born around then. I looked over at her, but she didn't show any sign of offence. She was leaning forward, listening intently to what Martin was saying. 'The guy who ran the company had a load of these brick-shaped bottles made. With beer in, of course. But when they were empty there were enough to build, like, a hundred little houses on an island where some people didn't have anywhere to live. They were specially designed so they fitted together and were strong enough.'

'So what happened?' Mrs Gyer asked. 'Why didn't they carry on making them?'

'I'm not sure. I think I read something about people just preferring prettier-looking bottles,' Martin said.

'It sounds like Mr Heineken was ahead of his time. I'd like to think people's priorities have changed since then...' Mrs Gyer mused. 'But somehow, I doubt it.'

It was my turn. My heart was thudding as I unrolled my giant graph against the front of the table and my notes trembled in my hands, but I found I didn't want to sit behind the paper screen this time. I wanted to be able to see Mrs Gyer's intelligent grey-blue eyes and I wanted her to see *me*.

When I'd finished speaking and she asked me why I'd chosen that idea, I mentioned the woods at Much Wheadle being chopped down to make space for new houses and said I could just *see* that there were too many people, even in my own small corner of the world. I didn't tell her about my aerial view from the roof of the flats, since I wasn't supposed to go up there. Besides, that was my secret.

'Well, you've certainly pinpointed the heart of the matter, the root cause of so many of our problems' said Mrs Gyer. 'But here's the big question, Louis. How would you do it? How would you go about reducing human population?'

I'd already given this plenty of thought. 'I think it has to come from the top. Every government needs to introduce policies to limit family size to one or two children, max. Like China did. I don't think you can rely on people to do that by choice, 'cause they wouldn't stick to it. And I'd make sure that people everywhere had access to contraception, too. And schools would have to teach kids about contraception and the population crisis, because people just don't seem to even *know* about it.'

Mrs Gyer was considering me with her eyes narrowed, as if she was trying to see — as if she *could* see — inside my head. 'There are a lot of politicians and religious leaders who would argue against what you're suggesting. It's not easy to get people to do things they don't want to do.' She hadn't asked a direct question, but her expectation of my response hung in the air between us.

'I think "easy" is a luxury we don't have any more,' I said. 'Humans, I mean. I called it a crisis because I think that's exactly what it is, even though people don't like talking about it. It might not be easy but we have to do something, before it's too late.'

There was a long moment where Mrs Gyer just stared at me. Despite the intensity of her gaze, I didn't look away. There was a connection. An understanding. I wasn't really aware of the other three people in the room and I certainly wasn't thinking about any possibility of winning the two hundred pounds. I just sensed that she *got* it, and maybe she knew people in Phoenix who could do something about it.

'Thank you, Louis,' she said, bursting the bubble that had briefly seemed to enclose the two of us. 'Thanks all of you. I've really enjoyed meeting you.' She glanced briefly at her watch and stood up. Mr Jones leapt to his feet as if he'd been stung on the backside by a wasp. 'I have another school to visit now so I have to go, but I'll be in touch within the next twenty-four hours about the prize.'

All she left behind was a light, flowery scent. But Eve Gyer had really made an impression on me.

10:59:14

How to Spend Two Hundred Pounds

It turned out that I *did* have the pleasant problem of working out what to do with two hundred pounds, after all. When Mr Jones made the announcement after registration the next morning, I'd been so prepared to applaud Sunila or Martin that I actually clapped once or twice before realising that Mr Jones had spoken *my* name. So then it looked like I was chuffed with myself, which made the moment even more excruciating than it would have been anyway.

Mr Jones gave me one of his big nerdy grins and joined in the applause. I was sure he would have looked just as pleased if either of the others had won, but I sensed he was proud of me, at least for overcoming my nerves.

Sunila was gracious and made a point of coming over to say, 'Well done, Lou.'

A few other people followed suit, echoing Sunila or saying things like, 'Nice one.'

Jay, true to form, sneered, 'What're you gonna spend the cash on then, Lou*ise*? Maybe a collar with a bow on it, little teacher's pet?'

I never usually dignified any of Jay's taunts with a response and this time was no different, but Martin appeared at my side and said, 'Maybe he'll buy you some sugar to put on your sour grapes, Jay.'

*

Dad was over the moon. So much so, that I thought he was going to hug me when I told him the news. I'm pretty sure *he* thought he was, too. Poor guy, compelled to keep his emotions hidden for no good reason whatsoever.

'Wow, Lou. I couldn't be more proud of you, son. Wow! That's so cool. Good for you!'

'Beats a tin of kidney beans,' I quipped, and he laughed.

'What a birthday present,' he said. It was my eighteenth birthday in less than two weeks. 'Still sure you don't want a party? You could have a corker now!'

We'd talked about this before, when the Phoenix prize wasn't even a factor. 'Still sure. There's not really anybody I'd want to invite, so it wouldn't be much of a party.' I wasn't sad about it. There was a difference between being a loner and being lonely.

'Well, it's up to you. But it's your eighteenth. Big occasion. Even if you just have a couple of mates over, have a few beers and some laughs. As long as you don't annoy the neighbours too much...'

'Thanks Dad. I appreciate the thought, but I don't need a party. And it's not really what kids in Mareton *do*.' I realised I had very little idea what kids in Mareton did. I only knew that, whatever it was, I had no particular interest in doing it with them.

Later, when Dad had left for his night shift and I was in bed, waiting for sleep, I pondered what to do with the prize money. There was a new book that I'd been wanting to buy, the latest in a series I'd been reading. Okay.... only one hundred and ninety-two pounds left. This was ridiculous. Two hundred pounds wasn't a huge sum and I was sure every other kid in my class could have spent the money ten times over without any trouble at all. Must try harder.

I thought about what I wanted, what I needed, what I enjoyed.

We were far from well off, yet I'd never lacked any essentials and had never been one to covet material things anyway. When I was fifteen, I'd found myself a part-time job so that I could start earning. It was only four hours a week, working as a kitchen assistant (washer-upper, in other words) on Saturday lunchtimes at one of the busy pubs in town that had a restaurant. They paid above minimum wage and I liked the other staff, so I'd stuck with it ever since and sometimes did a few extra hours for them here and there if they needed me. They never had a problem with me taking odd weekends off as long as I gave them plenty of notice, and I'd saved enough money to get myself a mobile phone — nothing flashy, but it did everything I needed it to do — and pay the monthly charges without having to ask Dad for help. The pub was called The Swan, but it was known locally as The Goofy Goose thanks to a dodgy touch-up job that had been done on the painted sign outside, which had improved the swan's flaking plumage but given it a daft, slightly cross-eyed expression. I realised my thoughts were wandering — hopefully a harbinger of sleep — and returned to the subject of what to buy with my prize money.

I liked playing computer games but it wasn't an obsession and I already had a fairly decent console, a gift for my sixteenth birthday from Dad, thanks to one of his mates at work who was a keen gamer and was selling his old console second-hand. I'd been delighted with it, especially since the mate's idea of 'old' was about eighteen months: barely a toddler. And I had a fair few games to keep me entertained. Hmm, what else, then? I liked walking, especially when I went to visit Auntie Cheryl, but that was hardly a hobby that required a lot of specialist equipment. Maybe some half-decent walking boots would be a good idea. I'd seen some cool-looking ones in a shop in town for about thirty quid. Wow. Last of the big spenders, me. And a bit of a boring old fart, at the grand old age of seventeen. I sighed and rolled over in bed.

I finally worked out what to do with the money just as I was drifting off to sleep.

The next morning, I got up as soon as my alarm went off,

checked a few prices and things online and made a very satisfying little list while I had breakfast. It was surprising what you could do with two hundred pounds when you put your mind to it.

The post was delivered just before I left for school. I flicked through the usual junk mail, put what looked like an electricity bill on the kitchen table for Dad, and was surprised to find an envelope addressed to me. It was the cheque from Phoenix. They were certainly efficient. There was a letter from Mrs Gyer with it, which I stuffed into my rucksack as I was running late.

I forgot about the letter until lunchtime, then read it while I ate my sandwiches. Mrs Gyer congratulated me on winning the prize and said she'd been impressed by my insight. She must have had to write loads of these letters but it didn't seem like a standard copy-and-paste job. The second paragraph said that she was keen to follow up with some of the winners in her region and would be happy to explain more about Phoenix's operations if I was interested. I was invited to attend an informal meeting with her at Phoenix's Mareton office in about three weeks' time. There was an email address for me to confirm my attendance. I thought I may as well go along. Mrs Gyer certainly wasn't the pompous jobsworth I'd expected, and I found I was looking forward to meeting her again.

*

Apparently, Lady Luck was still smiling on me. I bought the next *two* books in the series I'd been reading because the shop had a 'buy one, get one free' deal on. I treated myself to a pair of walking boots and found that the ones I'd had my eye on were reduced by ten pounds in a sale. I also booked a table for three at The Goofy Goose — where I got staff discount on food — and treated Dad and Auntie Cheryl to a slap-up meal on my birthday. It was a lovely way to celebrate my eighteenth and Dad made a big thing of buying me my first legal pint of beer.

Afterwards, back at the flat, while all three of us were still full, slightly tipsy and laughing together, Dad presented me with a small wrapped gift. He was looking very pleased with himself and exchanged a couple of knowing glances with Cheryl while I tore off the paper. Inside were two identical keys on a keyring. I looked up at him, puzzled.

'Downstairs,' he said, cryptically. He could barely contain his excitement.

We all went downstairs. I had no idea what to expect. The only thing I could think of was a car, but I didn't really need one and couldn't afford all the running costs. Not to mention the driving lessons and the fact I'd have nowhere to park—

My thoughts were interrupted as we reached the ground floor and walked out of the building. Dad went and stood proudly beside a shiny black moped. I was speechless.

'Like it?' he asked anxiously, after a few moments.

'I love it!' I assured him, walking around it. 'It's great, Dad. Absolutely great. But it's too much.' The bike wasn't brand new but it looked to be in perfect condition and must have cost more than Dad could afford on his wages.

'Nonsense,' he said, grinning at me. 'I've been putting a bit aside for years. Saving up. For this, or something… for you. After all, it's not every day your only son turns eighteen.'

I hugged him, hard, whether he liked it or not. And then Cheryl joined in and the three of us must've looked like right idiots hugging and laughing right there under the streetlights. It was brilliant.

Back upstairs in the flat, Cheryl produced a large square present from her huge overnight bag, and I opened it to find a smart black motorbike helmet.

It was the best birthday ever.

The last thing I did with my prize money was take Dad to see Mareton Town Football Club play a home match against Whiteford Wanderers. It was a proper boys' day out and we both enjoyed spending some quality time together. I even had enough left to buy us each a pie and a pint at half-time. I'd always had a pretty good relationship with Dad, but I was aware that it had been subtly changing recently. Strengthening. As I watched him, engrossed in the game, I worked out what was different. He seemed more relaxed, somehow.

I had wondered if we'd have enough in common when I grew up, what with my disinterest in football and so on, but actually it felt as if we were becoming closer. Perhaps subconsciously Dad felt more comfortable interacting with another adult and was relieved that his days of worrying about how to raise a child were officially over. It couldn't have been easy for him as a single parent. Mum used to be the one who made sure I had packed lunches and clean school uniform, who checked my symptoms if I wasn't well, who patched up scraped knees and dried my tears. Then she was gone — too suddenly for us, not suddenly enough for her — and Dad had to cope with his own grief as well as having sole responsibility for a bereaved, introverted ten-year-old who cried himself to sleep at night and asked all the angry impossible questions. I knew I would never fully understand everything he'd done for me.

He stood up to inform one of the Mareton midfielders who'd just passed the ball to a Whiteford player that he was 'about as much use as an inflatable dartboard'. I smiled at him fondly.

It wouldn't have mattered to either of us if Mareton Town had lost the match. According to Dad, that was the one thing they did well. But my uncanny good luck held and both of us were delighted to witness their only home win of the season, and I cheered as wholeheartedly as the rest of the die-hard fans.

10:59:15

Lunchtime

A classified location in North Korea

The food in the staff canteen at the nuclear weapons facility was reliably awful, and today's lunch was no exception.

'Hey, come back. You're miles away.' Ri Joo-Won waved his spoon in front of his colleague's face.

Mun Chong-Hae jumped slightly, flashing a secretive smile before shovelling another spoonful of rice into his mouth.

'What's going on? You've been distracted all morning.' Ri Joo-Won was intrigued by his friend's unusual behaviour. They had worked together for more than eight years and knew each other well.

'I can't say. Not here.'

Ri Joo-Won looked around, pretending to casually stretch his back. All of the other workers at nearby tables were engrossed in their own conversations and the canteen was filled with the hubbub of voices.

'No one's listening.' His curiosity was aroused now. 'This is probably the safest place to talk on the whole site. Come on, what is it?'

Mun Chong-Hae took another mouthful of food. In truth, he was bursting to share what he knew, and Ri Joo-Won was right:

this was probably not the worst place to do it, where his voice would be drowned out by others.

Extending his arm across the narrow table, he said, 'Did I show you the watch my wife bought for my birthday?'

Ri Joo-Won leaned in. The two men's heads were almost touching as they studied the wristwatch Mun Chong-Hae had worn every day for several years.

Mun Chong-Hae pointed at the dial and spoke softly. 'Pretend to be interested. I hardly even dare to say this aloud.'

Ri Joo-Won played along, nodding. 'Mm, I've always liked it. Okay, now tell me.'

Mun Chong-Hae slowly unbuckled the watch while he mumbled, 'My wife has a cousin who lives in China. She married a politician there whose father is—'

'Hold on. Your wife married a Chinese politician?'

'Of course not, idiot. Her cousin did. Anyway, it doesn't matter,' Mun Chong-Hae said impatiently. 'The father-in-law is highly placed in the Politburo, and… Well, you know how you're always complaining that our nuclear weapons will never be used? Let's just say you should be careful what you wish for.'

'What?'

'Shh!' Mun Chong-Hae turned the wristwatch over and leaned in still further to show his friend a non-existent inscription on the back. 'There's talk of war with the West. Serious talk.'

Ri Joo-Won was stunned. Yes, he had often expressed frustration with the arrogance and greed of Western civilisations, but… war? For all his brave and dangerous talk, the thought terrified him. He pictured the faces of his two young children and suddenly felt quite ill.

Mun Chong-Hae refastened his watch around his wrist and sat back with an excited gleam in his eye, clearly delighted that he'd managed to shock his opinionated friend into speechlessness.

*

London, England

The Right Honourable Philip Deakins MP polished off the last mouthful of a chicken-and-bacon baguette and started clearing the resultant debris of crumbs from his desk. He used one pudgy finger to wipe a splat of mayonnaise from the report he'd been reading, leaving a greasy smear across the close-printed text. He sighed irritably and licked his finger. This was one of many reasons why he preferred to go out for lunch.

The subject of the report was the recent explosion of a huge chemicals factory in Delhi. It made grim reading, but it hadn't affected his appetite. He picked up the phone and instructed his assistant, Jayne, to bring him a couple of doughnuts and some Earl Grey tea.

Deakins skimmed through a section about the horrific effects of the incident on the people who lived and worked in the Indian capital. The figures were astounding; the estimated death toll was already approaching four million and was still rising. Weather conditions on the day of the explosion had meant that toxic fumes had drifted slowly through the most densely populated areas of the city, causing severe blistering and damage to the victims' airways and lungs. Still, he already knew most of that from the news bulletins.

Initial fears of a terrorist attack appeared to be unfounded. Public interest in the tragedy had waned rapidly since it was announced that it was almost certainly just the result of an unfortunate industrial accident. So far, investigators had surmised that a spark must have set off a chain reaction along a network of gas pipes at the factory, and no evidence of sabotage had been found. Based on the aerial images of the devastated area, that was hardly surprising.

Deakins flicked through to the final pages of the report. Where was that damned girl with his tea and doughnuts? It didn't look as though the Delhi explosion would cause any significant environmental repercussions for Britain, thankfully. The cloud of toxic fumes had long since dispersed and he noted with relief that most of the UK's imports from India were not food-related. There would be potential shortfalls in goods such as metals, machinery and clothing, but those were somebody else's problem.

There was a knock at the door and it swung open as Deakins set the report aside.

'Ah, Jayne. A man could die of thirst around here, you know.'

He studied the young blonde as she slid a tray onto the front edge of his desk. It occurred to him that she'd taken to wearing trousers and high-necked tops these days, instead of the skirts and blouses that he used to admire.

Jayne looked up at him briefly with a tight-lipped smile. 'Sorry, sir. I had to take a call from the PM's office.'

She didn't comment on the crumbs all over the front of her boss's shirt or the blob of mayonnaise on his cheek, and left the room before he discovered that her letter of resignation was one of the items on the tea tray.

10:59:16

Buzzing

I was about to learn that Eve Gyer had a habit of blowing people's expectations right out of the water.

As I rode the bus across town after school to attend my informal meeting with her, I watched Mareton's familiar busy streets slide past on the other side of the grimy windows and wondered what the next hour would bring. I had no experience of the corporate world, but I imagined that even the Mareton branch of a huge multinational organisation like Phoenix would be pretty formidable. I pictured things I'd seen when big companies were featured on TV: a cavernous reception area with lots of polished marble, gleaming glass and chrome; a portal to a sophisticated world populated by intimidatingly competent professionals doing important jobs.

I got off the bus at one of the business parks on the outskirts of town. There was a sign listing all the companies that had offices there and a sketch map of the layout with numbered blocks. Phoenix was in Unit 13 and, sure enough, their familiar logo of Planet Earth cradled by two flaming hands came into view on the outside of a nondescript two-storey building as I walked around the next corner. The main door's panels were made of opaque black glass, and a neat sign at eye height instructed me to "Please press buzzer", with an arrow pointing towards a little metal panel to the side. There were two buttons: one for Phoenix and one for Wiggett & Steele, Solicitors. I pressed the Phoenix button and was rewarded with not only a buzz but also a loud click, some crackling, and then a 'Hello?' from a disembodied male voice. I leaned close to the metal panel and told it my name, then waited. Thirty seconds later, the door was opened by Mrs Gyer in person.

'Louis, how nice to see you again,' she beamed, looking as if she really meant it. Unlike most people I'd met, I found it difficult to imagine her saying anything she didn't mean.

'Come on in,' she said, ushering me along a short hallway and through an internal door that opened directly into a large, bright, open-plan office. A dozen or so people were either sitting at desks or standing and talking. A few of them looked up and smiled.

'I don't know about you, but I could murder a cup of tea,' Mrs Gyer said, walking ahead of me towards one of several doors leading off the main office area.

'Yes, please. Tea would be great, thanks.'

I followed her into a small kitchen, where she flicked the switch on a kettle and set about finding two clean mugs. I felt a bit like a satnav system when you take an unexpected turn and it says, 'Recalculating'. Everything was so... normal. We chatted a bit about what I'd done with the prize money while she made tea.

Mrs Gyer and I sat at a round table in a small meeting room beyond the kitchen and she looked at me with those piercing eyes of hers, reading me. I wondered what she saw.

'So, Louis. After your presentation, when I asked you how you'd go about reducing human population, one of the things you mentioned was educating people. I'm interested to know why you think that's important.'

Needing a moment or two to marshal my thoughts, I tried to take a sip of my tea but discovered it was approximately the temperature of molten lava by scalding my top lip. Smooth.

'Um... I just don't think enough people realise that we really are facing a crisis. I don't understand why we're not talking about population, working out what we should all be doing about it. I mean, it's *such* a big deal and it's already affecting us massively, but it's as if everyone's pretending the problem doesn't exist.'

'Go on,' Mrs Gyer said.

'Well, we should at least be educating people so they won't make the situation even worse. It seems to me there's pretty much an automatic expectation that most of us will have kids one day. It's just what people do. The vast majority of humans sort of sleepwalk through life. We should be teaching people to question that, shouldn't we?'

I made it a question because I was suddenly conscious that I was making a lot of grand sweeping statements and I was keen to hand the conversational baton back to Mrs Gyer. She had a knack for getting you talking.

'Yes, I think we should. Absolutely. It's refreshing to hear someone express that view,' she said. 'I like the sleepwalking analogy, that's very apt. Tell me more about what you mean by that.'

'I think we — most people, I mean — go through life just accepting certain things. We follow the same path everyone else does, just because that's what society says we're supposed to do. Not many people stop to question things. We eat certain foods. We eat our main course before our dessert. We eat breakfast at breakfast-time and lunch at lunchtime. We get a job, get married, have kids, just because that's what people *do* when they grow up. We think we're in control of our own lives, choosing our own destiny, when actually it's like being on one of those rides when you're little: there are buttons to press and a steering wheel you can turn but they don't actually make any difference whatsoever. They're just there to create the illusion that we're deciding where we go, when actually we could sit back and do nothing at all and the ride would still take us along the same predetermined route. The only way to take control is to get off the ride, think for ourselves and do our own thing. But that's not what people are supposed to do. So most of us don't.'

Mrs Gyer was nodding gently. She'd written a couple of things down in an A4 notebook while I was talking. Now she tapped her pen against her lips thoughtfully as the silence stretched out, and I wondered whether I should say anything else. Or whether I'd already said too much. I sipped my drink, cautiously this time.

'One second, Louis,' she said, and left the room. I finished my mug of tea. She came back with a tall man in tow. 'Louis, I'd like you to meet Tomasz Kowalski.' The tall man shook my hand and I recognised him as one of the people who'd smiled at me when I first arrived. 'Tom is the manager of our Mareton office.'

The three of us talked for over an hour, and it was cool. Tom and Eve insisted on me addressing them by their first names, which felt a bit odd initially because I was used to a school environment. I really enjoyed being with people who understood what I was saying and were obviously on the same wavelength, and I learned a lot more about all the things Phoenix did. Then Tom asked what my plans were when I finished school and I felt like an awkward teenager again, rather embarrassed saying that I still wasn't sure what I wanted to do. It seemed lazy and irresponsible, somehow. Eve asked if I was considering university; I said I wasn't sure my exam results would be good enough and, regardless, I wanted to get on with doing something real.

Eve glanced at her watch. 'Yikes! Ten past five already. I need to make a call before close of play. Sorry to have to dash off, Louis. I've really enjoyed our meeting today.' She shook my hand, picked up her notebook and pen, and gave Tom a questioning look. He nodded at her and she smiled broadly. 'I'll leave Tom to finish up.'

'Eve's great, isn't she?' Tom said, after the door had closed behind her. 'No one knows how she manages to take such a personal interest in everything. There's an in-joke that there must be at least three Eve Gyer clones. Not that that would be a bad thing.'

I smiled. 'So she covers the whole of the south of England?'

'She covers the whole of the UK. She's based in London with the other directors, but she makes sure she visits the regional offices as often as she can.'

I was confused. 'Sorry, I didn't know. The letter gave her title as Regional Coordinator for Southern England.'

'Oh, no worries.' Tom waved his hand dismissively. 'She never makes a big deal of job titles. That was the role she was fulfilling for the schools project. Actually, she was one of the founding members of the company and now she heads up Phoenix UK.'

I swallowed. People were just people, regardless of labels. I knew that. But I thought back to my pre-presentation nerves and was glad I hadn't known earlier that Eve Gyer was one of the top bosses of a huge global corporation.

'So what do you think? Interested?' Tom asked. I wondered if I'd missed something he'd said. He read the incomprehension on my face and burst out laughing, but not unkindly. 'She didn't tell you this was an interview, did she?'

'Er... an interview?'

'Classic!' Tom laughed again. 'Oh, that's typical Eve, that is. She sent me an email the day she met you at the school, talking about your clarity of perception. Seems you made quite an impression on her. I've been looking for someone to join the team here and she thought you might be the ideal candidate.'

I had the disorienting feeling you get when you look down at your feet on the sand as a wave rushes out beneath you.

Tom was still talking. 'Anyway, I agree with her, so... Well, the job's yours if you want it.'

10:59:17

Climate Change

The next few months bustled past in a tedious flurry of revision and exams. My main subjects were maths, physics and geography. When I listed them people tended to say, 'Oooh' in that three-tone way that meant they were impressed. However, those subjects were just the ones that came relatively easily to me because they had a heavy bias on facts and logic. I'd have been completely lost in most others. Sunila, for example, was taking English language, English literature and history. For me, those would have been the academic equivalent of a walrus trying to play an accordion. It helped a lot knowing I had the job at Phoenix to go to as soon as I finished my exams, regardless of my results, and the fact that the pressure was off undoubtedly helped me perform far better than I would have done otherwise.

Before all of that, I'd applied for my provisional driving licence and passed the compulsory basic training so that I could start riding my moped. The sense of freedom it gave me was intoxicating. No more organising my life around bus timetables, no more queuing at vandalised bus stops with miserable-looking commuters, no more searching for the least stained seat. Simply knowing that I could go where I wanted, when I wanted, made me profoundly happy. Most of my journeys were within a few miles of home but I didn't feel trapped in Mareton anymore. In giving me that amazing birthday present, Dad had opened the cage door and I knew I could escape if I chose to, so that even staying became liberating. The world was my oyster. Or, rather, a fifty-mile radius of Mareton was my whelk. For me, for now, that was enough.

My new-found freedom, the prospect of an interesting career with Phoenix, the knowledge that I'd soon be emerging from the long tunnel of compulsory education, even the relaxed rapport I had with Dad these days, all combined to give me a sense of lightness and excitement. I was on the brink of a new chapter, optimistic and eager. Little Louis Crawford was all grown up and ready to go.

I gave Brad, the manager at The Goofy Goose, a couple of months' notice that I'd be leaving. When I finished my last shift, on a sunny Saturday after an exceptionally busy lunchtime, he surprised me with a leaving gift and a card filled with farewell messages from everyone in the team. Feeling self-conscious and really moved, I tore open the large parcel while they all crowded around me in the kitchen. I'd worked there for three years but only as a part-time washer-upper and it hadn't even occurred to me that I'd get any kind of a send-off. The staff and some of the regulars had had a whip-round and bought me a warm waterproof jacket to wear on my bike. It was black with wide reflective strips around the sleeves and back, and I was chuffed to bits.

Brad had asked me a few times over previous months whether I'd be interested in waiting tables or working behind the bar after I turned eighteen, but I told him I was much more comfortable helping out in the kitchen, behind the scenes. Brad hadn't wanted to take no for an answer and on one occasion had said, 'You're just the sort of person we need: polite, reliable, sensible.'

He'd intoned the last three words like a really unexciting version of the FBI's 'fidelity, bravery, integrity' motto and I'd had a sudden mental image of a headstone bearing the epitaph: "Here lies Louis Crawford. Polite, reliable, sensible". I wasn't particularly bothered what people thought of me — that was their problem, not mine

— but it sounded so *boring*. I was happy to be all three of those things, but I didn't want to have a boring life.

If I'd known what lay ahead, I might have been more careful what I wished for.

*

The sunny spring raised false hopes and in fact preceded one of the wettest summers on record. The news was full of stories about localised flash floods and rivers bursting their banks, with speculation about global warming. I was as concerned about climate change as anyone, but found some of the coverage ridiculous and said so to Dad.

'I suppose rain in England is hardly news,' he conceded, flicking channels while we were sitting together in the lounge one weekend.

'The main reason it causes more flooding nowadays is that we've cleverly covered most of the country with concrete, so the water has nowhere to go,' I said.

'Hark at you, with your sarcasm and your "nowadays". You sound nearly as old and grumpy as me!'

Dad continued poking the TV remote every few seconds, giving us snippets of a cooking programme, various adverts and a lame sitcom with canned laughter to let you know when it was supposed to be funny. Then we watched a couple of minutes' footage of someone's seaside garden slumping off the edge of a low cliff, with a doom-laden voiceover.

'Poor buggers,' said Dad.

I was still in rant mode. 'People focus on the wrong stuff.'

'How d'you mean?'

'The world's vast, ancient forests are either being chopped down or going up in smoke — whole ecosystems lost for ever — and that hardly even gets a mention. That's the kind of thing we should be worrying about, not somebody's garden shed dropping off an eroded cliff into the sea because some numpty built it too close to the edge.'

Dad was chuckling at me. 'Calm down, Mr Geography A-level. Climate change has been happening for millions of years. Ice ages have come and gone, the oceans have risen and receded—'

'Yes, and that gives people an excuse to dismiss the whole subject. But if you look at the changes that humans are causing, that's really scary stuff. We're to blame for a lot of the extreme weather we're getting. The climate isn't just changing naturally, we're changing it. And we need to wake up.'

The following week, England's lost sheds and damp ankles paled into insignificance when the headlines were dominated by the news that a big dam had burst somewhere in China. Dad and I dunked biscuits solemnly while we watched one of the bulletins.

'Let's cross live now to our correspondent Matt Drake in Chongqing,' said the perfectly groomed presenter, Andrea something, turning to a large screen behind her that showed a map of the area and then a bedraggled reporter standing outside in pouring rain. 'Matt, what's the latest there?'

'Andrea, everyone here is struggling to comprehend what's happened. The immediate focus is of course on helping the vast number of people affected by the disaster, many of whom are still in mortal danger. However, as you can see, it's still raining heavily and that can only hamper the rescue efforts further downriver.'

'And what can you tell us about the cause and scale of the disaster, Matt?'

'The cause appears to have been a huge explosion in at least one of the thirty-two massive turbines within the Three Gorges hydroelectric plant on the Yangtze River, which breached the dam. The Three Gorges is the world's largest power plant and was only completed in 2012.' The soggy correspondent's voice continued over library footage showing aerial shots of an enormous dam. 'Such an explosion should not have been possible, according to early reactions from experts. The extent of the disaster is not yet known, but the reservoir was at full capacity after weeks of high rainfall and the floodwaters will certainly have caused unprecedented damage and loss of life in the many cities and communities further down the course of the Yangtze River, which include Wuhan, Nanjing and of course Shanghai, China's biggest city.'

'Dreadful news indeed, Matt,' said the studio woman smoothly. 'Are there any estimates yet regarding the death toll?'

'China is notoriously secretive, so we may never know for sure. When the Yangtze flooded in 1931, the official death toll was around 145,000 but it has been estimated that in fact up to four million people may actually have died. Flood protection measures have increased since then, but so has the population, and this latest disaster will undoubtedly have a catastrophic effect on one of the most densely populated areas of the planet.'

The drenched reporter disappeared from the screen and the camera returned to Andrea's sincere-looking face.

'Thank you, Matt. And at an emergency press conference earlier today, the President of the United States, Charles Wentworth, has already expressed his deepest sympathy for the people of China and pledged humanitarian aid. We will of course bring you more news on this, our main story, as soon as we have it.'

'Blimey,' said Dad, and I couldn't think of anything to add.

10:59:18

The Stablemaster

Ken Burford was a man with secrets. Members of the public who passed him in the street paid him no attention whatsoever, because he looked utterly ordinary and because they didn't *know*. They didn't know that he'd spent decades steadily worming his way into the most influential and dangerous of military and political circles. They didn't know that he'd manipulated the President of the United States, no less, into giving the green light to his outrageous proposals. They didn't know that Ken's lust for power and violence had been indulged beyond his wildest dreams, or that there was more to come.

Two of Burford's 'Four Horsemen' had already been unleashed upon an unsuspecting world.

The explosion at the chemicals factory in Delhi had gone exactly according to plan and there were no loose ends, no evidence of deliberate sabotage, no accusatory fingers pointed towards America. Ken had to admit that President Wentworth had done a creditable job of sympathising to just the right degree and had come up smelling of the proverbial roses.

Then, of course, the dust had barely settled over India's now-slightly-less-populous capital when Ken Burford's boss, General Barrett, had managed to press their advantage and get the go-ahead for Horseman Number Two: the destruction of the Three Gorges Dam in China. In terms of sheer numbers of casualties, this was the most ambitious 'accident'. And again, it had gone without a hitch, thanks to Burford's meticulous planning and daring execution. He felt like a god, with the power to snuff out human lives on a whim, yet he could move among mere mortals with absolute anonymity and impunity. What a rush.

*

Like most monsters, Ken Burford had started small, although the tell-tale signs were there for anyone who cared to see them. His wealthy parents weren't unduly concerned when, as a toddler, he poked one of his mother's knitting needles through the head of his favourite teddy bear. They simply bought him two new teddies and berated the nanny for not keeping a close enough eye on the child. When the replacement bears were found with all of their little furry limbs detached, the nanny was fired, and the parents sent the new one out to purchase an expensive set of wooden building blocks for their heavy-handed little angel.

In those days, Ken Burford wasn't Ken Burford. He was Howard Mayhope Carmichael. Little Howie was born and raised in Chestnut Hill, an upmarket suburb of Philadelphia, and had everything a child could wish for; everything except his parents' affection and attention. He learned to live without the former and gained the latter when he threw his expensive building blocks out of his playpen with sufficient force to destroy a top-of-the-range TV and a valuable antique vase. It may have been the wrong kind of attention, but even that was better than nothing.

By the time Howie was five years old, he'd gone through six nannies and a lot of toys, and his parents had been asked to withdraw him from three different nurseries. Mr and Mrs Carmichael were therefore hugely relieved when their darling boy became suddenly quieter. His destructive tantrums disappeared almost overnight. They were supplanted by a brooding sullenness that should have been even more worrying, but at least now the furnishings remained intact. In truth, Howard's mean streak had merely taken a more subtle turn and he'd learned that he could derive greater entertainment from being sneaky and spiteful.

The rest of Howard's school days passed with surprisingly little drama, apart from the one time he was expelled for breaking another boy's arm. Lies and crocodile tears helped him get away with many other incidents of nastiness and, whenever those didn't work, he knew he could rely on his parents' money and influence to smooth any ruffled feathers or fractured bones.

Later, Mom and Pop spent eye-watering sums on private therapists for their troubled teenager. To give the psychiatrists their due, they very quickly worked out that their unpleasant young client had simply been starved of parental love and recognition. However, they were understandably reluctant to tell the Carmichaels this and kill the geese that were laying them such fat golden eggs, so they hinted at it in only the vaguest and most tactful terms, and suggested that a substantial number of further sessions would almost certainly be beneficial.

One Saturday when Howard was in his late teens, he was sitting in Pastorius Park throwing stones at pigeons — one of his favourite anger-management techniques — when he heard some sort of commotion coming from a nearby street. He went to investigate and found himself caught up among a group of youths marching towards the city hall. They were waving placards and chanting something about rainforests. Howard had no interest in their cause, but he found their shouting and rebellious energy exciting. After that, he actively sought out protest marches and soon learned that they provided excellent opportunities for causing trouble. He joined a couple of local groups and at first his parents were delighted that their heir was finally taking an interest in something. Their disappointment and exasperation resurfaced, however, when Howard always seemed to find himself in the middle of any violence or vandalism, although it was presumably just bad luck that the protests in which he participated never ended peacefully.

By the time he turned twenty-one, Howard Carmichael had acquired a bad reputation and a criminal record that included breach of the peace, incitement to violence, destruction of property and three counts of assault. His parents just about managed to keep him out of jail but were nearing the end of their deluxe tether and, during a furious argument, they threatened to disown their wayward offspring. Howard told them he didn't need their money. He left home, moved to Washington and reinvented himself as the inconspicuous Ken Burford.

And now, twenty years down the line, his nasty secrets were still safe. Nobody knew what a dangerously screwed-up sociopath he really was: not his estranged parents, not his boss General William Barrett, not President Wentworth… not even Ken himself.

He bought a newspaper and noted the latest headline about the Three Gorges Dam disaster with no emotion other than personal pride in a job well done. Then he smiled to himself as his thoughts turned to the remaining two Horsemen, champing at the bit and awaiting their master's command.

10:59:19

Work Begins

After seven years at Mareton School, finding myself in an environment where I actively *wanted* to engage with the people around me was a novel experience. It wasn't until I started my new job at Phoenix that I realised the extent to which, before then, I'd had a constant nagging sense that I didn't belong. By the end of my first week the calendar had ticked over into July and stepping into the Unit 13 offices each morning no longer felt alien. On the contrary, it was rather like setting foot on a new planet I'd discovered where everyone spoke my language and I felt as if, at last, I was exactly where I was supposed to be.

It wasn't the first time I'd started a new job, but I'd viewed washing dishes at The Goofy Goose as nothing more than a way to earn some money, at least initially. At Phoenix, it wasn't like that. I found I was far more anxious to make a good impression and get things right, hoping it might be the start of something big, something in which I could invest part of myself. Right from the outset, even before I knew how horrendously accurate that would turn out to be, it was more than just a pay packet.

'You'll find that Phoenix operates somewhat differently from most conventional businesses,' Tomasz Kowalski told me on day one. 'Despite the size of the organisation, we don't have hierarchies and layers of management except where they're truly necessary. Here in Mareton, for example, all fifteen staff — oh, sixteen now, including you — report directly to me. We're a team, in other words. Nobody needs much supervision. We all understand what needs doing, we *want* to do it, and we work together to get it done.'

'Okay…' I said uncertainly.

'Sounds corny, I know, but it works. If you've got the right people, that is. And Phoenix prides itself on having the right people.'

I smiled, acknowledging the indirect compliment that I must be one of the right people. Whatever that meant.

'And… what will I actually be doing?' I asked. 'What's my actual job?' The offer documents I'd received through the post hadn't specified a job title.

Tom laughed. 'Fair question. But I don't know the exact answer to that yet.' I gave him a quizzical look. 'It largely depends on you,' he continued. 'You'll spend the first couple of weeks shadowing existing members of the team so we can suss out your strengths and preferences and you can get a better idea of what we're all about, then we'll decide where you can add the most value and take it from there.'

I wasn't really any the wiser. Not that I had much to compare it to, but even to me this all seemed unusually and disconcertingly vague.

'You look confused,' Tom observed.

'I am, a bit. I suppose I was sort of expecting to be given a list of tasks. You know, as some kind of office junior.'

'I'm probably not explaining things very well. Sorry, Louis. Okay… For starters, everyone does their own basic admin stuff, so there's no such thing as an office junior here. But most companies do focus on the job. They think about what needs doing, they write up a nice neat job description and then they try to find someone who fits the bill. At Phoenix, we turn that whole concept upside-down, pretty much. Like I said, we focus on finding the right people and then work out where and how we can best use them. Sounds nuts, I know, and it would probably just cause chaos in a lot of companies, but it works like a charm here. When everyone's consistently got too much to do then I know I've reached the point where I need an extra pair of hands, but not having to fill a specific job means we can look for the kind of person we want to be part of our organisation.'

For the first time in my life, nobody was trying to give me a label and stick me in a pigeonhole. I could certainly live with that. It all seemed unconventional, yet logical, and logic was my home turf.

'So, what are the qualities that make someone right for Phoenix?'

Tom grinned. '*Now* you're starting to ask the right questions! And a questioning mind is one of the main things we look for. It's more than just intelligence, it's big-picture thinking, common sense, open-mindedness, being prepared to challenge what other people take for granted, that sort of thing. Then there are qualities like loyalty, flexibility, integrity and trustworthiness. Oh, and a sense of humour's essential. We work hard here, but it's important to have fun, too.' There was Tom's easy smile again, as if to prove the point.

'Sounds brilliant,' I said, meaning it.

'Good. Right, talking of working hard, I need to crack on. We'll have plenty of other chances to chat. Meanwhile, here's a list of who you'll be shadowing over the next week or so, and right now I'll introduce you to Pam, who'll sort you out with a code to access the building and a few other bits and bobs like that.'

*

Spending eight hours a day with people is a good way to get to know them, and by the end of my first month at Phoenix I already felt that I knew my colleagues at least as well as I'd come to know my peers at school. More than that, the team had become like a second family to me. In his role as manager, Tomasz was the father figure, despite being barely thirty. Pam was the mothering type, a natural organiser and skilled coordinator who made sure everything got done and was always on hand with sound advice on any subject. I reckoned she probably had to be over sixty, although it was hard to guess her age because she wore trendy clothes and certainly didn't act like any sixty-year-old I'd ever met. She was involved in all the jokes and banter that went on between the rest of us.

When Tom had described the 'right people' qualities to me on my first day, I'd briefly pictured working with a bunch of clones if we all had those attributes in common, and the image had stirred a fleeting yet sinister discomfort. However, those worries evaporated almost immediately. In fact, you could hardly have wished for a more eclectic mix. The Mareton office was like a living advert for equality and diversity: including Ross who was in a wheelchair after a motorbike accident eight years earlier, and Chris who had seemed like one of the most conventional members of the team until he floored me by casually mentioning the fact that he'd started life as Christine, not Christopher. None of that mattered. They were all, indeed, the right people and if we were a family, we were a very happy one. Most of the time.

'God, why do people have to be such… such *arseholes?*'

It was a wet, grey Thursday morning at the beginning of August and Chris had just stormed into the office, uncharacteristically ten minutes late. His rhetorical question didn't seem to have been addressed to anyone in particular. He plonked himself down at his desk, next to mine.

'What's up? You okay?' I asked. Arseholes was a strong word by Chris's standards, so I knew he wasn't.

'Don't ask. Ugh. Idiot.'

'Charming,' I said, although I guessed the insult wasn't meant for me.

'Not you!' Chris stood up again and shrugged out of his wet jacket, which he hung on the back of his chair. 'The idiot cyclist who just damaged my car.'

'What happened?' Ross asked from his desk nearby.

Chris sat down and ran a hand through his rain-spiked hair. Pam produced a cup of coffee for him and perched neatly on the edge of Chris's desk.

'Come on. It can't be that awful. Drink this and tell us about your arsehole,' she said, winking. Everyone, including Chris, had to laugh.

'I was waiting to pull out of Norton Street; you know, by that junction where they've been digging up the road for God knows how long. I'd clocked a couple of cyclists coming towards me, riding along the pavement, and the one in front was looking back, chatting to his mate. I mean, if you're moving forwards, *look* forwards, for Christ's sake! But no, this genius just rode straight into my front wing and sort of flopped forward over the bonnet, and we both stared at each other in disbelief through the windscreen, with the wipers going nineteen-to-the-dozen. I started getting out of the car — despite the pouring rain, I might add — to check that this dipstick wasn't hurt, and you know what he does?' We shook our heads obligingly. 'Before I've even fully opened the door, he just rides off! My first thought was that I was glad he was okay, but then I noticed a dent in the wing of my car and a huge great scratch on the bonnet.'

'Oh no!' exclaimed Pam.

'Right through to the bare metal, it is. So I shouted after the guy as he's pedalling off down the pavement with his mate, and the cheeky sod only flicked me the finger.' Chris took a despondent sip of his coffee.

'Arsehole,' I agreed.

'World's full of 'em, sadly,' said Ross, wheeling himself over to give Chris a consoling pat on the shoulder.

'Don't you wish you could live on an island and choose the people you wanted to share it with?' piped up Grace from further down the office. She'd been the newest member of the team until I arrived and was only about six months older than me.

'Oh yes!' Pam agreed enthusiastically.

'Mm, an arsehole-free zone,' said Chris wistfully into his coffee mug.

'I can think of one major problem with an arsehole-free island,' said Ross.

'What?' challenged Chris.

'Constipation.'

10:59:20

The Birds and the Bees

The wet summer continued until I couldn't remember the last dry day, the last time everything wasn't damp, the last time I opened the curtains and saw blue skies. A general sodden gloom seemed to have settled heavily on everyone like a thick layer of grey mud.

Not that you could feel too sorry for yourself when every time you turned on the TV you were jolted out of your self-pity by news of the latest death toll in China. The Three Gorges Dam disaster had already officially claimed over a million lives and the international media speculated that the actual figure could be at least five or six times that many. The number of fatalities was still rising because of diseases and the massive loss of crops and livestock. How tragic to survive the catastrophe itself and then die of starvation or cholera.

I found it bizarre that UK news programmes never failed to mention the fact that at least twenty-three Britons had died in the tragedy. What did it matter? It was the same with that awful factory explosion that killed so many people in India. Were British lives worth more than those of other nationalities? Perhaps it was intended to make the drama seem less distant, to bring it closer to home. It was true that the sheer scale of the disaster dehumanised what had happened, and I realised I had no concept of what the loss of a million — let alone five or six million — people really meant, especially on the other side of the planet. I'd reached the point weeks earlier when news about the Three Gorges Dam bored me. I felt guilty admitting that, even to myself. But it didn't stop me flicking over to watch something more entertaining.

Being brutally honest, it just wasn't my problem. I'd donated a hard-earned tenner to two of the many fund-raising initiatives that had sprung up to help the relief efforts in India and China so I'd done my bit, and I reminded myself of those good deeds every time I chose to watch a mindless sitcom instead of yet more aerial footage of miles of flooded land and ruined cities. The devastation was on a scale that washed away the significance of every personal tragedy, despite the inevitable 'iconic' photograph that tried to capture it. In the case of the Three Gorges Dam, the picture that had come to personify the catastrophe was of a terrified-looking boy holding a young calf; the two were marooned on the roof of a farmhouse that had become a tiny treacherous island amid the swirling brown floodwaters. I'd seen that image so often that I'd acquired an immunity to it.

*

There was another downside to the incessant rain. As keen as I was to ride my moped, the novelty of clambering into and out of dripping waterproofs soon wore off. Enduring two bus rides a day with the great unwashed of Mareton was almost as unpleasant but at least I was dry when I arrived at work and didn't have to inflict bundles of wet nylon on my colleagues.

One morning, I climbed aboard the X56 bus at the end of Cuthbert Street and squeezed past a plastic-swathed pushchair to a free seat behind its owner and her friend. The two young women were chatting about babies and I had no option but to listen to their conversation while the bus splashed through town and the windows steamed up.

'You dunno what you're missing,' Ms Pushchair was saying.

'Nah, not my thing,' said the friend dismissively. 'Might change my mind one day, I s'pose, but I don't think I really want kids.'

'How can you even *say* that? They're just so *cute*.' Ms Pushchair leaned forward and punctuated the last word by prodding her infant's nose, which was just about the only body part visible amid all the waterproofing. 'Aren't you, Joshy-woshy? You're so *cute*. Yes you are. Oh you are. You're Mummy's cutesy-wutesy Joshy-woshy.'

The friend looked as nauseated as I felt.

'He's lovely, Shaz,' she said, to stop the mother babbling at Joshy-woshy. 'I'm not saying he isn't. It's just… well, I like my job, for one—'

'They have to keep it open for you. You could go back after.'

'Yeah, but then I'd have to pay for childcare. Besides, I just don't *want* kids. Me an' Pete wanna have some more holidays and all that, before we even think about starting a family. And even then, I'm not sure I—'

'That's a bit selfish, innit?' challenged Ms Pushchair.

'What d'you mean, selfish?'

'Having kids is what we're all here for, innit? Otherwise, what's the point? I couldn't wait to get pregnant.'

'I'm not criticising your life choices, Shaz,' said the friend. 'I just don't think it makes me a bad person if I choose not to have kids, that's all. Each to their own, an' all that.'

'So you're denying life to your baby, then,' stated Ms Pushchair, getting bolshy.

'*What?*' Again, the friend's expression — incredulity this time — mirrored my own.

'You're sayin' that a few nice holidays with Pete are more important than the life of the baby you could have if you weren't so selfish.'

'I don't believe you sometimes, Shaz. Honest to God, I don't.'

'Well it's true, innit?'

This was the most entertaining and infuriating bus ride I'd had in a long time.

'Nah, it's not true. It's rubbish,' retorted the friend.

'Why is it?' demanded Ms Pushchair.

'Because in that case I could argue that if you decide not to have any more kids after Josh—'

'Oh I want at least three,' said Ms Pushchair, as if she was talking about handbags, or doing the world some kind of favour.

'Okay, so by your argument, then, you're gonna be denying life to your fourth child. And your fifth. And so on.'

I cheered silently for the friend and had to forgo the pleasures of more pearls of wisdom from 'Shaz' because the bus had reached the industrial park. I silently wished Joshy-woshy luck as I squeezed past the buggy. With Shaz as his mother, he was definitely going to need it.

*

At lunchtime that day, I went into the office kitchen to put the ham and cheese sandwich I'd brought from home into the sandwich toaster. While I waited for the gadget to do its thing, I watched the rain trickling down the large windows that filled the back wall. Outside, the view of other buildings was relieved by one small birch tree that drooped miserably under the oppressive grey clouds. Inside, there were comfortable seats arranged around a couple of low tables in front of the windows and — as well as being used as an informal meeting area — this was where most of us ate lunch. I was the first, today. Grace and I had fallen into a routine of eating together, mostly because we tended to take our breaks at the same time. I enjoyed her company and found I was looking forward to telling her about the ridiculous conversation I'd overheard on the bus.

I took the first bite of my toasted sandwich just as Grace walked in, and discovered that it's impossible to look cool when you're desperately sucking air into your mouth to limit the scalding effect of melted cheese.

'You okay?' she asked, seeing my bright red face and watering eyes.

'Mm. Hot,' I managed, fanning my hand in front of my mouth and rushing over to fill a mug with cold water. She laughed.

By the time I started relating the conversation between Shaz and her friend, Chris and Pam had joined Grace and me in the kitchen.

'Gawd almighty,' said Chris when I'd finished. 'Some people shouldn't be allowed to breed.'

Pam sighed. 'Hear, hear. That's why Phoenix has been lobbying politicians for years to impose a limit on family size, even if it's just by structuring benefits and things to favour smaller families.'

'Huh. And instead we've got the opposite,' said Chris, polishing a red apple on his trousers as if he was about to bowl it. 'Only yesterday I saw an article about a couple bragging — *bragging* — about the fact they have eighteen kids and they can claim loads of benefits. There were pictures of the huge house they live in. Their whole lifestyle, holidays and all, is basically funded by Taxpayers-R-Us. Makes me sick.'

'That's the trouble,' agreed Grace. 'If you leave it to choice, it's the intelligent, enlightened people who decide not to reproduce because they can see that Earth is already overburdened. Which means that the idiot masses continue to breed like rabbits and we end up clinging to an obese, wheezing, polluted planet that's not only overpopulated but also overwhelmed by stupid people. Ultimately, the effect is that we're not reducing the population, we're just dumbing it down.' The rest of us were nodding. 'Sorry. I know that sounds horribly snobby and judgemental.'

'Oh, let's face it, we're all snobby and judgemental,' said Pam. 'Besides, you're absolutely right. Having kids is the biggest decision of our entire lives, yet even supposedly clever people don't really give it very much thought at all. Look at me, for example. I mean, I went to uni back in the days when that was relatively unusual, especially for a girl.'

'Must've been tricky, sitting in lecture hall seats wearing those crinoline skirts,' quipped Chris.

'Oi, cheeky!' Pam aimed a playful swipe at Chris, which he avoided, grinning. 'Anyway, I met Harry at uni and we got married, but we'd pretty much made up our minds not to start a family. We were having fun and enjoying our freedom, you know? But then a couple we knew had a baby and they kept raving about how amazing it was. Harry and I both got kind of broody, I suppose. Sounds ridiculous, and it was, in hindsight. But before I knew it, I'd put all my ambitions and dreams on hold and was the mother of two young kids. Not that I'd be without them, of course — I love them, and my grandchildren, to bits — but I'd be lying if I said I've never wondered what sort of a career and adventures I might have had if we'd stuck to our guns.'

Chris grunted. 'It's like my sister, Angela. Always said she never wanted kids. Always. Now they've got three and she and Clive, her spineless fool of a husband, never stop whingeing about it. Drives me mad every time I see them, so I try not to. I asked her once why they'd had kids if that wasn't what they wanted. You know what she said? "Clive's mum kept dropping hints about grandchildren." I was like, wow, seriously? *That* was your reason for creating three more human beings? Jesus. I know plenty of people who put more thought into what they're going to wear to a party or what they want for lunch. I just don't get it. When she was younger, Angie was always going on about saving pandas and tigers from extinction. Now all she's done is added to the problem.' Chris got up, shaking his head, and I wasn't sure whether the look of disgust on his face was because of his sister or the browning apple core in his hand.

'Apparently over a hundred species of living things become extinct every day, which is something like a thousand times the rate that would die out naturally without humans,' I said, remembering a fact I'd learned for my presentation at school. 'I wonder why pandas and tigers get all the attention.'

'Because they're big and cute and fluffy,' said Pam. 'I bet most of the species that die out are probably plants and insects that hardly anybody realised existed in the first place.'

'But they matter,' said Grace quietly. 'They all matter. They're all part of some huge, complex food chain somewhere. I do worry sometimes that, while everyone's busy having babies and campaigning to save pandas and tigers, we're going to find that we've inadvertently wiped out things like bees and other insects that pollinate all our fruit crops. It's only when that happens that we'll realise we backed the wrong horse.'

'Or panda,' I said, picking up my empty plate.

Lunchtimes at Phoenix were never dull.

10:59:21

London

There were two reasons why Monday the fifteenth of September was notable for me. Firstly, I awoke to a forgotten brightness pressing through my bedroom curtains. I threw them open and, sure enough, the sun was beaming down so brilliantly from a high blue sky that even Cuthbert Street looked good. It was like being reunited with a long-lost friend. And secondly, it was the day I found out that the world as I knew it was about to end.

My immediate thought after seeing the sunshine was that I could use my moped to get to work for the first time in ages, but then I remembered that I wasn't going to the office. Sod's law, as it was a great day for a ride. Instead, I was meeting Tomasz and Grace at Mareton station so that we could travel together by train to Phoenix's UK Head Office in London. Even so, I was tempted to take the bike, but I couldn't remember seeing any lockers at the station and I didn't want to have to carry my helmet around with me all day. I was stir-crazy after such a wet summer, though, and the last thing I felt like doing was sitting on a grimy bus. The train station was only a twenty-minute walk from Cuthbert Street and after I'd got ready I still had plenty of time, so I set out on foot, relishing the warmth of the sun on my back.

Two or three strangers smiled or said good morning as I passed —

behaviour unheard of in Mareton — and I half expected someone to burst into song like some Disney musical. It seemed that the sudden change in the weather had lifted everyone's mood. The only person who appeared completely oblivious to it was Gandalf, the old homeless guy who had haunted the streets of the town like a bearded ghost for as long as I could remember. Ironically, he spent most nights bundled in the doorway of an empty apartment block that could have housed him and a hundred others in comfort if some bureaucrat hadn't decreed that it should be boarded up. As I passed him that morning he was busy poking through the contents of a litter bin, with one proprietorial hand on the old supermarket trolley in which he kept his collected treasures. For the first time ever, I wondered what the world looked like through Gandalf's eyes. And what his real name was.

I enjoyed the walk and got to the station just after eight o'clock, ten minutes before I was due to meet the others for our 8:28am train. I spotted Tomasz as soon as I entered the ticket hall, but he was engrossed in a conversation on his mobile phone, so I hung back, not wanting to interrupt.

'…no concerns about Grace. She tends to speak out more, so I'm pretty sure about her views. I'm just not a hundred percent sure how Louis will handle it.'

I couldn't help overhearing what he was saying and wasn't sure what to do. He still hadn't seen me and was now listening intently to the person on the other side of the call.

'I know, I know. Look, he'll probably be fine with it all. He's bright and committed, but it's the moral dilemma he might struggle with. I mean, I don't think he'll freak out or anything—' There was another pause while Tom listened and I stood as far away as I could in the small station foyer, feigning interest in a rack of postcards near the news kiosk. Who the hell bought postcards of Mareton? 'Yeah, okay. Thanks Eve. Don't worry, I'll keep a close eye on them both. Anyway, I'd better go, they should be here soon… Yes, see you later.'

I bought a bottle of water that I didn't really want — Sunila

113

would have been so grumpy with me — and then turned around, pretending to scan the foyer. It felt dishonest, but I would have hated Tom to think I'd deliberately eavesdropped on his conversation.

'Louis!' Tom waved to catch my attention.

'Oh, hi Tom! Just got here.' I waggled my water bottle in front of his face, inexplicably. Feeling awkward, I opened it and took a sip. 'Mm, that's better. I walked.'

'Lovely day for it,' he said, oblivious to my clumsy acting.

Thankfully, Grace came through the door at that moment, her long dark hair tied back as usual into a neat ponytail that bobbed as she walked over to us.

'Morning,' she beamed. 'Gorgeous out there.'

The train was nearly full, but we managed to get three seats together after several people got off at the next stop. Tom spent the rest of the thirty-five-minute journey chatting to Grace and me about what to expect from our visit to Head Office. We were on our way to attend the Induction Workshop, which was known internally as the *Noobs' Conference*. Phoenix held an annual event for all new employees so that everybody attended one at some point during their first year with the company. Tom explained that it was intended as a formal welcome to the wider organisation, and an opportunity to meet the big bosses and get to know a few people from other offices.

I was looking forward to whatever the day held in store. Maybe it was just the sunshine, but I felt really happy and excited. The slight unease that I'd felt over Tom's comments during his telephone conversation was already forgotten. And whenever I looked across at Grace, sitting opposite me on the train with her knees almost touching mine, her brown eyes were sparkling, and I could tell she shared my sense of anticipation.

Phoenix's UK headquarters in central London were seriously impressive. As we entered the modern building via its big revolving doors made of glass etched with the company's logo, I was proud that I was part of it all. Only a tiny part, but still, I wasn't just a visitor: I belonged.

Grace's heels clicked on the polished floors as we walked past clusters of low, comfortable-looking dark blue chairs and approached one of the two receptionists sitting behind a huge desk. The back wall of the atrium was dominated by a giant full-colour version of the Phoenix globe cradled in fire-tipped hands.

'We're here for the induction workshop,' Tom said to the smiling receptionist.

'Through to your left, twelfth floor,' she said, gesturing with a manicured hand towards a bank of chrome security turnstiles barring access to the elevators that were visible beyond.

At a small desk in front of the turnstiles, we were greeted by a smartly dressed security guard. Tomasz signed us in and was handed three pre-printed identity passes on dark blue lanyards. While Tom dished them out, the guard instructed us to wear them around our necks at all times, after we'd used them to release the turnstiles. Mine, neatly printed with "Louis Crawford" in large letters and "Mareton" in a smaller font underneath, triggered a satisfying click when I held it near a magnetic reader on top of the barrier.

It was all very slick and efficient. Almost intimidatingly so.

There were four lifts on this side of the building, and one of those on our right announced its availability with a discreet ping almost immediately. I turned towards it, but Tom stopped me with a hand on my arm.

'The ones on this side are more fun,' he said, pressing the button to call one of the elevators on our left. Before I could ask what he meant, the brushed steel doors slid silently open and we could see that the lift had a transparent back wall. 'Hope you're not afraid of heights.'

'Wow, cool!' said Grace, stepping in, and we watched London fall away below us as we ascended smoothly to the twelfth floor.

Five minutes later we had taken our places three rows from the front in a plush auditorium with about two hundred banked seats facing a small stage, which was empty except for a lectern near the front and a backdrop of large screens showing the Phoenix logo.

Sitting between Tom and Grace, my anticipation mounted while we chatted and watched most of the other seats fill up. I felt like a kid on a special outing to the cinema.

Let the show begin, I thought to myself, grinning at Grace beside me as the lights dimmed slightly.

10:59:22

Plan A

At exactly 9:30am a tall man strolled to the centre of the stage and an expectant hush settled over the lecture theatre. He wasn't wearing a suit and tie, just smart dark trousers and an open-necked shirt. His black hair was peppered with silver and his neatly trimmed beard was completely grey. A whisper washed through the audience like a breath of wind through trees, but I couldn't catch what it said. For a full minute, the man scanned the faces in the room carefully, not looking for anyone in particular, just looking. We waited, and I was rather envious of the relaxed confidence it must take to hold a couple of hundred people's attention without saying a word. Then he broke the spell with a warm, genuine smile that made sense of the lines on his face.

'Good morning. For those of you who don't know me, I'm Roger Vee, and it's my honour and privilege to lead this company.'

Grace nudged my arm and mouthed 'Wow' at me. Roger Vee was the reclusive, almost legendary head of Phoenix. Famous for not wanting to be famous, he shunned personal media attention and always insisted that other employees got the recognition they deserved. He was supposed to have told a journalist once, politely but firmly, 'All I do is steer the ship; go and talk to the people who keep the whole thing afloat.'

By all accounts he was a brilliant businessman who, despite his unconventional and sometimes controversial approach, had led the company unerringly during more than thirty years at the helm. It was a well-known success story; in those three decades, Phoenix had become a household name all over the world and a global force in just about every eco-friendly field you could imagine, and probably a few you couldn't.

It was as if he'd followed my train of thought. 'It's been quite a journey. Several centuries ago,' he said with an amused twinkle in his eye, 'when I was in my mid-twenties, I gathered a small disorganised bunch of geeky environmental activists who thought they could change the world. And that's exactly what we did. It's amazing what you can achieve when you believe in what you're doing and you ignore all the people who keep telling you it can't be done. For the first time in my life, I was doing something that made complete sense to me. Something truly worthwhile.'

I caught myself nodding. Roger Vee's last two sentences had summed up my own feelings since I'd joined Phoenix. He was a compelling speaker. Nothing he said seemed rehearsed or stale, even though he must have told his story countless times before.

'Back then, what we lacked in knowledge and finesse we made up for in passion and daring, and we did some good stuff,' he continued in his pleasant American accent. 'Really good stuff. Things that made a difference. Things we were proud of. Our reputation grew and our intrepid little band attracted new members, but we weren't as careful about recruitment then as we are now. Some of them were only in it for the adventures and they went in search of confrontation, using our aims as an excuse to cause trouble. And, boy oh boy, they caused plenty. Fighting court cases for criminal damage and assault wasn't what I wanted to spend my life doing, and we lost all the credibility and momentum we'd worked so hard to build up. Our fledgling enterprise was suddenly bankrupt in every possible sense and my friends were quick to distance themselves from the whole thing, chalking it up to the folly of youth and going their separate ways.

'As for me, I found it harder to move on. My family urged me to grow up and get a proper job, but that would have meant admitting defeat and turning my back on things I believed were really important, and I couldn't bring myself to swallow such a bitter pill. Left alone among the ruins of my shattered dreams and ambitions, I... Well, let's just say I became very disillusioned for a while.'

Roger Vee paused with his eyes downcast, remembering. The audience was silent, subdued by the echoes of this engaging man's heartache.

'But you already know the story doesn't end there,' he said, brightening, and the mood in the room lifted instantly. 'Phoenix was born from the ashes of that experience and I'd learned some valuable lessons. Since then, I've chosen the people who share this journey with me extremely carefully. Passion and drive are essential but they must be harnessed by judgement and integrity. Intelligence and excellence must be tempered by humility and respect. Open-mindedness and independent thinking won't get you very far without the courage and self-awareness it takes to pursue the path less travelled. Each and every one of you,' Roger scanned our faces again, 'is in this room because we believe you have those qualities. And the main purpose of dragging you here today is to make sure you understand — *really* understand — what Phoenix is all about.'

I stole a sideways glance at Tomasz. Although he must have heard Roger Vee speak several times before, he looked just as spellbound as the rest of us. A slight smile lit his face and his eyes shone in a way that suggested he'd walk over hot coals for this man. And I suspected that most Phoenix employees, myself included, would be willing to follow in his smouldering footsteps.

'I learned the hard way,' Roger went on, 'how important it is to focus constantly on what you're ultimately trying to achieve and remember why you're doing it, without getting caught up or lost along the way in all the nonsense you have to wade through to get there.

'Money's one of the biggest distractions. People become blinded by it, and it becomes an objective in its own right instead of being a means to an end. It's a tool, not a goal. So, no one's going to bore you today with graphs and statistics about our financial performance and profitability, because money's merely a by-product of what we do here, not the reason we do it. I'm sure our shareholders would disagree with me, but they seem pretty happy with the amount of our by-product that ends up in their pockets.

'A lot of businesses try to solve the problem of maintaining focus by coming up with a mission statement. It usually takes several expensive lunches for their marketing people to decide exactly which words are the right ones to capture what the company's all about, then they write this magical sentence down and it either gets filed away and forgotten, or plastered everywhere and ignored. The words are meaningless unless people live them and make them real every day. That's why you won't find Phoenix's mission written down anywhere. But it is, and has always been, to help create a better, more sustainable world for a managed human population.'

More than ever, I felt elated by the sense that I was precisely where I was supposed to be, and proud to be part of an organisation that was such a force for good in the world.

'I'm now going to hand over to my colleagues Eve Gyer and Rashid Iqbal, who will summarise all of the incredible things we've achieved in pursuit of that mission and explain why — no matter what our shareholders might think — Phoenix is a big fat failure.'

I'd been ready to applaud enthusiastically at the end of Roger's inspiring speech, but that last word hung shockingly in the air. Instead, as he left the stage, a few uncertain claps petered out among the confused murmuring that filled the auditorium.

Over the next hour, Eve and Rashid — a bearded man wearing a neat blue turban — tag-teamed seamlessly in a fascinating presentation about the many projects in which Phoenix was involved. Their words were accompanied by images and video clips on the huge screens at the back of the stage, and the scale and scope of the company's activities around the world was mind-blowing.

Then, in contrast to the busy colours and activity portrayed previously, the screens suddenly went dark. Single spotlights picked out Eve and Rashid on the stage.

'As Roger said earlier, we've pursued a clear aim: to help create a better, more sustainable world for a managed human population,' Eve reminded us. 'That last part has always been critical. And we have failed.'

Eve looked to Rashid and he continued, 'All of the work we've done to help replant forests, protect natural habitats, research alternative energy, manage waste, produce food more efficiently, etcetera... All of that addresses the symptoms of an overpopulated planet, not the cause. Every hard-won achievement is negated by the inexorable growth of the human population. No matter how fast we develop new technology, no matter how we strive to implement solutions, mankind's efforts to solve its own problems are always overtaken and left hopelessly behind, choking in the dust of a species that seems intent on reproducing at any cost.'

Eve took up the story. 'Phoenix hasn't ignored this part of its mission. Far from it. We started at the top, campaigning directly with governments all over the world and pushing to get the issue of overpopulation on international agendas, but we've failed. When the internet took off, we were optimistic about its potential as a tool to raise awareness and stimulate debate but again, despite our best efforts, we've failed. We've also worked directly with communities to educate people about birth control and increase access to contraception, but it's not enough.'

'There are a lot of reasons why we and other organisations with similar agendas to ours have failed,' said Rashid. 'We could blame the democratic governments whose politicians are all too aware that their power is dependent on the people who vote for them; they know that the introduction of unpopular policies would bring a swift end to their leadership. We could blame the wealthy and influential elite who benefit from the existence of more consumers; they've certainly been known to censor and discredit those who campaign for population control. We could blame religious indoctrination, social conditioning, the media…' Rashid shrugged his shoulders. 'I could go on, and all of those factors play a part, but ultimately it is people themselves who are unwilling to listen, to understand, to change. Joe Bloggs — the ordinary man in the street — is the planet's most dangerous enemy. Society has been telling him for thousands of years that large families are indicators of health, wealth and happiness, so it's no surprise that he squeals about his human rights if anyone dares to suggest that he should have fewer children.'

Eve cut in smoothly. 'But the thing that's going to rear up and smack Joe Bloggs squarely in his complacent face is our old friend exponential growth. Here's how we try to explain it. At exactly ten o'clock, a scientist places a single bacterium in an empty petri dish.' The screens showed a simple animation of this, before zooming in as if we were looking down on the dish from above. 'Every minute, the number of bacteria doubles.' On the screen, the single cell divided into two, and then the two divided to make four. This process continued steadily in the animation while Eve went on, 'We tell Joe Bloggs that it takes exactly one hour for the petri dish to become completely full. We ask at what time the dish will be exactly half-full and Joe answers confidently, "Half past ten".' She paused.

I frowned at Grace beside me. She met my gaze, shaking her head, and we whispered simultaneously, '10:59.'

The rest of the audience was doing the same, and Eve waited until the room was silent again. 'Of course, Joe's logic is fatally flawed. The dish will be half-full at *10:59*. I don't need to explain that in our analogy Earth is the petri dish and the bacteria represent the human population. Poor Joe and Mrs Bloggs and all their little Blogglets are in for a nasty shock when they find out first-hand how quickly the problems of overpopulation will escalate.

'Back in our petri dish, the bacteria will continue to multiply until they either run out of nutrients or are poisoned by their own waste and it seems that, despite our supposed cleverness, the human race is hell-bent on doing exactly that. *Exactly* that. Why would we possibly choose such a depressingly sad fate for our near descendants when it's within our power to avoid it? When we put this to Joe Bloggs, he refuses to believe that things are really that bad, or that his own actions can make any real difference. Or he argues that growth can be sustainable if we simply apply our brilliant intellects and amazing technology to the more efficient use of resources. The fact is that we're already in a situation of massive overshoot where we're using up the Earth's dwindling assets increasingly rapidly and, as Rashid said, however clever we are about it, our innovations will not be exponential but our growth will be. Even a planet full of geniuses could never hope to keep pace.

'And, ladies and gentlemen, I think you'll find…' Eve turned towards the screen as the doomed petri dish was replaced by a real-time digital clock whose seconds were ticking away. '…that it's already 10:59.'

I checked my own watch. She was right.

10:59:23

Fallout

I hadn't even thought about whether I was hungry or thirsty until we were told that a short refreshment break was next on the agenda, and then coffee suddenly seemed like the best idea in the world. The coffee was good and the cups were small, so I made my way to the serving table to get refills for myself and Grace (Tom didn't want one), forced to take a slalom route between the knots of people who were chatting animatedly in the open area outside the auditorium. I felt terribly grown up. It was a good feeling.

Turning away from the serving table, armed with two very full cups plus a couple more ginger cookies to replace the ones we'd already eaten, I almost collided with someone who had come up behind me. We both watched helplessly as a miniature tide of coffee heaved itself over the sides of the cups despite my attempt to steady them, and the other person deftly plucked the two cookies off the saucers before they even got their feet wet. I looked up gratefully to find Eve smiling at me.

'Hello Louis,' she said, holding the rescued cookies. 'Can I help?'

Mumbling my thanks, acutely aware that I was pink with embarrassment, I led Eve back to where Grace and Tom were waiting.

''Scuse fingers.' Eve handed one of the biscuits to Grace, who threw me a bemused look as she relieved me of one of the swamped cups and saucers.

'Mugs,' Eve declared, holding out the other cookie to me between an elegant finger and thumb. 'That's the answer. If we had some proper mugs instead of these silly little cups and saucers, they wouldn't need to fill them so full. I shall have to have words with the management.' She winked. 'Anyway, back in a mo'.'

She disappeared into the throng but reappeared beside us with her own coffee while we were still laughing.

'Don't you dare dunk that cookie, Louis, not after my heroic efforts to keep the damn thing dry.'

'I wasn't—' I started to protest, then saw the twinkle in Eve's eyes.

'So, what do you think of it all so far, Grace?' she asked, sparing me.

'Really interesting. And powerful. I can't believe people don't act when they're confronted with such compelling facts. Why haven't those arguments worked?'

How come Grace could effortlessly produce words like 'compelling' while I always managed to act like a clumsy, mumbling buffoon? I concentrated on sipping my coffee without splashing the contents of the saucer on my clean white shirt.

'The simple answer is that people don't want to hear those things,' Eve said. 'Even if they know it's all true, they'd rather cling to even the weakest counter-arguments than face such a troubling reality. They seem to think that the problem might somehow go away if they keep on refusing to acknowledge its existence.'

'So meanwhile, it gets worse and worse,' added Tomasz.

At that moment a siren sounded and all conversations ceased. I assumed it was a fire alarm, but it stopped almost immediately. Just a test, maybe.

'Ladies and gentlemen,' Rashid spoke loudly from the other side of the room. 'Let's imagine the siren you just heard was a warning that a nuclear bomb will land very close to our current location in exactly one hour's time. You have some important decisions to make before then. If you look on the reverse of your ID pass, you'll see the name of your group facilitator and the colour assigned to your break-out group. Please join your facilitators without delay. The clock is ticking.'

While Rashid was speaking, Eve and Tom had moved quickly to the front of the room to join the row of other managers who were acting as facilitators. Each of them was now holding a laminated coloured disc above their head. There was a general buzz while the rest of us checked the backs of the ID passes hanging around our necks. Sure enough, in small print, mine said "Eve Gyer. Blue." Grace's read "Tomasz Kowalski. Yellow". I was surprised at the strength of my disappointment that we weren't going to be in the same group.

'Oh well, see you at lunch, I guess,' she said.

'If we haven't been nuked,' I replied, pulling a face.

*

Eve led me and the other nine members of Blue group to a small meeting room along the corridor. She didn't need to tell us to treat the scenario seriously; her uncharacteristically grave expression did that.

'A nuclear bomb will land near here in…' she checked her watch, '…approximately fifty-five minutes. The good news is that you have a bunker. The bad news is that there are ten of you and the bunker can only take six, maximum. You need to decide who will be saved and who will be left outside to die.'

The situation was fictional, but Eve's sombre tone and stark summary were discomfiting, nonetheless.

'Here are your roles.' Eve fanned out some slips of paper and offered them to us face down. 'A few of them are gender-specific so, if you pick one that's inappropriate, we'll swap them in the interests of realism, okay?'

We all chose a slip at random. Mine said that I was a survival expert with lots of useful skills, but that I wasn't sure I wanted to live in a world ravaged by nuclear war and wouldn't fight for a space in the shelter.

'I'm a heavily pregnant woman,' declared a big, bearded guy opposite me, holding up his slip of paper. There were a few giggles.

'Of course you are, Jack,' said Eve, deadpan. 'Swap with Carine, would you?'

The girl standing next to Jack exchanged slips with him. She had short spiky hair and a pierced nose, and she didn't look too chuffed that he'd made her pregnant.

'Everybody else okay?'

We nodded.

'The roles aren't a secret,' Eve continued. 'Here's a list of them. You might find it useful to make your own notes as we go.' She handed out A4 sheets and pens. The sheets were printed with a list of the ten roles, with space to write pros and cons against each of them. 'There are no right or wrong answers, and only one rule: you must reach consensus as a group on who will be saved. You have,' she checked her watch again, 'fifty-one minutes. The bunker is in that corner of the room,' Eve pointed, 'and the six occupants must be in there safely by the time the bomb drops.'

We looked at each other for a few seconds, unsure how to begin.

'Go!' urged Eve.

'Right,' said Jack assertively, taking a seat at the head of the rectangular table. We all followed suit and sat down. 'Let's start with the obvious, shall we?' He looked down the list of roles in his hand, already scribbling notes. 'Who's the survival expert?'

I raised my hand. Jack read my name from my ID pass.

'Well I guess you're safe then, Louis,' he said. 'We're gonna need your skills. Everybody agree?'

Three or four people nodded.

'Actually, I'm not sure I want a place in the bunker. And it's Louis with a wiss, not a wee,' I said. For once, I didn't blush.

'What?' Jack stared at me.

'My name's pronounced Lou-*wiss*. And I'm not sure I want to

127

survive a nuclear attack. Maybe that's not a world I want to live in. I'm happy to give some of you a few survival tips, though,' I said, improvising. If anyone had told me a few months ago that I'd be speaking up like this in front of a bunch of strangers, I'd have refused to believe it. A bird swooped past outside the window, high above the city, the movement catching my eye. Or perhaps it was a small pig flying by.

'Oh. Er, cool. Well that's still a no-brainer, then. Louis can stay behind,' said Jack, crossing things out on his piece of paper.

'Hang on, Jack,' said a blonde woman. The name on her badge was Jayne Fletcher-Harris. 'It's not just your decision. We're all entitled to our opinions and I think maybe we should try and persuade Louis to go into the bunker with us. If he's a survival expert, his skills might mean the difference between life and death for the rest us, if not in the bunker then afterwards, and putting his wants above the needs of the group seems pretty selfish to me.' She looked at me and smiled lopsidedly. 'Nothing personal, Louis.'

Before I could say anything, the guy on my right spoke up. His name was Ali, according to his ID.

'I disagree. I don't think we should force Louis to do something he doesn't want to do. Not only would that mean denying a place to somebody who really wants to survive, but also he might be really miserable in there and we've got to share a bunker with him for however long.'

'Yeah, and if Louis's survival skills are all about stuff like building shelters and making fires and spit-roasting squirrels, that's not even gonna be relevant to us,' added someone else.

'Good point,' Jayne said. 'Um, Eve?' Eve was sitting apart from us, listening to our conversation and making notes. 'Are we allowed to ask you about the bunker? What facilities we'll have? And how long we'll need to stay in there?'

'It's high time somebody did,' Eve said, extracting a printed sheet from among her papers. 'Yes, you are! I suggest you all jot this down on the back of your sheets. You'll have to remain underground for anything up to three months, depending on how close you are to ground zero. The shelter's equipped with lights, an air filtration system, a small generator and a limited amount of fuel to run it, a radio, rations of food and drinking water, bed-rolls and blankets, a chemical toilet, a first aid kit, a radiation monitor, emergency batteries and a few basic tools. Forty-seven minutes left.'

'Look, we've only talked about one person so far,' Carine pointed out. 'We don't have time for this. Maybe we should just draw straws or something. At least that way it's fair.'

'But Louis doesn't even want to go in!' Jack protested.

'If we leave it to chance, we might end up with six blokes in there,' said a curly-haired woman called Sara.

'What's wrong with that?' asked a freckly ginger kid who hadn't said a word until then. It was a first for me, not being the quietest one in a group.

'For all we know, we might be the only survivors,' Sara explained with exaggerated patience. 'And if we've only saved half a dozen men, it's bye-bye human race.'

The conversation got going properly after that but, the more we discussed each character's case, the more we realised there were no straightforward answers.

Several people thought Carine should definitely be saved simply because she was heavily pregnant, but others argued against it. There might be problems with the birth that we weren't equipped to deal with and, if Carine or the baby didn't make it, we'd have a corpse in the bunker. Even if the birth went smoothly, there'd be no food for the baby if Carine couldn't breastfeed for some reason, there were no nappies, plus we'd all be stuck in an enclosed space with a crying new-born to add to our woes.

Ali's character was a sixty-eight-year-old retired man who volunteered to stay behind because he'd already lived a full life. Sara's character was Ali's wife, who wouldn't go into the shelter without him.

'Cool,' said Jack, inappropriately. 'That's another obvious decision, then. And if Louis, Ali and Sara are all willing to stay, then we only need one other person. Any more volunteers?'

'Does it say in your notes what you did before you retired, Ali?' I asked.

'Yeah. I was a mechanic and handyman. And before that, a radio operator in the army.'

'And you, Sara?'

'It says I was a nurse.'

'Well, we might need all those skills!' exclaimed Carine.

'Not to mention nearly a hundred and forty years of life experience between them,' Jayne added.

'And they were prepared to sacrifice themselves for other members of the group,' I said. 'If I had to be stuck in a bunker for three months, I'd want to be with decent people like that.'

The debate raged on with surprising ferocity. At times, everyone was trying to speak at once. When things got heated, some members of the group withdrew and stopped contributing for a while, focusing on making their own notes. Jack, our self-appointed leader, was one of those. I kept hoping he'd get us back on track, but he sat doodling and looking sulky.

With less than five minutes to spare, it was Jayne who stepped up to summarise the arguments and helped us finally reach agreement — or at least acceptance — that Carine and I would stay behind, along with a nutritionist and a local celebrity. It was unexpectedly poignant watching the others walk away to the corner that represented the bunker.

Eve spent a few minutes debriefing us afterwards and congratulated us for the result we'd achieved.

'Did we get it right, then?' Jack asked.

'As I said at the beginning, there are no right or wrong answers with something like this,' she replied, 'but you tried hard as a group to listen to everyone's opinions and weigh everything up within the time available. It's tricky to balance emotional and practical considerations, isn't it?' We all nodded. 'And you often find that the seemingly easy options aren't necessarily the best ones. It's always so interesting to see how people react to such dilemmas.

Short non-negotiable timescales, not to mention the prospect of imminent death, force us to focus on what really matters, however uncomfortable that may be.'

It had been an intense hour. I noticed that Carine looked almost tearful; maybe she was feeling the effects of her fictional hormones. As we left the meeting room and headed back to join the others for lunch, Eve tucked her folder under her arm and put a discreet, comforting hand on Carine's shoulder and started chatting to her about the weather.

I brought up the rear, thinking that the notes Eve had made during that session would make fascinating reading.

10:59:24

Plan B

Lunch was a noisy affair. The polite conversations that had taken place earlier over coffee were a muted memory. Surviving a nuclear bomb together had well and truly broken the ice, and now the open area outside the auditorium was brimming with lively discussions about who'd been saved and sacrificed during the past hour. Clutching a paper plate full of tasty morsels from the buffet table, it took me a few minutes to find Grace and Tomasz in the throng. When I did, we too compared notes.

'Oh my God, I can't believe you guys didn't save the pregnant woman!' Grace gave me an incredulous look over the top of a triangle of sesame prawn toast she was about to eat. 'That's pretty brutal.'

'We had good reasons,' I protested, feeling like some sort of monster. 'It would have been too big a risk: to her, the baby, and the rest of us, potentially. Who got left behind in your group?'

'The celebrity, the older couple and the vicar.'

'Sounds like the beginning of a really bad joke,' said Tom, popping a cherry tomato into his mouth.

A short while later, the babble was silenced by the insistent *chink-chink* of someone tapping a glass with a metal teaspoon.

'Ladies and gentlemen,' Rashid was saying loudly. 'Ladies and gentlemen, please can I have your attention?'

The room quickly fell silent and, apart from a handful of people darting over to deposit empty plates and glasses on the buffet table, everyone turned respectfully to face Rashid.

'It certainly seems that we've had a productive and thought-provoking morning.'

There was a murmur of agreement.

'We're about to start the afternoon sessions. Again, you'll be working in smaller groups, but not the same ones as before. Please listen up, and would the following people accompany me?' He carefully and clearly read out a list of about twenty names. The only one I recognised was Jack's. The group sorted themselves out and Rashid led them off along a corridor, like a duck trailing a load of ducklings.

When they were out of earshot, Eve directed the rest of us to go back into the auditorium. A queue formed as we were funnelled through one half of the double doors, and I wondered why they hadn't opened the other one. Chatting quietly, we shuffled obediently forward.

'Are your phones still switched to silent?' Tomasz asked. Grace and I both nodded. He had checked the same thing with us before Roger Vee's presentation first thing that morning, which now seemed ages ago.

As we moved closer to the door into the lecture theatre, I could see that something was going on just beyond it. Whatever it was, it explained the delay. We stepped through. Four people were standing immediately inside the room. One was directing the incoming audience with polite instructions. Another was standing behind a large table; efficiently, he got us to write our names onto paper bags, and then sealed our mobile phones and any other electronic gadgets inside and sorted them into tubs. Beyond him, the other two were a man and a woman who quickly checked bags and pockets and skimmed our clothing with some kind of handheld scanner.

What on earth was this all about? A tingle of apprehension

zipped down my spine, but Tomasz looked reassuringly unfazed.

Just ahead, Eve was directing everyone to take seats in the auditorium. When we'd all done so, she strode purposefully down the aisle and stood behind the lectern at the front of the stage. She waited until the security team had left the room and closed the door, taking the tubs of phones and gadgets with them. Eve was wearing her serious look again.

'Sorry about the security measures, folks, but what I'm about to tell you is highly confidential. You'll soon see why. Please remember that you signed legally binding confidentiality and non-disclosure agreements when you joined the company.'

I exchanged a glance with Grace. In her eyes I read the same mixture of puzzlement and excitement that she must have seen in mine.

'In fact, it's no exaggeration whatsoever to say that you are about to be entrusted with one of the biggest secrets in history. You are in this room because we believe you are bright enough and strong enough to both understand and safeguard it.' Eve was choosing and speaking her words with emphasis and precision. 'We've selected each of you with enormous care and assessed your capabilities to play a vital role in what lies ahead. Nevertheless, the secret is one that we burden you with only reluctantly. We know that it will weigh heavily.' She paused, and an expression of profound sorrow clouded her face. 'I realise I haven't given you any specific information to go on, but if anyone wants to leave before we take things further, you are absolutely free to do so and someone will escort you to join Rashid and the other group. They'll be spending the afternoon brainstorming new ways in which we might address the challenge of population control.'

Heads turned but nobody moved to leave. I suspected that, like me, they were now burning with curiosity, despite the sense of dread that Eve had bestowed upon us. It was a bit like driving past a serious car crash: you couldn't help wanting to look, even though you knew you might later wish you hadn't.

Eve waited for a few seconds, scanning the faces in the room, and then nodded once. 'So be it.' She took a deep breath.

I realised my whole body was tense and made a conscious effort to relax in the comfortable seat.

'We've invested decades in trying to influence and educate people all over the world in the fervent hope that the increasing human population could be brought under control. We were optimistic at first. After all, surely everyone would soon see that the problem was real and would be eager to do something pro-active about it. We've dedicated countless hours, Phoenix's brightest minds and most persuasive ambassadors, millions of pounds... But, as we explained to you this morning, our best efforts — and those of numerous other organisations and individuals — have failed. It's painful to acknowledge it but it's an undeniable fact.

'That was Plan A: to get the world to see sense and take voluntary action to control the runaway growth in human population before it started causing too many insurmountable problems. It should have been easy. However, our approaches weren't welcomed. In many cases, we couldn't even persuade people to discuss or consider the subject.'

Once more, Eve's attractive face was contorted by sadness and deep emotion. We were silent, hanging on her every word, waiting to be let in on the big secret.

'Eve's being polite about it.' Roger Vee materialised from the shadows at the side of the stage. 'To be honest, we were dismayed by the blind, stubborn, sometimes aggressive resistance we faced.' He joined Eve behind the lectern. 'So a few of us started reluctantly developing a Plan B. We hoped desperately that we would never need to use it. We've put it off for as long as possible, but sadly the time has come. Already, much of the damage humans have done to the climate, to the natural environment, to Earth's resources, and to other species is irreversible.

'We won't keep you in suspense any longer, except to say this: Plan B will shock you. It will, quite rightly, appal you. But please hear us out. By the time you leave this room, we believe you'll be on board.'

I was impatient now, to the point of feeling irritated. What could it possibly be, this secret plan that was so momentous and terrible? I wished Eve and Roger would just cut to the chase. After such a build-up, it was bound to be an anticlimax.

I was wrong.

Eve spread her hands. 'Put bluntly, Plan B is to cull the human population in order to save the world.' She paused to let her words sink in. They didn't. I wasn't even sure I'd heard her correctly.

'We know that things can't continue as they are without rapid escalation of all the problems associated with overpopulation,' she went on. 'We are at 10:59. We are facing full-blown crises caused by pollution and destruction. Our climate, our oceans, entire ecosystems… they are teetering on the brink of catastrophic collapse. We *must* face these facts. They can no longer be put off as problems for future generations to deal with. It's time to clean up our own mess.

'Humans have proved beyond doubt, over many decades, that we are incapable of the self-control necessary to keep our own numbers and consumption in check.'

I was trying to take in what Eve was saying but my brain hadn't really got past the word 'cull'. I'd heard about culling animals like seals and badgers. That was bad enough. They couldn't cull humans. Could they?

Eve was still talking. 'It's time to join the dots, even if they do lead us to a highly controversial and unpalatable conclusion. Control measures must be enforced. Someone, somewhere — or rather, everyone everywhere — needs to put the survival of humanity and Earth as we know it above convenience and popularity. Destroying the planet is *not* one of our human rights. The days of being too squeamish to acknowledge that stark reality are over.'

Eve looked into the audience and someone near the front put their hand in the air.

'Yes, Alan?'

'Is this another fictional scenario? Another test?'

'Sadly, no. This isn't a test. It's real.'

'So what are we talking about, here? I mean, what exactly? Are you proposing to drop a nuclear bomb somewhere? Is that what this morning's little exercise was in aid of?'

'No, Alan. God, no. For all kinds of reasons. Not least because that would target a specific geographical area and any kind of bomb is a disgusting way to kill people.'

'Are you suggesting there's a *good* way to kill people?' Alan, whoever he was, sounded incredulous.

'Actually, yes,' Roger stepped in. 'If people must be killed, you're damn right there are good and bad ways to do it.'

The stunned silence that had hung over the audience like a fog began to dissipate and a low murmur of voices throbbed in the room. It made me think of a swarm of bees. An uneasiness that I didn't want to think of as fear started to nibble at the corners of my thoughts.

Roger lulled the swarm with calm authority. 'Ladies and gentlemen, you deserve our honesty and I promise you'll have it. Absolutely. You can ask questions and be as confrontational as you like, and we will provide answers. But first, allow us to explain Plan B in a little more detail.' He looked to Eve to continue.

'Over the years, we've considered just about every option you can think of,' she said. 'Back in the very early days, there were certain people within our own organisation who believed the time had already come for direct intervention. We parted company with them because they were proposing a frightening variety of possible actions. Putting fertility inhibitors in drinking water supplies, for example. We refused because that would be indiscriminate and cruel. Think of the heartache of couples desperate to have a baby. Besides, it would almost certainly be counter-productive because some of those people would have fertility treatments and end up with three or four children when they might naturally have stopped at one or two.

'Another proposal we firmly rejected was to trigger disasters that would wipe out sections of the population. Roger and I have known people who believed that was a perfectly valid thing to

137

do. You've only got to look at what's happened recently with the chemical factory explosion in India and the dam burst in China to understand something of the environmental destruction and long-term suffering caused by those sorts of things. And again, one relatively small segment of humanity is affected disproportionately, while everyone else carries on as before. In real terms, for all the pain they cause, things like that barely put a dent in the global population and the underlying problems remain unaddressed.'

There was a battle raging quietly inside my head. My superlogic was nodding along calmly, unable to find fault in anything Eve was saying, while another part of me wanted to get up and run as far away from this surreal situation as I could possibly get.

'So our Plan B involves the release of a virus. Not some horrible neuro-toxin or anything like that.' Eve raised her voice so that it would carry above the renewed murmuring of the swarm. 'It's an influenza virus. One that kills quickly and humanely—'

'Oh well, that's fine then!' This time, Alan didn't bother putting his hand up. He interrupted Eve with angry sarcasm. 'Biological warfare. Wonderful. Well, you can count me out. I won't play any part in killing people.'

'And we wouldn't dream of asking you to,' Eve said sweetly. 'What we want all of *you* to do is *save* people.'

10:59:25

Inescapable Logic

Having snatched the wind out of Alan's sails before he could really get going, Eve continued calmly. 'The mechanisms and personnel needed to introduce the virus are already in place. You won't be expected to have any direct involvement with that.'

A weird chill spread over the back of my neck and I felt vaguely nauseous. She was serious. This was really happening.

'What we want you to do is administer a vaccine that will *protect* people against the new flu virus,' she said. 'All of you in this room will be among hundreds of thousands of Phoenix employees worldwide who have been selected specifically to *save* people. Many of you are here because of the schools project; that was our final push to find enough personnel to administer the vaccine ahead of the release of the virus. Sessions like this one are happening in every country. You're here because you wanted to change the world and we're going to give you the opportunity to do exactly that, on a scale that you've almost certainly never imagined. Your role is a vital one and a positive one: you'll be ensuring that the best of the human race survive to safeguard the future of every species and the planet that is our home.'

Eve paused, scanning the sea of shocked faces.

'We know it's a lot to take in,' said Roger.

That had to be the understatement of the century. I felt as though I was reeling from a physical blow. My head was fizzing as my brain tried to process everything. I had a million questions, but they were all half-formed, tangled, adding to my confusion. Judging by the stunned silence in the auditorium, everybody else was struggling too.

'All we're asking for now is that you hear us out.' Roger's tone was confident, not pleading. He'd had years to get used to this idea. He'd clearly sold Plan B to hundreds of other recruits already and, actually, I found that reassuring. To the best of my knowledge, Roger Vee wasn't some fanatical misguided zealot evangelising a personal cause; both he and Eve were sane, respected, level-headed people. Weren't they? I was at least prepared to listen to what they had to say. And so, it seemed, were my colleagues.

'As I said this morning,' Roger went on, 'Phoenix prides itself on recruiting people who are able to think for themselves, who aren't afraid to challenge things. That's you. We know you're full of doubts and questions. Frankly, we'd be disappointed if you weren't. I promise that most of those will be addressed by what we're about to tell you, but afterwards we'll welcome anything you want to ask or say. Would Plan B have been an easier sell to a bunch of mindless "sheep" who we could practically brainwash into helping us with implementation? Hell, yes. But easy isn't always right. We're confident that Plan B is as polished and thorough as it needs to be because it's been challenged by people like you, and refined and perfected as a result.'

As soon as Roger finished speaking, he looked to Eve and she picked up her cue to continue. 'We've found that the best way to run this session is to anticipate some of the questions we know you have. Let's start with the big ones about the justification for such drastic measures.'

She pressed a button on a discreet hand control and words stretched across the screens behind her:

"Is Plan B really necessary?"

'I could spend the rest of the afternoon presenting just a

fraction of the evidence which proves that the answer to this is "Yes",' she said. 'But I won't, and I don't believe I need to with this particular audience. You know the facts. You know that we're already in a dangerously untenable situation. You know that we've already reached a state of global ecological overshoot where we're running out of critical resources. You know that we're already causing irreparable damage to biodiversity and climate and to the Earth itself.'

Behind Eve, various headlines such as "Ten Billion People Before 2050" and "Humans are Driving the Next Mass Extinction Event" flashed on the screen. And then there was a cartoon of a miserable-looking, battered Planet Earth waving a white flag of surrender.

'Sadly, Plan B *is* necessary. We wouldn't be talking to you about it if it wasn't. It's necessary because we as a species have failed quite spectacularly to control the growth of our own population. It's necessary because, despite the signs that have been staring us in the face for decades, there are still no indications that the human race will take meaningful action until it's far too late. And the depressing reality is that, even if by some miracle we could get the whole world to start controlling population growth right now, the impact of that control wouldn't start to make a big difference for several generations, by which time there might be nothing left to save.'

I was still very aware of the conflict going on inside me. My superlogic was sitting back, cool and relaxed, with an air of 'I told you so', while my socially-conditioned side was racing around in panicky little circles with its fingers in its ears, hoping there wasn't any history of heart problems in the family.

A new question popped up on the screen:

"What about all the counter-arguments?"

Eve continued. 'Some people refuse to acknowledge that population growth is a problem. They quote an array of counter-arguments but, basically, these can all be consolidated under three main umbrella headings. We call them the "Three Ts": Texas,

Technology and Transactions.' As Eve spoke the words, they appeared across the top of the screen.

'The first "T", Texas, covers all the redistribution arguments. You may have heard people say that you could fit the entire human population of the world into the state of Texas, so surely there must be plenty of room for everyone. The first part of that statement is technically correct. The area of Texas is roughly seven-point-five trillion square feet, so seven-point-five billion people would have a thousand square feet each, which equates to an area about ten metres by ten metres. There's a big "but" there, though.'

Grace leaned over and whispered, 'It's America. There are probably quite a few big butts.'

I smiled at the inappropriate joke and realised that I'd almost forgotten Tom and Grace and the rest of the audience were there. I'd been so engrossed in what Eve was saying and preoccupied with trying to get my head around the bombshell that she and Roger had dropped in our laps.

'The Texas argument is meaningless. Physically fitting somewhere is very different from living somewhere. You could *fit* ten people into a telephone kiosk, but even one person couldn't *live* there. Our ten-metre squares in Texas — which are shrinking every day — wouldn't allow for streets, shops, schools and other infrastructure, for starters. But the minor detail the Texas argument conveniently overlooks is the fact that it takes hundreds of times as much physical space to produce the food and energy that each and every person requires to support even an average lifestyle.

'If you doubt the world is full, think about how much time you spend sitting in traffic jams or trying to find a parking space. Look out of the window and see all the people living and working in little boxes stacked on top of each other. Notice how many new housing developments are being built. There's no denying that habitable land is in increasingly short supply. Even if it was feasible, redistributing people would not solve the problems of overpopulation. And redistribution of wealth and resources isn't the answer either; that's basically communism, and history has taught us to approach that model with extreme caution.'

Below the word 'Texas' on the left side of the screen there was an aerial image of an overcrowded city street. The pavement was invisible beneath teeming pedestrians and the road was completely covered by nose-to-tail vehicles. I felt claustrophobic just looking at it.

'Technology, then. Technology will save us!' Eve exclaimed, moving on to the second of the Three Ts as a photograph of a white-coated scientist in a laboratory appeared under the central heading.

'We humans are so smart, we can just "clever" our way out of this mess. Yes, we're smart. We've come up with countless brilliant innovations and some of those *are* helping us to tackle the challenges of overpopulation. We can harness solar energy, we can coax higher yields from our crops, and so on. But as Rashid said this morning, we can't keep pace. With net growth of 240,000 people every single day, as fast as we solve one problem, another ten appear. And the solutions themselves have their own side-effects and resource requirements.'

I recognised the net growth statistic from my own presentation back at Mareton School just a few short months ago, and my superlogic nodded sagely while it joined dots and ticked boxes in my brain as Eve carried on talking.

'"Ah, but necessity is the mother of invention," say the technologists. "Wait until we're under pressure. Humans will be able to solve everything just as soon as the you-know-what starts hitting the fan." Newsflash: it already has, and we haven't. The only technological innovation I can think of that might help us now is a time machine. And, with the world at 10:59, time is another crucial resource that we're rapidly running out of.

'Another Technology argument is that we needn't worry about overpopulation because, by the time things get really bad, we'll be able to move to another planet. Really? And that's okay? Once we've finished chopping down the trees, wrecking the food chains, toying with genetics, destroying habitats, altering the climate and polluting the oceans, it's okay for us to just bugger off and leave every other living thing to die in our wake? Having utterly vandalised an entire planet, it's okay to go and do the same somewhere else?'

I hadn't seen Eve angry before. Her eyes flashed and her passion was contagious. I noticed I'd clenched my fists.

She took a calming breath before she continued speaking. 'Besides, having the technology to facilitate space travel is one thing. Finding another habitable planet is quite another, let alone evacuating billions of people. You really think everyone would get to go? And that's before we even stop to consider whether we'd be happy and have a reasonable quality of life on another planet.

'No. Technology can help us to alleviate some of the symptoms of overpopulation, but it is not the solution to all our problems.'

Our attention was drawn to the right-hand side of the large screen behind Eve as a graphic appeared below the Transactions heading. It showed a Monopoly game board superimposed over lots of graphs and spreadsheets.

'The Transactions umbrella covers the economists' arguments that we *need* population growth to fuel socioeconomic development. The bean counters see the world as a huge elaborate trading game which relies on continuous transactions for the production and distribution of wealth although, as in any game, there are more losers than winners.

'Economists pepper their arguments with abbreviations like "GDP" and fancy terms like "demographics" and "dependency ratios" that most of us don't fully understand. So, not wanting to look silly, we duly assume that the economists must be jolly clever people and must therefore be right when they say we need even more humans on the planet. Let's dig beneath the big words and summarise the things they're actually saying.

'Thing one: the fastest population growth rates are seen among the poorest people, and they can't buy lots of *stuff* and boost the global economy.

'Thing two: people are living longer and, if they have fewer children, that gives us an ageing population which puts increased burdens on pensions and healthcare.

'Thing three: we need more humans grouped together in urban environments to achieve economies of scale and to get busy cooperating and producing and innovating and solving the world's problems. The clever economists miss the irony that these problems stem from the fact that there are too many people in the first place.

'Thing four: all we actually need to do is focus on reducing excessive consumption. Well, nobody's tried to crack that particular nut before. And good luck with that.

'Thing five: we need more people in order to be able to feed, clothe, house, educate, employ, and entertain more people. Hmm.'

I found myself smiling. I couldn't help enjoying Eve's biting sarcasm, and wished economics had been this entertainingly explained when I was at school.

'All of the economics arguments go around in circles. Maybe that's the point. Maybe they want to get the rest of us chasing our tails while they line their pockets so they can afford to emigrate to a five-star space station when things get really nasty. Protecting the interests of trade and commerce won't save us then. Our clever bean counters will still be preoccupied with inventing big words, calculating gross domestic product and worrying about the performance of their stock portfolios when we finally realise we've sawn through the branch we're sitting on.

'Money is an artificial construct, a human invention.' Throughout the session, Eve had been moving around the stage addressing us all, but now she came forward and scanned a section of the front row. She pointed, choosing someone. 'Can I borrow you for a minute?' A guy with a thick mop of wavy blond hair stood up slowly and Eve beckoned him up onto the low stage. 'Could you lend me some money? Ten or twenty pounds, perhaps?'

Mop Man looked comically dubious, prompting laughter from the audience. The atmosphere in the room was lighter; the earlier tide of shock and outrage over Plan B had receded for now. Mop pulled a slim wallet from the back pocket of his crumpled trousers, opened it and peered inside.

'You'll get it back,' Eve said, smiling.

Mop hesitantly extracted a ten-pound note.

'Ten whole English pounds. Thanks.' She plucked the note from his grasp and looked at it, then pointed to a line of small print. 'Could you read out what it says just there, please? Nice and loud.'

Mop peered at his tenner. 'I promise to pay the bearer on demand the sum of ten pounds.'

'Ha! You see? It's literally an I.O.U. from the Bank of England. A token. Your ten-pound *note* is just a piece of plastic. It has no material value. It merely *represents* tangible wealth. That wording dates back to the days when you could exchange your promissory note for the equivalent in gold coins. Today's banks won't do that, you'll find. It's not real. And most of our money these days isn't even as physical as this.' She held up the note. 'It's all online, virtual, merely numbers on a computer screen.

'Thank you.' Eve handed Mop Man his tenner and gestured for him to return to his seat. 'Basing an argument to keep producing more humans on the need to keep generating numbers on a computer screen is utter madness. All the money in the world will mean nothing if we plunge the Earth into famine, destruction, war and disease.

'You may also hear references to predictions that the number of humans will reach a natural plateau at some conveniently movable point in the not-too-far-distant future. Even if we all keep popping out offspring at the same rate, the population will somehow magically level out while granny's busy knitting another set of bootees for grandchild number twelve? Even if those predictions are true, is it wise to sit back and wait for the population to stabilise at around, what, eleven billion? Fifteen billion? Remember, it's already 10:59. Before we reach any fabled plateau, we'll have comprehensively destroyed, corrupted and poisoned our own environment.

'Which brings us to the last big question.' Eve pressed a button and the Three Ts faded from the screens, to be replaced by:

"What will happen if we do nothing?"

Eve looked solemn. 'The writing's on the wall, as the saying goes, even if everyone's pretending they can't read it as they bustle past looking for more sand to stick their heads in. If we do nothing, the problems we're currently facing — congestion, water shortages, pollution and so on — are quickly going to pale into insignificance. If we continue refusing to learn the lessons that nature is trying to teach us, we will be looking at unprecedented droughts, floods, plagues and famines. Climate change will make more of the planet uninhabitable. We'll be looking at food riots. We'll be looking at global economic crisis. Fossil fuels are running out fast. Nations that have been built on oil wealth will be thrown into poverty. Migration of refugees will increase drastically. We'll be looking at growing social and political unrest and the collapse of so-called civilised society. We'll be looking at wars and pandemics that will dwarf the horrors of the past.

'Mental and physical health issues are increasing. We've never understood more about nutrition and health, yet our diet of highly processed foods and our insistence on banishing all germs from our environment have left us poorly equipped to fight off illness. Meanwhile, diseases are crossing from animals to humans because of habitat destruction and intensive farming, and they will spread ever more easily and quickly because people live in such close proximity to each other.

'So you see, it's going to happen anyway, and in an infinitely less humane, less manageable way. By controlling it, we'll be doing the human race an enormous favour. We can ensure it's over quickly. We can be prepared to clean up and help the survivors make better lives for themselves and for future generations.

'Plan B sounds absolutely monstrous at first, of course it does. But the logic behind it is inescapable. And the alternatives — including doing nothing — are ultimately far more cruel and frightening.'

As Eve finished speaking, the attentive silence gave way to the hum of voices. The swarm was stirring once more.

10:59:26

Freedom

In North Korea, Ri Joo-Won and Mun Chong-Hae were eating lunch together in the site canteen, as they did most days. It was the only time and place they felt they could talk without too much risk of being overheard.

Even at lunchtimes, both men were always careful to keep their voices down and make their conversation appear casual to any observers. The guards who patrolled the site were constantly watching, alert for the slightest misdemeanour. You had to be wary of your colleagues, too. People were actively encouraged to report anyone they suspected of wrongdoing, and it was literally more than your life was worth to arouse suspicion.

Only a few months ago, a young man from their section had mentioned he was worried that innocent comments he'd made to someone might have been taken the wrong way. It had started as some lame joke about the weather in South Korea, but he'd meant nothing by it. Of course not! He loved his country and its revered leaders, just as everyone did. The following day, the young man was not at work. The official story was that he'd been taken ill, but no one had seen him since. No one asked what had become of him. No one wanted to know the answer to that question.

Ri Joo-Won had grey shadows under his eyes. He often had

trouble sleeping, but recently his insomnia had been worse than usual.

'Are you okay, my friend?' Mun Chong-Hae enquired.

Ri Joo-Won took a sip of water and gave his colleague a bleak look. 'Fine. Just another headache, that's all.'

They ate in silence for a minute or two.

'How is your family?' Ri Joo-Won asked.

'Very well, thanks. And yours?'

'Yes, they're fine. What about your wife's cousin? The one who lives in China.'

Understanding dawned on Mun Chong-Hae's face as he recalled their previous conversation about her being married to a member of the Chinese Politburo. 'Ah. As a matter of fact, my wife is very worried about her.'

'Oh? Why?'

'Did you hear about the big dam that burst? The one on the Yangtze?'

'Yes, I heard something about that.'

'My wife hasn't had any word from her cousin since that happened.' Mun Chong-Hae lowered his voice further. 'She's afraid the accident might be much worse than the news reports suggest.'

Ri Joo-Won slowly chewed another mouthful of his lunch while he considered this.

'I sincerely hope your wife's cousin is safe, but…' He stopped, hesitant to make any reference to what they'd spoken about before.

'But what?'

'I just wondered… If the dam burst was really bad, do you think it might affect… that other thing we talked about?' Until now, Ri Joo-Won hadn't liked to push for more news about China's plans to launch a military attack on the West, but he'd been able to think of little else, and the terror of what it could mean for him and his family was driving him crazy.

Mun Chong-Hae looked downcast. He covered his mouth to cough and kept his hand there while he spoke. 'I suspect at the very least it will delay things for quite some time. If the dam burst is as big a disaster as we fear it might be, then the Politburo will have more urgent priorities. It's a shame. It's about time those American dogs got the kicking they deserve.'

Ri Joo-Won hid his relief and finished his meal. Not for the first time, he found himself thinking about everything the North Korean people were taught to believe, and whether it bore much resemblance to the truth. He wondered what life was really like in other countries.

'Do you think it's possible to miss something you've never had?' he murmured.

'Absolutely,' Mun Chong-Hae replied. 'I've never been rich, and I miss money all the time. And there was a beautiful girl I used to see on the tram when I was at university... Why? What do you miss, that you've never had?'

Ri Joo-Won shook his head and said something in a low whisper.

'What? I didn't hear you.' Mun Chong-Hae leaned closer.

'Freedom.'

Both men knew that Mun Chong-Hae could report Ri Joo-Won for that. It was a sign of the trust the two friends had in each other that they ever mentioned such things, but looking over your shoulder was a way of life. You lived in fear that the Bowibu, the secret police, would come to your door. And they wouldn't only drag *you* away to a re-education camp; they'd take three generations of your family, just to make sure.

In North Korea, freedom was an impossible dream. If you dared to dream of it, you'd better make sure you didn't talk in your sleep.

10:59:27

Questions and Answers

Roger re-joined Eve in the centre of the stage. He gestured for quiet and got it, more or less.

'Okay, let's take some questions and comments. Eve and I have radio mics but the acoustics in here are pretty good so everyone should be able to hear you if you speak up clearly.'

Before he'd finished, a forest of hands had appeared. If Roger was even remotely daunted, he didn't show it and picked someone sitting almost directly in front of me.

A large man stood up and spoke in a loud, deep voice. 'You make a very strong case; I don't think any of us would deny it. But, whatever the justification, you're proposing mass murder. I, for one, am struggling to get past that.' He sat down again.

I nodded, relieved that I wasn't the only one. I couldn't wait to find out how Grace felt about all of this.

'That's understandable,' said Eve. 'It's drummed into us from a very young age that the deliberate killing of humans is wrong. Religion tells us murder is a sin, even though millions of people have been killed in the names of various deities. The law tells us murder is a crime, yet millions have been killed in wars under the orders of world leaders and we're told that doesn't count. Everyone's willing to bend the rules when it suits them. Generally speaking, ending another human life is wrong, of course it is. But there are circumstances when it can perhaps be justified: in self-defence, to avoid unnecessary suffering, or when it's for the greater good.'

'We used the word "cull" earlier,' Roger cut in. 'It's another emotive word, but the practice of selective slaughter to reduce the population of certain species is accepted — or at least overlooked — by the majority of us as a necessary intervention. In the UK, seals are culled to prevent them from eating too many fish. Deer are culled to prevent them from damaging crops. Badgers are culled to prevent the spread of disease to cattle. Hedgehogs have been culled to prevent them from eating the eggs of rare birds. We choose to ignore the fact that those animals' numbers are only excessive in the first place because we've killed off their natural predators or otherwise meddled with the food chain. And we choose to ignore the fact that by far the biggest threat to the food stocks and rare species we're trying to protect comes from humans themselves.' He paused. 'So... who culls the cullers? There is no one to cull humans, even though our own population is completely out of control.'

'But we are starting to reap the deadly rewards of our vandalism of the natural world,' said Eve. 'As I said earlier, humans are going to die anyway because our environment is polluted, our resources are dwindling, our social structures are crumbling, our very climate is changing, and we're creating a perfect storm for the spread of diseases. And those will be horrible deaths over a long and terrifying period. So yes, we *are* talking about mass murder. I'm not going to stand here and insult anyone's intelligence by trying to deny it. But culling the human population in a quick, humane and managed way will ultimately save mankind. It will save countless other species from extinction. And it's the only thing now that will save our world while there's something left worth saving.'

A noticeably smaller forest of hands sprouted from the audience. Roger selected one of them and a strikingly attractive black woman stood up to my right.

'Saving the world sounds like the plot for a Hollywood movie. And I can't help thinking that, if this was a film, Phoenix wouldn't be portrayed as heroes. The good guys would be the ones trying to stop you. Aren't you worried that one or more of us might do just that? What if we decide to blow the whistle?'

'No, we're not worried,' said Roger, and he certainly didn't look it. 'For two main reasons. Firstly, we believe that everyone we've told about Plan B is intelligent enough to understand that, when all the facts are considered, it really does represent the best long-term option for the human race and the entire planet. And secondly, even if someone did blow the whistle — hell, they could hire a whole brass band — we've used all of the considerable experience and resources at our disposal to think through every possible scenario and take every precaution to ensure that the release of the virus will go ahead. Nothing can stop the implementation of Plan B.'

There was that chill down the back of my neck again, and my heart skipped a beat or two.

Roger was still talking. 'I completely understand why whistleblowing might occur to people. Plan B is in a league of its own, beyond anything that's come before. I'd be the first to admit that it's not politically correct or morally acceptable by any normal standards. But normal standards are hopelessly inadequate now. We *must* face the unpleasant truths, we *must* think the unthinkable, precisely because we've failed to make any of the more palatable solutions work. We had plenty of those opportunities but they've been squandered. Believe me, everyone at Phoenix wishes wholeheartedly that Plan B wasn't necessary. Everyone here cherishes life and absolutely thinks it is precious, worth protecting and nurturing. And, although it may sound ironic, that's precisely why we're doing this. The people who succumb to the virus will not die in vain. It's not over-dramatic to say that we're acting to safeguard the survival of the human race. We're not threatening the world, we're saving it. Just as literally and as surely as in any Hollywood movie.'

Every word Roger and Eve had said made complete sense to me, but the secret they'd shared with us was absolutely terrifying, nonetheless. I felt like I needed much more time to get my head around it, if only to try and rationalise with the social conscience I didn't know I had.

Roger was taking another question on the other side of the auditorium.

'Can you tell us more about the virus? And the vaccine?'

'We have someone lined up to do just that,' said Roger. 'But before we introduce him, are there any more questions about other aspects?'

A few hands went up. One of them was immediately beside my right ear and for a split second I wondered whether my own body had betrayed me.

Eve looked in our direction and said, 'Yes, Grace?'

'When is all this going to happen?' She voiced the question that was now uppermost in my mind, too.

'That's the one thing we feel it's best not to be too specific about,' Eve replied. 'But it's only fair to give you some indication. Less than a year.'

As the swarm started buzzing again, Roger quickly said, 'Okay. We'll be stopping soon for a comfort break and you'll all have plenty of chances to ask more questions before the end of the day. But first, allow me to introduce one of Phoenix's top scientists, Ben Griffin.'

The man who walked onto the stage didn't look like a top scientist. He wasn't wearing a white lab coat, for starters, and he was young, maybe not even thirty. However, as Eve and Roger exited and the newcomer took their place in the spotlight behind the lectern, I realised that he must be at least ten years older than I'd first thought.

'Okay, let me tell you a bit about influenza in general and the Phoenix virus and vaccine in particular. Feel free to raise your hand if you've got any burning questions as we go, but let's try and get to tea and biscuits as soon as possible.

155

'I'm sure all the ladies in the audience already know there's a big difference between the common cold and influenza. Gentlemen, I'm sorry to be the one to break it to you but man flu isn't really a thing. Proper flu basically gives you all of the delightful symptoms associated with a bad cold, plus fever and pains. It makes you feel very poorly indeed. Every year, ordinary seasonal flu causes severe illness in… well, would anybody care to guess how many people?'

A few hands went up, and Ben took guesses ranging from one hundred thousand to two million. Then the actual number appeared on the screen behind him:

3,000,000 to 5,000,000

'It's estimated that between three and five million people get seriously ill from flu every single year,' he said. 'And up to half a million of those people will die from it, especially among high risk groups like the under-fives and the over-sixty-fives. Half a million deaths annually, and it doesn't usually even hit the headlines.'

The screen changed to show a photo of people walking along a city street wearing surgical masks to cover their mouths and noses.

'Flu only really makes the news when it's a pandemic: a new strain of the virus that affects whole countries or continents. These are the ones that scare us, the ones we give names to as if they're tropical storms: swine flu, bird flu, Asian flu.'

Another image appeared. It was a black and white photograph of a very large, very full hospital ward staffed by nurses wearing old-fashioned uniforms.

'The deadliest flu pandemic hit in 1918,' Ben said. 'Anybody care to guess how many people died in that one?'

Somebody near the front guessed five million.

'You can probably multiply that by ten.'

There were audible gasps around the room.

'Yup. That one alone wiped out fifty million people worldwide. In fact, the highest estimates are a hundred million. Plus it came hot on the heels of the First World War, which had already killed another sixteen million.

'But here's the really interesting part: I'm not alone in suspecting

156

that the 1918 flu pandemic may have been a previous attempt to cull the human population, long before Phoenix even existed.'

Louder gasps. It had been quite a day for shocks.

'There were a lot of unusual factors that point to a deliberate infection. Firstly, it spread worldwide at a time when international travel was less common, and there's significant evidence to suggest multiple points of origin on different continents. Secondly, it hit in summer and autumn, while most naturally occurring influenza outbreaks happen during winter. Thirdly, the sector of the population most severely affected was healthy young adults, not the very young, the very old and the very ill who would normally be expected to perish. And fourthly, there were two or three waves of the disease, each involving even deadlier strains of the original virus. All things considered, I really don't believe we're the first to attempt something like this.'

Hands sprouted and Ben picked one.

'So why try the same again, if it didn't work before?' someone asked.

'Because in 1918, whoever was behind that influenza pandemic didn't do a very good job,' Ben replied matter-of-factly. 'If the 1918 outbreak was a culling tool, then it was a relatively slow, cruel and ultimately ineffective one. Some victims lingered so long that they contracted secondary bacterial diseases. Many became seriously ill for a while and then recovered. Only twenty percent of those who were infected actually died. And even if the highest estimates of one hundred million deaths are accurate, that was still only about five percent of the total population at the time. I know it sounds callous to say so, but that virus wasn't deadly enough.'

Ben paused but there were no hands. There were no words.

'The Phoenix virus,' he continued, 'is virtually one hundred percent effective. And it kills quickly. Even in 1918, there were stories of people going about their everyday lives feeling perfectly well and being dead by the next morning. With our influenza strain, the onset of fever is rapid and usually leads to collapse within about an hour. While the person is unconscious, their respiratory system becomes inflamed and they suffocate without any awareness of pain or discomfort. In actual fact, the body's own immune over-reaction tends to ensure that the impact of the virus is fatally accelerated, in what we call a cytokine storm. It's—'

Ben broke off as a woman near the stage stood up suddenly.

'How do you know?' she said in a rather shrill voice. She didn't sit down again.

'We've carried out extensive tests. More than enough to be sure that—'

'On animals, presumably,' the woman interrupted. 'How do you know they didn't suffer? And how do you know it will affect humans the same way?'

'No. Not on animals,' Ben stated gently. He was every bit as cool, calm and collected as Roger and Eve had been. 'For two reasons. One, Phoenix doesn't condone animal testing. And two, only humans get influenza, even though some strains are mutated forms of viruses found in birds and pigs, hence the terms "avian flu" and "swine flu".'

The woman was still on her feet. 'So you're telling us you've already used this virus to kill humans?'

'Yes. They were—'

'Did they know?'

'Madam, they were volunteers. We found volunteers — plenty of them, actually — among men and women of all ages who had been diagnosed with terminal degenerative illnesses or suffered injuries that drastically affected their quality of life. They were people who wanted to choose when and how their lives ended. They knew exactly what they were doing. The virus was administered under controlled conditions in secure locations in Belgium, Luxembourg and the Netherlands, where human euthanasia is legal.'

'So they were seriously ill anyway, then. How can you be sure the virus will affect healthy humans in the same way?'

'We deliberately didn't select anyone whose immune or respiratory systems were compromised. We know the virus works. We know the vaccine works. We've tested both, beyond any possible doubt. In fact, neither failed in any of our tests. There's too much at stake to get this wrong, so we've gone to enormous lengths to make absolutely sure we get it right.'

The woman slowly sat down.

'Thank you,' Ben said, sounding like he meant it. 'Those were really good questions. The virus is proven; anyone who's exposed to it will certainly develop the disease within a few days. The vaccine is also proven; anyone who receives it will have guaranteed immunity to the new flu strain for at least a couple of years. Either course is irreversible once the virus or the vaccine is administered. And this is going to be really fast. There will be no slow, agonising deaths. The pressure on worldwide health services will be intense but brief. If everything goes according to plan — and there's no reason to think it won't — the flu outbreak will be initiated simultaneously in multiple locations on every continent, and within an estimated maximum period of three weeks, the Phoenix virus will have done its job. There's no ongoing threat; there'll be no time for it to mutate and we know that flu tends to disappear abruptly once the hosts have died out. The disease will be naturally eradicated as soon as all unprotected humans are dead.'

Ben's last word echoed around the room with a fitting air of finality.

The thing that scared me the most was that I couldn't see any flaws in the plan. Phoenix's monstrous proposition was a viable reality. Eve, Roger and Ben had logical, reasoned answers to every question and it was increasingly obvious that everything had been well thought out over the course of many years by far bigger brains than mine.

Besides, they weren't asking our permission. Plan B was going to happen, whether we liked it or not.

10:59:28

Desirable Survivors

A neat rope barrier had materialised across the exit from the atrium outside the lecture theatre, and we were escorted to the bathrooms in batches. Our comfort break purposely didn't coincide with that of Rashid's group, who weren't in on the secret: the huge, awful secret. Phoenix's discreet but effective security personnel were everywhere and, for now, we weren't allowed to discuss anything to do with Plan B outside the auditorium. Since that was the only subject any of us wanted to talk about, the open area where tea was being served was unnaturally quiet and everyone beetled off back into the lecture theatre as soon as they'd got their drinks. Tomasz, Grace and I stood at the rear of the room, glad to stretch our legs.

'So how are you guys doing?' Tom asked, flicking his concerned gaze alternately between Grace and me. 'Hell of a thing, huh?'

I raised my eyebrows. 'You could say that.'

There were similar little huddles all over the auditorium and it dawned on me that this was why new employees were always accompanied by their line managers to the Noobs' Conference.

'How long have you known, Tom?' Grace asked.

'About Plan B? Two years. Although they hadn't pinned down the final details then.'

I was incredulous. 'How do you even…? I mean, knowing something like that is going to happen. How do you just carry on as normal? How do you live with it and talk to people and pretend everything's okay?'

'I was like you at first. I remember how shocked I was. It was so far outside anything in my experience that I just couldn't take it in for a while. Everybody feels that way.'

'Glad it's not just me,' I said. 'I keep wondering if this whole day is some elaborate dream. Or nightmare.'

'So what is it they actually expect us to do, Tom?' Grace asked. She sounded almost excited about it. 'I know we're supposed to get involved with vaccinating people, but how? And how do we know who should be immunised? And where will we have to go, and when?'

'Oh God, are we gonna have to stick needles into people?' It hadn't occurred to me until that moment. 'I can't even watch when they do that on the telly.'

Tomasz was shaking his head and smiling. 'Don't worry, Louis. We won't have to wield syringes. And Grace, you'll have answers to all those ques—'

'Ladies and gentlemen? Please re-take your seats.' Ben Griffin's voice came through the sound system.

Tom stayed close to Grace and me, like an anxious mother hen with a couple of chicks, as we added our empty cups to the untidy collection on the tables at the back of the room and then went to sit down again. He seemed relieved that neither of his chicks had thrown a fit of hysterics or run screaming from the auditorium. Not yet, anyhow: I wasn't prepared to discount the possibility. I was about to ask whether there had been any extreme reactions in the past, but just then the lights dimmed and Ben returned to centre stage.

'Thanks, everyone. Right, you'll be glad to know there's not much more from me, just five minutes to give you a bit more info about the practicalities of administering the vaccine. And after that, Eve and Roger will say a few words about the selection process and answer any final questions.'

Grace leaned closer to me and whispered, 'I still can't believe all this.'

I was getting to like her leaning close. 'I know. Me neither,' I whispered back.

'One question we've been asked before is why we've waited until now to move ahead with Plan B,' Ben said. 'And while it's true that some of the damage caused by overpopulation would have been reduced if we'd acted sooner — deforestation, climate change, pollution, extinctions and so on — Phoenix obviously wanted to give Plan A every possible chance. I suppose it's a bit like deciding when to have a beloved family pet put to sleep; you wait until every available treatment has been tried, until you're certain that all hope of recovery has passed and the animal's quality of life is really starting to deteriorate. And even then, it's a tough call.'

The way Ben spoke these last words, you could tell he'd experienced such a situation personally. I hadn't. The only pet I'd ever owned was a goldfish — which I'd named Woof as an early act of rebellion against adults' obsession with pigeonholing — and I didn't remember being particularly traumatised when, aged nine, I'd caught Mum flushing its little orange corpse down the loo.

Ben's expression lifted. 'But there was another reason we waited, too. We kept coming up against the stumbling block of a suitable delivery method for the vaccine. Syringes were the obvious choice but they're invasive, you need trained personnel to use them, and the disposal of used needles is a problem. Edible vaccines in tablet form are neater, but we still had the issue that we could only persuade people to accept them *after* they knew the flu virus was a risk. We'd be waiting for people to come to us, and they could have already contracted the disease. Ideally, we wanted to be able to administer the vaccine prior to releasing the virus, so that we'd have a much better opportunity to protect the right people. But immunisation by stealth is a tricky business. We considered introducing the vaccine into water supplies or via airborne inhaled delivery systems, but those methods are indiscriminate. We'd have far less scope to target desirable survivors.'

I shifted in my seat, instinctively uncomfortable with the term 'desirable survivors'. It sounded sinister and elitist.

'It's only very recently that an ideal solution has been developed by our own scientists. This is brand new, leading-edge stuff. Ostensibly we were working on a pain-free administration system for a hepatitis vaccine that would avoid contaminated waste, but in fact it was all done with Plan B in mind from the start. It's perfect and it's finally ready to go, not a moment too soon. It's a microneedle array.'

Ben's enthusiasm for scientific innovation was obvious. On the screen behind him, a photo appeared that made me think of a bed of nails with lots of neat rows of vicious-looking spikes. I found it difficult to associate the image with anything 'pain-free'.

'This is a close-up, of course, taken through a microscope. A small patch that can fit on a fingertip is coated with about a hundred microneedles, each one extremely fine and less than a millimetre long.' A new picture showed a tiny transparent spiky pad balanced on the end of someone's finger. 'The needles can be coated with the vaccine which, by the way, isn't sensitive to temperature changes so it doesn't need to be refrigerated during storage or transportation. Then the coated patch is simply pressed against the surface of the recipient's skin where the microneedles enter the outer layer and detach. There's no sensation of pain, as the needles aren't long enough to reach the skin's pain receptors.'

Someone put their hand up and Ben paused to take the question. 'Don't the microneedles cause irritation?'

'No, because they're actually made of a type of sugar. They dissolve harmlessly in the recipient's skin within a few minutes, and the vaccinated person never knows a thing about it.'

I had to admit it sounded clever and futuristic. I could understand why Ben was excited about the breakthrough.

'Could I borrow a volunteer for a moment?' He picked someone from the front row and extended a hand to help a slim, short-haired girl up onto the stage. 'What's your name?'

'Chen.'

'And how does it feel to have a hundred microneedles embedded in the back of your hand, Chen?'

'What?' The girl looked anxious and stared closely at her hands.

'Don't worry, it was a blank array. The patch wasn't coated with anything.' Ben looked pleased with himself. 'But when I helped you up just now… Well, that's how easy it is.'

'No way! I didn't feel a thing!' the girl exclaimed, still peering at her hands. 'Is that it, there? That little pinkish mark?'

Ben moved closer to inspect the area she was pointing at. 'I don't think so. Wasn't it your right hand that I touched? He gently turned Chen's arm as he examined her skin. 'But now you have a second blank array in your left arm.'

'Hey!' She stepped back quickly, snatching her arm away from him. 'Where?'

Ben chuckled at her reaction. 'Thank you, Chen, for an excellent demonstration.' He gestured for the girl to go back to her seat and, while she did so, he held his hands up and peeled off what looked like normal sticking plasters from each of his middle fingers. 'That's all there is to it, folks. We've perfected these small plasters with an array of dissolvable microneedles set into the centre. They're unremarkable to any casual observer. When you're ready to immunise someone, all you do is flick off the protective cap and away you go.' On the screen behind him, a slow-motion close-up video showed a thumbnail levering off a clear round cap to reveal the prickly patch of microneedles underneath. 'The cap is rigid enough to protect the array, but it's made of water-soluble gelatine — the same stuff they use to make capsules for drugs — so it can be safely discarded.'

They really did seem to have thought of everything.

'When you leave here today, you'll be given a few blank array samples like the ones I just used on Chen so that you can try them out and practice using them.'

Roger and Eve walked onto the stage as Ben finished speaking.

'Ben, thank you,' said Roger.

There was a spontaneous round of applause as Ben made his exit. It still felt inappropriate to be applauding anything to do with Phoenix's drastic plan, but I joined in. Ben was very likeable, and what his team had achieved in scientific terms was worthy of applause, regardless of its application. Which sparked another unsettling thought.

'Hey, those microneedles would be great if you wanted to poison someone,' I whispered to Grace as the clapping died down.

She gave me a resigned look. 'I guess pretty much anything can be misused. Didn't Alfred Nobel believe his invention of dynamite would bring about world peace? Humans are rubbish.'

My semi-flippant comment had backfired, albeit less spectacularly than Nobel's naïve intentions. Before I could say anything else, Roger started speaking again.

'Even though it may not be the done thing in today's politically correct world, I bet we've all thought to ourselves at some point that certain people shouldn't be allowed to reproduce. Haven't we?'

I was sure I wasn't alone in agreeing with Roger's rhetorical question, and in calling specific examples to mind. A couple of weeks previously I'd been getting some food shopping for Dad and me, and there was a woman in the supermarket who made it an even more miserable experience than usual. She had three kids. There was a toddler squirming in the seat at the front of the trolley, crying and screaming constantly at the top of its lungs while the mother ignored it completely. The two older children were allowed to menace other aisles, running around, bashing into people, shouting to each other and grabbing things off the shelves. By the time this delightful family got to the checkout, the woman was openly swearing at her loathsome offspring while she piled frozen pizzas, tubs of sweets, microwaveable burgers, crisps and fizzy drinks onto the conveyor.

'The animal kingdom has its own checks and balances in place, of course,' Roger continued. 'Natural selection generally ensures that the best of any species has the most opportunity to breed. The fittest, cleverest, most advanced, hard-working and well-adapted are more likely to survive and find suitable mates. The weak and the lazy don't tend to make it, and so the species improves and evolves over time.

'Also, unlike us, animal populations in the wild can't easily override the natural limits on their numbers. When they run out of food or habitat, the ones that don't get dinner die of starvation, and the ones without a safe, cosy little burrow get eaten. Sounds cruel, but that's what ensures the survival of all the others. Animals can't artificially screw up the balance by dialling out for a take-away when there's no grass left or building a new kind of high-rise den to create extra living space and protect them from the big bad wolf. And the ones that are fit and strong and smart enough to defend their dens and their dinners are the best of the bunch, so it's their DNA that carries through to the next generation.'

Again, my superlogic was so comfortable with all this that it was now reclining, wearing fluffy slippers. My socially-conditioned side was poking me with a sharp stick and muttering half-remembered horrors from history lessons about Nazis and selective breeding.

Eve took up the story. 'Because we've opted out of natural selection, the human race is regressing. Hereditary illnesses and defects are passed on, faulty genes are multiplied, health problems become increasingly prevalent. We're not for a moment suggesting that imperfect humans shouldn't survive. On the contrary, some of the most brilliant, wonderful people I have the privilege to know inhabit flawed or damaged bodies. We're simply stating facts here. Humans have made Mother Nature's quality control department redundant and that has undeniably weakened us as a species.'

Yes, my superlogic was loving this crazy day. Every word we'd heard was summing up and validating things I already knew were true, things I'd worried no one else understood. My superlogic was now cracking open champagne, celebrating the fact that I wasn't alone, that I was among people who not only got it but were doing something about it. It was just a shame that my fears and social-conditioning were being party poopers.

'In an ideal world, you'd choose the best of humanity to continue the species,' said Roger. 'Plan B is going to give us precisely that opportunity, an unprecedented chance to cherry-pick the people who will carry the baton forward in this human race of ours. So what are the qualities we should be looking out for?'

Silence. Was this another rhetorical question?

Apparently not.

'Come on! What are people's best attributes? What behaviours make a *good* human being? We all know what they are. Shout 'em out!'

After another pause, someone said, 'Compassion?'

'Good, yes! Compassion. What else?' Roger was pacing along the front of the stage.

'Decency!' a woman shouted.

'Yes, decency. Keep 'em coming.' He beckoned with both hands as he paced.

'Kindness.'

'Imagination.'

'Selflessness!'

'Courage!'

'Respect.'

'Excellent. You see, when you strip away all the stuff that doesn't matter, we all recognise the basic qualities that make good humans. And who can deny that this world would be a better place with more of those kinds of people? Or rather, with fewer of the opposite kinds?

'When it comes to it, one of the things you guys are going to worry about the most is how you'll know who to vaccinate. But you already know. Deep inside, you know. You're looking for people who demonstrate those attributes we've just listed so easily. People who *care*, regardless of their gender, race, appearance, religious beliefs, age, financial status, social standing, physical abilities… People who care about themselves and others, people who care about having a positive impact on their world, even in small ways.

'We're not Nazis. We're not seeking to exterminate any particular group of people because we think the colour of their

167

skin or the nature of their faith or the country they happen to have been born in makes them less deserving of life than us. We're not terrorists. This isn't about tyranny or persecution or power or world domination. No one at Phoenix stands to gain anything from this other than a habitable future, an opportunity to heal our world, more time to learn and get it right. There will be no inhumane treatment or prolonged, unnecessary suffering. But if we're going to do this at all, we may as well try to do it *right* and take the opportunity to improve the human race, if only to reduce the chances of history repeating itself.

'When you leave here today, look around you. See the human species for what it has truly become. Look at all the good, decent people trying to do the right thing every day, only to see their best efforts negated and swamped by the rising tide of those who don't give a damn about anyone else, the hordes whose selfish and small-minded greed is the real plague on our planet. They are parasites, taking as much as they can get and contributing nothing to society or to the future of the species except the further burden of their grasping offspring. See all of that, and then look inside yourselves to decide what's right and what's wrong.'

'Wow. Harsh,' I whispered to Grace.

'But true,' she whispered back.

A woman in front of us raised her hand and coughed to get Roger's attention. 'I get what you're saying,' she said as he acknowledged her. 'I really do. But… Well, you're making human life seem so cheap.'

'On the contrary,' Roger replied smoothly. 'Human life has become far too expensive and nature is getting a poor bargain. In fact, we cannot meet the cost without bankrupting the planet. I know it sounds horrendously judgemental, but there are so many corrupt, lazy and stupid people in the world that the many nuggets of wisdom and benevolence are lost among them. We've regressed to a point where it's increasingly difficult to find examples of integrity and compassion. We've made our*selves* cheap.'

Phoenix had answers for everything, it seemed.

'And,' added my superlogic smugly, 'damned good ones, at that.'

10:59:29

A Breath of Fresh Air

By the time Eve brought the final afternoon session to a close, I felt like I'd spent years in that auditorium. I thought my head might actually burst from having Phoenix's enormous secret squashed inside it.

Eve had assured us that we'd have follow-up discussions locally at a later date before we'd be expected to immunise anyone, but in the meantime she suggested we might find it helpful to talk — in extreme confidence — with other Phoenix employees who knew about Plan B. We were reminded that Rashid's group were *not* in on it, and we were taught a signal by which we could recognise those in the know. Anyone wanting to talk about Plan B had to subtly curl one hand into a fist, with their thumb poking out between their middle finger and ring finger. The response from someone who recognised the signal was to touch their left earlobe with their right hand, or vice versa. I wasn't the only person in the room who had trouble taking this bit seriously. It seemed more *Austin Powers* than *James Bond*. However, Eve assured us that the system had been in successful use for more than a decade.

The audience's anger had abated. The mood was still a long way from light-hearted, but the earlier outrage had been transformed under the hammer blows of Phoenix's relentless logic into something approaching acceptance. The pensive, serious faces slowly dispersed towards the exits to begin the task of digesting all the food for thought we'd been given.

Tomasz, Grace and I were among the last to leave. On our way out of the lecture theatre we collected our mobile phones in their labelled paper bags, and I wasn't surprised to see that recycling bins had been placed nearby for the rubbish. We were also each given a small envelope containing three wrapped plasters. They looked so ordinary in their packaging that no one would suspect they incorporated Ben's state-of-the-art microneedles. I tucked mine carefully into my wallet while Tom stowed his in an inside pocket and Grace zipped hers into her small shoulder bag.

'Are you two okay?' Tomasz asked when we'd put our phones away.

Grace nodded.

I shrugged. 'I think so.'

'I could really do with seeing Eve for a quick word in private before we head off, if you guys don't mind. Shouldn't be more than ten or fifteen minutes, tops. There's a staff cafeteria down on the tenth floor. If you want to go and grab a coffee or something, I can meet you there.'

'Actually, I could use some fresh air.' I suddenly felt quite claustrophobic despite the spacious proportions of the Phoenix building. 'If it's okay with Grace, I think I'd rather wait for you outside.'

'Suits me,' said Grace. 'I've had enough tea and coffee for one day, anyhow.'

Tom nodded. 'In that case, don't go down to the street. There's a roof terrace. It's nice up there.'

'Perfect,' I said.

'Take the lift to the top floor. When you come out, there are stairs leading to the terrace. I'll meet you up there. I won't be too long.' Tom hurried off to catch Eve, who had just emerged from the auditorium.

I was very glad Tomasz was with us in London — his quiet

presence had been a constant source of reassurance — but he was still the boss, and I felt more relaxed once Grace and I were on our own. We were the only ones in the glass-fronted lift. The numbered buttons on the sleek control panel went up to fourteen, then there was one marked "T".

'Top, I guess,' I said, pressing it.

'Terrace?' Grace suggested.

'Ah, yes.' Feeling slightly stupid, I looked out over London as the lift rose. 'Trumpets?' I offered.

Grace looked at me, straight-faced. 'Turkeys?'

And then we were giggling together like a couple of schoolkids.

The roof terrace was really nice. The sky was a richer shade of blue than it had been that morning and there wasn't a cloud in sight. It was hot in the sunshine but at this altitude there was a light breeze blowing. We walked over to the edge, which was guarded by a waist-high parapet topped with a glass and chrome safety barrier. Grace obviously wasn't bothered by heights either and we spent a few minutes in companionable silence just taking in the views across the glittering, seething city and breathing in the warm fresh air. Not that the air above a place like London can accurately be described as fresh. Regardless, it was exactly what I'd needed and I felt revived.

About half of the roof space was cordoned off, the domain of industrial-looking structures that presumably housed air conditioning equipment and the like, but the rest had been prettied up with large, well-tended tubs of plants and tall shrubs, interspersed with wooden trellis panels and fancy garden furniture. When we'd first arrived on the terrace there had been a man nearby talking loudly into a mobile phone, but he'd disappeared and now we had the roof to ourselves. We sat on chairs that weren't as comfortable as they looked, surprised at the heat of them through our clothing. We both sighed contentedly at exactly the same moment and smiled at each other. I suddenly felt oddly self-conscious under Grace's gaze and ran a hand through my hair.

'This is cool,' Grace said, crossing her slim legs and closing her eyes as she tipped her face towards the sun. 'Up here, Plan B feels a million miles away.'

'Shh!' I looked around nervously, even though I knew we were alone. Now that we were sitting down, I couldn't see the whole terrace because the area near the stairs was screened by shrubbery.

Grace made a dismissive gesture. 'It's fine. There's nobody else around.' Now she was looking at me pointedly. She had her hand against her chin, and I noticed that her thumb was poking between her clenched fingers. She made it look really natural. With an exaggerated show of casualness for comic effect, I scratched my right earlobe with my left hand. We both laughed, although I could see how the signals could work.

'You seem really fine about it all,' I remarked.

'I am, pretty much. Why? Did you think I wouldn't be?'

'No, it's just… I dunno. I keep thinking I'm okay with it. I mean, everything they said to us today makes perfect sense to me. But I suppose I still can't believe it. That all those people are really going to die.' I almost whispered the last word.

Grace shrugged. 'I was shocked at first. I think everybody was. But then… Well, people die anyway.'

'Yeah, but not like this! I can't even imagine it.'

'Me neither. But, like you said, everything Roger and Eve told us is true. There's no question that it's ultimately for the greater good. It solves pretty much everything, and it's the only thing that does. As scary as Plan B is, the results of doing nothing would be far worse. Besides, there are plenty of people I won't weep for.' She said the last sentence as if she had specifics in mind.

'Ouch. Such as?'

'Oh, no one in particular. Just… certain *types*, you know?'

'I can think of a few, yeah. But you said that like there's a story behind it.'

She sighed. 'There is. And it still makes me angry.' I could read the emotion on her face. 'It's not that big a deal really, but… well, my grandparents died a couple of years ago, within four months of each other. My mum's mum and dad. It was such a tough time for her. They were very close and she really misses them. Anyway, Dad and I wanted to do something nice for her, so… she's always wanted an Acer.'

'A laptop?'

'No!' She smiled. 'It's a tree. A Japanese maple. There are different kinds, but they're really pretty. Delicate leaves. You know?'

I didn't, but I nodded anyway.

'They're quite expensive, which is why Mum never bought one for herself, but Dad and I clubbed together and gave her two of them, saplings, on Mother's Day this year. She cried when we said we thought she could plant them close together, to remember Nana and Grandad. She was so chuffed.'

I had no idea how any of this related to what we'd been talking about or made Grace angry, but I let her talk.

'Mum said she knew just the spot for them, near the front fence, and the three of us worked together digging holes and planting these pretty little trees…' She trailed off.

'And?' I prompted, after a moment.

'Less than a week later, Mum phoned me in floods of tears. Some hateful person had walked past and broken both of them in half. You could see where the main trunks had been deliberately snapped.'

I was speechless. Grace wasn't.

'I mean, who *does* that? It's not even like they got anything out of it. All they did was ruin something for someone else. I suppose that's the definition of mindless vandalism. I don't think I've ever felt so much hate for anyone. In fact, I know I haven't. *Bastards*. Those trees were living things, and Mum was so upset. People are disgusting.'

'Wow, Grace. That's awful.'

'It's depressing, having to share the world with people who are capable of doing stuff like that. You know? So the prospect of wiping some of them off the face of the Earth… Yeah, I have to admit I'm not averse to the idea.'

'Blimey. I hope I'm never in your bad books,' I said, in an

attempt to lighten the mood.

'Sorry. I know they were only trees, but—'

'No, don't be. You're absolutely right.'

'I know that what Phoenix are planning to do is… Well, it's unthinkable. But, like they said, those millions of people won't die for nothing. They'll be helping to save the world. Doing something useful, for once. And, between you and me, I'm actually glad I can play a part in it.'

'Me too, I think.' I said, almost envious of Grace's unexpected brutal streak.

'It's going to be a fresh start for the human race. An opportunity to get it right. A beginning, not an ending.'

'Yeah, that's true. And at least our priority is finding the people who should *live*. We get to focus on the positive.'

I lifted my head, certain that I could detect the unpleasant stink of cigarette smoke on the breeze.

'Exactly,' Grace said. 'There are plenty of people in this world who deserve to survive. And they deserve to do so on a thriving planet, not a dying one. Not one that's being steadily and systematically destroyed by the kinds of morons who'll go around breaking something beautiful just for the hell of it.'

At that moment Tomasz appeared, making me jump.

'Hi guys. Sorry I've been a while. You two ready to go?'

As the three of us left the roof terrace I noticed a man sitting near the exit, smoking a cigarette. Although he didn't look our way, as we passed him I recognised Jack from my nuclear bunker group. Tom was chatting to us about train times, but I wasn't taking in what he was saying. I was too busy wondering how long Jack had been there and worrying whether Grace and I had said anything he shouldn't have overheard.

10:59:30

Jack

Jack West had always come second. He was the second child of pushy parents whose favourite hobby was bragging about their first child's achievements. Malcolm and Caroline West never left Jack in any doubt that his role in life was to follow inadequately in his older sister's golden footsteps. Elise was the first-born, and no one had ever bothered trying to pretend that she wasn't first in her parents' affections. Jack had come along four years later, something of a surprise and something of a disappointment, which had rather set the tone for the unfortunate boy even before day one.

Malcolm and Caroline loved to entertain and threw frequent dinner parties. Many of Jack's early childhood memories involved sitting on the stairs watching grown-ups drinking wine while their hosts regaled them with tales of Elise's achievements and Jack's shortcomings. The child listened as guests were told how Elise had been walking when she was only nine months old, was potty-trained by the age of two and could read, write and count to twenty before she started school. But Jack's chubby little face reddened and withdrew into the upstairs shadows whenever someone was jovially reminded that he had still been crawling at two, didn't learn to scribble his own name until he was five, and occasionally wet the bed even now.

The Wests spectacularly failed to realise the impact their behaviour had on their children. While Elise flourished with the loving support and encouragement of her doting parents, Jack could never do enough to earn his fair share of their praise, no matter how hard he tried. And he had tried very hard indeed. Trying and failing becomes a bitter endeavour and it meant that Jack was a miserable baby, a bad-tempered toddler, a withdrawn schoolboy and an angry teenager. It never once occurred to Malcolm and Caroline to attribute any of this to their own treatment of him, and instead they frequently bemoaned the fact that he'd just always been a difficult child.

Consequently, Jack had spent his entire life wanting things he couldn't have. More than anything, he wanted his parents to talk about him to their friends with affection and pride. It didn't seem too much to ask, but his clumsy efforts to impress them only served to make Elise shine brighter still. Perhaps if he'd stopped trying to compete in such an uneven race and focused on pleasing himself instead of them, he might have stood a chance at happiness.

Jack may have been resentful of his sister's success, but he loved her. She was a kind, good-natured person and always had time for her little brother. Elise wasn't quite the star her parents believed her to be, but it's amazing what you can achieve when you know people believe in you. She'd studied hard, gained a good degree in English and Journalism, and secured a graduate trainee role with a national newspaper. Now, at the age of twenty-eight, she was enjoying an interesting career as one of their online reporters, starting to move away from fluff pieces and prove her capabilities in investigative journalism. She made a point of phoning Jack once a week and always seemed genuinely keen to hear his news.

Towards the end of secondary school, Jack had made a useful discovery: you didn't necessarily have to be good at something in order to tell other people how to do it. A maths teacher by the name of Mr Cottersby, who had once famously insisted to a bewildered Year Nine class that a kilometre was longer than a mile 'Because a mile is one, and a kilometre is one-point-six', was the most domineering person in the whole school. Jack — whose years of observing people had actually made him fairly perceptive — noticed that the teachers who were least confident about their subject knowledge tended to cover up with bluster and an air of authority. Mr Cottersby did it badly, but there were others who blagged their way through pretty well. Jack tried the same tactic and, in doing so, unearthed a talent as a natural leader that was as much of a revelation to him as it was to everyone else. By the age of sixteen he had grown tall and strong, despite the weight of the huge chip on his shoulder, and his physical presence combined with his newfound assertiveness transformed him from a grumpy, insecure kid into an apparently self-possessed young man in the space of a few short months.

University was compulsory in the West household and, although Jack was reluctant to spend another three or four years studying, it at least served to defer the moment when he'd have to decide what he wanted to do with his life and, more to the point, start actually doing it. In fact, university was the making of Jack West. A fresh start in a new place, living away from home for the first time, gave him a chance to try out a different version of himself. He made the most of it. He oozed confidence and took every opportunity to demonstrate his leadership credentials, securing positions as the head of several student groups and clubs, and he cultivated relationships every bit as carefully as he cultivated facial hair. By the time he realised that he'd finally given his parents something to brag about, that no longer seemed like the most important thing in his life.

After Jack graduated, it was Elise's new husband who spotted an advertisement for jobs at Phoenix and suggested that he should apply. Freshly armed with a mediocre business degree and a non-specific ambition to work in management, Jack could see that the career prospects in a massive multi-national corporation operating in a growth market were potentially not too shabby. As a young boy he'd shown some interest in the environment, putting out food to encourage wild birds, policing the family's recycling habits and briefly tending a patch of garden, but he'd dropped such activities when he reached the grand old age of ten and began to worry that other people might consider these hobbies uncool. However, when he attended the interview he put his charisma and blagging skills to good use and built this experience into a lifelong passion for ecology that even he found convincing.

Eleven months on, Jack was getting by in a junior role at Phoenix's Head Office in London, spending his days showing an even newer recruit how to sort items of incoming mail and deliver them around the building. With only a little embellishment, this enabled his parents to boast that their son was already helping to run the company's communications centre, so that was something. But, although Jack cared a great deal what people thought of him, his parents were no longer highest on his list of priorities. He was on his way, earning money of his own, climbing the ladder slowly but surely. And this particular ladder — planted firmly in the central hub of a prestigious international organisation — was surely going to lead to great things. Jack knew that the post room was merely the first rung. His daily rounds gave him the opportunity to meet a lot of influential people in the business, and he worked hard at remembering names and making a good impression. He was also well aware that knowledge is power, so he soaked up information like a sponge while he was sorting and reading letters, avidly followed office gossip, and generally made a point of knowing what was going on.

So what bothered him the most about the conversation he'd overheard on the roof terrace between Louis-with-a-wiss and his pretty little girlfriend was that it suggested they knew something he didn't.

Jack had been disappointed to find the terrace almost deserted. He'd taken up smoking more because it was a great way to eavesdrop on all kinds of interesting conversations than because he enjoyed sucking nicotine into his lungs, and he had little interest in what two kids from some regional office might have to say. Still, it was nice to have a break in the sunshine and he actually quite fancied a cigarette, so he sat down and lit up while the girl was wittering on about something to do with trees. But then she'd made that comment about a company plan — he remembered she'd used the word 'unthinkable' — and his ears had pricked up. And then… What was it she'd said? 'Those millions of people won't die for nothing; they'll be helping to save the world.' What was that all about? The two of them had mentioned playing a part in whatever it was, so how come they were involved and he wasn't?

Frustratingly, their boss had arrived at that point, but Jack's curiosity was piqued. He stubbed out his cigarette distractedly after they'd gone. Something was going on and he wasn't part of it. He had no idea what it was, but he was sure as hell going to find out.

10:59:31

Ignorance is Bliss

The world had changed. Or maybe I had. The journey back to Mareton with Grace and Tomasz should have felt pretty much like the morning's trip in reverse, but my whole perception had shifted. In the morning I'd quite enjoyed the sense that I was one of the rats in the race, at one with the other commuters, engrossed in the purposeful experience of getting from somewhere to somewhere else. As we negotiated the rush hour at the other end of the day, it was as if I was watching the scene from some kind of external perspective, going through the motions but detached from everyone else's superficial scurrying. And, while other passengers chatted and whinged about their work, the three of us sat mutely staring out of the windows, forbidden from speaking of what had transpired during the past few hours.

Tom made a couple of attempts at unrelated small talk but soon gave up. I felt kind of numb. I was just trying to keep up with the thoughts that were racing through my head, making the train's progress away from London towards the coast seem sluggish by comparison. I supposed that nothing would ever be quite the same again.

Before the three of us parted company at Mareton station, Tomasz took us aside and quietly reminded us of the need for confidentiality. We were not to discuss the afternoon sessions with anyone at home. We weren't allowed to make references to any aspect of Plan B via phone or email either, just in case. Phoenix's secret seemed to weigh even more heavily as it hit me that I'd have to keep it hidden from Dad.

'Feel free to chat about the nuclear bunker exercise if you want to,' Tom said. 'A lot of companies use that kind of team activity. And general stuff, of course. Just nothing about—'

'Don't worry. We know,' said Grace with a lopsided smile.

'I've deliberately kept tomorrow morning free, so we can talk more then. Try not to think about it too much in the meantime.'

Grace laughed humourlessly. 'Fat chance of that.'

'Yeah, okay. But don't let it drive you crazy. It gets easier, I promise. The plan's existed for years. The only difference now is that you know about it.'

'Talk about "ignorance is bliss",' said Grace.

I was wondering whether I ought to confess to Tomasz that someone might have heard us talking up on the roof earlier. I wasn't sure that Jack had heard anything incriminating but I was kicking myself for possibly having blown it before we'd even left the building, after we'd been told in no uncertain terms how important—

'You okay Louis? You're awfully quiet.'

'Hm? Oh, I'm fine. Honestly, I am. Thanks Tom. I'm just… Well, you know.'

'Yeah, I do. Look, we'll talk tomorrow. Try to get a decent night's sleep.' He patted me on the shoulder, concern furrowing his brow. 'Do either of you need a lift home?'

'No, thanks,' I said automatically. I realised I was hoping for another chance to talk to Grace.

'No, thanks,' she echoed. 'My mum's picking me up.'

Tom said goodbye and we watched him stride away.

'Quite a day, huh?' I offered.

A car beeped from the drop-off zone.

'Sorry, that's Mum. See you at work tomorrow.'

Grace was gone before I could even reply.

While other commuters flowed around me, I stood on the pavement for a minute or two, feeling irrationally disappointed, weirdly emotional and very much alone. Just me and my big, ugly secret.

I was so preoccupied that I barely even remembered walking home. My thoughts kept meandering, interrupting each other and tripping over themselves in my brain, incomplete and getting nowhere. I made an effort to clear my head before I turned my key in the door and put what I hoped was a carefree expression on my face.

That evening, I ate supper with Dad but didn't have much time with him before he had to head off for his night shift at the factory. Between mouthfuls of the chicken casserole he'd made, I described Phoenix's smart London office building with its fancy glass lifts and roof terrace, and told him a little bit about the nuclear bunker team session.

When he left, I missed him.

After dinner I did the washing up and then settled on the sofa to watch some TV, thinking that Tom's recommendation of a decent night's sleep was rather optimistic, all things considered. The next thing I knew it was almost seven o'clock the next morning and I awoke to some dismal bloke on the telly droning on about politics. My neck was stiff, my clothes were creased, and my cheek was wet with drool. On the plus side, I felt rested, the sky was blue again and it was a brand-new day.

Over breakfast I realised it was the sheer magnitude of Plan B that kept threatening to overwhelm me. I couldn't imagine seven and a half billion human beings in the first place, so trying to grasp the implications of lots of them dropping dead within a couple of weeks of each other was utterly impossible. But it was the responsibility of other people at Phoenix to think about the big picture. I decided the only way to maintain any semblance of sanity was to focus on my own miniscule role in the whole thing, since that was the only bit I'd have any control over. My job was to concentrate on my little corner of the world. If this whole mind-blowing scenario did play out — and there was a big part of me that didn't believe it really would — my worrying about the entire planet wouldn't serve any purpose whatsoever. And if it was going to happen, there was nothing I could do to stop it. Or was there? Should I be trying to? Would I, if I could? More big, impossible questions. I sighed and went to the kitchen sink to wash my cereal bowl.

Driving to work on my moped was a pleasure in the sunshine, but I was more acutely aware than ever that there were too many people in Mareton. I wasn't yet confident enough on the bike to do much weaving through traffic, so most of the time I was stuck behind cars and trucks, breathing their exhaust fumes while we all crawled along. It was such a joke that this was called *rush* hour. I looked around at other drivers sitting in their tin boxes and watched pedestrians stepping over litter or staring at mobile phones while they walked. I couldn't help noticing that nearly everyone looked miserable. I supposed I was lucky to enjoy my job.

I pulled into the car park at the industrial estate, having decided that I'd ride my moped out to visit Auntie Cheryl the next time she had a free weekend if the weather was still nice. A longer run on open roads, riding between trees and fields instead of lamp-posts and buildings might be just what I needed.

Tomasz kept his promise to spend the morning with Grace and me. We closeted ourselves in the meeting room, equipped with large mugs of coffee, and spent a lot of the time talking about how the vaccination programme would work and who we'd be targeting. Phoenix's usual meticulous planning was in evidence as Tom showed us an annotated map on his laptop and explained how every regional office had been given a clearly-defined geographical area to cover. Each employee who knew about Plan B would be allocated their own section of this area and, once the immunisation was ready to be rolled out, would spend their days systematically visiting all the communities in their section. Tom didn't know exactly when this would happen, but he guessed it would be fairly soon. He mentioned that the company's pharmaceutical divisions had been in full production since Ben's research team had completed testing on the microneedle array a couple of months back.

'Oh my God, I forgot about the plasters!' I exclaimed, putting my hand to the pocket where I kept my wallet. 'I couldn't wait to have a proper look at them when I got home last night. I can't believe I completely forgot.'

'I've tried two of mine already,' said Grace, grinning. 'They're cool. Amazing when you look at them closely. I tested one on myself as soon as I was in my room. Ben was right, you really don't feel a thing. So then I put another plaster on and waited for a chance to try it on my mum. I was so aware of it. I felt like I may as well have had a big flashing light on the end of my finger, but she never even noticed. I touched her arm while I was helping to clear stuff off the table after dinner and she didn't bat an eyelid, just carried on talking about what a shame it was that some of the potatoes weren't quite cooked through.'

Tom went on to tell us that, for years, Phoenix had been compiling lists of key people, doctors and counsellors, writers and artists, farmers and gardeners, teachers and community leaders; people whose skills and values would be important to the human race after the virus had done its thing. Immunising the specific individuals on this list — and, where appropriate, their immediate families — would be the responsibility of managers like Tom. He would also be vaccinating people like crematorium workers to ensure that large numbers of bodies could be cremated quickly. I didn't want to think about that too much, but of course it would be necessary if the plan went ahead.

There was all kinds of stuff I hadn't even considered. Basic facilities and communication infrastructures would be safeguarded. Tom also mentioned teams of people who would be given the task of checking and clearing buildings afterwards, helping to remove bodies from homes so they didn't just rot there, and turning off electricity and gas and water supplies wherever they were no longer needed. There'd be vets who would go around with these teams euthanising pets so they wouldn't die slowly of starvation and neglect after their owners had gone. Talking about such things really brought home the grim reality of what Phoenix intended to bring about. I couldn't decide if it was reassuring or sinister that every possible implication seemed to have been thought through.

Grace asked whether the vaccination would be given openly en masse in places like schools. It seemed a perfectly reasonable question until Tom pointed out that this would actually be a bad move, since it would potentially create a lot of orphans, many of whom wouldn't be able to fend for themselves. An imbalance of very young people who needed to be cared for and couldn't contribute much to the new societies would put a huge strain on limited resources. And children weren't automatically good people, Tom added. I thought of some of the kids I'd been at school with, who I knew had been bullies and vandals and troublemakers from a very young age, and knew he was right.

Our job would be to immunise ordinary people who came from all walks of life and, wherever possible, we would look for opportunities to vaccinate whole families, so as to reduce the heartbreak of personal loss. Those last words hit me hard. I couldn't help recalling the deep, crippling sorrow that Dad and Cheryl and I had experienced when Mum died. Echoes of it still haunted us eight years later. I knew the grief would never completely go away; its pervasive black tendrils had run deep inside me until it had become a part of who I was. I didn't want to imagine that on a worldwide scale. I didn't want to play any part in inflicting that kind of suffering on anyone.

Tom was still keeping a watchful eye on us, and he must have seen the sudden wave of doubt crash over me. His tone became gentler. 'No one's pretending this is going to be easy. The survivors are going to face a tough time, especially at first. They'll have to watch others fall ill and die, and weather the inevitable unrest and challenges that will follow the pandemic. Some will wish they'd caught the flu themselves. People will have to get through the immediate future before they can start building a brighter one. But it *will* be brighter. Remember all the things that Eve and Roger said yesterday. Don't ever lose sight of the fact that the whole purpose of Plan B is to save the world, quite literally, from a fate worse than death. And there will be lots of measures in place to give people the best possible chance of moving on from this and thriving in a healthier, happier environment.'

Amid all my swirling doubts and fears, my superlogic stood strong and immobile like a lighthouse in a storm. I drew strength from knowing it was there, and Tom's words helped to remind me of it. My superlogic knew that the people at Phoenix weren't monsters. My superlogic knew that Plan B was a brave and genuine attempt to save humanity from itself: an initiative born of necessity and compassion, not cruelty. Prejudice and personal gain didn't feature in any of their thinking. This wasn't a hare-brained scheme for world domination, it was a carefully designed solution to the wholesale destruction of the planet by a single species that had grown far too big for its boots. Never mind our carbon footprint, we were grinding the earth to dust beneath our size seven-and-a-half-billion clodhoppers.

'God, it's 12:15 already,' Tom said, breaking my fanciful train of thought as he checked his watch. 'We'll have plenty of chances to talk more, okay? I'm meeting my partner for lunch today, so I've got to dash. It's her birthday.' He stood up. 'Any final questions before I shoot off?'

'Just one for now,' said Grace. 'Does everybody here in the Mareton office know about Plan B? Can we talk to them about it?'

'That was two,' said Tom, smiling. 'But they're good ones. No, there's one person here who doesn't know, so you can't speak openly in the office. Always use the hand signals. If someone doesn't respond correctly, it either means they don't know about it or it's not safe to talk.'

'Can we ask who the one person is?' I said, intrigued.

'Sure. Who would you think it is?'

I thought for a moment. 'Pam?'

Tom chuckled. 'What made you guess it was her?'

'She talks about her family a lot and she's… Well, she's an older lady.'

Tom laughed again. 'Actually, Pam's known about Plan B for a lot longer than I have. She's one of its strongest supporters. Yes, she's got two children and I think it's three grandchildren, and she wants a better world for them. You can certainly talk to her about it. In fact, I'd recommend it.'

'So who…?' Grace began.

'Loretta. Don't mention anything to Loretta.' Tomasz picked up his empty coffee mug and opened the meeting room door. 'Gotta dash, guys. See you later.'

I hadn't had many dealings with Loretta, although she'd introduced herself and always seemed pleasant. She was one of Phoenix's alternative energy specialists and spent a lot of time out of the office. I wondered why she hadn't been let in on the secret.

Grace and I took our cups to the kitchen. Pam was in there, getting a large plastic tub out of the fridge. She opened the lid to reveal a delicious-looking cheese salad. There was nobody else around, for now. Grace expertly gave the Plan B signal and Pam casually adjusted her left earring with her right hand. She smiled. 'Welcome to the club, you two.'

We only had a few minutes to chat to her about our day in London before the kitchen started getting busier.

'One piece of advice: read the news,' Pam said, rummaging in the cutlery drawer for a fork. 'It helps. There are more than enough depressing stories every day to make you realise the world could be a much nicer place. And a few to remind you of the people who absolutely deserve one.'

10:59:32

Ignorance is Torture

Jack's sleuthing was going badly. Three weeks of tactical charm and persuasiveness had got him precisely nowhere.

He'd started by making a list of people within the London office who'd attended the recent induction workshop, then he had sought out those who hadn't been with him in Rashid's group after lunch, and chatted with them about the day in deliberately casual tones. A couple of them had seemed rather guarded when Jack steered the conversation to the afternoon sessions but they all gave the impression they'd talked about similar topics: namely, new ways to raise awareness of the need for population control. And yet, despite his lack of progress, Jack was more certain than ever that something was going on. When he'd pressed for examples of the ideas the other groups had come up with, the people he was talking to invariably became vague and found excuses to cut the conversation short. And they all named either Eve Gyer or Roger Vee as their group leader. That struck Jack as odd, too. If there had only been two other groups, they would have had to be a lot larger than Rashid's. Why not split the numbers evenly?

He could feel his frustration growing, permeating him like an infection. He absolutely *hated* not being in the know. The thought that someone had decided he shouldn't be trusted with whatever it was… that was driving him crazy. How dare they? He knew he was becoming increasingly distracted and paranoid. Several people at work had remarked recently that he didn't seem his usual cheery self. And he wasn't sleeping, either. His nights were tormented by dreams where he was back in the school playground, left outside a big circle within which his peers whispered tantalising secrets that he couldn't quite hear and then laughed in his face when he begged to be included.

The words he'd overheard on the roof terrace ran through his tortured mind in a constant loop. A thousand times a day, he heard the sweet voice of Louis-with-a-wiss's girlfriend saying, 'Those millions of people won't die for nothing, they'll be helping to save the world'.

Speculation always led Jack to the same destination: he became convinced that Phoenix was involved in a plot to launch a nuclear attack of some kind. How else did you kill millions of people? And the bunker exercise had to be a clue. He had a nagging feeling about the significance of that session. No matter how many times he replayed it to himself, he couldn't find any flaws in his own performance — he'd stepped up, taken the lead and almost single-handedly steered the group to a successful outcome, for Christ's sake — yet he apparently hadn't made the grade as far as Eve high-and-mighty Gyer was concerned. Being judged as not good enough despite your best efforts was a situation Jack was all too familiar with, and all the old feelings of inadequacy and resentment that he'd worked so hard to bury came rushing back. He found it increasingly difficult to be civil to Eve when he saw her around the London office. The woman seemed to see right through him.

The only person Jack could confide in was his sister, and he'd been excited to tell her about his investigation and theories, feeling sure that Elise would be supportive and interested. However, during their weekly telephone chats she'd implied more than once that he must have misheard or misinterpreted the rooftop comments, and suggested he should drop the whole thing. In their most recent conversation she'd expressed concern that Jack's 'obsession', as she called it, was unhealthy, and even suggested that perhaps he should see a doctor. Basically, she didn't believe him. That was what it boiled down to, and Jack was immensely hurt by what he saw as a betrayal from the one person he'd thought he could count on.

He knew he was onto something — something big — and he became more determined than ever to prove that he was right.

He needed to work on his interrogation skills, though. The subtle approach hadn't worked so far. There was only one person left on his list — Sophie Pearce, a nobody in the accounts department — and he decided he'd have to use more devious tactics this time. He devoted his attention to working out how he could trick this girl into letting something slip. It shouldn't be too difficult.

Accounts occupied the whole of the seventh floor of the Head Office building, and it took a few discreet enquiries to find out where Sophie Pearce sat. As luck would have it, her desk was on the end of a row, next to one of the main walkways through the department.

Jack whistled tunelessly as he waited for the lift to carry him and his loaded post trolley up to the seventh floor. Before the doors opened, he donned his friendliest smile and flicked the switch on his charisma. Thanks to the open-plan office layout, he could see the back of Sophie's head almost as soon as he entered the department. Her long mousey brown hair was woven neatly into a single thick plait and she was on the phone. Damn it. He'd have to wait until she was finished. He made a meal of saying good morning to the manager of the accounts payable team and took his time finding the bundle of invoices for them, even though he knew exactly where it was among the neat stacks of sorted correspondence on his trolley. He exchanged insincere greetings with a couple of other people he recognised, keeping a careful eye on the girl as he got closer. Yes! She'd finished her call. Jack sped up along the walkway and deliberately dislodged a small pile of loose envelopes onto the floor right beside her desk. Tutting, he bent down and started picking them up. She leaned down and retrieved a couple of them to help him.

Jack looked into her eyes. Their faces were only inches apart. He gave her a grateful smile. 'Thanks.'

'No problem,' she said, already starting to turn back to her work as he gathered the last of the envelopes and stood up.

'Hey, it's Sophie, isn't it?'

She looked up at him uncertainly. Her eyes flicked to the ID pass hanging around his neck, but the lanyard was busy with two other laminated cards and a couple of pens. 'Yes. Sorry, I don't…?'

'Jack. I work in the comms centre. Although I guess that's kind of obvious.' He pulled a face, gesturing to the trolley full of letters. 'I recognise you from the Noobs' Conference.'

'Oh, right. Yes.' She smiled politely.

'Interesting day, wasn't it?' He gave her a conspiratorial wink.

'Very.'

Jack dropped his voice. 'And the whole thing with… Well, you know. Pretty cool being trusted with something like that, isn't it?'

Sophie was frowning. Jack noticed that she kept looking at his hands, for some reason.

'What d'you mean?' she asked. Her own hand was lightly clenched, and her thumb was sticking out between her fingers. The gesture sparked a very early childhood memory for Jack, when his grandad used to pretend to steal his nose.

'Oh, it's okay,' he said. 'I'm in on it.' It suddenly occurred to him that perhaps the hand thing was a sign of some kind. He copied the gesture, just in case.

Sophie was still frowning, watching him carefully. 'In on what?'

Damn this silly cow. Jack was getting irritated. Why couldn't she just take the bait? He forced himself to be patient and pleasant. 'Fine. I get it. This isn't the time or the place to talk about it, right?'

'I'm sorry, I have no idea what you're on about.' She turned back to her computer and started scrolling through a spreadsheet.

He changed tack. 'Look, I didn't mean to put you on the spot. I was just trying to make conversation, that's all. I noticed you at the induction day because… well… d'you fancy going out for a drink sometime?'

She looked up at him again but he couldn't read her expression. He treated her to one of the smiles he practiced in front of the mirror at home.

'Thanks, but I'm seeing someone. And I don't mean to be rude but I really need to get this finished.' Sophie gestured to her computer screen and started scrolling slowly down the spreadsheet again.

Jack gripped the handle of his trolley, barely managing to hold his frustration in check. What a cheeky bitch, shutting him down like that. He at least managed to salvage what was left of his dignity by refusing to let little miss prissy pants have the last word.

'Your loss, babe.'

*

One of the first people Jack had questioned was Max, the other recent recruit who was based in Phoenix's communications centre. Max was newer, younger, and shorter than Jack and he didn't have a degree, so it was only right that Jack looked down on him both literally and figuratively. During the first few weeks of them working together, Max had invited Jack to join him and his friends on a couple of nights out but, although Jack didn't have much of a social life, he wasn't interested in wasting time with a group of youngsters when there was a career ladder waiting to be climbed. Instead, he set his sights on ingratiating himself with some of the more influential people in the organisation. His efforts had yet to yield any social invitations per se, although it was surely only a matter of time. He'd taken up golf at university in anticipation of such occasions and had recently signed up for a few very expensive lessons, persuading his parents to pay for them as an early Christmas present. Both he and they viewed the extortionate sum as a worthwhile investment.

On the way back to the post room following Sophie's rejection, Jack started pondering a new idea that had been sparked by his conversation with her. He didn't know why he hadn't thought of it before.

At lunchtime, Jack quickly scoffed a sandwich and then went out for a walk. London was its usual clogged self and the streets around the office were definitely no exception; the traffic was a mess of stationary cars and aggressively hooting taxis, and the pavements were thick with meandering tourists, dawdling shoppers and impatient businesspeople. Jack pushed and weaved his way through the throng towards a pub that he knew hosted tribute bands once a week. He needed to find something that might appeal to Max's dodgy musical tastes. The place was absolutely heaving and, as soon as he stepped inside, he knew it would take him the rest of his lunch break just to reach the bar in order to enquire about their live music nights. Thankfully, looking around, he spotted a large chalkboard up on the wall that announced forthcoming events with a generous sprinkling of overenthusiastic punctuation:

*"Tuesday 14th Oct — They're back!! Our very own Sister Act!! Don't miss **NUN DIRECTION!!***
The lovely ladies from St Mary's will be here again performing songs from your fave boy band!!"

Good grief. That definitely wouldn't do. Jack craned his neck over the chattering pub crowd and read on.

*"Tuesday 21st Oct — **LEONARD SKINHEAD!!**"*
*"Tuesday 28th Oct — **LADY HAHA!!**"*

Leonard Skinhead might have suited Jack's purposes but he wasn't sure and, besides, he didn't want to wait that long to put his idea into action.

There was one other venue Jack knew of that was a possibility. Another ten minutes of barging through pedestrians and a couple of wrong turns finally brought him to a quieter side street and a less trendy pub called The Wild Rabbit. The crazed-looking bunny pictured in the sign outside looked more than just wild; it had a distinctly homicidal gleam in its painted eye. Jack was running out of lunch hour and shoved his way rudely to the bar, where the harassed-looking barman studiously ignored him in favour of two giggly women wearing low-cut tops who were apparently ordering drinks for half of London.

Eventually the man came towards him but infuriatingly said, 'Yes mate?' to another customer beside Jack, a fat guy in a loud striped shirt.

Before Stripe Guy could order, Jack spoke up. 'Sorry, could I just—'

'Hey! Wait your turn,' said Stripe Guy.

'Look, I'm not buying drinks,' Jack said, pulling up to his full height and giving Stripe what he hoped was an intimidating look. At least he had the barman's attention now. 'D'you still have live music here?'

In response, the barman thrust his designer-stubble-clad chin towards the end of the bar, where Jack could see a small stack of bright pink flyers. The top one had a large brown ring-shaped stain on it where someone had stood a drink on the pile, but Jack grabbed one from further down and then escaped back out into the sunshine.

He was due back at work in just over five minutes and glanced at the flyer as he hurried along. The Wild Rabbit didn't go in for exclamation marks. The piece of paper stated, economically, "8pm Wed 15th Oct at The Wild Rabbit: Tara and her Cobnuts". The rest of the badly-photocopied page was dominated by a poor-quality photo of a punk girl with a lot of piercings and an impressive Mohican hairdo. She looked as if she was about to take a bite out of the microphone she was holding.

Jack smiled to himself as he folded the pink flyer and tucked it into his trouser pocket. Tara looked perfect. He walked back into the Phoenix building, decidedly sweaty but only a couple of minutes late.

'Hey Max, you doing anything Wednesday night?' Jack threw

the question casually to his colleague when he got back from collecting outgoing mail later that afternoon.

'Um… don't think so. Why?'

'You like punk music, right?'

'Some of it, yeah.'

'Apparently these guys are pretty decent.' Jack fished the crumpled flyer out of his pocket, opened it out and tossed it onto the desk towards Max. 'They're doing a gig at the Rabbit this week. Fancy it?'

'Er…' Max gave Jack a sideways glance as he picked up the flyer. 'I didn't know you were into this kind of stuff.'

'Oh, yeah. I've got pretty eclectic tastes. I was gonna go with a girlfriend but she's blown me out. So I thought of you.' That sounded a bit dodgy. 'It's about time we had a couple of beers together. You know, get to know each other better.' God, that sounded worse. Damn it.

'Sure, why not. Beats sitting at home in front of the telly.' Max said cheerfully.

Jack breathed a sigh of relief. Game on.

10:59:33

The Wild Rabbit

The photo of Tara that had been used on the flyers was out of date by a decade or two. In the flesh — which had to be well into its forties but was still perforated with an array of metalwork — she looked somewhat less anarchic. Disappointingly, her Mohican was noticeable by its absence; instead, her short hair had been gelled into slightly droopy spikes that stuck out all over her head at odd angles. It was purple, though. Her outfit comprised a short tunic dress made from irregular patches of denim and other fabric that were held together with hundreds of safety pins. Below this unique item of clothing, Tara's skinny legs were clad in ripped black tights and ended in a pair of battered Doc Marten boots. The overall effect was slightly absurd, but you had to give the woman points for effort.

The Wild Rabbit was less busy than it had been on Monday lunchtime, and Jack and Max were able to find seats at a table surprisingly easily. A lot of their fellow music-lovers were considerably older than them, and Jack sipped his first beer with a growing sense of foreboding while they waited for Tara to get her Cobnuts in order. The latter were two middle-aged gentlemen who didn't look punky at all. The keyboard player wore a black t-shirt with a picture of a moose on the front stretched over his beer belly, and the balding guitarist had an embarrassing comb-over and his jeans were held up with rainbow-coloured braces.

In preparation for this evening, Jack had spent a thoroughly unpleasant Tuesday night swotting up on punk music, since that was inevitably going to be a topic of conversation. After a few hours on the computer at home, wincing and fast-forwarding through snippets of what sounded to him like a punch-up in a glass factory, he wasn't much the wiser. He would just have to try and steer the chat onto other subjects, which was of course what he needed to do anyway.

Max was grinning at him over the top of his pint. 'Never would've had you pegged for a punk. Not in a million years.'

'Well, I'm not. Not really. Like I said, I just have eclectic tastes. Some of the music's pretty cool, that's all. It… um… just does something for me.' *Makes me want to cut off my own ears, mostly,* he added to himself.

'I know what you mean. I love the energy.'

'Oh yeah, absolutely. The energy's awesome.' Jack suddenly felt old. He found himself hoping Tara and her Cobnuts weren't going to be too loud. It was going to be a long night.

'So who d'you listen to?'

Jack was ready for this one. 'To be honest, a lot of it's just stuff I've just added to my playlist and I don't even know who it's by. A few of the old classics, of course. Pistols, Clash, Ramones.' Max was nodding. Jack was glad he'd done some homework. 'And then there's… um… oh, I think I've got a few Green Day tracks, some Offspring, stuff like that.' Jack felt a twinge of panic, having exhausted all of his newly-acquired knowledge within the first five minutes, but Max seemed convinced.

'Wow, cool. Toy Dolls?'

'Er…' Jack was thrown. Was that a punk band? It didn't sound like it. He made a non-committal gesture and took another swig of lager.

'Oh man, I love Toy Dolls.' This wasn't a statement Jack had expected to hear tonight. 'Nellie the Elephant just makes me feel so alive.' And there was another one.

Since Jack had absolutely no idea how to respond to what Max had just said, he offered to go and buy more drinks. Max had insisted on getting the first round.

'No, you're all right. I'm fine with this one for a bit.' Max raised his glass, which was still two-thirds full.

'Nonsense. I may as well get us another one in before the band gets going.' Jack went to the bar and bought two more pints of lager. There were a few standing people and a pillar between him and the table where Max was sitting. Perfect. Jack waited until the barmaid had turned to serve another customer and then he quickly drew a small flat bottle from his pocket and poured a generous slug of vodka into one of the beers before returning to the table.

'There you go, mate.'

'Cheers, Jack.'

'No probs. Now we're all set.'

At that moment, the Cobnut with the rainbow braces struck a loud chord to get everyone's attention and Tara stepped up to the microphone. 'Evenin' all,' she said in husky tones. She had quite a pleasant voice when she was speaking. When she was yelling the lyrics of well-known songs it was markedly less pleasant, at least as far as Jack was concerned. Whatever he'd expected, it wasn't this.

Tara, Moose-Belly and Braces applied their distinctive musical talents to a bizarre range of material. Nothing was sacred. Over the next hour, everything from the national anthem to popular hymns was given the Cobnuts treatment. Taking his lead from Max, Jack clapped as enthusiastically as everyone else at the end of each over-amplified track, then went back to sipping his beer and praying for the interval. The only time his applause was genuine was when, at long last, Tara said, 'Back in five. Don't run away,' and disappeared off in the direction of the ladies' toilets.

Max was grinning. 'What a pile of shite!' he exclaimed happily.

'Yeah, sorry mate. I th—'

'Brilliant! What a buzz!' Max stood up. 'My round.'

Still not entirely sure whether Max loved or hated Tara and her

199

discordant Cobnuts, Jack sat in a state of bewilderment and waited for his ears to stop ringing. Max deposited two full glasses on the table and then went to find the gents', giving Jack the opportunity to discreetly spike his beer with another big dash of vodka. As soon as his drinking buddy was back from the loo, Jack planned to steer the conversation to Phoenix.

Max plopped back into his seat. 'Blimey, this is going to my head tonight.' He drained the last of his previous pint. 'I haven't eaten since lunch. Want some crisps or something?'

'Nah, I'm fine, thanks.' Jack was keen to talk while they had the chance, but Max was already on his feet again and making his way to the bar. After about five minutes, he returned with two large bags of crisps and accidentally knocked the table as he sat down, spilling some of Jack's fresh pint of lager.

'God, sorry mate! Here, swap. I haven't touched mine yet.' Before Jack could protest, Max picked up Jack's less-than-full glass and took a hefty swig, pushing his own across the table. 'So, what d'you think of the band?'

Jack didn't know what to say. 'Um, yeah. They're—'

'A one, a two, a one-two-three-four!' Without preamble, Tara launched into the second half of her set.

Jack sipped the spiked beer miserably. Between the effects of the alcohol and the volume of the music, he was barely able to process any coherent thoughts beyond a vague hope that he wasn't suffering permanent damage to his hearing. Perhaps this hadn't been such a good idea, after all. Following an inexplicably aggressive rendition of "Morning Has Broken", he went to the loo and then bought two more lagers. This time, he spiked both glasses with what remained of the vodka before returning to the table. What the hell.

In the end, it wasn't until they were walking to the tube station at the end of the night that Jack had another proper chance to talk to Max. By that time, neither of them could walk in a straight line and Jack was struggling to remember what it was he'd wanted to say. Whatever it was, he was going to have to raise his voice above the loud ringing in his ears.

'So, Max. Look, mate. I wanna… Look, we're mates, right?'

'Yeah Jack. Course we are. An' we gotta do this again. I'm gonna be honest, it was a lot more fun than I thought it'd be.'

Jack belched. 'Ooh pardon. Yeah, but look, Max. About Phoenix. This thing they're planning—'

Max stopped dead. He looked at Jack, frowning as he focused on his face. He waggled a finger. 'Uh-uh. No shop talk. It's a boys' night out.'

'I know, I know. But when's it gonna happen? That's all I wanna know.'

Max's frown grew deeper. 'I dunno.' He took a few wavering steps along the pavement. 'Are we goin' the right way? God, I could murder a kebab. With silly— I mean, chilli sauce.'

Jack lurched after Max and grabbed his shoulder to stop him walking off again. Max turned, did an ungainly pirouette, lost his balance and sat down abruptly, then burst out laughing. Jack tried to help him up, but it was like trying to lift a giant water balloon. Max was helpless with booze and laughter. Suddenly, all of the failure and frustration of the past couple of weeks bubbled up inside Jack and his temper erupted. The next thing he knew, he had grabbed Max by the front of his shirt and was shaking him, holding his upper body off the ground, shouting into his stupid, surprised face.

'Don't play dumb with me! Is it a bomb? It's a bomb, isn't it? Tell me! Just tell me!'

There was a pregnant pause while Max stared blearily up into Jack's angry red face. 'I dunno what the hell you're talkin' about,' he said, and then dissolved into fresh fits of laughter.

Jack managed to resist the urge to punch him. Instead, he released Max's shirt and let him drop. There was a sickening thud as the back of Max's skull made contact with the pavement. The infuriating giggling stopped abruptly.

A few passers-by had given the two drunken young men a wide berth, but now three or four people were right beside them, asking if everything was okay. Jack felt ill. How had everything become so messed up? Suddenly weary, he slumped against a lamp-post, watching resignedly as things went even further off the rails. Max was groaning. A woman was leaning over him where he lay on the ground. Someone else was speaking into a phone, asking for an ambulance. Somewhere in Jack's head there was a voice urging him to run away, but he didn't have the energy or the coordination to heed it. Instead, he bent over and vomited into the gutter.

*

The next day would have been awful even without the worst hangover Jack had ever experienced. He'd somehow made it to work on time — at least in body — despite not having fallen into bed until around four o'clock that morning. Now he was sitting in the post room with his head in his hands, wondering how he was remaining upright and wishing fervently that he'd stayed at home.

Max was off sick. No surprises there. Jack hadn't left the hospital until he knew Max hadn't suffered anything more serious than a nasty bruise and a mild concussion. Jack didn't envy his workmate's even worse headache, although he probably had stronger painkillers to tame it with and was almost certainly asleep in a comfy bed. Max's parents had arrived just before Jack left and had given him some distinctly unfriendly looks even before they saw Max's ripped shirt and the lump on the back of his head. By that time, Jack was desperate to be horizontal, and he certainly didn't feel inclined to hang around offering explanations.

He sipped his third cup of strong black coffee, half-heartedly sorting post into piles, reflecting on all the reasons he had to feel wretched, and worrying about what Max would say when he came back to work.

As it turned out, Jack could have avoided the whole fiasco. In the end, finding out what the Phoenix plan was really all about was ridiculously easy.

10:59:34

Killing Time

Ken Burford stared through the magnified scope of his high-powered rifle. He took a slow breath, savouring the moment, watching his target move casually beyond the crosshairs, oblivious to his deadly presence. Letting his breath halfway out, he squeezed the trigger and the shot rang out, shattering the peace of the ancient Montana forest.

He lowered the rifle and wandered over to the kill. The deer looked up at him with belated alarm in its limpid eyes and Burford watched the animal impassively while the fatal bullet-wound finished its work. It was only another whitetail. He'd been hoping to find a black bear or at least an elk today, but it didn't really matter. Anything to alleviate his impatience while he waited for Horseman Number Three to be given the go-ahead.

The guide came up to congratulate his client, and the two men in their bright orange jackets gazed down at the carcass for a few seconds.

'There's a mountain lion been spotted up near the ridge, if you fancy trying for it,' said the guide.

'Well, what are we waiting for?' Burford replied.

*

Hunting usually put Ken in a good mood, but he still felt twitchy and unsettled when he got back, as if there was an itch he couldn't quite scratch. It had been a while since the first two Horsemen had carried out their murderous business in Delhi and China under his orders, and the sense of power was addictive. General Barrett was pushing for another green light, but the press attention and the still-rising death toll in both locations had given President Wentworth a serious case of cold feet.

So, meanwhile, Ken found himself killing time. When he wasn't hunting, he kept himself occupied spying on people. Much of it was legitimate intelligence work for his paymasters at the Pentagon, although he derived greater personal pleasure from snooping on those who had wronged him in the past.

With the resources he had at his disposal, it hadn't been difficult to set up a couple of hidden cameras in his ex-wife's lounge and kitchen, and he regularly watched the footage for a few hours, fast-forwarding through the boring bits. It was like a reality TV show, but with the added satisfaction that she had no idea he was still keeping an eye on her.

The illegal wiretap he'd placed on Roger Vee's mobile phone was less entertaining. Nevertheless, Ken made a point of going through the recordings at least once every couple of weeks in his office at home. It was mostly tedious dialogue relating to Phoenix business and, in the years he'd been eavesdropping, there hadn't been anything he could use. Still, Ken lived in hope of hearing something incriminating. Oh, how dearly he would love to bring that man down. Just as his ex-wife had kicked him out, so had Roger Vee, and the sting of rejection had never abated.

Ken had still been Howard Carmichael back then. He'd joined Roger's little environmental protest group in the early days and had genuinely admired the man's passion and drive. They'd become friends and Howard had been one of the regulars at their meetings and marches. Howard's ideas and enthusiasm had been welcomed for a while, until things went sour and Roger Vee had turned out to be just as timid and pathetic as everyone else. So what if Howard had smashed a few windows and started a fight or two during the protests? Roger had bailed him out and then told him off like a naughty schoolboy. And just because Howard's ideas were more ambitious than anyone else's didn't make them any less valid. Roger should've been grateful, but no; instead he'd told Howard to leave and never return. Ken still thought that putting something in the drinking water to make people infertile — especially in backward countries like India and Africa — had been a perfectly reasonable suggestion. Roger obviously wasn't as dedicated to controlling population as he professed to be.

The most galling thing, of course, was that Roger Vee had somehow turned Phoenix into such a massive commercial success. He must be worth a small fortune, and the whole world knew his name and his virtuous reputation. But nobody was that squeaky-clean. Nobody. And if there was dirt to be found that would bring Roger Vee crashing down from his lofty pedestal, Ken wanted desperately to be the one to find it. So far, he'd come up empty. There had been no affairs, no hint of any financial wrongdoing… Nothing.

A while ago, Ken had thought he might be onto something. There had been an anomaly: a late-night call to Eve Gyer, the woman who headed up Phoenix in the UK. Roger Vee's familiar voice had sounded strained — emotional, even — when he'd said, 'I'm not sure we can afford to wait any longer. Please tell me I'm wrong, but I think we have to set Plan B in motion.' Then Gyer had said, 'I hoped this day would never come.'

So what was this 'Plan B' of theirs? And why did they both sound so reluctant about it? It had to be something big. The days when Roger Vee did anything on a small scale were long past.

Recently, Ken had been listening to his illicit recordings with greater diligence. He hadn't been able to glean any further clues, which told him loud and clear that a secret was being carefully kept, and this aroused his curiosity even further.

Ken grabbed a cold beer from the fridge and sat at his computer to listen to the latest soundbites. The voice he loved to hate filled the room, talking to a series of colleagues about solar energy and climate change and ice in Greenland, and asking after someone's sick kid. Then there was a very brief call from Eve Gyer, the woman in the London office. She said, 'I think we need to start pinning down timings.' Roger Vee responded, 'I know. I'll talk to Raleigh.' And that was it; no hellos, goodbyes or chitchat, which was unusual.

So who was Raleigh? Ken pulled up a huge spreadsheet listing Phoenix employees and ran a search. The only near-match was someone called Ray Farleigh, based in Malaysia. Ken listened to the recording again, thinking perhaps he'd misheard the name. No, Roger had definitely said, 'I'll talk to Raleigh.'

Ken flicked to his internet browser and entered the search terms "Phoenix" and "Raleigh". The screen filled with images of a massive modern factory building. Apparently Phoenix's main pharmaceutical production facility was situated in Raleigh, North Carolina.

Ken sat up straighter and took a swig of his beer. He'd picked up the scent of something interesting, he was sure of it. He began tapping on his keyboard.

Oh, how he loved the hunt.

10:59:35

Naughty or Nice

The moped breezed along in the direction of Cheryl's house at Much Wheadle. Once I'd managed to extricate myself from the tangled web of traffic around Mareton, the roads stretched away invitingly between long hedgerows splashed with autumnal browns and golds. The weather was turning cooler but bright sunshine sparked off the polished instruments on the front of the bike as I opened her up and then dived through pools of shadows cast by huge trees. The ride was every bit as enjoyable and exhilarating as I'd imagined it would be, and I couldn't help grinning to myself — to the extent that the padded interior of my helmet would allow — as I left the town and my cares far behind.

'So how's the job going?' Cheryl asked as soon as we were settled into folding chairs in her pretty garden, with supplies of hot tea and thick slabs of her delicious home-made lemon drizzle cake within easy reach.

'Really well, thanks. I'm enjoying it.'

'Honestly?' She'd always been able to read me like a book and seemed to sense that I was holding something back, but of course I couldn't tell her what it was.

I laughed. 'Yes, honestly. I really am. I had no idea what to expect but it's even better than I hoped it'd be. The people are great and the work itself is fascinating. I'm learning so much and getting involved with lots of cool stuff.'

Cheryl smiled, satisfied with my response this time. 'Like what? Tell me.'

'Well, so far I've mostly been working with a guy called Chris. He cracks me up, you'd like him.'

'And what's his job?'

'Phoenix doesn't really go in for titles but he's one of their waste specialists.'

Cheryl pulled a face. 'That doesn't sound like a very nice job.'

'It's way more interesting than you'd think. And waste is a huge problem. I mean, massive.' I took a bite of the moist, tangy cake on my plate.

'That I can believe. Even living on my own, I'm always amazed how much rubbish ends up in my bin. And that's not from being wasteful or eating lots of convenience foods or anything. It's all the plastic, it just mounts up. Every single thing you buy is wrapped in layers of the stuff these days.'

I told her about the enormous waste processing plant that Chris had been helping to get up and running. Situated to serve three different counties, it would divert hundreds of thousands of tonnes of rubbish that would otherwise end up in landfill, extracting recyclable materials and incinerating the rest to generate electricity. Even the ash from the furnaces would get recycled into building materials. 'This is the third one Chris has been involved with, apparently, so he's one of the top experts in the country now. The engineers from the new plant are on the phone several times a day, asking his advice about something or other.'

'And yours, I bet.'

'God, not yet. I just help Chris out, really. There's so much more to it than you'd think. But I'm learning fast.'

'You always did.' She was ridiculously biased, but it was touching. It struck me then how supportive she'd been over the years and how much I'd come to value her sound advice and enjoy her easy company. I wished I could talk to her about the whole

Plan B thing.

'Thanks, Cheryl.' I was getting used to dropping the 'Auntie' bit. 'You know, for... Well, just for everything. You've always been here for me. I don't think I've ever really thanked you for that.'

She flapped her hand in a dismissive gesture. 'Of course I'm here for you, Lou. You're my nephew and I love you to bits. Besides, your mum made me promise I'd look out for you. Not that she needed to.'

It hadn't occurred to me that Mum would have asked that of her sister, but I found I could picture the conversation. I could almost hear her voice. She'd known she was dying. And, once she could no longer pretend that the cancer wasn't going to win, she'd spent the last months of her life getting things in order, making sure Dad and I would be okay, saying what she needed to say to all the people she cared about. I realised that I was only now beginning to understand a little of what she must have gone through. When she'd tried to have those 'soppy' conversations with me, I'd rejected them, often angrily. Now, I regretted having pushed her away. Back then, at ten years old, the last thing I'd wanted to do was face the fact that I was losing her, and I'd found any excuse to avoid those meaningful chats that sounded too much like goodbye.

I looked across at Cheryl. Her face and her expression were so much like Mum's in that moment that I caught my breath. Tears threatened and I turned away, unsure why I felt the need to try and hide my feelings but blinking furiously nonetheless and suddenly needing to be very busy with the teapot that stood on the tray beside me.

'Shall we have a top up?'

*

I'd adopted Pam's suggestion of reading the news. She was absolutely right: it was a daily reminder of all the reasons why Plan B was necessary. From specific stories about individuals to national issues and world trends, I scanned the articles with a new sense of

209

perspective and realised that the planet was indeed in a pretty sorry state and it was all mankind's doing.

There were reports of record-breaking traffic jams. There were pictures of ridiculously crowded beaches and cities. The need for housing was being mentioned more often and micro-flats were becoming a thing. Pollution was causing growing concern, even in places where it had never been a serious problem before. Depression and mental health issues were on the rise. Crammed shanty towns wallowed in poverty and disease. Waiting lists for medical treatments were growing. No one knew what to do with the growing tide of refugees fleeing from a varied assortment of wars and catastrophes, including those displaced by the recent disasters in India and China. Forests were still being destroyed, if not by chainsaws then by fires. There were attacks by wild animals near diminishing pockets of their remaining habitat. Now and then, another species was reported as extinct or endangered. Climate protesters and environmental activists were doing their best to raise awareness, but they may as well have been yelling at cows.

I wondered for the umpteenth time how anyone could possibly fail to see that our planet was already perilously overcrowded. I reckoned that the people who were still waiting for signs that things were reaching crisis point must be going around with their eyes shut. They'd be the same ones who'd be wailing, 'Why didn't anybody warn us?' when it was too late.

I read about babies and young children who'd died or been injured because of their parents' neglect, cruelty or sheer stupidity. There were wars, there were threats of more wars, there were murders, thefts, acid attacks, rapes, strikes, protests and riots. Ignorance, petty-mindedness, prejudice, corruption and religious fanaticism were common denominators on every continent. In short, people were busier than ever doing horrible things to each other.

I read that President Wentworth in the United States was being criticised for withdrawing from global talks about climate change and for pledging yet more US troops to fight in some long-running civil war in the Middle East. Having previously been praised for his humanitarian response to the awful industrial accidents in India and China, it looked like he was out of favour again. He seemed a weak and insubstantial leader, easily blown off course by any prevailing wind, and his popularity bobbed up and down with every change in the weather. The populace was fickle, but then so were politicians, I reflected despondently.

Updates on the situations in Delhi and the Yangtze flood plain were very few and far between. I presumed that people there were still dying or struggling to piece their lives back together, but it was old news now. There were more important things to write headlines about, like so-called celebrities choosing the wrong outfits to wear, lamenting the break-up of their latest short-lived relationships or divulging their beauty secrets and dietary habits.

The online comments about news items made even more depressing reading, if that was possible. For every insightful and constructive observation, there were invariably at least twenty other remarks that completely missed the point, took offence, slagged off someone else, or otherwise reinforced my worst fears about human nature.

Within a couple of weeks, I'd found myself really hoping the Phoenix virus would be unleashed. I read about the child abusers, the thugs who beat up little old ladies, the people who inflicted unspeakable suffering on animals, the terrorists who drove vans into crowds of families, the crime lords who profited from the misery of others and the drug pushers who wrecked lives. Was it wrong to wish those people dead and gone from the world? Maybe. But I knew I wasn't alone in wishing it, regardless.

However, just as Pam had said, there were a small number of stories that restored my faith in humankind. Not many, thanks to the insatiable appetite of the masses for murder, misfortune and scandal, but a few.

I read of a homeless man who, despite having no shoes, walked across a town to escort a lost child safely to a police station. The police officer bought a pair of trainers for the homeless man and drove him to a shelter.

There was also a woman who anonymously picked up the tab in a pub restaurant for a meal eaten by a group of exhausted firefighters who'd been busy saving lives.

Another story that moved me was about a young man from a poor neighbourhood, who was trying hard to make a better life for himself and his family and walked five miles to and from work in all weathers. Someone offered him a lift one day and was so impressed by the man's attitude and effort that they raised money to buy him a used car and a year's worth of fuel and insurance.

Those were the people I wanted to share the world with. Those were the people who deserved to survive.

But how the hell was I supposed to find them? Reading news stories was one thing. The news was literally black and white. If you assumed the reporters' often biased identification of the heroes and villains was correct, then sure, it was a doddle to decide who deserved to live or die. Walking around Mareton or Much Wheadle was a less extreme experience and I balked at the prospect of playing God, even on a small scale. I remembered Roger Vee saying that the thing we would worry about most was how we'd know who to vaccinate, and he'd been right. Who was I to make such decisions?

Riding my moped to work one morning, a woman in a big flashy car was too impatient to wait for a traffic light and she almost wiped me out. Braking hard, I consoled myself by thinking, *No vaccine for you!* And then, later in the same journey, a van stopped to let me pull out into the slow traffic and the driver waved me ahead of him with a courteous gesture and a friendly smile. I decided he was someone worth saving.

Before I knew it, I'd developed a habit of thinking *no* or *yes* as I observed everyone, like Santa knowing who'd been naughty or nice. It was true that a seemingly insignificant action or gesture could tell you a lot about someone. The person who bothered to hold a door open for you… yes. The person who didn't smile or thank you when you held a door open for them… no. It became almost like some sinister game.

But the prospect of *actually* having the power of life and death over people? That responsibility didn't sit comfortably with me at all. It disturbed my days and plagued my dreams at night, and I was going to have to talk to somebody about it before I went stark raving mad.

10:59:36

What are Friends For?

By the time Max came back to work on Monday, Jack's hangover was long gone but he was a wreck, nonetheless. His paranoid imagination had been busy for the past four days, conjuring every possible scenario. He had spent a miserable weekend at home alone, wishing he had Max's mobile number… Wondering whether Max would report him at work for bullying… Wondering whether Max's parents would convince their injured son to press charges for assault… Wondering whether Max had lapsed into a coma and died. Twice he'd actually phoned the hospital but hung up before they answered. So when Max breezed into the comms room on Monday morning wearing his usual lopsided grin, Jack felt a confusing rush of relief and irritation. He was desperate to talk about what had happened, but the pair barely had time to acknowledge each other before their boss walked in.

'Ah, good. Max. Borrow you for ten?' Charmaine Beesley was Phoenix's communications manager. Ironically, her own style of communication was to speak in abbreviated staccato sentences as if there was a tax on words. She smiled briefly and beckoned to Max before turning on her heel and marching out, clearly expecting him to follow. He flashed Jack a grimace before hurrying after her.

Jack's unease returned in full measure while he sorted the post and loaded the trolleys. Max wasn't back by the time Jack had to set off on his morning rounds of the building. Given Charmaine's infamous efficiency, that could only mean that Max was doing most of the talking, he reflected grimly.

Shortly before eleven, Jack spotted Max re-stocking copier paper at the other end of the marketing department and pushed his trolley over to him. 'Everything all right?' he asked anxiously.

'We need to talk,' said Max, looking uncharacteristically solemn and doing nothing whatsoever to alleviate Jack's worries.

'Okay.' Jack waited expectantly.

'Not here.' Max glanced around. No one was paying them any particular attention but there were several people within earshot. 'I'm nearly done with this. How about you?' He looked at the almost empty mail trolley.

'Yeah, just the third floor and then I'm finished.'

'Right. See you back in the comms room in about ten minutes. And try and avoid Charmaine until then, if you can.'

Max hadn't seemed hostile, yet Jack was convinced he must have reported last Wednesday night's events in terms that wouldn't do Jack any favours; if not to his parents or the hospital or the police, then certainly to Charmaine.

At last, the two of them had chance to talk.

'So what was your meeting about?' Jack asked.

'Oh, she called it a return to work interview. It's standard practice, apparently, whenever anybody's been off sick. Just asking for a few details and checking I'm fit for work, basically.'

'And are you? I mean, are you okay?'

'Yeah, I'm fine.' Max shrugged. 'They kept me in hospital for observation for a few hours and then discharged me. I was a bit confused, apparently, so they gave my mum a leaflet about concussion, but I think it was mostly the beer. That was some strong stuff they served in that place, wasn't it?'

'Um, yeah.' Jack said, studying his fingernails. 'Very.'

'Anyway, I had the mother of all hangovers on Thursday and still felt like my head was gonna explode on Friday. I lived on

215

painkillers for two days, but I was pretty much back to normal by the weekend.' Max gingerly prodded the back of his head and winced. 'I had a hell of a lump, but it's gone down now.'

'I'm glad you're okay,' said Jack, realising that he meant it. 'So… what did you tell Charmaine about how it happened?'

'That's the thing. Trouble is, that beer went straight to my head for some reason and I don't actually remember what happened. I mean, I do up to a point, with the band and everything, but then it all gets majorly blurry.'

Hope dawned in Jack's eyes. 'Oh. Well, what *do* you remember?'

'Not much from later on, to be honest. Just being in the pub… and then walking down the road… and after that it's just snippets, really. And God only knows what we talked about. I've got this weird memory of you leaning over me and yelling something about a bomb, right in my face… and me thinking that was absolutely the funniest thing ever.'

'Wow, I don't remember that,' Jack said carefully. 'To tell you the truth, I was off my face as well. That lager they serve at The Wild Rabbit should come with a health warning.'

'Damn straight.' Max rubbed his head again.

'So what was Charmaine's reaction to all that?'

'God, I didn't tell *her* all that! I happen to like this job and I'm not even out of my probation period yet. There's no way I was gonna tell her I ended up having to take two days off sick because I got falling-down drunk on a Wednesday evening! That's why I needed to talk to you. Did you say anything to her about it on Thursday or Friday, when I was off?'

'No.' Jack frowned. 'I don't think I even saw her. I've got a feeling she was away on a training course or something.'

Relief lit Max's face. 'That's the best news I've had all day. Will you cover for me, if she asks? She knows we were together. I'm not asking you to lie, exactly. Just… Please don't mention the state we were in, okay?'

'Um, okay. Sure. So how did you say you ended up banging your head?'

'I just told her I slipped on something, maybe some greasy food someone had dropped on the pavement. I said I didn't remember much about exactly how it happened because, you know, head injuries and all that. So if you're okay to stick to the same story? I mean, hopefully she won't even ask you but, you know, just in case.'

Jack felt as though a big black cloud had lifted. He allowed himself a chuckle and said, 'Sure, Max. No problem.'

'Thanks, mate. You're doing me a huge favour. Cheers.'

Jack smiled. 'What are friends for?'

*

'Houston, we have a problem.'

Eve Gyer had asked the Human Resources manager, Lisa Scott, for a private word. The two women had worked together for several years and they were now sitting alone in a meeting room, but as a precaution Eve gave the hand signal that meant she wanted to discuss something to do with Plan B. Lisa rubbed her left earlobe between her right thumb and forefinger to acknowledge the gesture.

'Do you know Jack West?' Eve asked.

'Yes. Graduate trainee in the comms centre.'

'That's the one. He's our problem.'

'Really? That's a shame.' Lisa seemed disappointed. 'I thought he had potential.'

'So did I,' Eve agreed. 'He was in my group for the bunker exercise at this year's induction workshop. He took the lead, and at first I was quite impressed.'

'That fits with the feedback I've had from Charmaine. After his last review, she told me that people really seem to like him and she could easily see him moving up into a supervisory role within a few years.'

'Jack has a lot of excellent qualities. But something's off.' Eve frowned. 'I can't quite put my finger on it, but I just get the

217

impression he's not entirely genuine. I noticed in the bunker session that he tends to focus on quick fixes and easy solutions, even if they're not the best things to do. He got quite sulky when things didn't go his way. And he displayed a lack of compassion and judgement. Without those, authority is a dangerous thing. During the exercise, Jack's prime motivators seemed to be personal gain and self-preservation. Anyway, for all of those reasons I decided *not* to include him in the group that was told about Plan B.'

Lisa was nodding resignedly. Eve had demonstrated on countless occasions that she was a formidable judge of character. 'Okay. Well, as I said, that's a disappointment. But why is he a problem?'

'We think he knows something. We don't know exactly what, or how he found out, but Sophie from the finance department came to see me last week—'

'Sophie Pearce?' As HR manager, Lisa prided herself on her knowledge of the employees who worked in Phoenix's Head Office.

Eve smiled indulgently. 'Yes, that's her. A very astute young lady. By the sounds of it, our friend Jack West made a rather clumsy attempt to chat her up. However, what prompted her to report it was that he was dropping hints and asking questions that suggested he wanted to talk about Plan B. When she gave him the hand signal, he didn't seem to know the correct response. He definitely noticed her gesture, though. He repeated it back to her.'

'Oh my God. That could be disastrous! If he gives someone the signal…' Lisa trailed off.

'Quite. And I've been making a few discreet enquiries and it seems that Jack's been digging for information with several other people, too.'

'Oh no!'

'I don't believe he's found out very much. At least not yet. And even if he did, there's a limit to how much damage he could do to our plans at this stage.' Eve uncrossed her legs and leaned forward in her chair. 'But he could be… an inconvenience. So here's what I want you to do.'

'What did you tell them?' Jack demanded angrily.

Max backed away instinctively, eyes wide as Jack loomed over him. 'What d'you mean?'

'You ask me to cover for you and promptly go and drop me right in it!'

'I… What? Honestly, mate, I have no idea what you're talking about. I swear!'

Max's confusion seemed so genuine that Jack hesitated. 'How d'you explain this, then?' he said disgustedly, throwing a folded sheet of paper which landed at Max's feet. While Max retrieved the letter from the floor and read it, Jack flung himself into a chair and ran his hand through his hair, glaring malevolently at his younger colleague.

Max appeared even more bewildered when he'd finished reading. 'I don't understand,' he offered miserably. 'What are you having a go at me for?' He handed the letter back to Jack at arm's length, as if he was feeding a tasty titbit to a hungry dog that had big teeth and no manners.

'Oh come on, Max, it's not that tricky. HR want to talk to me about allegations of harassment. A formal disciplinary hearing, for God's sake. Strange coincidence that you had your little chat with Charmaine yesterday, don't you think?'

'But I didn't s—'

'If you decided to make up some story that I pushed you over last Wednesday rather than admit you were drunk, just say so, then at least I know what I'm dealing with here.'

'Hey! Why the hell would I do that? I thought we were mates!'

'So did I,' Jack retorted sulkily.

'Look, I didn't say anything like that, I swear. I have no clue what this is all about.' Max's worried expression brightened. 'Tell you what, it says you can be accompanied by a colleague. If you like, I'll come to the hearing with you and put them straight.'

Jack looked up at him. Perhaps he'd misjudged Max. He

219

reasoned that it would be pretty difficult for the company to make a harassment allegation stick if the person he was presumably suspected of harassing was his chosen companion. 'You'd do that?' he asked.

Max smiled tentatively, relieved that the storm seemed to be abating. 'Of course! Like you said earlier: what are friends for?'

10:59:37

Hearing

The day of Jack's disciplinary hearing was also the day he finally found out about Phoenix's big secret.

Jack was in a meeting room with the woman from HR, Lisa Scott. They were enduring a horribly uncomfortable silence while they waited for Max to join them; he'd been called away on some urgent errand at the last minute. Time ticked by. Jack was more anxious about this whole business than he cared to admit, and worried that it might stunt the growth of the illustrious career he'd envisioned for himself.

He was reminded of sitting in the dentist's waiting room. The silence stretched out painfully. At least the dental surgery had a fish tank and a few well-thumbed magazines to look at.

After another excruciating minute, Lisa made an attempt at small talk to relieve the tension. 'So, what did you think of the induction workshop the other week, Jack?'

'Um, yeah, it was good,' Jack replied distractedly. He just wanted to get the meeting over with. Where the hell was Max? Maybe he should suggest starting without him.

'Eve told me you did well in the bunker exercise,' Lisa said brightly.

Praise was oxygen to Jack and he paid full attention, pride

pulling at the corners of his mouth. 'Really?'

'Oh yes. She said you took the lead.'

Jack sat up taller in his chair. 'Well, I… Somebody had to.'

Lisa smiled back at him. 'Whose group were you in for the afternoon sessions?' she asked conversationally.

That was when it hit Jack like a ton of bricks. Of course! He'd been going about this all wrong, focusing on the other newbies who'd been at the same induction workshop as him. Why hadn't he realised before? There was a good chance his peers would know he *wasn't* in one of the groups that was let in on the big secret, whereas he was in a building full of hundreds of longer serving employees, many of whom didn't know him from Christopher Columbus and probably had the inside knowledge he craved. Pieces started falling into place. His mind was racing.

He decided to take a chance. 'Er, Roger's. Yep, I was in Roger Vee's group.'

'Oh cool, so you know about the plan, then. What d'you think?'

Jack felt as if the floor had shifted under his seat, but he forced himself to remain outwardly calm. He'd spent all this time trying so desperately to find out the truth and now it was being handed to him on a plate. If only he'd known it could be this easy.

'Well, it's… um…' What the hell could he say that wouldn't give the game away?

Lisa smiled and rescued him. 'Still sinking in? I know. I was lost for words, too, when I first heard about it. You get used to the idea after a while.'

'I suppose so. It's a pretty big deal, though.'

'Of course. It's huge. But you just have to keep reminding yourself it's for the greater good.'

'Yes, that helps.' Jack had been wishing Max would hurry up and get here; now he was hoping his companion would be delayed for a while longer so that he could fish for more information. 'It's just… Well, you know, all those people.'

'Oh God, I know. It's going to be awful.'

When Lisa then casually mentioned what the plan entailed,

Jack was simultaneously triumphant and horrified. He just about managed to keep his reaction hidden, despite feeling suddenly dizzy and nauseous.

'But won't they know it's us?' he blurted.

Lisa didn't seem to have noticed his shocked expression. 'Not if everything goes according to plan. You know the plan, Jack. Nothing's traceable. It'll just go down as the biggest natural disaster in human history.'

At that moment, there was a timid knock on the door and Max's apologetic face appeared. 'Sorry,' he said. 'Did I miss anything?'

*

It took every ounce of self-control Jack could muster to sit through the short disciplinary hearing. What Lisa had said about Phoenix's intentions had completely floored him and his mind kept wandering. Luckily, the harassment allegation was all a bit of a storm in a teacup, anyway. And Max had been right: it was nothing to do with him.

'Jack? Did you hear what I just said?' Lisa asked.

'Er… yes. Sophie Pearce. Girl in accounts.'

'Yes. She made it very clear that she didn't want to get you into any trouble, but she did find your behaviour inappropriate and we're obliged to take these things seriously. You do understand?'

'Of course. It's fine. It won't happen again.'

Max hadn't uttered a word since he sat down and was merely acting as a witness, turning his head between Jack and Lisa like a spectator at a tennis match.

'Well, okay then,' Lisa said. 'In light of your assurances and the fact that Sophie told us there was no unwanted physical contact, I think a formal verbal warning is appropriate. I'll confirm it in writing—'

'All right. That's fine.' Jack couldn't wait to get out of the room.

'You have the right to appeal if you—'

'No, it's fine. Really.' Both Lisa and Max were staring at Jack

223

and he realised he wasn't being very subtle. 'Sorry. I didn't mean to sound abrupt. It's just… Look, it was a complete non-event, that's all. I shouldn't have asked her out. I accept the warning and now I just want to put this whole thing behind me and move on.'

'Well, okay then,' Lisa said again. 'If there's nothing else you want to say, I think we're done.' Jack was on his feet before she'd closed her notebook, and out of the door by the time she'd stood up.

'Hey, wait up!' Max had to jog along the corridor to catch up with Jack on the way to the lifts. 'I never knew you had a thing for Sophie Pearce. Wouldn't have thought she was your type.'

'She's not.' Jack was stabbing the lift call button repeatedly. His efforts were rewarded with a soft ping and the doors slid open.

'I think she's spoken for anyway, mate,' Max offered as they stepped inside. 'I'm sure I've seen a photo by her desk of some bloke with his arms round her. And not in a brotherly way, if you catch my drift.'

'Hm?'

'Did you even hear a word I said? What's the goss? What went on with you and Sophie? Come on, spill!'

'Nothing to tell.'

'But something must've—'

'Look, just drop it, Max!' Jack snapped, then immediately relented as his workmate recoiled like an eager puppy that had had its nose smacked. 'Sorry. This whole thing's been stressing me out, that's all, and I just want to forget about it. Okay? Thanks for coming with me and everything.'

The lift pinged again as the doors opened and Max trotted along at Jack's heels all the way back to the post room.

*

Later that afternoon, Lisa Scott tapped on the open door to Eve Gyer's office and correctly interpreted the older woman's warm smile as an invitation to enter the room and sit down.

'So, tell me.' Eve leaned towards her visitor. 'How did it go with our inquisitive young friend Mr West?'

'Just as you predicted.' Lisa summarised her conversation with Jack while Eve listened attentively, turning a sleek ballpoint pen between her fingers.

'Sounds like you handled it perfectly.'

Lisa nodded resignedly. 'And what about Max? Is he okay?'

'Ah, Max. You know, beneath his ingenuous exterior, that boy's actually very sharp.' Eve smiled. 'I hope I kept him away from the hearing for about the right amount of time?'

'Yes. But... Are you still sure we should've told Jack—'

'Let me worry about that.'

10:59:38

What If?

The prospect of having the power of life and death quite literally at my fingertips, thanks to Ben Griffin's clever microneedle plasters, was starting to pose a serious threat to my sanity. Playing the 'naughty or nice' game in my head helped a little and had taught me that it was surprisingly easy to spot clues about people's underlying natures. Pam's tip about reading the news had been useful too. But there was so much more to it than that.

What if I vaccinated someone awful? Even murderers, rapists and paedophiles probably held the door open for people sometimes or let them out in traffic now and then.

And what about all the good, thoroughly deserving people I'd be bound to miss? There could be a modern-day Mother Teresa living right here in Cuthbert Street for all I knew, and it was entirely feasible that she'd be at home polishing her halo on the day I was dishing out salvation.

What if I vaccinated a child and missed its parents?

What if I saved someone who'd be devastated beyond bearing when they had to watch the rest of their family die?

What if I didn't save enough people?

What if I saved too many?

'What if' was threatening to destroy me. What if, by the time I was supposed to get out there and save the good people of Mareton with my microneedles and my flawed judgement, I was sitting in a padded room drooling on myself, incapable of doing anything more than rocking backwards and forwards and humming the *Spongebob Squarepants* theme tune over and over again?

Impossible questions swirled constantly around my brain like particles in a snow-globe. It was exhausting. Thankfully it had been a really busy few weeks in the office, so at least during the days I'd had other things to focus on. The downside of the general busyness was that nobody at work had been able to spare much time to chat.

One Friday evening, as the office was starting to empty and I found myself feeling almost panicky, dreading another quiet weekend with nothing but my snow-globe thoughts to occupy my steadily unravelling mind, I spoke to Tomasz.

'Tom? Sorry to bother you. Can you spare a minute?'

He didn't look up from his computer keyboard. 'Sure Lou. Gimme one sec, I just need to get this email sent off.'

'Of course. I'll be at my desk.'

More than ten minutes passed before he came over. We were the only two left in the office by then; nobody stayed late on a Friday if they could help it.

'Sorry Lou. I had to get that done before the weekend. What's up?' he asked. He looked wrung out. I felt guilty burdening him with my problems.

'It's just… I'm feeling a bit… I dunno. Overwhelmed, I guess.' As I met his eyes and attempted a smile, my bottom lip wobbled unexpectedly. I swallowed, fighting to get a grip on my wayward emotions. Perhaps tackling this with my boss wasn't such a good idea after all. I looked away. 'I'm sure I'll be fine, though. Sorry. I should let you get home.' I stood up, feeling pathetic.

Tom didn't move. We were now standing face-to-face and I could read nothing but sympathy and understanding in his expression. 'No. Let's talk,' he said firmly. 'I would say let's get out of here and go for a pint somewhere, but then we couldn't say what needs to be said. So the best I can offer is caffeine and maybe a chocolate Hobnob. How's that sound?'

This time I managed to smile without the wobble.

We sat in the kitchen for almost an hour and I felt much better after our chat. Tom assured me that I wasn't alone in feeling the way I did, and told me that in fact there was another counselling session planned for everyone early the following week. Apparently, Phoenix had produced a video that would be shown to all the staff who'd be doing the vaccinations, covering many of the questions with which I'd been torturing myself. It was uncanny how the company always seemed to anticipate my needs. They were always one step ahead, to a degree that was almost creepy.

The counselling for the Mareton office happened the following Tuesday. It was typically well organised. Tom had kept the whole day free and the rest of us were split into two groups; half of us did the session in the morning while the others covered the phones, then we swapped in the afternoon. Loretta — the only member of our team who didn't know about Plan B — was out for the whole day surveying possible sites for a new offshore wind farm.

We watched the half-hour video first and then had a couple of hours to discuss things afterwards. The film that Phoenix had produced was slick and professional, much to no one's surprise, and had been circulated to regional managers all over the world as an encrypted digital file. It was basically a series of staged questions and answers, with a couple of Head Office employees asking the questions and Roger Vee and Eve Gyer responding. No bells, no whistles, no animations or acronyms. The video concisely summed up most of the things I'd been worrying about, plus a few I hadn't even thought of. And it was brutally honest. No punches were pulled. Roger and Eve talked about deaths and survivors in straightforward terms. There wasn't a single mention of people 'passing away' or other beating around the bush. There was no shying away from reality, no dressing up or dumbing down of the facts. The result was shocking, yet somehow reassuring.

The lively discussion that ensued was enormously helpful, too. Chris, Pam and Grace were in my group and it was comforting to hear people I really liked and respected voicing the same doubts and concerns that had been driving me nuts. I realised I'd been foolish — and wrong — to assume that I was especially fragile when it came to handling such emotive issues. We were all thinking, feeling, caring human beings, and we'd all had plenty of sleepless nights over Plan B.

'I'm so glad they confirmed that we'll be able to vaccinate our close family and friends,' I said. This was one of the many, many things that had been causing my insomnia. 'Although it feels kind of biased. Like we have an unfair advantage.'

'We do,' Tomasz responded, 'but there's a practical reason for it as well. Our roles won't be over once the virus has done its thing, you know. That's just the start. So the company doesn't want us moping around. There'll be a lot to do, and Phoenix people will be better prepared than most to help the world move on.'

Chris snorted. 'Prepared is probably an overstatement, at least in my case. I must admit I really struggle to imagine what the world's gonna be like afterwards. It's like there's a huge great mountain range in my head. I can imagine getting to the top, but on the other side everything's covered in fog.'

'Ooh Chris, how poetic!' teased Pam, reaching for another biscuit from the tin in the centre of the meeting room table.

'I have my moments.' He grinned self-consciously.

'It's a good description, though,' I said. 'I feel the same way.'

'Me too,' said Grace. 'But I don't think that's a bad thing. We'll have a… Well, I was going to say a blank canvas. It won't be exactly blank, but everyone will have a chance to make a fresh start.'

'I can think of another good reason for letting Phoenix employees protect their own.' Pam waved the biscuit as she spoke, liberally sprinkling the table with crumbs. 'The kinds of families that produced people like you lot have got to be worth saving. And people like you don't choose idiots and wasters to be your friends. I know we're a modest bunch, but let's face facts: Phoenix recruited all of us because we're basically good people. Good people generally come from good people. And we tend to recognise other

229

good people when we see them.'

'I still can't help worrying about that last part,' I said. 'What if I get it wrong?'

'You will. We all will.' Tomasz was standing near the window and adjusted the vertical blinds to let in more of the feeble late-October sunlight. 'As Roger said in the video, it's not an exact science. It would be totally unrealistic to hope that we can save all the good people or get rid of all the bad ones. That's not what's expected of us. Our task is to give the good people a fighting chance, that's all. At the moment there's a lot of evidence to suggest they're increasingly outnumbered, not by "bad" people necessarily, but by those who contribute nothing to the world or to human society. The purpose of the vaccinations is to safeguard the future of the human race and to redress the balance.'

Chris added, 'I liked what Eve said in the film about small signs of integrity, kindness and respect. It's not about grand gestures or making a big show of being charitable. In my experience the people who shout the loudest about their good deeds are often just trying to make themselves look good. It's more basic than that. We'll be targeting the parents who've bothered to teach their kids to say please and thank you. The kids who share their toys. That sort of thing. Even just people who'll give you a smile when you pass them in the street; how rare is *that* these days? They're the ones who'll probably help others without expecting anything in return.'

And so it went on. The key messages from that momentous afternoon in London a couple of months back were reinforced and many of the fears that had haunted me since then were put to rest. Or at least they were persuaded to lie down for a while. I was never going to feel at ease with Plan B or my part in it, but at least I knew that was okay and everyone else was in the same boat.

At lunchtime, despite what we'd been discussing, our little group came out of the meeting room laughing. Somebody had referred to a segment in the video about not discriminating on any grounds other than behaviour. Factors like race, religion, gender, social status and age were irrelevant. At that point, Pam — the oldest person in the room by a considerable margin — had put on a hilarious voice and said, 'Exactly. I may be ancient enough to remember when the Dead Sea was only sick, but I could teach you youngsters a thing or two about growing your own parsnips and making one sausage feed a family of four for a week.'

*

Lying in bed that night, feeling more relaxed than I had in weeks, I realised that despite all the talk I still didn't truly believe that something as big as Plan B could actually happen. Maybe it wouldn't. Did I hope, deep down, that someone or something would stop it? My heart lurched when I wondered if it was already too late for that.

The one thing we still hadn't been told was when the virus would be unleashed. But I sensed that Phoenix's monstrous plan was reaching its final stages, and things like the roll-out of the counselling video only fuelled that feeling.

10:59:39

Needles

On Thursday the thirtieth of October, I had an appointment with the dentist. This was noteworthy since I have a problem with dentistophobia (that must be a thing, right?) and I tend to avoid my dentist unless absolutely necessary. She's evidently used to this, and counters people's reluctance with relentless cheerfulness while she prods their exposed nerve endings with a metal spike.

During my lunch break, I lay in the dreaded chair feeling ridiculous in a waterproof bib and tinted plastic safety glasses, attempting to answer my dentist's questions with inarticulate squawking sounds while she invaded my mouth and I tried to avoid staring directly up her freakishly large nostrils. After a cursory glance at my x-rays she smiled broadly and told me I needed a filling, then happily pushed a syringeful of local anaesthetic into the gum above my nagging molar. If I'm completely honest, it really didn't hurt that much, but it was a very uncomfortable sensation and, as she pressed the injection gradually deeper, I became convinced that the needle was going to pop out somewhere near my eyeball. I emerged from the clinic twenty minutes later feeling violated and certain that the numb side of my face had swollen to at least three times its normal size.

The other reason the date was memorable was because, when I

got back to the office, there had been a delivery during my absence and I noticed half a dozen brown cardboard boxes stacked near Tomasz's desk. With a jolt, I realised the flu vaccine had arrived, even before Tomasz confirmed it. The reality of Plan B roared towards me like an express train, blasting away my denial and my hopes — or were they fears? — that it might not actually come to pass.

Every time I glanced at the boxes that afternoon, my heart skipped a beat. Between being very aware of their ominous presence, massaging my numb face, and trying not to lisp or dribble, I found it almost impossible to concentrate.

Tom was too preoccupied to notice that I wasn't getting much work done. He spent the afternoon dishing out the first supplies of the vaccine plasters to each of the employees. Loretta was out of the office again so there was no need for any particular discretion, but Tom called us into the meeting room one by one.

'Here you go, Louis,' he said, handing me a white cardboard packet slightly larger than a deck of playing cards. Printed in green on a white background, the box read:

SafeWorld
50 sticking plasters
Sterile • Hypoallergenic • Biodegradable

It felt like an important moment as I took the packet from him. 'Thankth.' Stupid numb lips.

'How's the tooth?'

'Fine. Thorry, I'm thtill a bit numb.'

He smiled. Gesturing to the box I held in my hands, he asked, 'You okay about this?'

'Yep.' The terse answer sounded teenagerish even to my ears, but it was better than 'Yeth'. I might have said more if I hadn't been embarrassed by the antics of my uncooperative tingling lips. I might have said 'No, I'm still full of doubts and worries and there have been plenty of times when I've wished I'd never got involved

233

with Phoenix at all and was still dossing about in blissful ignorance like any other normal eighteen-year-old out there.' Then again, I might not.

'Just remember all the training and counselling sessions, okay?' Tom was checking a list as he spoke. 'You're clear about the areas you're covering? You've got your map so you can keep track?'

'Yep.'

'Start with family members to get your confidence up. And don't forget to use one on yourself, of course. Let me know whenever you need more.'

I smiled lopsidedly and nodded. Tom was perceptive enough to realise that I was orally-challenged and didn't comment on my silence.

'Everyone in all the Phoenix offices around the world will be sharing ideas and learning points now that these are being rolled out, so let me know if you have any problems or suggestions. Or if you just want to talk. When you've regained the power of speech, that is.' He grinned at me.

I tried to grin back, managed what felt like a Popeye-style grimace, and left the meeting room clutching my innocent-looking packet of fifty SafeWorld plasters.

Unlike the shiny pink prototypes we'd been given to try after the Noobs' Conference, these were clear matt plasters. I wondered why, and then realised they needed to be unobtrusive regardless of the wearer's skin colour. Clever Phoenix. The design was well thought out in other ways, too; the plasters were the perfect length to overlap slightly around a fingertip and they adhered well, but they were also easy to remove and didn't leave your finger feeling sticky. The circular gelatine cap protected the microneedle array until you flicked it off to administer the vaccine.

I was inspecting one of the plasters in the office kitchen when Grace walked in and came over to me.

'Cool, huh?'

'Very,' I agreed. 'It's hard to believe something so small can protect someone against a deadly disease... Although I suppose the flu virus itself is microscopic too.'

'I had a dream a few nights ago where I was skipping around and dabbing loads of people with the vaccine. I didn't even need the plasters; I was just using my fingertips. We were all on a huge merry-go-round at some kind of theme park; it was one of those proper old-fashioned carousels with the painted horses that move up and down on poles. Somebody was chasing me, trying to stop me, but it was easy to hide in amongst all the chaos and I was carrying a cheap stuffed toy, a big weird-looking duck, under my arm to help me blend in. God knows why. It made sense in the dream. Anyway, all the people I'd touched suddenly started falling off the horses and I realised I'd been giving them the disease instead of the vaccine. I woke up in a panic, scared of my own fingers.' Grace looked at her hands.

'How awful,' I said. 'And that thought's crossed my mind a few times, too. I don't think Phoenix would do that to us, though. Do you?'

'Oh no, it was only a dream. I'm not really worried about it. The company's earned my trust so far. But it just shows how these things play on your mind, doesn't it?'

'Maybe that's the twist in the whole plot: maybe the company's gained our trust up until now so they can use us to spread the virus,' I said.

Grace laughed. 'You've been watching too many movies. Besides, if this flu of theirs is as contagious as they say it is, spreading it this way would be overkill. Literally. Actually, I can't wait to get started. Want to be my first victim?' She held up her forefinger in front of my face and I saw that she was wearing one of the plasters. 'I'll do you, and you do me.' Her cheeks flushed pink as we both registered the innuendo.

I'd already given plenty of thought to the question of whether I'd want to survive Plan B. I wasn't sure what the future would hold, but I was burning with curiosity to see how — and whether — Phoenix's grand scheme would play out. I guessed there was also a built-in survival instinct programmed into all human beings.

Not only that, at my age I felt like my life was only just getting properly started. Damn right I wanted to live.

'Sure. Why not?' I said, and carefully wrapped the first SafeWorld plaster around my fingertip. I flicked off the gel cap and Grace did the same with hers. Then we stood there for a few moments looking at each other and feeling self-conscious. Grace offered her left hand, fingers spread, palm down. I mirrored the action, suddenly solemn.

'On three?' she asked, and I nodded. 'One… two… three.' We touched each other with the microneedle pads and then giggled.

That was the first time I saved her life.

10:59:40

Ticking Boxes

Despite the fact that he still hadn't been allowed to let his two remaining Horsemen out of their stables, Ken Burford was in a fine mood. He and General Barrett had been subtly working on the puppet President, and it was surely only a matter of time. On the drive out to Raleigh, Ken had been thinking of possible further targets once the original four had been addressed and, by the time he pulled up to the big metal gates of Phoenix's main pharmaceuticals plant, he'd envisaged an apocalypse wrought by a whole herd of his own covert Horsemen.

The gates slid open and Burford eased the car towards an inner set of gates beyond. A well-built man in a smart uniform emerged from the guardhouse and stepped up to the window of Ken's car as he applied the brake.

'Good morning, sir.' The young guard immediately noticed the prominent blue and gold logo of the Federal Drug Administration on the visitor's dark blue shirt. 'How may we help you today?'

Ken smiled and removed his sunglasses. *I have nothing to hide.* He resisted the temptation to touch his false moustache and passed an ID wallet to the security man.

'FDA spot check. Name's Ron Miller.'

The guard studied the ID. 'Is anyone expecting you, Mr Miller?'

N R Baker

'Well now, it wouldn't be much of a spot check if they knew I was coming, would it?' Ken chuckled good-naturedly.

The guard handed back the ID. 'I suppose not, sir. May I ask what it is you're here to check?'

Ken pressed the moustache against his top lip, disguising the gesture to make it look as if he had an itchy nose. 'Of course. It's to do with the latest CGMP regs. CFR Title 21 stuff. Just routine, really. Need to make sure you guys are applying the new Part 520 quality controls.' *Blind 'em with science.* 'I'm sure everything's up to standard, but you know how it is. Somebody's gotta tick all the little boxes.' He'd practised the lies until they rolled easily off his tongue.

'Thank you, sir. One moment, please.'

The security man disappeared into the guardhouse and returned a couple of minutes later with a printed visitor pass on a clip.

'Please wear this at all times while you're on site. The visitors' parking lot is ahead and to your left. I'll ask Gene Washington, our quality manager, to meet you in reception. Have a good day, sir.'

Ken couldn't help feeling a wave of relief as he drove through the inner gates. He'd passed the first hurdle and was on Roger Vee's territory. Nervous excitement was making his palms clammy. There had to be a clue here in Raleigh as to what Phoenix's mysterious 'Plan B' was all about, and Ken was determined to find it. He didn't know exactly what he was looking for, but he was counting on recognising it when he saw it.

Gene Washington had been employed in quality control at Phoenix for nearly fifteen years and he enjoyed talking about his work. He welcomed 'Ron Miller' almost literally with open arms and gave him a guided tour of the vast production facility that lasted more than three hours. Ken was utterly bored within ten minutes. He had to keep reminding himself that this was all in a worthwhile cause, and he was certainly getting a detailed look behind the scenes. Thankfully, Gene did most of the talking and didn't ask 'Ron' too many awkward questions. Ken had downloaded an official-looking FDA checklist onto a tablet computer and spent

238

a lot of time staring at the screen, scrolling through pages, typing notes and entering random ticks into random boxes. Gene seemed convinced.

Most of the pharmaceutical products manufactured at the plant had fairly obvious environmental or humanitarian applications. Phoenix made things like contraceptive pills, vaccines and water purification tablets, many of which were distributed to developing countries at low prices that barely covered the manufacturing and shipping costs. Perhaps Roger Vee really was a saint.

After three of the most tedious hours in Ken's entire life, he hadn't seen anything that struck him as remotely suspicious. His stomach rumbled loudly.

'Gee, I'm sorry Ron, you must be getting peckish. Time flies when you're having fun, eh? Can I buy you lunch? The staff restaurant here's pretty good and we can carry on afterwards—'

'No, no,' Ken cut in a little too quickly. 'That's kind of you, Gene, but I'm afraid I really have to get back on the road. Got another one of these to do on the opposite side of town this afternoon.'

'Well, if you're sure.'

'Absolutely. Besides, I think I've seen all I need to see here.'

'I'll walk you back through to reception, then,' Gene said. 'Quickest route from this part of the site is to cut through dispatch. This way.'

Ken followed his host through a set of double doors and into a busy dispatch area dominated by hundreds of brown cardboard boxes. Employees in hi-viz vests buzzed around on forklifts, feeding the boxes into several big trucks whose cargo areas gaped hungrily at a series of loading bays.

While Gene marched ahead, greeting some of the dispatch workers by name, Ken noticed that a great many of the boxes were marked 'SafeWorld'.

'What's in all these?' Ken asked, catching up with Gene.

'Sticking plasters. Fully biodegradable.'

Ken frowned. 'I didn't see those in production.' It seemed that

Phoenix made a heck of a lot of sticking plasters.

'We didn't get to them. They're made in the last unit, along with the sterile gel dressings we manufacture to treat burns. Lunch is still on offer, if you want to—'

'No, it's fine. I really do need to head out.'

*

Roger Vee had a definite soft spot for his head of security. Thandi Mbela had excelled in a field traditionally dominated by men, rising rapidly to her current role and earning the respect and friendship of her colleagues along the way, thanks to unerring instincts, sharp eyes, and a wicked sense of humour.

She was justifiably proud of her achievements and made no secret of her past. Ten years earlier, Thandi's baby boy had died. The young mother struggled to come to terms with her tragic loss and sank into a destructive spiral of depression, drug addiction and homelessness. Luckily, she ended up at a rehabilitation centre that happened to be the pet project of one of Roger Vee's neighbours. Thandi fought to overcome her demons and, with counselling and support, got herself clean and regained control of her life. At a neighbourhood social, Roger had been told the story of this likeable young woman and how she'd taken it upon herself to investigate the theft of some of the rehabilitation centre's equipment. Within a week she had not only identified the thief but had also gathered enough evidence to get him arrested. Hearing this, Roger had offered to give her a one-week trial as a security guard. Eight years on, they had become firm friends and he now relied on her to run Phoenix's US security operations.

'Hey, boss!' Thandi greeted Roger with a hug when he entered the security control room. Her two colleagues grinned, used to this unconventional behaviour.

'You wanted to see me?' Roger asked, also smiling.

'Yes. Thanks for coming down. Look, it might be nothing, but something about this man just… Well, it seems to me he's as fishy as a hatful of anchovies and I wanted to flag it up to you, just in case.'

'Okay. What man? Tell me.'

'Right. Well, Marcos — he's the new guy working the main gate at Raleigh, really good guy — phoned me earlier today. They had some inspector from the FDA turn up to do a spot check. Everything looked perfectly legit; he had the uniform, the ID, and he spent the whole morning walking around the facility with Gene Washington.'

'So... Why all the anchovies?'

'Here's the thing. Marcos asked what this guy was checking, and he started spouting abbreviations.'

'It's the FDA, Thandi. They love abbreviations.'

'Yeah, but he said he was there to check that we were complying with Part 520 quality controls.' Thandi looked pointedly at Roger, clearly enjoying herself.

Roger shrugged. 'Don't ask me. I've only memorised parts one through five hundred.'

'Marcos looked it up. Part 520 deals with *animal* drugs.'

Roger narrowed his eyes. 'Okay... I'm impressed that he looked it up, but maybe he got the number wrong.'

'He's pretty sure he didn't. He wrote it down straight after the guy said it. And then later, when there was a lull in visitors, he looked it up just out of plain ol' curiosity.' Thandi looked triumphant, proud of her subordinate.

Roger wasn't convinced. 'I can see why that might give you a whiff of an anchovy or two, but not a whole hatful.'

Thandi laughed. 'After Marcos phoned me, I contacted my friend at the FDA and asked him to check the guy's name — Ron Miller — against their records. The FDA currently has two auditors called Ron Miller.' She paused for effect.

'And?' Roger obliged.

'One of them's a woman whose full name is Veronica Miller, and the other one is the same colour as me. Our fishy visitor didn't even have a suntan.'

Roger's expression became serious. 'Got a picture?'

Thandi turned to her computer and pulled up an image of a middle-aged white man with sandy hair and a prominent moustache.

'This is a still from the camera at the security gate. We don't have any better ones from CCTV inside the plant because our Mr Miller conveniently wore his FDA baseball cap the whole time and looked down at his computer a lot.'

Roger leaned in to study the picture. It pricked something at the back of his mind, but the man was a stranger. 'Never seen him before.'

'I'll show you the video segment that the still was taken from.' Thandi started clicking her computer mouse.

'Can you email it to me? I'm going to be late for a meeting.'

'Sure thing, boss.'

'Good work, Thandi. Run the photo past one of our police contacts, too, will you?'

It was evening before Roger had chance to check his emails. The message from Thandi said that the police had matched the photo to someone called Kenneth Burford but his records were classified. Frowning, Roger opened the video file and watched the short clip several times. Something about the man's expression or mannerisms struck him as familiar. Roger played the clip again. Years fell away and an unwelcome ghost from his past looked briefly into the camera.

Roger pressed pause, his eyes widening in recognition. 'Howard?'

10:59:41

Touching

English people, generally speaking, aren't big on physical contact, and this fact was suddenly a major problem for me. If you start touching complete strangers, especially in a town like Mareton, you're likely to get some very peculiar reactions. Or arrested. I imagined it was easier for my colleagues in other European countries where I had the impression that people were far more demonstrative and it was considered perfectly normal to go around kissing random passers-by on both cheeks. The facial ones, at least.

Another thing English people aren't big on is cold weather, despite the fact that we get so much of it. As soon as the thermometers dip to 'a tad nippy', weather forecasters start urging caution, the media digs out stock photos of cars stuck in snowdrifts, supermarket shelves are emptied of bread and milk, and out come the coats, scarves, gloves and woolly hats. There's always one hardy eccentric wearing shorts in a blizzard, but otherwise there is precious little British flesh to be seen on display outdoors in November. I realised there must be similar challenges in countries where women wore hijabs and burqas. Anyway, unless I could come up with an excuse for touching people's faces, the lack of accessible bare skin was a problem. Nightclub queues were an obvious exception and presented an opportunity, I supposed, but the brainless bimbos who tottered around wearing next to nothing weren't at the top of my list of targets to perpetuate the human species. Good grief, was I eighteen or eighty? This whole thing was turning me into a grumpy old man.

So yes, it was all very well being tasked with saving lives but — however much I wanted to do so — when it came to it, the practicalities presented quite an obstacle.

Vaccinating Dad and Cheryl was easy. As luck would have it, the weekend when I visited Cheryl, she was involved with a coffee morning to raise money for the air ambulance service and she introduced me to lots of her local friends and their families. Although I was nervous and couldn't believe I was finally bestowing immunity on people for real, all the introductions and plate-passing made it reasonably easy to use my magic microneedles. That was my first major success and I was glad I'd had the foresight to ask Tomasz for another box of SafeWorld plasters. Much Wheadle wasn't in my area but we'd been told we could protect friends and family regardless of location, since the worst that could happen was that they'd end up getting vaccinated twice.

Having safeguarded some of Cheryl's friends, I was keen to do the same for Dad, so I tagged along with him on a pub outing with some of his mates from the factory. All the people I'd heard him talking about — Steve and Bob G and the others — were really decent guys. I offered to help carry drinks from the bar to the table where we were sitting, and they had no idea that that I was passing them life along with their pints of lager.

It was a weight off my mind, getting started and knowing that Dad and Cheryl and their close friends were immunised. Now all that remained was for me to turn my attention to the thousands of warmly-clothed members of the general public who occupied my assigned area of Mareton.

Thanks to all the weeks of observing people's behaviour and playing my theoretical game of 'naughty or nice', deciding in principle who among them would deserve the vaccine and who wouldn't, I found it easier than I'd expected to choose people. Anyone who dropped rubbish in the street or hawked and spat where someone else was about to walk... no. Whilst it seemed ludicrously harsh to condemn a person to death for discarding a sweet wrapper, behaviour like that was almost invariably a sign of a generally uncaring and selfish nature. Those who cared enough to parent their children properly, help a stranger up a step with a buggy or a wheelchair, give up their seat on the bus... they were my targets. Actually getting my hands on them was quite another matter, but I learned quickly.

It was easier to make physical contact appear casual and accidental in crowded places. Shopping centres were good, because they were busy and people tended to leave their gloves off while they were in and out of the shops. The malls and supermarkets also attracted a wide cross-section of inhabitants from the town and neighbouring villages and I saw lots of family groups together, especially at weekends.

Having personally experienced the soul-rending pain of losing a close relative, I probably tried too hard at first to vaccinate whole families. It was almost impossible, and I had to force myself to accept that bereavement was going to be a fact of life for everyone. I supposed it already was. No matter how diligent I tried to be, there would always be a grandparent, sibling, aunt, uncle or close friend who got missed, and it wasn't — it couldn't be — my responsibility to save people from grief. That was a road to madness, and I felt like I'd already taken more than enough steps down that path. I knew that the intention was for the survivors of Plan B to assume they must have had some kind of natural immunity to the virus. No one would know they'd been chosen to live.

Ideas were circulated within Phoenix. One that worked quite nicely was to carry a pocketful of small papers with fictional names and phone numbers written on them. You could go up to someone nice and say, 'Excuse me, I think you dropped this,' and vaccinate them as you handed them the scrap, then walk on. I wrote out loads of them and wondered whether anyone actually tried to phone Andy on 07865-whatever.

I was still reading the news; it had become part of my daily routine. Early one morning, spooning cereal into my face while I skimmed over all the boring stuff about reality TV 'stars' and life hacks — I decided I could manage without "Twenty Things You Never Knew You Could Do With a Lemon" — I spotted a familiar face under the Local News heading. Gandalf, Mareton's resident tramp, was pictured sitting at the bottom of the town hall steps, his long beard angled by the breeze, his gaze a million miles away and his beloved shopping trolley piled with loot. I read the article with interest.

The man, whose improbable real name was apparently Randolph Bannister, had found a lost wallet in his wanderings and, despite the fact that it contained over one hundred pounds in cash, had delivered it intact to the owner's home address a couple of miles across town. Although he'd simply dropped it through the letterbox and immediately turned to leave, the owner had seen him and rushed out to thank him. He'd tried to give him some cash as a reward, but the offer was politely refused. In the end, Gandalf had accepted a hot meal by way of recompense.

The following day, I sought out Gandalf and — on the pretext of returning an old saucepan lid that had fallen off his trolley — touched his dirty, weathered hand with my microneedles. I figured he had as much right as anyone to survive, and deserved to do so more than many.

One overcast Friday lunchtime in mid-November, I went into the town centre to buy some stamps from the post office. I found myself walking behind an elderly couple who were hand-in-hand and chatting away happily to each other. They seemed lovely people; you could just tell, from the way they were and from snippets of things they said. The pair entered the post office ahead of me and, while we were waiting in the queue, the woman took a purse out of her handbag and dropped several coins on the floor. I helped her gather them up and took the opportunity to use a SafeWorld plaster on her when I deposited them in her hand. Her husband also thanked me, commenting on how unusual it was for people to help each other these days, and I quickly flicked the cap off another plaster before he shook my hand. Two more worthy survivors in the bag. Result.

Walking back to the office, I found myself wishing for a scenario where I would have a reason to shake lots of people's hands. An idea began to take shape and, later that afternoon, I suggested it to Tomasz.

'We could sell handshakes for charity. It's just a gimmick, but it might help us to vaccinate more people, including whole families. It could work in places like shopping centres at weekends.'

'Yeah, I like it,' Tom said enthusiastically.

'I was thinking maybe we could come up with some kind of catchphrase, like "Handshakes for the homeless" or "Help with a handshake". I don't know. I'm not very good at stuff like that. People could shake my hand and stick a pound in the collecting tin. I know we don't really need to be collecting the cash, but we could give it to charity and—'

'I think it's a great idea. And it might help a lot of other Phoenix employees to give the vaccinations, too. The company might even be willing to sponsor the initiative. Maybe publicise it, too…' Tomasz trailed off, considering possibilities. 'Leave it with me. Good work, Louis.'

Half an hour later he was standing beside my desk, holding a hand over his mobile phone with, apparently, someone connected on the other end of the call. 'I floated your handshakes-for-charity idea with Eve, and she loves it. She wants to know if you can be at Head Office for two o'clock on Monday to finalise the details and talk to her about marketing.' He looked at me enquiringly, a twinkle in his eye.

I gave him an apprehensive look and said nothing.

'He'll be there,' he told his phone.

10:59:42

Scoop

Elise Hayes (née West) checked her watch yet again and decided she'd give her brother just five more minutes. Jack was almost half an hour late, and sitting alone at an unpleasantly sticky table in a crowded London coffee shop was not Elise's idea of a good time. She picked up a plastic stirrer and poked at the brown-edged froth that lined the bottom of her empty cup.

'You finished with that, love?' A harassed-looking waiter scooped Elise's oversized cup and saucer onto a large tray that already bore a precarious pile of crockery, and disappeared towards the swing doors that led to the kitchen. A couple of seconds later, a loud ceramic crash told Elise that she wasn't the only one having a bad day. The other patrons winced and there was a brief lull in their noisy chatter.

Ugh. Enough of this. Elise took her mobile phone out of her bag and started typing another text message:

Where are you??? Can't wait any longer. Sorry. Call me later.

'Sorry I'm late! The underground was a complete nightmare.' Jack materialised beside her, slightly out of breath. Despite rushing, his face was cold from the outside air when he leaned over and kissed her on the cheek.

'Well of course it was. It's Friday night. What d'you expect? I was just about to leave. Why didn't you answer my texts?'

'No signal on the Tube. Sorry Sis. Lemme get you a drink.'

'I've had one, thanks,' she said frostily, stowing her phone. She wasn't ready to forgive him yet.

'Aw, come on, don't be grumpy with me. I got here as quick as I could. How about a blueberry muffin?'

'Choc chip. And another cappuccino.'

Jack grinned. 'Be right back.' He strode off to join the queue at the counter.

Elise sighed. *Bang goes my evening*, she thought. She had to admit she was intrigued to find out what he wanted to talk to her about. He'd been very secretive when he'd phoned her, asking to meet somewhere in town after work. She'd been quite worried about him lately; he'd seemed really out of sorts for the past couple of months, although she hadn't seen him in person for a while. He was certainly in a good mood today. She hoped he wasn't having an affair with a married woman or something.

'Here you go, Sis.' He slid a loaded tray onto the table and placed a huge chocolate muffin in front of Elise, and then sat down opposite her.

'Blimey. Thanks Jack.'

'My pleasure.' There was that boyish grin again.

'You look like the cat that's got the cream. So what's this all about, then? I can't stay too late. I told Mark I'd be home in time for dinner. Not that I'm going to need any after this.' She took a bite.

Jack looked at her. Glanced around to check no one was eavesdropping on their conversation. Leaned in close. 'You remember I told you that Phoenix were up to something?'

'Oh Jack, no! Not this again!'

'It's different now. I've heard it from the horse's mouth. And you're not gonna believe it.'

'What d'you mean, the horse's mouth? I thought you were going to drop all this nonsense.'

'I wish it *was* nonsense. But on the plus side, you and I are

249

going to make an absolute fortune out of it if we play it right.'

'Jack, you're not making any sense.'

'Elise, what I'm about to tell you is pretty much the biggest news in the history of the world. I'm going to be the guy who saved the day. And you're going to be the famous journalist who broke the Phoenix story.'

During the few weeks since his disciplinary hearing, Jack had been doing some research. After his sister's previous scepticism, he was determined to impress her with facts this time and had rehearsed his pitch to make it sound as convincing as possible. Even so, twenty minutes later she remained dubious.

'Okay, okay, enough.'

'But Elise—'

'Jack, hang on.' Elise frowned, chewing her lip. 'This can't be true. It just *can't*. It sounds like the plot for some far-fetched disaster film.' Her brother looked crestfallen and her heart went out to him. 'Look, I'm not saying I don't believe you. Tell me again what the HR woman said to you. Are you sure you heard it right?'

'Yes! I've told you, the first thing I did when I got back to my desk was write down her exact words so I'd remember. Don't forget, I'd tricked her into thinking I was already in on the secret at this point. And then she told me that people would just assume the whole thing was a natural disaster. She said, "Nothing's traceable."'

Elise absent-mindedly picked up an escaped chocolate chip from among the crumbs on her plate and popped it into her mouth. 'This is insane, Jack. If it's true then this is huge. It's beyond huge.'

'I know, right?' He sat back, watching her intensely.

'I still don't understand what's in it for them. What would Phoenix stand to gain from something like that?'

'That's the bit I'm not a hundred percent sure about,' he admitted, leaning in again. 'Maybe they wouldn't, directly. But they're always banging on about overpopulation and using up the Earth's resources, and all I can think is that this would wipe out a lot of the biggest consumers on the planet.'

Elise shook her head, incredulous. 'It's just horrible. Millions of people...'

'Yeah. And it all fits. That's what that girl on the roof must've been talking about back in September after the induction workshop. *Now* do you believe me?'

'I don't *want* to.'

'But you do, right? So will you run the story?'

'Slow down, Jack. I'll need to think this through. And I mean really carefully. I'll need to do some research of my own. And maybe have an off-the-record chat with someone in our legal department. I won't mention any specifics, of course. I'd like to talk to my editor, too...' She trailed off, deep in thought.

Jack was delighted. 'We're gonna be rich and famous, Sis.'

'Not to mention saving millions of lives.'

'Of course. That too.'

'Give me a couple of days. And I'm not making any promises, okay?' Elise glanced at her watch and gasped. 'I've got to run. Mark's going to be sending out search parties.' She stood up, put her coat on and slung her bag over her shoulder. 'Did you hear me? No promises.'

'Okay. There are other journalists, you know...' he teased, getting to his feet.

'Don't you dare!' She stood on tiptoes to kiss his cheek, then turned and walked quickly towards the exit but stopped in her tracks and came back to the table.

'What did you forget?' Jack asked.

'Be careful, okay? If it *is* true, this is a hell of a big deal and somebody might try to stop you blowing the whistle.'

He smiled at her genuine concern. 'I'll hire a bodyguard first thing in the morning.'

'I mean it, Jack!' She lowered her voice to an anxious whisper. 'If these people really are planning to murder millions of innocent citizens, they're certainly capable of silencing one person who's out to spoil their fun. Please be careful.'

He wrapped his arms around her. 'I will, Sis. I promise.'

10:59:43

The Power of Speech

'Look, Elise, if you think this newspaper would even *consider* publicly accusing a company like Phoenix of something so far-fetched without some kind of proof... Are you crazy? Jesus, this thing has "libel suit" written all over it! The lawyers would have my guts for garters, right before we both get thrown out and the whole paper goes bust. Forget it.'

Robert 'Dutch' Holland had been in the journalism game for too many years to take chances. He was surprised and, frankly, rather disappointed in his promising young reporter. He eased his rotund frame back into his office chair and ran his fingers through what was left of his hair.

'But Dutch, my source—'

'I don't care what your source thinks he heard, or who he heard it from. Unless he's got video evidence of Roger Vee himself dancing naked and brandishing a signed confession, I'm not buying it.'

Elise silently cursed her brother for putting her in this situation. 'Please, Dutch. It might be nothing, but if it does turn out to be true it'll be the scoop of the century for us.' She gave her boss one of her best smiles. 'All I'm asking for is permission to go and speak to the Phoenix employee who leaked the information to my whistle-blower. I promise I'll be the very soul of discretion and diplomacy.'

He sighed dramatically. 'You'd better be,' he said, acquiescing. 'We're talking eggshells, you understand me? Kid gloves.' Elise nodded eagerly. 'And you needn't think this is any kind of victory, young lady. You don't take this any further without my say-so. And if they deny it, you lick their boots like they're leather lollipops and back the hell away from this whole ridiculous thing, and don't waste any more time on it. And I still want that other piece, about the corpse in the basement, on my desk by Friday. Am I making myself clear?'

'Crystal. Thanks Dutch.' She beamed and left his office before he could reconsider.

*

Elise's relief was short-lived. The HR manager at Phoenix, Lisa Scott, had taken her call but then flatly refused to meet, suggesting that Elise should contact the company's press office. When Elise mentioned that she wanted to discuss something Ms Scott had said to one of their employees, Jack West, the woman politely but very firmly brought the call to an end and hung up. However, there had been a pregnant pause before she did so, which caused Elise to wonder whether there might be something to Jack's wild allegations, after all.

Damn. Jack was going to be horribly disappointed when she told him she hadn't got anywhere, but what more could she do?

Putting her brother's conspiracy theories out of her mind, Elise resumed work on her article about some human remains that had been found in the cellar of a swanky house in Chelsea during renovations. She'd been at it for almost an hour when her phone rang.

'Elise Hayes,' she said distractedly, cradling the phone with her shoulder while she continued cutting and pasting paragraphs on her computer screen.

'This is Lisa Scott, from Phoenix,' said a female voice in her ear.

Elise instantly forgot about bones and basements. 'I'm willing to meet with you.'

'That's great! Where?' Elise scrabbled for a pen among the papers on her untidy desk.

'Here. Phoenix Head Office.'

'Really? We can meet somewhere else if it's easier,' Elise offered, surprised.

'No. Come to the office. I've been interviewing candidates for a couple of vacancies. If anyone asks, you're an applicant for the finance role.'

'Okay, perfect. When would suit you? I can come over this afternoon if you like.' Elise didn't want to give the woman a chance to change her mind again.

'No, not today. Tomorrow morning. Can you be here at 10:30?

Elise was scribbling on a notepad. 'Absolutely. Tomorrow, 10:30. I'll be there.'

'I'll tell Reception I'm expecting you for an interview.'

The line went dead.

*

Elise sat on one of the comfortable blue chairs in Phoenix's seriously impressive foyer, doing her best to look like an applicant for a job in finance. She didn't have to feign pre-interview nerves; now that she was here, she felt daunted. Every inch of her present surroundings exuded world-class professionalism. Phoenix was an international household name, known and respected for doing all sorts of worthy environmental stuff, and they had to be one of the biggest employers in the country, if not the world. Surely Jack must have got it wrong. It was funny to think that her younger brother was somewhere in the building. She hadn't told him she was coming here today.

She shook off her unease and reviewed her notes. She'd managed to find out a little bit of background on Lisa Scott, despite the common name and the fact that, unusually, the woman didn't seem to have any social media accounts. People's inexplicable compulsion to share every banal, intimate detail of their lives had certainly made things easier for journalists, Elise reflected. The only readily-available public information about Lisa Scott related to her well-established career in human resources; more than seven years with Phoenix and five with another large corporate before that—

'Mrs Hayes?'

Elise looked up, closing her notebook, and immediately recognised Lisa Scott from a photo she'd seen of her on the company's website. 'Yes.' She stood up, smiling. 'Please, call me Elise.'

'I'm Lisa Scott,' the woman said pleasantly, shaking Elise's proffered hand. 'This way, please.' Elise followed the smart skirt-suit and carefully tamed curls towards a bank of lifts. Lisa Scott seemed pretty self-composed for someone who was about to spill the beans on such a heinous plot and had invited a journalist right into the lion's den. The lift arrived, the sleek doors whispered shut and, in accordance with English etiquette, the two women studiously ignored each other all the way up to the thirteenth floor.

Elise's doubts nibbled at her while she walked in Lisa's wake along a corridor lined with doors, most of which were open or ajar and afforded glimpses into spacious private offices. The whole place smacked of class without being opulent. It was everything, in fact, that Elise would have expected from the national headquarters of a major global organisation.

Lisa stopped at the end of the corridor, gesturing for Elise to enter the room ahead of her. As she did so, Elise was surprised to find that it was already occupied. She turned in bewilderment as Lisa left, closing the door behind her.

'I... I think there's been some mistake,' Elise faltered, trying to master a wave of something that had evolved rapidly from uncertainty into panic.

'No mistake, Mrs Hayes. Please take a seat. How would you like your coffee?'

Elise glanced at the closed office door again before sitting down slowly. 'I'm sorry, but who…?'

The older woman on the opposite side of the large desk was standing with a coffee flask in one hand, her elegant silhouette framed against the bright city skyline.

'Where are my manners? I do apologise. I'm Eve Gyer, one of the directors here. Cream and sugar?'

'Just black, please.' Elise didn't particularly want to drink coffee with this person but hoped the caffeine would help to steady her jangling nerves. What the hell was going on? 'I thought I was having a… an interview. With Lisa Scott.'

'Please relax, my dear.' Eve handed her the cup of coffee and sat down, studying Elise. 'I trust we can speak freely to each other?'

The question threw Elise. 'Of course. But—'

'As soon as you mentioned Jack's name to Lisa on the phone, she guessed what this was all about. You're Jack's sister, yes?'

'I—'

'It's no great mystery; you're listed as an emergency contact on Jack's personnel file. Lisa recognised the name and made the connection almost immediately. She's very good at things like that.' Eve smiled disarmingly. 'And I wouldn't mind betting that you're here to ask me whether we're planning to bomb Yellowstone National Park and trigger a huge volcanic eruption that will wipe out most of North America.'

Elise had believed that people's jaws only dropped in cartoons. She realised her mouth had fallen open and closed it again.

'I'm so glad you came in to see us,' Eve went on. 'We've been rather worried about poor Jack just lately. Such a likeable young man and we're very happy to have him on board, but he's developed some very strange ideas over the past month or two and hasn't seemed quite himself. And then of course there was the disciplinary hearing. I don't think he took that very well.'

'Disciplinary…?' Elise was trying to keep up, and failing. Jack hadn't told her anything about a disciplinary hearing.

'Oh, it was nothing serious. Just a harassment allegation,' Eve continued airily. 'These things happen. But Jack seemed rather thrown by the whole thing. It was just before the hearing that he told Lisa about this bizarre bomb theory of his. And then of course the disciplinary warning put rather a dent in his pride. Is there any history of mental illness we should be aware of?'

The caffeine was apparently doing its job and Elise was starting to regain some of her composure. 'Wait. What? It's not *Jack's* bomb theory. At least… Well, he told me he overheard something after that big induction event, weeks ago, something about millions of people dying. And then…' She faltered. 'He said it was Lisa Scott who told *him* about the thing with the Yellowstone supervolcano.' It sounded ridiculous now, even to her ears.

'Oh dear.' Eve's expression darkened in consternation. 'Well, I can see why you're worried about him and, as I said, I'm very glad you've come to talk to us. It's great to know that he has such wonderful support from the family. Perhaps some counselling would help him. If you'd like, we can arrange something — in complete confidence, naturally — through the company's employee healthcare scheme. And of course a little time off would be no problem at all. We just want him to get well. I'm sure he'll be fine once he gets over this little blip. A lot of young people find it overwhelming when they start work and have all the responsibilities of adulthood suddenly thrust upon them. Poor Jack. You have my personal assurance that we'll do whatever we can to help him.'

Elise was stunned. She felt close to tears and had no idea whether it was because of her concern for Jack, her embarrassment at having made a fool of herself, or the shock of everything veering so unexpectedly and spectacularly off course. Floundering, she said, 'So there's nothing to it, then? The whole bomb thing, I mean.'

Eve smiled sympathetically. 'Well of course not. Goodness, can you even imagine how dreadful that would be? I don't know much about these things but, quite apart from all the people and animals and plants that would perish, I should think the ash cloud alone would affect climate and crops all over the world. Why on earth would Jack believe we'd do such a thing? What possible reason could we have? It makes no sense. I mean, Phoenix provides solutions for an overburdened planet. If there was a dramatic reduction in population, many of the things we're working on wouldn't be needed.

'To put it crudely, Elise, this company makes a lot of money and creates jobs for employees all over the world thanks to the very fact that there are so many people. The more, the merrier.' She gestured to the flask on the table between them. 'Can I pour you some more coffee?'

10:59:44

Black Ice

Jack wasn't angry when Elise told him about her visit to Phoenix and her conversation with Eve Gyer. People got angry when they burnt the toast. *Angry* didn't even come close to describing Jack's emotional state.

He'd worked so damned hard to convince Elise that he really was on to something. He *knew* he was. After he'd tricked the HR woman into telling him what Phoenix was planning, he'd done a ton of research into supervolcanoes in general and Yellowstone in particular. But it had all been for nothing. All of his effort and conviction had been casually brushed aside by a few words from Eve Gyer's smart mouth. Of course the woman had denied everything. What had Elise expected? A full confession? He'd been doing his sister an enormous favour by gifting her the scoop. Fine. If she wasn't interested, he'd find someone who was. He'd sell his story for a fortune to another newspaper that recognised a major scandal when it saw one.

Jack had been pacing around his small apartment like a caged animal since Elise left, taking occasional gulps from a large tumbler of cooking brandy clutched too tightly in his right hand. He never usually drank spirits. There were beers in the fridge, but he'd needed something stronger after his sister's brief visit. He shouldn't have kicked her out like that. He knew she was trying to help, but she'd stood there patting his arm and explaining that she'd waited until tonight, Friday, to tell him about it so that he'd have the weekend to think about things... And when he'd read the pity in her expression — *pity!* — he'd felt such rage rising inside him that he'd been afraid he might hit her. At this very moment she was probably crying to Mummy and Daddy, breaking the news that their son was losing his marbles. Not that they'd care; they'd have yet another story of his latest hilarious failure to entertain their pretentious friends with. He had thought he'd buried his childhood insecurities deep and left them far behind, but it turned out they'd been right here all along in a very shallow grave.

Phoenix. He'd come to hate his employers. Phoenix had to be stopped. Somehow, they had to be exposed for the murdering frauds they really were. The thought of working away meekly in their post room, pretending nothing was wrong, sickened him. He never wanted to set foot in that building again, yet he knew his best chance of foiling their plans was to be there on the inside. He realised he was holding the brandy glass dangerously tight and relaxed his grip, taking another swig, trying to force himself to calm down, to marshal his dark thoughts into some kind of rational order. But the rage... the blinding rage refused to subside. On the contrary, he could feel it building. Hardening. The brandy tasted revolting, but he swallowed another mouthful, the burning bitterness suiting his mood.

It always came back to Eve Gyer. She was the focus of all his misery. She was the one who'd destroyed his credibility with his own sister and poisoned her against him. Elise: the only person he'd always believed he could count on. Gyer, the treacherous witch, had robbed him of that one comfort by convincing her that he was cracking up. And this evening, the more Jack had insisted to Elise that Phoenix really were planning to perpetrate the unthinkable and bomb Yellowstone, the more Elise had given him that awful, condescending, *pitying* look.

The rage was choking him now. It was too much... a demon

inside him, clawing to be released. It tore at his ragged thoughts until he couldn't bear it any longer. He wanted to scream. He wanted to smash the glass he was holding into Eve Gyer's knowing face. He raised his hand to hurl the empty tumbler against the wall, but then something came adrift inside his head. Somewhere in the circuits, a fuse had blown. The rage was still there, blacker than ever, but now it was cold. It was black ice in his veins. He lowered his arm and set the glass down very gently on the table.

*

That same Friday, on the other side of the Atlantic, Ken Burford was given the Phoenix vaccine.

Ken never usually visited malls. They were invariably full of idiots and he preferred to shop online. It was pure chance that he'd missed lunch that day and, driving home wondering what to have for dinner, passed a sign for a fried chicken restaurant inside a nearby shopping mall.

Ken never usually chose to eat in at places like that. He didn't enjoy being around other people and preferred to get take-out. It was pure chance that he'd just had his car valeted and didn't want it stinking of greasy food.

Ken never usually cleared his own table. He figured that's what the restaurant staff were paid to do. It was pure chance that, while eating his chicken, he'd noticed a girl handing out flyers next to the area where diners were invited to deposit their rubbish and empty trays. For something to do, he'd found himself watching her. She was attractive and unreasonably cheerful, and was obviously one of those touchy-feely people; he saw her chatting to family groups, handing out her flyers and crouching to talk to the kids and give them high-fives. What had aroused Ken's curiosity was that, every few minutes, the girl did some weird thing with her fingers, threw something in the trash, and then turned away to rummage in her bag for a while before thrusting more leaflets at the next group of shoppers.

261

Unable to think of a logical explanation for the girl's odd behaviour, Ken took his tray over to the rack and tipped his rubbish into the bin nearest to her, glancing inside as his chicken bones landed among some papers and a small white box with a green logo: SafeWorld. It was the same brand name he'd seen printed on the stacks of boxes in the dispatch area of Phoenix's pharmaceuticals plant in Raleigh. Sticking plasters, the quality guy had said.

While his mind raced, Ken pretended to re-tie his shoelace while he watched the girl hand out flyers to another family group. He was missing something… but what? Playing for time, he took his mobile phone from his pocket and faked a call as the girl greeted an older couple who were walking by. Then she made a fuss of a baby in a buggy and gave flyers to the parents. After that, she discreetly pulled at each of her fingertips in turn and threw something in the trash. Did she have plasters on all her fingers? Why would she? It made no sense.

Ken carried on his side of the fictional telephone conversation. 'Well I know, but I thought your mother was coming over *next* Friday.' He kept talking while the girl turned to rummage in her bag, which was on the floor against the wall behind her. 'No, no, it's fine, honey. I'm at the mall now, so I'll pick something up here.'

As the girl stood and turned with a fresh handful of flyers, Ken went to leave, still holding his phone to his ear. 'It's pretty busy but I'll be home as soon as I can.' He hurried past the girl, knocking her arm hard enough to spill leaflets everywhere.

'Oh jeez, I'm so sorry, miss.'

Ken bent to pick up a few flyers that had fallen near the girl's bag and, while she was busy gathering others, he quickly peered inside. There were two more SafeWorld packs, one of which was open. He snatched two or three of the plasters and slipped them into his pocket, then gave the girl the leaflets he'd collected.

'I really am sorry. I wasn't watching where I was going.'

'No harm done,' she said, smiling. She touched his hand as she took the flyers from him. 'Thanks for helping me pick them up.

Here, take one: it's about a charity market this weekend.'

Ken feigned interest. 'I'll be sure and check it out.'

'Great. Have a nice evening, sir.'

*

Ken Burford's phone barely rang once before he snatched it up.

'Alex. What've you got for me?'

It was Sunday evening, but Alexandra Connors didn't mind working weekends. The facility was always quieter than during the week and she usually had the lab to herself to catch up on things. This weekend had been more interesting than most.

'These plasters are amazing. Whoever developed these… Well, they're—'

'What's amazing about them?' Ken interrupted.

'The rough patch in the centre? It's a microneedle array. Tiny sharp points that can be coated with the substance you want to deliver.'

'What substance?' Sweat broke out on Ken's forehead. He'd been feeling rather off-colour for a day or so; had that little bitch at the shopping mall poisoned him?

'I want to run a couple more tests before I can be certain. At first it looked like a virus…'

Biological warfare? Ken's thoughts were racing. He was thrilled at the prospect of having found something that might bring Phoenix and Roger Vee crashing down, and simultaneously terrified that he'd been infected with some awful disease.

Alex was still speaking. '…But I'm pretty sure it's a vaccine. The plasters are a vaccine delivery system. It's genius, actually—'

'What kind of vaccine? Against what?'

'Influenza. You could easily immunise millions of people using these.'

Ken's heart sank. So Roger Vee was doing good, yet again. The guy was a regular boy scout.

'Okay, Alex. Let me know the final results when you have them.

And remember, this is strictly classified.'

'Of course. Something's odd, though. Like I say, I need to run these other tests, but… It looks like this is a vaccine against a strain of flu we've never seen before. Where did these plasters come fr—'

Ken hung up.

10:59:45

Break

I shouldn't have said yes to the second cup of coffee. I'd expected a short meeting with Eve, but I'd been sitting in her office talking about the handshakes-for-charity idea for about forty minutes. For the last ten of those I'd been increasingly preoccupied with the undeniable fact that I was desperate for the loo.

Apparently, after Tomasz called her on Friday, she'd asked some guy in the Head Office marketing department to give the idea some thought; they'd branded it "Helping Handshakes", which wasn't great but it was certainly better than anything I'd come up with. Then Eve had suggested that any money we raised could go towards research into Parkinson's disease because of the shaky hands that are often a symptom of the condition. The marketing guy had been working on some promotional material and, when Eve picked up the phone to ask him to bring the mock-ups of the posters to her office, I seized the opportunity to nip out for a bathroom break.

Hurrying along the corridor, I passed someone walking in the opposite direction who I recognised but couldn't place. I said hello but the man's eyes were vacant, and he carried on as if he hadn't seen me. Suit yourself, I thought. While I was in the toilets I ran his face against my mental database but still couldn't come up with a name. He wasn't someone I knew well, but I'd definitely seen him before.

On the way back to Eve's office, it suddenly clicked. It was Jack, from the nuclear bunker exercise at the Noobs' Conference. He looked a bit different — slightly thinner, maybe — but it was definitely him. Pleased with myself for solving that little puzzle, and mightily relieved to have an empty bladder, I tapped on Eve's door and entered.

I picked up straight away that something was wrong but couldn't immediately determine what it was. It seemed it was a day for brain-lag. Jack was in the room, standing beside Eve. His left hand was on the headrest of her office chair and he was leaning over her slightly. I assumed he must have brought the colourful posters that were now spread out on the desk. Jack's dominant stance and the fact that he was standing too close to her might have been what initially struck me as odd. He looked up at me as I entered the room and his expression was no longer blank but full of emotions I couldn't read. Eve's face was pale.

If you've never been exposed to extreme situations, I suppose your mind refuses to accept what your eyes are seeing, searching for rational explanations and almost stalling when there aren't any. You imagine what you might do in certain scenarios, but for most of us those situations come as such a shock when they're real that we don't react as we imagined we would. I had the weird feeling that my brain was running in slow motion, trying to catch up with what the rest of my body could somehow sense.

'Come in and close the door, Louis-with-a-wiss.'

Jack's voice was a low growl. At the Noobs' Conference he'd been assertive and quite loud. Now, there was a new quality to his voice. Not quite a tremor, but a discordant edge like a bow drawn slowly across an overtightened string.

'Jack, what—?'

'Shut up. Sit down.'

I obeyed, registering at last that, with his right hand, Jack was holding the sharp point of a metal letter opener to the centre of

Eve's throat.

I couldn't take my eyes off the point of the paperknife, where it was pushed into Eve's neck. I saw with relief that there was no blood, so he hadn't pierced her skin. Not yet. Her head was pressed against the high back of her chair. She couldn't move.

I had no idea what to do. So I did nothing.

'It's okay, Jack.' Eve's voice was tight but surprisingly calm. It was the first time I'd knowingly heard her tell a lie. Whatever this was, it was most definitely not okay. 'Please. Put that down and let's just talk.'

'There's been enough talk. Too much. You might be able to fool everyone else, but you can't fool me.'

'No one's trying to fool anybody, Jack.'

'Shut up! Just shut up.' Jack pressed the letter opener harder against Eve's throat and I held my breath, dreading the seemingly inevitable moment when it must puncture her stretched skin.

I couldn't believe this was happening. I didn't dare say anything. Not that I could think of anything *to* say. The silence grew for a few long seconds, in which I willed my sluggish brain to come up with something useful. It refused.

'You fooled Elise, made me look ridiculous to her, so now... What else can I do? This is all I can do. I didn't want this. This is your fault. It's all your fault.' Jack sounded utterly miserable, as if some part of him was an unwilling passenger along for the ride.

Who was Elise? What was Eve's fault? I had no idea what this was about.

I was sitting quite close to the front of Eve's expansive desk and my legs were out of Jack's line of sight. I wondered whether I could somehow get my mobile phone out of my trouser pocket without him noticing. Unlikely. And then what? Dial 9-9-9. Except I wouldn't be able to talk to whoever answered. They might hear what was being said but it wouldn't make any more sense to them than it did to me. Would they be able to trace the call, or did that only happen on TV? And what if Jack heard them speaking? Bad idea. A text message might work. Could you text the police? I didn't know.

Eve's phone rang, making us all jump.

Jack looked panicked for a moment and then snapped, 'Leave it!' All three of us stared at the phone as it continued to ring. He changed his mind. 'Okay, answer it. But just say you'll call them back. Just that.'

Jack moved the paperknife away from Eve's throat to allow her to lean forward and pick up the phone. I could see a small dark purple mark on her pale skin. As soon as she put the handset to her ear, Jack held the sharp metal point in a new position below her jawbone.

'Eve Gyer,' she said, sounding almost chirpy.

A pause.

'Actually, John, sorry to interrupt but I'm right in the middle of something. Could I possibly call you back a little later?'

Another pause. Jack visibly applied more pressure.

'Will do. Speak to you then. Bye for now.'

She ended the call and went to return the phone to its base unit, but couldn't reach. Jack kept the knife pressed to her throat. 'Leave it on the desk.'

Eve did as she was told.

I considered grabbing Jack's arm, pulling the letter opener away from Eve's neck and wresting it from Jack's grip, but the idea was stillborn. He was taller and much stockier than me and, even if I managed to get to my feet and lunge across the broad desk before he reacted, in trying to avoid me he might stab Eve. Or retaliate and stab me. Feeling desperately useless, I remained seated and pleaded silently with my superlogic to come up with a brilliant plan. My superlogic protested that logic had absolutely nothing to do with whatever was going on here.

Jack pressed harder and Eve winced.

'What do you want from me, Jack?' Her voice was strained now.

'I want you to call it off.'

'Call what—' A high-pitched sound escaped Eve's mouth as the knife bit deeper. Horrified, I watched as a drop of blood painted a fast red line down to her collar.

Jack either didn't notice or didn't care. 'Don't play dumb with me,' he snarled dangerously. 'I know what you're planning to do. I've known about it ever since I heard Louis and his little lady friend calmly chatting about how millions of people were going to die.' A frown flickered across Eve's pale forehead. Jack turned to give me a shark's smile: cold, deadly and utterly humourless. 'You remember, Louis. Up on the roof after the induction workshop.'

10:59:46

Nothing to Lose

'Eve, I'm *so* sorry. I had no idea...'

'Louis, don't—' Whatever Eve had been going to say to me was cut off by Jack applying more pressure to the letter opener. I couldn't take my eyes from the dark patch that was steadily flowering on the collar of her neat blue jacket.

'Shut up!' he spat venomously. 'I swear I'll kill you if you don't. I mean it. You and your smart words have taken everything from me. All of it. Everything that mattered is gone. My sister, my career...'

He stopped. I was terrified that Eve would fill the silence and get herself killed, so I spoke.

'I really am sorry, Eve. Grace and I honestly didn't know there was anyone around to hear us.' Jack allowed me to continue, no doubt savouring my distress. 'When we got to the roof terrace that day, it was empty. We checked really carefully. But then... I suppose we got engrossed, talking about the virus and—'

Eve widened her eyes, but the silent warning came too late.

'Virus?' Jack looked confused. 'What virus?'

Oh my God. I wondered how much worse this day was going to get. I didn't dare open my mouth again in case I did even more harm.

Jack was frowning, looking from me to Eve and back again. 'What about the bomb?'

It was my turn for confusion. Bomb? What bomb?

'Tell me!' Jack roared.

Maybe someone would hear him and come to our rescue. Any time right about now would do.

Eve tried to respond but only produced a squeak.

'Not you! I've had enough of your lies.' Jack then turned his malevolent gaze on me. 'You. Tell me. And it'd better be the truth, or I'll kill her.'

Eve closed her eyes; whether in despair, consent or pain, I didn't know.

I would have done just about anything to avoid having to watch Jack sink the blade of the letter opener any deeper into Eve's neck, and was no longer in any doubt that he was crazy enough to do such a thing. I spoke in a small, wretched voice, trying to give away no more than I had to, devastated that I'd already messed up so badly.

'I don't know anything about a bomb. There's a plan to spread a virus. It'll reduce the population and give the world a chance.'

Jack was staring at me. I could almost see the cogs turning behind his pale eyes, one of which was twitching constantly. 'No bomb. No volcano.'

Volcano? What the hell was he on about? His words sounded more like statements than questions, so I kept my treacherous tongue still.

'That whole thing... was a lie?' Jack's face went red, as if he himself was about to erupt.

Eve's agonised exclamation told me that the knife had been pushed further in. The dark stain was spreading more rapidly now over the right shoulder of her jacket.

I'd stood up before I realised it. 'No!' I yelled. 'Don't!'

Jack turned his shark-smile my way, but at least my outburst had stopped him. 'You stupid little idiot. You may have fallen for her filthy lies, but I won't. Can't you see? She's a monster! She's...

She's Hitler in a skirt! I'll be doing the world a massive favour.' He turned his attention back to Eve. Her eyes were still closed, more tightly now. She looked paler. Older.

'So get her to stop it, then,' I said loudly, trying to distract him. 'She's the only person who can prevent the virus from being released. The only one. If you kill her now, all you'll be doing is making sure the plan goes ahead.'

My eyes were fixed on his hand where it held the letter opener and I saw him relax his grip slightly. The blade was no longer silver. It was crimson.

He looked down at Eve. 'Is that true?'

'Yes.' It was a croaky whisper.

'How can you stop it? What do you need to do?'

'I…' She struggled to speak.

Jack withdrew the paperknife, but he kept it threateningly close. Blood seeped continuously from a small livid wound in Eve's neck. Seeping wasn't good but it was way better than gushing or pumping.

'I'd have to phone Ben,' she said hoarsely. 'Tell him we're calling it off.'

'Who's he?'

'Our head research scientist.'

'Do it.' Jack gestured to the phone handset lying on the desk. 'Now.' As Eve reached for it slowly, another thought seemed to occur to him. 'If there's a virus… there must be an antidote, right? Some kind of vaccine?'

'Yes.'

'Get him to bring some. Oddly enough, I don't trust you. I want protection.'

Eve picked up the phone and pressed a speed-dial button. The sharp point of the blood-smeared letter opener hovered near her ravaged neck.

'Ben? It's Eve. Listen carefully. The plan is off.' A pause. 'Yes, you heard me. It's off. We won't be going ahead with it. Understood?' Another pause. Jack tensed, prompting her to interrupt whatever was being said on the other end of the phone. 'I'll explain later. And Ben? Please bring some of the vaccine to my office… Yes, right now, please. Can you? Good. Soon as you can. Not the microneedles, the full dose. Okay? Thank you.' Slowly, she put the phone back down on top of the incongruously cheerful-looking posters that were spread on her desk.

I was still on my feet and had been watching for an opportunity to try and disarm Jack, but there hadn't been one.

He looked at me and pointed to a navy blue scarf that was hanging with Eve's coat on a hook near the door. 'Get that scarf, then sit down' he ordered. I fetched it and he told Eve to drape it around her neck. As she finished doing so, there was a loud knock on the door.

'No tricks,' Jack warned tersely.

Ben entered the room and I hoped that his superior brain would do a better job than mine had of sizing up the situation. Jack was still on Eve's side of the desk, holding the letter opener low, where Ben couldn't see it. He'd hurriedly wiped it and his bloody hand on the dark scarf. I willed Ben to notice the stain on the front of Eve's jacket that was just visible under one edge of the scarf, and there was a red smear on her chin.

'Is everything okay?' Ben asked uncertainly.

'Everything's fine,' Eve lied, speaking softly. 'We've just decided to call off the plan, that's all. Is that the vaccine?'

Ben was holding a slim metal case, slightly larger than a piece of A4 paper. 'Right here,' he said, walking over to lay the case on the front edge of the desk.

'Jack here works in our comms centre. He hasn't been immunised yet,' she said.

'But if the plan's been called off—' Ben started.

Eve interjected, 'Better safe than sorry, eh?'

Ben looked intently at her pale face. 'Of course.'

We watched as Ben opened the combination locks on the case, put on a pair of latex gloves and meticulously filled a small syringe from an unlabelled vial of clear liquid. I prayed Ben had realised that something was badly wrong and had brought a strong sedative instead of the vaccine.

Jack seemed to read my mind. 'Louis first,' he said.

'I've already been vaccinated,' I protested.

'Louis first,' Jack repeated.

Frowning, but apparently deciding not to question the fact that Jack seemed to be calling the shots both literally and figuratively, Ben got me to roll up my shirt sleeve, unwrapped a sterile swab and used it to clean my upper arm, then expertly administered the injection.

'Eve next,' Jack said firmly.

Ben looked at her questioningly, but she nodded. He didn't see her wince as she carefully shrugged her left arm out of the jacket.

Jack was keeping a close eye on Ben. 'Use the same vial.'

Ben took a fresh syringe from the case and filled it from the little bottle. After Eve's injection, Jack came around the desk and stood in the open area of the office so that Ben could give him the vaccine, observing as a third syringe was filled from the same vial of liquid. He must have dropped the letter opener on the floor next to Eve. Ben swabbed Jack's arm and gave him the jab.

I waited for my moment. Now that Eve's life wasn't in immediate danger and Jack was unarmed, I reckoned I could probably rush at him and at least knock him off-balance. He was nearly twice my size, but hopefully Ben would then help me overpower him. It wasn't a great plan, but it was the only one I had.

Jack looked down to unroll his shirtsleeve. It was now or never.

I launched myself off the chair and charged at Jack, hunkering down and aiming for his solid midsection. I'd never been any good at rugby tackles, but that was vaguely what I had in mind. He was standing less than two metres away from me so I couldn't get up much momentum. He yelled in surprise, took one small step backwards, and promptly retaliated with a hefty punch to the side of my head. I had a close-up view of his shoes before all the lights went out.

10:59:47

Bruised

Although I couldn't have been unconscious for more than a couple of minutes, Jack wasn't in the room when I opened my eyes. It was like falling asleep in the middle of a film and missing an important part of the action. Only with more of a headache. My left temple and cheekbone throbbed unpleasantly as Ben pulled me up into a sitting position on the floor.

'Eve…?' I enquired groggily.

'I'm here, Louis. I'm okay.' I was glad to hear her voice from somewhere above the looming bulk of her desk, where she was presumably still sitting in her chair. I started trying to stand, then decided to stay on the floor for a while longer. Having helped me to shuffle backwards so I could lean against the wall, Ben straightened up.

'Where's Jack?' I asked.

'Handcuffed,' Ben replied. 'Not a happy bunny. And he'll be even grumpier when the police get here.'

'What happened?' I gave the side of my face an experimental prod and flinched.

'I knew something wasn't right when I got Eve's call, so I instructed our security guys to stand by and come in here if I hadn't given them the all-clear within ten minutes. They burst in literally a couple of seconds after Jack thumped you. It was a pretty impressive right hook. How do you feel?'

'Unimpressed,' I said.

A knock at the door heralded the arrival of paramedics. In a blur of friendly yellow-and-green efficiency they attended to Eve and insisted that I should accompany her to the hospital to rule out concussion or a fractured cheekbone, and before I knew it the two of us were sitting in the back of an ambulance.

Eve looked terrible. Above the large white dressing that had been applied to her damaged neck, her face was grey and drawn. One of the paramedics was in the back with us, monitoring her attentively as we pulled away from the Phoenix building and our blue lights carved a slow path through the city's perpetual traffic.

'I'm so sorry, Eve. This whole awful situation is my fault,' I said miserably.

'Nonsense,' she croaked.

'But if I hadn't messed up on day one—'

'Louis Crawford, stop right there. None of us can turn back the clock and do things any differently, so there's absolutely no point worrying about what's already done and dusted. I'm so impressed with the way you handled yourself back there. You're an amazing, courageous person, do you know that?'

I didn't answer. I didn't feel amazing or courageous. I felt like I'd let everyone down. I felt small. I felt shaky, drained and scared. My head hurt a lot. I'd have burst into tears for less than a quid and was quite possibly going to throw up at some point in the very near future.

*

Dad came to get me from the hospital. Someone from Phoenix's HR department had phoned him to let him know that I'd been involved in an unfortunate incident with a disgruntled employee, which I supposed was a fair — if incomplete — summary, and that I was bruised but otherwise all right. He'd got the next train into

London. He took one look at my swollen face and puffy eye and pulled me into a rare hug.

By the time we got home to Cuthbert Street I'd managed to convince him that I really was okay. Nevertheless, he fussed over me and made me sit on the sofa with an ice pack against my face while he brewed tea.

'I had a call from some woman at your work,' he said, when we were both concentrating on dunking biscuits.

'Yeah, somebody in HR. You said.'

'No, after that. Eve something. She phoned me on my mobile while I was on the train.'

'Eve Gyer?' I asked, surprised. Surely she'd been kind of busy getting her damaged throat mended.

'That's her.' He took a bite of soggy gingernut. 'Nice woman. She said I mustn't let you worry about what happened. Said you're a remarkable young man and I should be very proud of you.'

I was stunned. Again. 'And what did you say?'

'I told her to tell me something I didn't already know,' he said, picking up the TV remote.

It was only later, when the painkillers had properly kicked in and I was lying in bed reflecting on the day's unusual events, that I realised I hadn't asked Ben about the injections. There was a warm patch on my arm where he'd given me the jab, but I had no idea whether the virus or the vaccine was now pumping through my veins. If it was the former, I supposed I was about to find out first-hand whether or not the SafeWorld plasters really worked.

*

The next morning I was almost disappointed that the faint bruising I could see in the bathroom mirror didn't match the pain in my face. I swallowed a couple of paracetamol tablets with my breakfast and headed to the office, hoping for a day distinctly lacking in angry homicidal co-workers. I gave Tomasz and Grace the edited highlights of what had happened in London and they were both

277

suitably shocked, and Ben phoned mid-morning to let me know that Eve had been kept in hospital overnight as a precaution but the injuries to her neck weren't serious. A low mood descended on me like a raincloud and, shortly after two o'clock, Tom sent me home to nurse my headache and get over myself.

Wednesday was better. With Phoenix's trademark efficiency, the Helping Handshakes posters arrived via courier and there was an email making all staff aware of the initiative — ostensibly just another fundraising programme the company was supporting. I contacted a couple of the big shopping centres in my sector of Mareton and got such a positive response that by that afternoon I was selling handshakes in one of them. It was busier than I'd expected for a Wednesday afternoon, and useful practice for the weekend when the crowds would be bigger, and I planned to spend longer dispensing handshakes to many and immunity to some. Despite the fact that it wasn't even December yet, the whole place was dripping with tinsel, fairy lights and special offers, and after only a couple of hours I was already sick of hearing 'Jingle Bell Rock' and I most certainly did *not* wish it could be Christmas every day.

I stationed myself in a different shopping mall on Thursday after I'd checked in at the office, done a couple of jobs to help Chris and picked up more supplies of plasters. I put a Helping Handshakes poster on a pillar and set up my small folding table and chair below it. I also had a collecting bowl — which I emptied frequently into a zipped money pouch that I wore around my waist under my sweatshirt — and a bin in which I could bag up the biodegradable wipes I was using to sanitise my hands, along with the tell-tale backing papers and caps from the plasters.

At lunchtime I exchanged a few handfuls of coins for lighter ten- and twenty-pound notes in the nearby shops, then visited the loo, washed my hands and sat on a bench to eat a sandwich. There were banners across several of the big stores' windows announcing their Black Friday sales. Ugh. That meant tomorrow would be stupidly busy. I was already dreading it, but it would be a good opportunity to vaccinate people.

Back at my post, I carried on dishing out my Helping Handshakes and met some genuinely nice people. I'd got the plasters down to a fine art now, quickly reapplying them below the table and flicking the gel caps off subtly before shaking the hands of worthy candidates. I'd just immunised a young couple and their charming toddler — not a pair of words I had often put together with any sincerity — when I spotted three teenagers approaching. My heart sank as I recognised Jay, my old nemesis from school days, who slid a sneering grin across his face as he made a beeline for me. Tagging along like belligerent geese in his wake were two younger lads: Flaky Ollie and another kid, Nemo, whose real name was Finn. I knew them because they belonged to the little gang that terrorised the steps in front of my building in Cuthbert Street, forcing anyone needing to enter to run the gauntlet of their skateboards, cigarette smoke and foul language.

My superlogic was sitting back muttering 'no-brainer', since Mareton would undoubtedly be a nicer place without these three geniuses in it. Not giving the vaccine to strangers was one thing; making a conscious decision to allow people I knew to die was harder, somehow. Showing off in front of the younger lads, Jay dug in his pocket for a pound coin and made a big show of going to put it in the collection. As he added the coin to the small pile already there, he grabbed a handful of money and ran off with it, shouting, 'Cheers, Lou*ise*!' over his shoulder.

Some people don't need any qualifications to become the architects of their own downfall.

10:59:48

Black Friday

The incident with Jack might have made me question Plan B all over again. Instead it did the opposite, making me realise that I didn't now want anything or anyone to prevent it. And if my eventful Monday hadn't had that effect, I'm pretty sure Black Friday would have done.

Reading some online news while I ate my breakfast, both the headlines and the adverts were all about the sales. Many major stores had opened their doors to bargain hunters at midnight, some voluntarily and others when the chanting packs of eager shoppers had forced their way in. There were video clips of crowds crushing against the glass, fighting to get to the front, and then of men and women brawling over high-tech toys and discounted widescreen TVs. It was carnage. One report showed two people lunging for the last gadget on a shelf. One of them, a man who was hampered by his beer belly, realised he was going to lose out and tried to stop his rival, a chunky blonde woman, by grabbing her hair. She took exception to this and walloped him, and somebody else nabbed the gadget while they were occupied. I watched the clip in disbelief, munching my toast.

When I arrived at the office, there was a lively discussion going on.

'I don't know how we have the nerve to call ourselves a civilised society,' Chris was saying.

Grace asked, 'People don't actually die though, do they?'

'Yes, they do!' Chris insisted. 'I read up about it when all this nonsense kicked off last year. Parents have shot each other in front of their families in arguments over parking spaces. A pregnant woman miscarried her baby after being knocked to the ground. People pushed past an elderly man who was dying on the floor. Children have been hospitalised. It's ridiculous. There was one guy — a shop worker — who got trampled in a Black Friday stampede. His colleagues appealed to shoppers to back off and let them help him, but they refused. They *refused*. They even stepped on the paramedics who were trying to administer CPR to the poor guy. People get crazy.'

'Trouble is, mob mentality kicks in,' Pam said. 'And when that happens you can forget rational thought, let alone compassion. Like you say, people get crazy.'

'Wow. These videos are downright scary,' Grace said from her desk, where she was watching news clips. 'Give me the mosh pit at a heavy metal gig any day. These idiots make that look like a quiet stroll in the countryside.'

Making a mental note to ask Grace about her musical interests sometime, I joined in the conversation. 'What I don't get is why we've adopted this delightful American tradition when there are scenes like this every year. You'd think it'd get banned when people are hurt and killed, but instead more and more retailers seem to think it's a great idea.'

'Yeah, because there's money to be made!' Chris said. 'Lots of other countries have started having Black Friday sales in the last few years, it's not just here. Apparently the international brands encourage it. Big surprise. What do they care about a few blood sacrifices to the god of profit? And there's no point trying to protest against these things; you may as well be talking to a brick wall.'

'Or yelling at cows,' Grace said, winking at me. I'd explained my 'yelling at cows' analogy in the office a few months back, and everyone had started using the expression.

'Exactly,' Chris agreed.

Pam added, 'And every year people just shake their heads over the latest casualties and carry on doing exactly the same thing on an ever larger scale. I tell you what, it's lucky we're the most intelligent species on the planet. Imagine what would happen if we were the stupidest.' She got up and walked into the kitchen, and the others turned their attention to their work, mumbling agreement.

I went into the kitchen to get myself a coffee and found Pam sitting with her head in her hands.

'Pam? Are you okay?' I asked, crossing the room to sit near her.

'Ugh, I'm fine Lou.' She looked up at me. Her expression was bleak, but I was relieved to see that her eyes were dry. 'Stuff like this just gets me down sometimes, you know?'

Pam gave the Plan B hand sign and I double-checked that we were alone before giving the response. She continued, 'This Black Friday insanity, the fact that people are prepared to trample each other to death for the sake of twenty quid off a new telly... What will they do when the stakes are higher and they're competing for their families' survival?' She sighed, and I nodded in sympathy. 'The world would be a better place without their kind. I know I shouldn't say things like that. I'm not supposed to despair that there are loathsome multitudes breeding indiscriminately and teaching their kids precious little except that society owes them a living. I'm not supposed to harbour a secret longing to eradicate them like the parasites they are, to leave a better world for those of us who want to look after it and show each other a little basic respect and decency.

'I know my sentiments are shocking when confessed to even the most open-minded of people. Good grief, people seem to get their knickers in a twist these days over the slightest thing that offends their delicate sensibilities; I'm sure all their underwear would spontaneously combust if they heard me talking like this. But, given the choice, of course I want my children to share their environment with people like those few brave employees Chris was telling us about who tried to save the life of their injured colleague. Otherwise my grandkids are either going to have to fight for survival against the grasping hordes or give up and let these locusts plunder and pillage until there's literally nothing left worth fighting for.'

She looked up at me and smiled self-consciously. 'Hark at me, wittering on. Sorry Lou. I'm sure you've got more important things to do than sit here listening to an old woman ranting.'

'On the contrary,' I said. 'I think you should be Prime Minister.'

Grace put her head around the door. 'Ah, here you are. Tomasz has asked us all to gather in the office. Some kind of announcement.'

Pam and I joined the knot of people in the middle of the open-plan office, wondering what was going on.

Tom looked serious. 'I have a piece of sad news and I've no idea how to break it gently, so I'm just going to say it.' He paused. 'Eve Gyer died this morning.'

10:59:49

Identity Crisis

In New York, Ken Burford turned up the collar of his overcoat against the drizzle that was blurring the Manhattan skyline. He walked another block, then the big revolving door moved easily at his touch and he strolled into Phoenix's international headquarters building like a man who had absolutely nothing to hide.

'Victor Chase,' he announced authoritatively to the smiling receptionist. 'I have an appointment with Roger Vee.'

*

In the security office, Thandi Mbela happened to glance at the CCTV monitor and broke off in the middle of an anecdote that had her two colleagues laughing.

'So what did you do next, Thandi?' one of the guards asked.

'I'll tell you later, Chuck. Zoom camera two for me, will you?' She peered intently at the image of the businessman who was signing in at reception. 'Well, well... I do believe I smell a hatful of anchovies.'

'What?'

Thandi was hurriedly flicking back through her notebook to find the names she'd jotted down.

'Watch the monitors and keep your radios on and your wits about you, boys. That guy right there could be trouble.' She straightened her tie and bustled out of the room.

*

Ken was sitting in the foyer. He'd waited years for this moment and was relishing it. Although the evidence was circumstantial, Alex Connors at the CIA labs had confirmed that the SafeWorld plasters were coated with a vaccine against a specific strain of flu that didn't exist in any of the international disease databases. Ken should have gone to his government colleagues with the information, but where was the fun in that? He'd been dreaming of confronting Roger Vee face-to-face and seeing the man's reaction, and no one was going to rob him of that pleasure.

His phone beeped in his pocket and he pulled it out. The screen showed a text message from an unidentified number that General Barrett used solely to convey updates about the Four Horsemen. It read: "Your horse is running in the third race". Finally, they had the go-ahead from President Wentworth for Horseman Number Three. Could this day possibly get any better?

'Mr Chase?'

Ken looked up to see a smartly-dressed female security guard approaching him.

'Mr Vee will see you now, sir. If you'd like to come with me, I'll escort you to the top floor.'

'I'm sure I can find my way,' Ken said pleasantly.

'All part of the service, sir.' Thandi assured him with a smile.

They were the only two passengers in the lift. Thandi pressed a button and the doors closed.

'Shame about the weather out there today, Mr Miller,' she said casually, with one hand resting on the nightstick that hung from her belt.

Ken's eyes narrowed. 'My name is Chase.'

'My mistake, sir. You're the spitting image of an FDA inspector by the name of Ron Miller who visited our Raleigh facility recently.'

Ken said nothing, calculating his options as the elevator ascended.

'Come to think of it, you also look rather like a man called Ken Burford,' Thandi said. 'Or is it Howard Carmichael?'

The reaction came as soon as she had spoken the name, and it was far swifter and more violent than Thandi had expected. Ken aimed a lightning punch at her face, and she barely had time to lean away from it. The blow struck her throat. She'd drawn her nightstick but it fell to the floor as she staggered heavily against the wall of the lift, clutching her neck. She tried to speak to her team on the other end of the radio, but found she could only produce a wheezing sound.

Ken realised he would have to abort his plans. Damn this woman! How the hell did she know who he was? He glanced at the panel in the elevator and saw that they were nearing the twenty-fifth and final floor. There was no time. The guard was struggling to drag air in through her damaged windpipe but she still did her best to kick and resist as, in one practised motion, Ken pulled her chin down to her chest and then twisted her head sharply.

He let Thandi's limp body drop to the floor and stood ready as the lift door opened on the penthouse level, braced for a welcome from another security guard. The hallway was empty. Ken was seething with rage but knew he must keep his cool and find a way to get out of the building. He quickly placed the guard's nightstick so that it would prevent the door from closing, and stepped across to another elevator on the opposite side of the passage so that he could head all the way back down again. As a precaution, he pressed buttons for floors four and eight. He should have a few minutes before the woman's body was discovered, but it would be pushing his luck to go straight to the ground floor and walk brazenly out through the main reception area.

A soft chime announced the lift's arrival on the eighth floor. There was no sign of any alarms or disturbance, so he allowed the doors to close again. The lift stopped on the seventh floor and two young women got in, chattering about something someone had said to somebody else. Ken excused himself politely when they reached the fourth floor.

He located the door to the stairwell and was about to enter when he heard a man's voice on the other side. Ken stepped back out of sight just in time as a security guard passed, mounting the stairs two at a time while he shouted breathlessly into a handheld radio. 'Thandi, are you there? Thandi, this is Chuck. Come in, over!'

As soon as the man had turned the corner, Ken yanked the door open and started trotting down the stairs. He reached the ground floor and continued on, following signs to an underground parking lot and emergency exit. Within minutes, he was striding purposefully away along the Manhattan sidewalk. His escape had been almost disappointingly easy. Phoenix really ought to improve their security.

His long-anticipated confrontation with Roger needn't be abandoned, merely postponed. Ken was determined to have his moment, to see defeat cloud the great Mr Vee's eyes, to savour the sweet taste of cold revenge. It would happen. He would come up with a new plan. Just as soon as the Third Horseman had fulfilled its destiny.

10:59:50

Letters from the Dead

Tomasz called me quietly to one side straight after the announcement. 'I've got something for you,' he said. 'A letter from Eve.'

'For me?' I looked at him, not understanding, still trying to make sense of the news. She couldn't possibly be dead. I'd been with her just four days ago. Maybe the wound in her neck had got infected…

'I had one, too. She enclosed this and asked me to give it to you after… when the news broke. Why don't you use the meeting room so you can read it in private?' Tom suggested.

I took the letter from him and walked to the meeting room in a daze. He had handed me a sealed envelope with my name handwritten in small, neat script on the front. Underneath was written: "<u>PLEASE DESTROY AFTER READING</u>".

London, Monday 24th November
Dear Louis,
There are some things I want you to know. Firstly, it was my choice to die now. I was diagnosed with cancer last year and was told there was nothing the doctors could really do for me, so the news you've just heard was a deliberate, informed decision on my part to avoid the slow

torture that the disease would have held in store for me. It had already begun, and I'm not good at being ill. Perhaps that seems cowardly, but I'm in no doubt that most people would spare themselves such suffering if they were fortunate enough to be given the option. I was one of the lucky ones.

And now I'll tell you another secret, although you might have already guessed… I was Plan B's first victim. It's quite fitting, really. The injections that Ben gave us in my office earlier today contained the virus, not the vaccine. I imagine that my official cause of death will be recorded as cardiac arrest resulting from blood poisoning, or something along those lines. The hospital will only know that I suddenly developed a high fever and they'll assume it was caused by an infection in that little love-bite that poor Jack gave me. Don't think too badly of him; he was a casualty of Plan B too, in more ways than one.

It was our intention all along that the virus would be released at the beginning of December, so today's events have merely brought things forward by one week, that's all. Ben knew what I meant when I asked him to bring 'the full dose', although he wasn't aware that I'd chosen not to give myself immunity.

Part of our reasoning with the timing was that the flu will have done its work and vanished before the end of December, so the new year will be a fresh start for mankind. Also, the highest populations are in the northern hemisphere and the cold winter weather will help to avoid the spread of secondary diseases. We've had years to think about all this. Years when we fervently hoped it would prove to have been wasted effort. Ah well, that ship has sailed, as the saying goes. By the time you read this, the virus will have been unleashed on every continent.

I would have liked to see how things turn out, of course. It would be dishonest of me to pretend otherwise. But that's my only regret, and I'm not afraid to die. Allow me a few thoughts on the subject of death, since there's about to be an awful lot of it. We all die; it's the one inevitability of our existence. I'm not sure that anyone truly fears death itself. What we fear is the unknown, the process of dying, the pain and indignity we might have to endure, the fact that we can't be sure what *face Death will be wearing when it comes to our door.*

Most of us don't get to choose how we die. But we do get to choose how we LIVE. That's all that really matters, and it's something within our control. Even when bad things happen, we can choose how we let them affect us. A good life has nothing whatsoever to do with how many years you're on the planet or how often you go to church or how much money you have when you finally cash in your chips. It's about trying in your own small way to do right and make the very most of the gift of life while you have it; it's about the decisions you make, what you do and say, the way you treat other living things; it's about working out who you really are and what makes you truly happy, and building everything else around that.

Anyway, enough of my views on life and death. I started writing this letter to you because you were there today, and I don't want you to feel any sense of guilt over what's happened. I'm afraid I've ended up writing rather an essay but please bear with me, there are just a couple more things I want to say before I sign off.

I was only ever a very small part of this grand plan of ours. It has been such a privilege to get to know you, Louis, and many other wonderful people like you. I am so proud of Phoenix's legacy. The months ahead will be immensely challenging, but don't doubt yourself. Remember that we've done this for all the right reasons: to buy time for the human race to learn from its mistakes and achieve its full potential, to protect all of the compassion and integrity and beauty and gloriously flawed brilliance that our species has to offer this world.

I won't personally get to see whether we learn to live in harmony with the rest of nature, whether we learn to explore the true power of our minds and spirits, but I can die in peace knowing that those things could *happen because of what Phoenix is doing now. I wish Plan B hadn't been necessary, I really do, but I believe in what we're doing with all my heart and soul. And I believe in you. You have no idea yet what you're capable of. There's such potency in youth; you're still becoming the person you're going to be. The world is yours, and it couldn't be in better hands.*

I want you to know that I met my end with a light heart and a

clear conscience. Now go and meet your future in the same way.
Thank you, Louis.
Eve

10:59:51

Virus

It took a few days for the burgeoning influenza epidemic to climb the hierarchy of news stories, a few days for it to be deemed more important and interesting than all the usual celebrity gossip and political posturing. At first it was no more than an afterthought in the regional bulletins, an 'Oh, and by the way, a local man died of flu'. But the growing number of regional dots were quickly joined, and when the virus had the audacity to claim the lives of a famous rapper and a popular TV chef, the panic began.

Watching the news with Dad was an odd experience because I couldn't share my inside knowledge. I wanted to be able to warn him how bad this was going to get and reassure him that we were safe. Not that he was even worried at first, as neither of us had ever tended to succumb to whatever lurgies were doing the rounds in the past. So when we watched the news together I had to feign an appropriate level of boredom.

'Our top story today: the death toll rises in the global flu outbreak,' Andrea the perfectly groomed presenter announced gravely as soon as the opening credits faded. 'Cases have now been reported in multiple countries including Britain, the United States, India and Australia. The original source of the disease has not yet been pinpointed and factors such as the frequency of international travel mean that it's possible it may never be discovered.'

Footage of people wearing surgical masks in crowded streets and queuing for vaccinations was shown while Andrea's smooth voiceover continued. 'Later in the programme we'll be talking to Dr Runjit Chaudhry, a virologist from the World Health Organisation, to find out more about what is believed to be a variant strain of the H1N1 virus that claimed at least eighteen thousand lives in 2009. Meanwhile, members of the public are being urged to take appropriate precautions.'

The camera turned to Andrea's co-host, an equally primped and polished man, who said, 'And, we may only be three months into the football season but Manchester City have already established an unbeaten record under new manager Javier Gonzalez...'

Dad's attention level increased and mine decreased in direct proportion, and I went to the kitchen to make us another coffee.

Less than a week later, the 'outbreak' had become a 'pandemic', Andrea the perfectly-presented presenter had become one of its victims, and Manchester City had suffered their first defeat of the season in a 'shocking' four-nil drubbing by underdogs West Bromwich Albion.

Andrea had heeded her own warning to take appropriate precautions, even though she was a bit famous and therefore not just a member of the public. She'd taken to wearing a surgical mask while she walked between her car and the TV studio. She wouldn't have been seen dead on any form of public transport, epidemic or no epidemic. She curtailed her social life and shopping habit almost entirely. There was that one Saturday when she indulged in a bit of pre-Christmas retail therapy with her best friend, Camille, but they stuck to the high-end boutiques and lunched at a very clean-looking restaurant. Andrea could have picked up the flu virus in any of those places but, in her case, it was actually a work-related fatality. Fabien, one of the studio's make-up team, passed on the deadly infection while he was applying face powder and hairspray, and telling Andrea how he'd booked a week off in January and was going to treat himself to a winter getaway, probably in the Canary

Islands. While he was inadvertently killing her, Fabien told Andrea he was leaning towards Fuerteventura. She said you couldn't beat Tenerife for the nightlife.

Fabien had also been careful, wearing a mask and washing his hands more than usual, just to be on the safe side. He'd picked up the virus from the television studio's main door handle.

It was John Simmons — known as Simmo to fellow members of the camera crew — who had coughed into his hand just before leaving the building ahead of Fabien. It was nothing, no more than a clearing of the throat, really. He didn't even realise he'd done it.

Simmo caught the flu from the TV remote at home, unaware that his flatmate, Spence, had already contracted the disease from a grumpy-looking elderly woman for whom he gave up his seat on the bus.

Mrs Patel, who didn't even thank Spence for his act of kindness, looked grumpy because she had a nasty headache and suspected that one of her neighbour's noisy kids might have given her a cold. If not that, maybe she'd picked up a bug of some sort from the handle of the supermarket trolley.

Mrs Patel was right about the kids. Children have a particular talent for making noise and spreading germs. A few days later, when the neighbour's irritating offspring had fallen uncharacteristically silent, Mrs Patel was breathing her last and was in no fit state to appreciate the peace and quiet.

And so it went on, all over the world. The flu virus was passed along like a juicy piece of gossip. It was transmitted passionately between lovers, carelessly from one complete stranger to another, whispered among friends, spat out and inhaled.

*

As the pandemic escalated, it brought out the worst in people. Shops were emptied of supplies as panic-buyers stripped the supermarket shelves bare, hoarding more than they could use and leaving others with nothing. I watched news footage of queues and then riots at doctors' surgeries, pharmacies and hospitals where flu jabs were being offered. I knew that Phoenix had supplied stocks of the virus — labelled as "vaccine" — to these outlets and in fact these clinics were helping to spread the disease even faster. I felt awful knowing that most of the people clamouring for salvation were merely hastening their doom.

There was a huge public outcry over the fact that vaccinations were offered to prisoners, but the protesters needn't have wasted their vitriol. The murderers, rapists, drug-dealers and thieves eagerly bared their arms for their lethal injections and, when they all died, the authorities simply assumed that the vaccine had come too late to prevent the spread of the disease in such enclosed environments.

The virus spread at a rate that made wildfire look downright lazy. There was plenty of advice about staying at home but, by the time governments started changing the guidelines to rules, it was already much too late. It soon reached the stage where everybody knew someone who had died from the flu and world populations realised that they were facing something completely unprecedented.

I'd carried on with the Helping Handshakes vaccinations for a while longer, determined to bestow immunity on as many people as I could, but by mid-December — when the retail centres would normally have been heaving with Christmas shoppers — there were so few people around that I stopped. Belatedly, people realised that survival was probably more important than buying new toys or scented candles or a thousand other things they'd never really needed in the first place. Even before full lockdowns were imposed, many shops were shut, partly because of the lack of customers and partly because their staff had either fallen prey to the illness or were too terrified to leave their homes. This effect grew as everyone realised the scale of the pandemic. Workforces were thinned by the disease and those who hadn't yet succumbed were intent on trying to protect their families. Public transport systems were grounded. Manufacturing ceased. The wheels of industry stopped turning almost completely.

It was the nineteenth of December when Dad fell ill.

10:59:52

Sick

'Get out!'

It was clearly meant to be a shout, but it came out as a croak. I was used to Dad sleeping at unconventional times, but he'd been in his room for hours and I thought I'd better wake him up.

'I brought you a cup of—'

'I mean it, Lou. Don't come near me. I've got it.'

I knew straight away what he meant.

'But Dad, you can't have it.' What could I say? How long had he been lying awake in this room, believing he was going to die? I was desperate to reassure him and stepped closer, intending to put the mug of tea on his bedside table.

He pulled the duvet up to cover his nose and mouth, and lunged to push me away. The tea went flying and the handle of Dad's favourite mug broke as it hit the floor. We stared at each other for a second before Dad started coughing into the duvet. He was still gesturing at me to leave and I did so, not wanting to distress him any further.

I pulled his bedroom door shut behind me and leaned against it. Now what? How could I reassure him that he hadn't got the lethal virus without telling him about Plan B? Did it matter anymore? Of course it did. What would he think of me? I'd known the epidemic was going to happen. I'd known people would die.

Dad was still coughing on the other side of the door. He sounded so ill. I was going to have to tell him. He needed to know he'd had the vaccine. And I should clean up the spilled tea, as well.

My hand was on the door handle when a terrible thought hit me. Maybe the vaccine hadn't worked on him. Maybe Phoenix hadn't even given us the real vaccine to distribute.

My head and my heart were both pounding. Dad had stopped coughing now, but the silence was worse. If Phoenix had deceived us all, then their treachery was even more monstrous than Plan B itself. I felt dizzy and sank to the floor.

'Lou? You still there?' His voice was hoarse. 'Don't come in!' he added urgently.

'I'm here, Dad.'

'Would you mind getting me some water? Put it just inside the door and I'll get it from there.'

'Of course. I'll be right back.'

I walked to the kitchen on autopilot and ran the cold tap while my mind whirled with fear, anger, disappointment, betrayal, sorrow, shame… How could I have been such a bloody idiot? I'd been sucked in by their lies and their compliments, fooled so easily into believing I was one of the good guys who deserved to survive. It had all made such sense to me. Was I immune? Yes, I must be, because I'd been injected with the virus that day in London. Or had I? I didn't know what to believe any more.

Everything was invisible: the virus, the vaccine, the secrets, the lies, the terror.

Oh God, this whole thing was overwhelming… Too huge, too awful… People were dropping dead all over the place, in their thousands. Hundreds of thousands. And now Dad… If anything happened to him, it would be my fault. It would destroy me.

I filled a pint glass with cold water and knocked gently on the door to Dad's bedroom.

'Remember, don't come in,' he said.

I put the glass down on the floor, then closed the door again and sat down against it. I heard him padding across the carpet to collect his drink.

'Dad?'

'Please, Lou. Please don't come in. I don't want you to catch this, son.' I'd never heard him sound so frightened, even when Mum was dying. It was horrible.

'I need to tell you…' My voice caught.

'Louis? Listen to me, kiddo. Let me do this one last thing for you, okay? If I've got this flu, I might… Well, I haven't heard of anybody surviving it. Go and stay with Cheryl for a bit. Maybe out in the country where there aren't so many people, you'll stand a chance.'

'No, Dad. I can't just leave you. Let me look after you.'

'No!' His violent reaction caused another coughing fit. I didn't trust myself to speak, so I waited for him to finish. 'Lou, you're my boy. My world. And I'm so proud of you. Of who you are. I'm not good at this stuff, I know, but I should've told you more often. I wish I had. And your mum would've…' He sniffed. 'She would've just…'

He broke off, and neither of us tried to say anything for a while. I knew he was crying, just inches away from me on the other side of the door, and tears were pouring down my face.

In the end, I stopped trying to hide my emotions and spoke through my sobs.

'Dad, I'm not going to leave you. I can't…'

'I won't be the person to give this damned virus to you, Lou. If there's even the smallest chance you might avoid it, I—'

'The flu is everywhere, Dad! And if I'm gonna get it, I'd rather catch it from you than from some complete stranger. You're all I've got. If I leave you to die alone, how could I live with myself?'

I heard a shuddering breath on the other side of the door.

A more convincing argument occurred to me. 'Besides, I could run away to Much Wheadle and find that all I've done is carry the virus there with me. I'm staying, Dad. And if this really is it, then at least we'll be together.'

There was movement, so I stood up and tried to wipe my face. I was a mess.

Dad opened the door and met my gaze. His pyjamas were all wrinkled, his eyes were red, and his cheeks were wet. He looked absolutely terrible. And absolutely wonderful. He shook his head, put his hands on my shoulders, and then pulled me into an almost unbearably tight hug. I hugged him back and we stayed like that for a while, sobbing onto each other's shoulders.

'I love you, Lou.'

I couldn't remember the last time he'd said it, or if he ever had. And yet, in my eighteen years on the planet, he'd never let me doubt that it was true.

'I love you too, Dad.'

*

The next few days nearly broke me.

Dad got worse. I didn't need a thermometer to know that he had a fever; whenever I got near, I could feel the heat radiating off him. He slept a lot, but never for very long without coughing or groaning, so neither of us got much rest. I did my best to look after him and make him comfortable, trying to cool him down, ensuring he had frequent sips of water, coaxing him to eat a little, dosing him with painkillers, and even helping him along the hallway to get to the bathroom. I'd never seen him so ill.

I begged him to let me take him to hospital or at least try to call a doctor, but we both knew there was no point. We'd seen the news footage. Hospitals were overflowing, forced to turn people away and lock their doors, while the medical staff put their own lives on the line trying to help those who were beyond saving. The official advice was to stay at home.

I spent a lot of time thinking and I found myself wanting to connect with people. I wanted to speak to Cheryl but there was no point in worrying her, and I was afraid she'd come to Mareton and then she'd get sick as well. I wanted to speak to someone at Phoenix, but the office was closed. I had mobile numbers for Tomasz, Grace and Chris, and I came close to calling each of them, but I simply didn't know what I'd say or what they could say to me that might possibly help. I wanted to speak to Mum.

The world closed in until it was just the flat, just Dad and me. I focused on caring for him, and we talked a little whenever he was awake. After the first disturbed night, I dragged my mattress through to his room and camped out there. That way I'd be with him if...

I tried to block the thoughts of what I'd do when he died, but they nagged and gnawed, and leapt out to ambush me in the darkest hours of the night.

I waited for my own symptoms. Every time my throat seemed a bit dry and sore, or I had a bit of a headache, I felt a weird mixture of terror and elation. I didn't want to die, but at least Dad and I would go together, and I wouldn't have to deal with his body on my own: at least, not for too long. But the vaccine seemed to have worked on me and I stayed healthy. In some ways, the prospect of living was even more frightening than the prospect of dying.

Having avoided watching the news for a day or two, I went back to it out of morbid curiosity and a desire to distract myself from my own situation.

10:59:53

Advent

In most places there had been concerted efforts to keep essential resources like food stores and hospitals open, but these were rapidly swamped and stripped of supplies. Families stockpiled canned and frozen food so that they could stay at home, and the world had gone into lockdown.

The steps Phoenix had taken to safeguard certain services gradually became apparent, at least to me because I recognised them. Crematoriums operated around the clock, with no time for the usual fond farewells and religious rigmarole. Power and communications were still up and running, and a few television networks continued to broadcast.

Teams of people who became known simply as 'cleaners' patrolled every town. In the early days they'd collected the bodies of those who had collapsed outside: the victims who'd been left to die by everyone else who was terrified of infection and had already learned that the fallen were doomed. Later, the same teams went systematically from one residential building to another, redistributing food supplies, removing corpses before they could start decaying, euthanising pets that would otherwise starve, and turning off electricity, gas and water supplies wherever they were no longer needed. The cleaners also acted as a data gathering service, providing statistics to the authorities and, where possible, recording the identities of those who had died. The teams spray-painted a red circle on the door of every home that had been cleared. There were an awful lot of red circles.

Everyone was paralysed by fear. I honestly think they'd have been less afraid if an army of hostile aliens had landed or if Godzilla was rampaging through the streets of Mareton. When your enemy is huge and noisy, you can at least try to run in the opposite direction. The flu virus was everywhere, an invisible and unavoidable threat, too tiny to be shot down or otherwise vanquished, its microscopic particles reaping an abundant harvest of human lives as they touched every corner of the globe.

It was a civilised apocalypse. There were no mushroom clouds, no explosions, no gruesomely dismembered bodies littering the streets, no bombed out buildings, no giant monsters, no space invaders. It was the flu. Death came softly and swiftly, exactly as Phoenix had promised, and gathered up souls. People died in hospitals or, in the majority of cases, at home in their beds. People died recumbent on their sofas in front of the telly, with the squawking of soap operas and gameshows as the soundtrack for their journey to the hereafter. The quiet, non-violent nature of it all and the fact that the deaths were hidden neatly behind bricks and mortar served to lessen the horror, the awareness of the shattering scale of it all. Everything *looked* normal, neat and tidy.

There were exceptions, of course. Drivers fell ill at the wheels of their vehicles and crashed into things. A number of small planes dropped out of the sky. And there was a popular rumour that President Charles Wentworth died sitting on a toilet in the White House with his expensive trousers around his presidential ankles.

The virus scoured the planet indiscriminately, snatching those in their physical prime along with innocent new-borns and tired spirits inhabiting brittle old bodies. Those with the means to do so fled to remote places, often carrying the virus there with them. Others barricaded themselves inside their homes and taped the gaps around doors and windows, unaware that their fates were already even more effectively sealed. The rich, the poor, altruists and psychopaths: no one was spared unless they'd received the real vaccine.

Dad started feeling better on the twenty-third of December. The next day, he was well enough to have a much-needed shower, and sat on the couch afterwards instead of going straight back to bed. His appetite returned that evening and we celebrated his recovery with a lasagne ready meal from the freezer. Nothing had ever tasted so good.

We were both a bit self-conscious about the fact that we'd believed he was dying, but neither of us really regretted our displays of emotion. The prospect of imminent death had been oddly cathartic. That night, Dad and I watched old movies and made inappropriate jokes about man-flu.

Just as everyone was beginning to wonder if this pandemic might actually wipe out the entire human race, it was over. In the scheme of things, it hadn't taken long. Within four weeks of Eve's death, the news programmes started reporting an abrupt drop-off in the number of victims. The people who were still around to watch the updates began daring to believe that they'd been spared. The virus had run its course and would now live on only in the scarred memories of its survivors and the newest pages of human history. Despite the shock of the tragedy, a fragile hope began to bloom, like wildflowers among gravestones.

On Christmas day, Dad and I went for a slow walk around the block. It was the first time we'd been outside the flat for ages and we were going stir-crazy. Flaky Ollie and his cronies were conspicuously absent from the front steps of our building and the streets of Mareton were eerily quiet. Apart from the two of us, the only things moving were pieces of litter, chased along Cuthbert Street by the bitter wind that nipped at their heels. I remembered the countless times when I'd yearned for silence, but now I almost missed the old familiar cacophony of traffic and trains, sirens and chatter. At least it would have drowned out the mournful wailing of the gulls that wheeled overhead.

We didn't stay out for very long. Back in the flat, we spoke to Cheryl on the phone and then in the afternoon Dad fell asleep in front of the TV.

Despite the cold, I went up onto the roof and sat for a while, alone with my thoughts, wondering whether Plan B had been a hideous mistake after all. The unthinkable proposition was now an unthinkable reality. As the short day began to dim, I huddled into my coat and remembered something Eve had said to me: that none of us can turn back the clock and do things any differently, so there's absolutely no point worrying about what's already done and dusted.

I watched the sun sink lower. It was a pale, watery excuse for a star that didn't so much set as merely dissolve resignedly into the horizon.

10:59:54

All Good Things

The Third Horseman was to be rather more subtle than its predecessors. As much as Ken Burford had enjoyed the theatrical explosions his pets had set off in India and China, too many big bangs might have aroused suspicion.

Ken pulled a damp handkerchief from the pocket of his trousers and wiped the sweat from his face. Despite the uncomfortable heat and humidity, he laughed aloud. There was no one around to hear him.

Everything was coming together beautifully. At first he'd been bitterly angry about what had happened at the Phoenix headquarters in New York. That stupid security guard had ruined his planned face-off with Roger Vee, and he'd been forced to run away like some punk kid caught shoplifting. But it had turned out to be a blessing in disguise. Some news of the worldwide flu pandemic had reached him even here, in the fetid jungles of Brazil, and an eerie stillness had gradually descended on São Paulo during the past fortnight. Ken had panicked initially. Not because of the corpses in the streets or because he was frightened of the virus — he was certain now that the girl in the mall had immunised him when she'd touched his hand — but because he had missed his chance to spoil Roger Vee's precious 'Plan B'. Then, during the time he'd spent in what passed for a five-star hotel in the sprawling city, he'd come to realise that things were actually turning out better than he could possibly have imagined.

Millions of people were dying of the flu and Ken had evidence that Phoenix had developed and mass-manufactured a vaccine against this specific strain of the H1N1 virus *before* the disease itself officially existed. That could only mean that they had also developed the virus. Ken was shocked that his saintly nemesis could possibly be behind such a devastating attack on the human population. Everyone thought that Phoenix was a force for good in the world. Ken could have contacted the Pentagon and let them handle it in his absence, but his fun had already been spoiled once. There was no way he was going to miss the opportunity to personally inform Mr Vee that little old Howard Carmichael was the one who would see him tried, convicted and probably executed for mass murder on an unprecedented scale. Roger would be publicly disgraced and vilified. Ken could picture—

'Cub to Alpha. Over.' The radio interrupted Ken's happy thoughts.

'Alpha receiving. Over,' he replied, putting high-powered binoculars to his eyes. From his vantage point on the jungle-clad hillside, he had a clear line of sight to the industrialised riverside in the valley below. He adjusted the focus until the lenses were filled with a sharp, close-up view of the huge factory that dominated the waterfront.

'Sun is hot. I repeat, sun is hot. Over.'

No kidding, thought Ken.

It was the pre-arranged signal to confirm that the Horseman had successfully laid the string of specialised low-explosive charges that would fracture an underwater pipeline, leaking thousands of gallons of organophosphate pesticide into the Tietê river.

He spoke into his radio. 'Roger that. Prepare for sunset. Over.'

'Received, Alpha. Willco. Out.'

Ken checked his Breitling watch, which had been a rare and expensive indulgence. 'Sunset' would take place in precisely twenty-seven minutes. It was the pre-agreed code word for the quiet detonation that would be triggered by the Third Horseman. By the time the leak was detected, the water supply to almost half of São Paulo's twenty million inhabitants — or however many the flu virus had spared — would have become highly toxic. Those who didn't die would almost certainly find themselves unable to reproduce.

Whilst this wasn't the most drastic of his Horsemen's antics, Ken derived a certain private satisfaction from knowing that his suggestion to Roger Vee of 'putting something in the water' all those years ago was finally coming to pass. And, let's face it, President Wentworth didn't care exactly *how* the population was reduced in countries other than America, as long as it took the pressure off resources and kept people too busy to target the US. If the flu pandemic was as serious as the sporadic news reports suggested, maybe Ken's whole operation was technically redundant… Not that he had any intention of aborting the mission.

Ken reflected on this dispassionately while he packed the binoculars away in his rucksack, along with his dog-eared copy of Ber van Perlo's *Field Guide to the Birds of Brazil*. He wiped his face again with the handkerchief, which bore an elaborate monogram of the initials JS. As far as the Brazilian authorities were concerned, Ken was a keen twitcher by the name of Jeffrey Sullivan. It was a perfect cover for this operation, although he had always hated birds and now hated São Paulo too. Still, the US government was funding his grand killing spree, within a couple of days he'd be back home in Washington prepping for the Fourth Horseman's mission and Roger Vee's dramatic downfall, and all the years of skulking in the shadows, of loneliness and waiting, would have been worthwhile. Even if he'd known that all commercial flights had been suspended, it probably wouldn't have dampened his spirits. Life was good… and about to get a whole lot better.

That evening was due to be Ken's last in São Paulo. The detonation had been confirmed and he'd be long gone by the time the water supplies became toxic. Having attended to the small matter of putting the Third Horseman out to grass in the same way as he'd done with Kyle Dempsey in Delhi and the guy in China — Ken couldn't recall his name — he showered at the hotel and then went out for dinner. During his birdwatching holiday, Ken had eaten regularly at a little place less than four blocks from the hotel. It wasn't great, but it was one of the few places still open, and they served a half-decent steak and had a surprisingly impressive wine list.

Only one more night in this cesspit of a city. He was in such a good mood that, on his way back, he threw a few coins onto the pavement for the urchins who hung around the more affluent districts begging for handouts. He left the starving children scrabbling on the dirty concrete and walked on, crossing the empty street to give the corpse of a female flu victim a wide berth.

On a sudden impulse, he took his mobile phone from his pocket and scrolled through his contact list to Roger Vee's home number, which he'd managed to find out some time ago. He looked at it occasionally, savouring the knowledge that he could intrude on Roger's peace of mind at the touch of a button. Tonight, the temptation to do so was a siren song in Ken's mind. Why not? Sure, a face-to-face meeting would have been ideal, but why deny himself this moment of gratification any longer? Besides, it was much safer than returning to the Phoenix building in New York and he'd still get to hear the shock in Roger's voice. Ken's usual self-discipline was taking a nap, thanks to the bottle of wine he'd enjoyed during his evening meal. He couldn't resist. He kept ambling slowly down the street, tapped the screen and held the phone to his ear.

'Hello?' The voice Ken knew so well spoke on the other end of the line.

'Roger.'

'Yes. Who is this?'

Ken had to suppress a boyish urge to giggle. 'I'm disappointed you don't recognise my voice. Although, it's been a while.'

'Sorry, no. Are you sure you have the right number?'

'Oh yes, I'm sure. You're the great Roger Vee, head of Phoenix, the humble do-gooder who's made a fortune from other people's misery.'

Roger was silent for a few long moments, and then… 'Howard?' There was a new, cold edge to his tone.

'Ah, there you go. I knew you'd catch up, sooner or later.'

'You murdered a good woman, someone I cared about. You'll pay for that. Justice will find you.'

'Oh, please. Spare me your pathetic promises of justice.' Ken was enjoying himself immensely. 'You can't touch me. No one can. I'm not the same person I was when you kicked me out of your precious little group, you know. You have no idea who I am now.'

'I know exactly who you are. You're a murderer and a coward.'

This time Ken laughed out loud. 'Well that's rich, coming from you.'

'What?'

'We'll get to that in a minute. First, I want you to know that your security guard died easily. She thought she was cleverer than me and that's the same mistake you've made. I'll never face trial for her murder because I have friends in extremely high places.'

Roger said, 'Sometimes it's more useful to have friends in low places.'

Abruptly, the line went dead. Had Roger hung up on him? How *dare* he? Ken was just getting started. He was only a block away from his hotel now and he crossed the deserted street, pressing redial as he walked.

Ahead, a scruffy teenage boy stepped out from a narrow gap between two buildings.

The youth held out his hands and pleaded pitifully, 'Um réal, senhor?'

Ken fished in his pocket, listening to the ringing tone of Roger's home phone. Why not get rid of the last of his loose change? He wouldn't be needing it.

The boy rewarded the benevolent tourist with a gap-toothed grin and took the coins in his left hand, then he punched Ken hard in the chest with his right and retreated a little way into the narrow alley.

'Hey! You ungrateful little—' Ken took a few steps after the beggar, still holding the ringing phone to his ear.

Something wasn't right. Ken didn't seem to have any strength in his legs and his head was swimming. His chest hurt where the boy had punched him, and he looked down. The handle of a knife was sticking out near the breast pocket of Ken's shirt. He lifted his head, squinting in the dim light of the alleyway, and frowned at the scrawny teenager who was loitering just out of reach.

'You have no idea who you're messing with,' Ken growled, trying to convey outrage and menace. The effort of speaking was excruciating.

He was going to throttle the kid. No doubt about that. But first he needed to lean against the wall, just for a minute. The phone slipped from his hand and clattered onto the cracked paving of the alley. He felt cold for the first time since he'd arrived in this godforsaken country. This couldn't be happening. Not like this. Ken was used to Hollywood endings. He hadn't even told Roger that he knew about the virus, not yet. And he damn well deserved that satisfaction. After everything. God, his chest really hurt. The pain and the cold were everything now. Someone would come. Soon. He slid down the wall until he was slumped on the filthy ground. So cold.

Ken's eyes closed. He heard no sirens, but somebody must have called an ambulance because he was vaguely aware of small hands undoing his expensive watch, removing his wallet, taking off his leather shoes. He hoped they'd pick up his phone. He still had to finish his conversation with Roger.

10:59:55

Dawn

More than once during the bleak no-man's-land between a Christmas that hadn't happened and a New Year that would go uncelebrated, I awoke to an unnatural hush and expected to see snow when I opened my bedroom curtains. There was none. Instead, it was shock and sadness that had settled on the world.

During that week and those that followed, there was a gradual realisation among the survivors that what had happened was stupendously, world-changingly massive. News networks quoted early estimates that the pandemic had claimed the lives of over four billion people worldwide. Approximately fifty-five percent of the total human population had been wiped out in under a month. The post-apocalyptic feeling dawned like a rising alien sun on those of us who were left.

I'd thought I was prepared. Well, as much as you could be for something like that. If nothing else, I'd known in advance roughly what to expect and had a little time to think about it, unlike most people. But it hit me nearly as hard as it hit everyone else, and possibly even harder in some ways because I'd been a party to it all. I should have known better. When Mum died, I'd thought I was ready for that. I'd known it was going to happen. Yet the reality of her absence from our lives had still hit me like a wrecking ball.

There was a sense that everyone was waiting for things to get back to normal, except that 'normal' had been pretty comprehensively redefined by the pandemic and was never going to be the same again. The survivors were forced to adjust, to recognise what really mattered. And it wasn't the things they had believed to be all-important. It wasn't jobs and money and being able to afford better houses, cars, clothes and holidays than your neighbours. It was life. It was the basics, the simple things. It was food and health and family. It was relationships and memories and experiences.

For now, at least, banks and building societies had suspended mortgage instalments and loan repayments. There were no moneylenders or debt collectors. With a sudden glut of houses and material goods literally there for the taking, there was no immediate *need* to earn money. Just as well, really, as there were fewer employers; many of the shops, factories and businesses that had temporarily closed would never open their doors again. People were forced to re-evaluate what to do with their lives, with their time, and many realised that what they'd been doing before was existing, not truly living.

Bureaucracy was gone, tumbled in an instant like a house of cards in a gust of wind. All the investors with their portfolios of stocks and shares in now-non-existent companies had lost everything: and yet they'd lost nothing. In truth they'd lost pieces of paper, numbers on a computer screen. I remembered Eve explaining it to the mop-haired guy at the Noobs' Conference. People had lost tokens for a monetary system that had been wiped out overnight, tokens for a game that nobody was playing any more. Those who could see that none of it had ever been real in the first place were able to move on. Those who had measured their whole lives by those fictional numbers were not.

There was an abundance of properties no longer needed by their previous occupants and, like human hermit crabs, people started scuttling around in search of more desirable homes as soon as they realised that there were unlikely to be any negative consequences, certainly in the short term. Families who had only been able to

313

afford small flats in the past could now take their pick of more spacious houses. Many did so, scrubbing the red circles off of their new front doors to denote their tenancy, although there wasn't the wholesale scramble that I would have predicted. I supposed there was probably a lingering fear that the virus might still be lurking among the soft furnishings of the dead, and perhaps some people found it too macabre or distasteful to pick over their deceased neighbours' belongings like vultures.

Others, adrift in a world they no longer recognised, gathered familiar things around themselves and clung to them as if they were a life-raft, unwilling to abandon the small comfort of a well-known environment. Dad was one of these. He refused to even consider leaving Cuthbert Street, despite the fact that there was no longer anything to keep us there. I wasn't remotely sentimental about the high-rise concrete box in which I'd grown up, but Dad seemed to believe that his cherished memories of Mum and of my childhood were somehow embedded in the flimsy walls of our unlovely building instead of being safely stored in his head and preserved in photos. So we stayed.

Things got worse before they got better. Although I'd never expected that the post-virus world would be perfect, it was disappointing to learn from news reports that Phoenix hadn't managed to wipe out all the idiots on the planet. There were ugly stories of violence erupting between a few morons who had set their sights on the same thing and deemed it worthy of fighting over. Shops selling electronics and jewellery were raided. What the hell were these imbeciles looting for? There was no market for fancy televisions and gold bracelets now that people could take their pick from the ample supply of such coveted luxuries, which were less desirable as a result of being readily attainable.

Clashes over food stocks had been anticipated and in many towns and cities the local authorities had assumed control of supermarkets and warehouses so that supplies could be doled out fairly sensibly. I wasn't surprised to read reports of panicking citizens, especially among first-world consumers who had absolutely no idea where to get food if it didn't come from a shop. Plenty of them would struggle if their dinners weren't pre-prepared for their convenience and neatly presented in attractive packaging; they wouldn't know where to start if you asked them to concoct a decent meal from raw ingredients, let alone being faced with the prospect of having to become hunter-gatherers in their barren concrete jungles. Securing ongoing food supplies was a priority for every community and, while that was being done, we were advised to freeze any remaining perishable essentials like bread, meat, and milk to avoid them being wasted.

Yet even at its worst, the world after Plan B was nothing like the doom-ridden post-apocalyptic depictions I'd seen in movies. As far as I knew, there weren't vicious gangs of bloodthirsty bikers terrorizing innocent travellers. There weren't unscrupulous crime lords controlling monopolies over key resources (apart from the local authorities). No, it soon became clear that our biggest short-term problems weren't dramatic enough for a Hollywood-style apocalypse; you didn't need many stunt-doubles or pyrotechnics to portray boredom and depression.

Phoenix had re-opened its offices early in January and I'd gone back to work, pleased to be doing something useful again and seeing my friends and colleagues. It was also a huge relief to be able to discuss the past few weeks with people who knew what had really happened, and I realised how isolated I'd felt being stuck at home with Dad. Now that the task of immunising people was over, we got busy reviewing all of the projects the company had been involved with before and establishing which of them were still needed.

The factory where Dad had worked stayed firmly closed, but I'd convinced myself that he ought to enjoy taking it easy for a while. After so many years on the night shift, he still tended to sleep during the day, and it was easy for me to ignore the signs that he wasn't coping.

One Friday afternoon towards the end of the month, I got home from work and the flat was quiet. I shut the front door silently, assuming that Dad must be snoozing. I heard a sniff as I tiptoed past the lounge and peered in, to see him sitting on the edge of the sofa with his head in his hands. He was wearing the same clothes he'd worn all week and he looked dishevelled, shrunken and utterly miserable.

'Dad? What's up?' I hesitated in the doorway.

'Oh, sorry Lou,' he said, sniffing again. 'I didn't hear you come in.' He looked up at me with such doleful eyes that my heart clenched.

'What's up?' I repeated, crossing the room to sit next to him.

'Nothing, son. I'm fine. Just a bit down in the dumps, that's all. Don't mind me.'

'I don't,' I said, and was rewarded with the ghost of a smile. 'C'mon Dad, talk to me. What's the matter?'

He gestured helplessly at the four walls. 'I'm not used to this. Just sitting here. I can't bear the silence, Lou. It's doing my head in. Even with the telly on. God, I'm not even making any sense.'

'It's fine, Dad. I get it.'

'What the hell am I gonna do? Looks like the factory's shut for good and it could be months before another job comes up, if ever. I just keep thinking, what's the point? You know? In carrying on, even. Honestly, you're the only thing left in this world to stop me wishing I'd died along with all the rest of 'em.'

'Don't say that.'

'Why not? It's true. Apart from you, I've got nothing left. No purpose.'

'What was your purpose before? To work at the factory? That wasn't a purpose, it was a way to earn a living. A *living*, Dad. Money to live your life with, not just pay the bills and sit in front of the TV until it's time to go and earn some more.'

He just looked at me mournfully, so I persuaded him to go and have a shower and put on some clean clothes while I delved in the kitchen cupboards for something I could cook for supper. By the time we sat down to eat my tuna and pasta creation, I'd had a brainwave.

'I reckon you should start a local football club, Dad. A new one.'

He stared at me, frowning. 'You what?'

'A football club. I was thinking about what you enjoy, what your interests are, and football was the first thing that came to mind.'

'Yeah but that's watching it. I haven't played for donkey's years.'

'You wouldn't have to play. You could coach. You know the game inside out, and there must be loads of youngsters around here who'd be interested. I bet some of your mates from the factory might be happy to get involved, too. They're probably at just as much of a loose end.'

'What do I know about starting a football team?' he said dismissively, but I could tell he was tempted by the idea.

'What's there to know? You spread the word and show a few kids how to kick a ball, and that's about it to begin with. It doesn't have to be anything fancy. You'd have something to do, you'd be seeing your mates and getting a bit of exercise, and you'd be doing a good thing for some of the people round here.'

We chatted about it all evening, and when I said goodnight he was starting to scribble lists of people he wanted to speak to and things he was going to do. I was relieved to see the positive transformation in him.

The whole world was beginning again and the last few hours had taught me the importance of seeing this as an opportunity. There would have to be lots of new beginnings — three and a half billion of them, in fact. And we were going to have to get a whole lot better at working together and supporting each other. There was plenty that needed doing, and doing it was the best way to avoid going stark raving mad.

I knew that Dad wasn't the only one struggling to come to terms with a different way of living, but I fell asleep feeling more optimistic about the future than I had for weeks. Naively, I assumed that most other people were probably also sensing that the worst was now behind us. I was about to find out that, for some, the dawn was still a little way off and they were enduring their very darkest hours of all.

10:59:56

Clouds

The next day, the first Saturday in February, I found myself thinking about Grace. Not that there was anything unusual in that; we'd become good friends and I often caught my thoughts drifting in her direction. She'd seemed oddly withdrawn since we'd been back at work and we hadn't had any opportunity for a private chat, and then yesterday Tomasz told us she'd phoned in sick.

We'd never had much contact outside work, but after breakfast I sent her a text message and she replied straight away.

Hey Grace. You feeling better?

Hi Louis. Not really but thanks for asking

I got little butterflies in my stomach, for no good reason. *What's up?*

Oh nothing. Everything. Meh.

How was I supposed to respond to that? *So… are you ill?*

I guess you could call it that, yeah

Maybe it was something embarrassing. *Want me to mind my own business?*

No

Well at least you've got the weekend to get better. Reckon you'll be in work on Monday?

Haha I doubt it

Was she seriously ill? I tried to sound casual. *Oh. That sucks.*

There was a delay before Grace replied.

Will you miss me?

I knew the answer to this one. *Yes*

Really?

Of course

A minute went by, feeling like longer, before my phone buzzed again.

You doing anything Lou?

You mean right now?

Yeah

Should I try to think of some cool activity I was about to engage in? Parkour? Abseiling? *Nope. Just chilling.*

Can we talk?

The internal butterflies came back. *Sure. Want me to call you?*

No. Can we meet?

Meet? Was she asking me on a date? Maybe I was getting ahead of myself. *Yeah, cool. I think the coffee shop in the High Street's open again now…?*

I don't want to be around other people. And I need to get out of here. Can I come to yours?

I looked at my room through fresh eyes, seeing the dated décor and the cheap furniture and the mess. *Um, yeah, I guess. It's not very nice… but you're welcome if you want.*

You live in Cuthbert Street, right?

How did she know that? I must have mentioned it. *Yes. Number 9. It's the building with all the graffiti on the front doors. 5th floor, flat 58. When d'you want to come over?*

Now. That ok?

Now? I'd been sitting on my bed but I leapt to my feet and picked up yesterday's socks and pants from the bedroom floor while I typed one-handed. *Sure*

See you soon then. 10 mins.

I quickly changed into my decent jeans and a clean sweater, gave my teeth a cursory scrub, and then rushed around tidying the flat as best I could. Dad grinned when he heard there was a girl coming to visit me, and he lent a hand with the housework. There'd been something weird about Grace's tone — not least the fact that she'd suggested meeting up — but I dismissed my odd sense of foreboding in my haste to gather dirty coffee mugs and straighten cushions.

She knocked very quietly on the front door, but I'd been listening out for her. I'll never forget how she looked that morning. It was one of those sharp, bright winter days and Grace was framed in the doorway with a shaft of sunlight kindling red flames in her dark hair. It was the first time I'd seen her with her hair down. She was bundled into a thick sheepskin flying jacket, with tight black jeans and black combat boots. Her breath made a halo in the frosty air. There were pink patches on her pale cheeks and there was trouble in her brown eyes.

I could sense Dad loitering behind me so I briefly made introductions. Then, on impulse, instead of inviting Grace in I grabbed my coat and joined her outside. It seemed perfectly natural to lead her up to my sanctuary on the rooftop, even though I'd never taken anyone else there. I found an upturned plastic crate for her to sit on and a broken wooden pallet for myself, and we leaned against the low structure in the middle of the roof that housed the lift machinery.

For a couple of minutes neither of us said a word. There was barely any warmth emanating from the wintry sun but, even so, it felt good to be outdoors after the stuffy flat. We watched the seagulls swooping and wheeling in the still air against a backdrop of clouds that looked like they'd been sculpted by some flamboyant chef, elaborate meringue confections in the pastel blue sky. I was starting to wonder how to break the silence when Grace spoke.

'Sorry to interrupt your weekend.'

'No, it's cool. Nothing to interrupt, really. I wasn't doing anything.' I wished I didn't sound so lame. 'It's good to see you.'

Grace was sitting with her hands thrust into her pockets, face tipped skyward, eyes closed. I noticed she had a few subtle freckles sprinkled across the bridge of her nose.

'So, are you still feeling ill?' I asked, when she didn't say anything.

'Kind of.' She took a deep sighing breath. 'It's nothing physical. It's just… I couldn't face work yesterday. I can't…' She stopped.

'Can't what?' I prompted gently.

'Did you see any bodies? Flu victims?'

'Yeah. I think most people did. Not close up, but I saw quite a few.'

'Who were they?' She still had her eyes closed.

'I don't know. I mean, I didn't know them. I saw a team of cleaners carrying a guy out of one of the flats on a stretcher. They'd put a sheet over him, but they were struggling a bit because he was a big bloke and the sheet had come half off his face. That was the first one. I saw a few like that. How 'bout you?'

'Mm. Same. The one I can't stop seeing is Alice. She was one of our neighbours, a few doors down the road. She used to babysit me sometimes when I was little.' Grace opened her eyes but turned her face slightly away from me. 'Just before Christmas, Mum asked me to deliver a card to Alice and check that she was okay. We used to sort of keep an eye on her because she was getting on a bit and she lived on her own. There was no answer when I rang her doorbell, so I dropped the card through the letterbox and then looked in through the lounge window. She was lying on the sofa and I… I thought she was asleep at first, but… her face was grey and kind of… *empty*… and I just knew…' She trailed off.

I wanted to comfort her and weighed my options. I wasn't sure she'd feel a pat on the arm through the sheepskin jacket, touching her leg seemed a bit forward, and I had no idea if she'd appreciate a hug. In the end I carried on being lame and merely said, 'It's always worse when it's someone you know, I guess.'

She rounded on me. 'You don't get it, do you? I should've vaccinated her! But I didn't. I forgot. I forgot about her, and now a good person is dead because of me. It's my fault! I was too busy being selfish and making sure my family and friends were protected, and then we had to get on with the immunisations in our sector and Alice wasn't in my sector so I never even thought about her. And later on it got to the point where I'd completely lost track of who I'd vaccinated and who I hadn't, and I was anxious not to waste the plasters by doing the same people more than once, but I should've remembered Alice. I should've! She was such a nice lady. And I keep seeing her empty dead face and knowing it's my fault. It would've been the easiest thing in the world for me to save her, the easiest thing, and I didn't do it.' Tears were rolling down Grace's cheeks and I put my hand on her sleeve whether she could feel it or not.

'I'm so sorry.' I had no idea what else to say, so I said it again. 'I'm so sorry.'

Grace shook her head. 'And now my brother's really, *really* upset—' She broke off, sobbing, fished a tissue out of her pocket and blew her nose.

'Because of Alice?' I asked, trying to be helpful. I didn't even know Grace had a brother.

'No, because of Greg! They've been best mates since primary school.' I assumed her brother's friend must have died too, but it was worse than that. 'He moved away for work, but they stayed really close. Cal was the best man when Greg and Fran got married.' Was Cal her brother, then? I was struggling to keep up but I just let her talk. 'Then they had Emma and they asked Cal if he'd be her godfather and even though we're not religious he was so chuffed. She was such a sweet little girl. And when the virus… When Fran and Emma both died… Well, Greg couldn't handle it. We heard on Thursday that they found his car and he must've… and now Cal's just… it's all too much, and he's just…'

The sobs took over and she buried her face in my chest. Suddenly I was rocking her in my arms, and I didn't even know how she'd got there. I desperately tried to think of something to say that would comfort her but came up empty.

'I wanted all this to happen, Louis. I *wanted* it. D'you remember? In the end I couldn't wait. And now it has, and it's awful. It's so awful. Everybody's too sad. I can't bear it. I thought Plan B would fix things, but everything's broken. More than ever. It's all broken. They've all gone and it's my fault. I should've… I'm sorry. I just want to go to sleep now and never wake up. Ugh, this bitter taste is disgusting. Makes you feel like throwing up.'

I stopped rocking her. 'What bitter taste?'

'It's disgusting.'

I held her at arm's length. Her head lolled forward. 'Grace? Grace!'

She looked up at me, frowning. 'You have birds in your hair.'

'Did you take something?'

'Why do you have birds in your hair?' She lifted her hand, then let it fall back into her lap.

'Listen, Grace. Tell me what you took. It's important.'

'Mum's sleeping pills. Lots. I wanna sleep.' She tried to return to the damp patch on my coat where she'd been nestled before, but I held her upright.

'How many? Grace, how many pills did you take? What were they called? Tell me!'

She made an incoherent sound and flopped against me.

My phone was downstairs in the flat. Not wanting to leave her alone, I searched the pockets of her jacket and found her mobile. Thank God. When I switched it on, I was prompted to enter an unlock code but there was a bypass feature for emergency calls. Heart pounding, I asked for an ambulance, briefly explained the situation and gave the address. When they asked for a flat number I told them I'd be waiting at the front entrance. Now all I had to do was pick Grace up and carry her down to the lift.

Well done, Louis. Well done for bringing a suicidal girl up onto the roof. Brilliant. My track record involving Grace and rooftops wasn't great, it had to be said.

I'd never picked up a girl before, in any sense of the term. Thankfully she was slumped on top of the crate that I'd given her as a seat, so it wasn't too difficult to lift her from there. I'd intended to sling her over my shoulder like I'd seen on TV, but it wasn't nearly as easy as people made it look, so I ended up carrying her in my arms like an overgrown baby. The stairs down to the top landing were tricky; the doorway was narrow and my passenger had way too many limbs sticking out at odd angles. She was fully unconscious now, heavy and uncooperative. The bulky sheepskin jacket didn't help, but I didn't remove it in case she got cold. I somehow made it to the lift, not daring to put her down, and rested her hip on the handrail to ease the burden while we descended creakily to the ground floor. There, I carried her out to the front steps and put her on the ground as gently as I could, then waited a couple of long minutes for the ambulance to arrive while I watched over her and gave her very strict instructions not to die.

10:59:57

Legacy

The medical staff quizzed me while they hooked Grace up to a drip and various monitors, then sent me back to the reception desk to provide her details; the ones I knew, anyway, which I realised weren't many. While I was wondering how to contact her parents, Grace's phone started buzzing in my pocket. The screen announced an incoming call from "Mum", which solved my immediate problem but gave me an unexpected stab of longing because I would never get a call from mine.

Grace's mum listened while I rapidly explained who I was, why I was answering her daughter's phone and what had happened. All she said was 'I'll be right there.' I asked if she could check her sleeping pills first and she phoned me back a couple of minutes later; she gave me the name of the drug to relay to the doctors and said she was pretty sure that no more than five or six tablets were missing.

It proved unnecessarily difficult to let my dad know where I was and what was going on. I very politely asked the woman at the reception counter — whose name was Barbara, according to the name badge pinned to the foothills of her intimidating bust — if I could possibly use her desk phone to make a very quick local call.

Barbara looked at me dubiously and said, 'I'm sorry, sir. You'll have to use your own phone.' She managed to make the 'sir' sound scathing rather than respectful. 'Outside,' she added firmly, efficiently conveying her strong disapproval of my previous use of a mobile phone in blatant defiance of the signs forbidding the use of mobile phones. The fact that my brief conversations with Grace's mum had potentially involved the small matter of life and death was clearly no excuse for my anarchic behaviour.

Understanding her scepticism, I explained that the device she'd seen me using wasn't mine and I was unable to make outgoing calls because I didn't know the unlock code.

'In that case, sir, there's a payphone on the second floor. Go to the end of this corridor, through the double d—'

Wanting to save some of Barbara's valuable time, I interrupted her directions and explained that I had no money on me, having had to bring my friend straight to hospital.

She eventually allowed me to make the call, muttering that she wasn't supposed to do so and was too busy to deal with such things. Anyone would think I'd asked her to donate one of her kidneys for my benefit. Resisting the temptation to point out that she could have saved plenty of her precious minutes by simply letting me use the phone in the first place, I dialled Dad's number. When I told him about Grace, he swore loudly in my ear and told me I seriously needed to work on my dating technique.

By the time Grace's parents and brother brought their anxious faces into the reception area I was able to give them the excellent news I'd had from the doctors that she was going to be fine, then I handed over Grace's phone and left.

There was no ambulance for the return journey and my only option was to walk the couple of miles across town back to Cuthbert Street. I didn't mind; the sun was still doing its best to take the edge off the day's chill and I had plenty to think about.

The familiar streets felt wide and alien now that they were no longer full of cars and pedestrians. A few of the strangers I passed waved or smiled at me; there was a cautious camaraderie among the survivors but it took some getting used to in an anonymous town like Mareton where people weren't in the habit of acknowledging each other's existence.

I saw a couple of flyers fixed to lamp-posts, advertising support groups for those who wanted to share their grief and talk about their experiences and loved ones. I was also aware that lots of towns and villages had established books of remembrance where people could create lasting records of local flu victims, and I could understand the desire to do so. Cheryl had mentioned that, in Much Wheadle, there was a big book in the village hall that contained a list of the inhabitants who'd died, with space for people to write comments. She'd told me that lots of the residents had added photographs and even embellished their entries with little poems and sketches. Somebody in Mareton had set up a social media page for the same purpose, which I supposed was a more modern approach but it seemed less of a tribute somehow.

As well as sharing their sorrow and their memories, the survivors were united by the realisation that the threat had passed and they needed to get on with their lives. I had a sense that the initial shock of what had happened was starting to ebb and people were beginning to look to the future. As if to prove the point, I caught the sound of laughter as I walked past a house. It was something I hadn't heard in ages.

I turned the corner into Jackson Street, absorbed in my thoughts. Red circles glared at me reproachfully from the majority of the doors. The icy breeze was stronger here and I hunched deeper into my coat and picked up my pace. Nearly home.

I was pleased that I'd handled the morning's crisis reasonably well and got Grace to hospital quickly without panicking. I'd always liked to imagine I'd stay calm in an emergency, but you never knew for sure until one actually came along. Although, come to think of it, there had been a few lately. I reflected on what had happened with Grace, conscious that it had affected me deeply in lots of ways. It had made me think about how much I really would miss her if she wasn't in my life. It had caused some of my long-buried emotions about Mum's death to resurface. And it had pierced the armour that I hadn't even realised I'd been wearing. The scale of the flu pandemic had had a numbing effect on me. So many people had died that life seemed cheap and arbitrary. The Phoenix counselling sessions had urged us to focus on the positives — those we'd saved — but in the end I'd immunised hundreds of people and felt distanced from them too, and carrying the secret of Plan B had isolated me even further. Everything that had been happening was so huge, so much bigger than any of us, that individual stories and personal tragedies had become blurred and trivial. Almost losing Grace had somehow brought everything back into focus because she *mattered* to me. Recognising that fact made me feel scared and relieved all over again.

I walked on, purposely calling to mind some of the individuals I'd immunised: a black-clad teenager who'd picked up a piece of someone else's litter and put it in a bin... a woman who'd reached something down from a supermarket shelf for a disabled man... the elderly couple in the post office... they all had their own stories. They were all important to someone. Personal stories were what made us human. We all lived and died; it was the details — the things we thought and said and did along the way — that made the difference, that defined us, that made our lives matter.

I stopped and looked around, momentarily disorientated, and realised I was at the far end of Cuthbert Street and must have walked straight past my own building.

*

By mid-March there was a definite feeling of spring in the air, of things itching to grow after lying dormant for too long, even in Mareton where trees were an endangered species.

In the news there were fewer reports of violence and suicides, looting and destruction, and more stories about communities that were re-establishing themselves. I watched a piece about a town in Suffolk where the residents had gathered to discuss the skills and resources they possessed between them and were now successfully operating an exchange system where people gave their time, expertise or labour in return for food, laundry and other services.

'We've gone back to traditional values, working together. We might never need money again!' exclaimed an enthusiastic gardener at the end of the item, brandishing a fistful of home-grown vegetables on cue and giving an awkward cheesy grin to the camera as he symbolically exchanged his carrots and onions for a loaf of bread baked by one of his neighbours.

I was pretty sure money was going to come back into fashion sooner rather than later, but there was certainly a lot to be said for a simpler way of life and helping each other out a bit more.

Plan B wasn't over yet. Tomasz had told us in February that the final phase was to try and ensure the remaining population's chances of success, but even he didn't know exactly how the company intended to achieve that. There had been a lot of chat in the office about how — and whether — it could be done, with most of us assuming it meant that Phoenix would continue lobbying and campaigning as it had done before. Now, hopefully, people would be more willing to listen, and the company wouldn't just be yelling at cows.

There was also 'PV1'.

PV1 was an hour-long film that Phoenix had commissioned. It eloquently summarised the world-changing impact of the pandemic and the opportunity it represented for the human race to make a fresh start. In this first post-virus year that gave the film its title, stunning footage and an impressive cast of world leaders and respected personalities were employed to urge everyone to learn from the mistakes of the past. It didn't preach, dictate or patronise; it informed and inspired.

PV1 was broadcast all over the world, with subtitles, at the end of March, and remained freely available online after that. The film was an unprecedented global collaboration with no national, religious or political agendas. Influential people representing every continent had united to convey a single important message to all humankind.

It was compelling viewing, brilliantly done, powerful and perfectly timed, and for weeks afterwards everybody was quoting from the film and talking about the parts of it that had made the most impact on them.

The familiar voice of a renowned presenter of nature documentaries summarised the impact of overpopulation on the environment while beautiful images of plants and animals and wild habitats filled the screen.

'We've spent billions searching for life on other planets when we've barely begun to appreciate the life on this one,' he said. 'We'll never know how many other species have already become extinct as a direct result of our actions, including many that we'd never even discovered. We still understand so little about the capabilities of other animals, many of which touch on the things that we believe differentiate us as humans. Bees have a sophisticated communication system, dogs can detect certain illnesses, elephants grieve and console each other when members of their herd die, fish and birds navigate their way across vast distances. And yet, despite these incredible feats and behaviours and countless others like them, we jump to the conclusion that animals aren't as clever and sophisticated as humans. In *assuming* our own intelligence, we are merely *proving* our own ignorance. The world is teeming with miracles and — if we truly *are* intelligent — we will seize this fresh opportunity to discover more of them.'

Another segment featured a much-loved actor who'd originally made his name starring in a movie that was on everyone's list of favourites. He said passionately, 'This whole thing needs to be a massive wake-up call for us. We need to recognise that we'd become like a bunch of lazy, spoiled kids. I think most of us just took it for granted that we could simply buy whatever we wanted and there'd be an infinite supply. We're not used to being accountable for the basic necessities of life. We've grown too complacent to bother about living in harmony with our environment.'

Fascinating behind-the-scenes footage from the filming of his movie were shown as he continued. 'When we were making that movie, I had the amazing privilege of spending time with the Mbuti tribespeople in Africa and I learned… wow, such a lot. That experience literally changed my whole perspective. They're so much better than we are at keeping things in balance because they *have* to be, you know? They have a far greater respect for nature than we do. The forest is absolutely sacred to them. I mean, they refer to it as "mother". Whenever they forage and hunt, they make sure they leave enough plants and animals behind to regenerate what they've taken, knowing that, if they don't, there'll be no more to take in the future. When they kill an animal, they're thankful for its sacrifice and they don't just eat the meat, they use every possible part of that creature for some purpose. They don't waste anything. Man, it really opened my eyes.

'Before I made that movie, I would've looked at people like that and called them primitive. I thought I was so much smarter. But then I met these eight-year-olds who had so many cool skills and so much knowledge about their world and I was like, what do I know? These kids know really important stuff and all I know is how to learn my lines and which buttons to press on the microwave when I want to make popcorn. I think we've all lost sight of what really matters. And maybe this pandemic was nature's way of restoring the balance.'

The new American president also appeared in PV1, as did several other world leaders. Dan Sagan had been Charles Wentworth's vice president and, despite over-whitened teeth and a slightly cringeworthy flair for the dramatic, he'd already shown signs that he would be a more solid and shrewd statesman than his predecessor.

'Like it or not, we've turned the page on a new chapter in human history, and now it's up to each and every one of us to write that story. We owe it to ourselves, to those we've lost and to future generations to give it a happy ending. I think we all have to be honest and acknowledge that that was never going to be the case before. We've gotta be the best we can possibly be. The funeral pyres have finally stopped burning and now, from the ashes, a new civilisation can arise, perhaps one truly deserving of the name.'

Although I knew that PV1 had been Phoenix's brainchild, their only obvious involvement was an appearance by Roger Vee.

'Above all, we need a conscience,' he said, over tragic footage of polluted oceans and burning forests. 'We've got to learn from our mistakes. We need to use our resources more wisely, be less wasteful, ban the use of non-recyclable plastics, clean up our act. But the single biggest mistake we could make right now is to think we don't need to control population growth. Even though the virus has reduced our numbers by more than half, the human race is only looking at a brighter future if we can maintain the total population at its *current* level. It would be all too easy to underestimate how quickly things could end up right back where they were. The world population now stands at a little under three and a half billion. That's the same as it was in 1966, which means that just fifty or sixty years from now — well within the lifetime of today's children — we could be facing all of the same problems all over again. We must embrace this chance to make the world better than it was before, by working together to achieve and *maintain* a balance between the human population and the fragile, beautiful environment on which we depend for survival.

'Let me finish with a quote: "We humans are marching blindly towards our own certain doom, even though we have eyes to see the disastrous road that lies ahead and the knowledge and power to choose a different path. It is entirely within our capabilities to solve the current crisis of overpopulation, but we must act now. Only time will tell whether we are wise enough to save ourselves."

'Those words were written back in 1966, when the population was the same as it is now, and already regarded as a "crisis".'

*

By late summer, whole areas of large cities around the world had been abandoned. I noted the trends with interest as people instinctively congregated in certain hubs or migrated to smaller towns and villages, like casting off oversized clothes after a drastic diet and finding something that was a better fit. I understood that they found comfort in each other's company and felt lost in the concrete mazes of sprawling urban environments that were still liberally sprinkled with red circles denoting empty dwellings. I'd read about places where deserted blocks of flats had already been demolished so that the tortured ground could be replanted with grass and trees, although there would be plenty of decaying ghost towns left to crumble over time.

Dad had finally been persuaded to leave Cuthbert Street in June. In the end it wasn't my doing but Steve's, his old friend from the factory. They'd been spending more and more hours in each other's company and Steve had been instrumental in helping Dad to make a success of the Mareton Marlins, his fledgling football club. Steve lived near the recreation ground they used for their training sessions and made a point of mentioning what a shame it was that the semi-detached house next to his was standing empty.

I considered striking out on my own but decided to allow myself to get relocated along with the rest of Dad's fixtures and fittings. I was enjoying my grown-up relationship with him and wasn't yet sure where I belonged in the world. For now, I was happy working at Phoenix and seeing where life would take me.

One gloriously warm Saturday in early September, I rode my moped to Grace's house to pick her up. We'd been spending a lot more time together and, as she slipped deftly into her usual place on the seat behind me, I relished the familiar thrill of having her arms around my waist and her body close to mine. We'd arranged to go and visit Cheryl but I was early and, out of curiosity, I made a short detour to Cuthbert Street. In the couple of months since Dad and I had left, the few remaining inhabitants of the high-rise blocks had also departed and an air of melancholy and neglect had taken up residence. The doors and ground floor windows of my old home had been boarded up.

We parked the bike outside, took off our helmets and walked towards the entrance. I touched the rusting handrail and was briefly haunted by Flaky Ollie and his mates; I could almost hear them swearing over the rumble and clatter of their skateboards. An eddy of wind lifted the litter by the doorway into a quick spiral, and I was sure I got a waft of stale cigarette smoke.

'D'you feel weird coming back here?' Grace asked, kicking at a broken chunk of tarmac.

'I suppose,' I said, shrugging off the memories. 'It doesn't feel like home anymore. It's just a building.'

Weeds had already sprouted through every gap in the paving, and more cracks had appeared in the concrete. I stepped back and looked up towards the roof, remembering the countless times I'd sat up there seeking a little room to breathe and had gazed down on a different world. I knew we were both remembering Grace's one and only previous visit, too, but we'd long since talked those demons to death.

I sighed. Cuthbert Street was finally filled with the silence I'd yearned for, but I still felt claustrophobic. Wherever I belonged now, it wasn't here. It had never been here.

We rode to Much Wheadle, enjoying the space and the speed and the sunshine, and the boundless freedom you feel when you're young and you have a whole world to explore and a lifetime in which to do it.

Later that afternoon, Cheryl sent the two of us off for a walk while she prepared supper. The countryside around the village was lush and green, full of birdsong and the scuffling of unseen things. We wandered through a swaying meadow and sat down under a big oak tree, then lay back in the long grass, talking about everything and nothing, and watching the way the soft breeze made the leaves flicker against the blue sky. It was a perfect day.

Heading back up the lane that would lead us to Cheryl's cottage, Grace stopped beside a field of grazing cattle while she removed a stone from her shoe. I climbed on the fence.

'Hey cows!' I yelled.

Most of them ignored me completely. They pretended I wasn't there and just carried right on munching grass like they hadn't even heard me at all. Some of them looked up and stared at me like I was some kind of weirdo for a few seconds before they put their heads back down and carried on. And a few of them acted startled, skittered away a little bit, and then stood there chewing, keeping a wary eye on me like I was definitely not to be trusted and probably dangerous. But before long they went right back to munching grass, like nothing had ever happened.

The End

10:59:58

Obituaries and Footnotes

Washington, USA

The popular rumour that President Charles Wentworth died sitting on a toilet in the White House with his expensive trousers around his presidential ankles was entirely true.

Research Vessel Phoenix, *Arctic Circle*

Don 'Mac' McIntyre and Steve 'Creepy' Crawley survived the pandemic, together with the two new research assistants who happened to be with them on their next voyage. There weren't many places on Earth that were beyond the reach of the virus, but a small boat puttering along off the shrinking coastline of Greenland was one of them.

Mac still makes a mean hot toddy.

North Korea

No one knows what became of Ri Joo-Won or his friend and colleague Mun Chong-Hae. North Korea keeps its secrets, and freedom is still a forbidden dream. However, the classified nuclear facility was mothballed after the pandemic and the missiles lie rusting in their silos.

London, England

Jack West would have been satisfied with his funeral. He was one of the very first victims of the virus, so the mourners were unaware of the risks and the ceremony was well attended. Jack would have particularly appreciated the moving eulogy given by his father, in which Malcolm West spoke of how proud he and his wife Caroline had always been of their son's achievements and their certainty that he would have gone on to great things, had the mystery illness not snatched him away in his prime. Malcolm didn't mention that Jack had died in police custody, or that an inquiry was ongoing.

Twenty-seven people caught the virus at Jack's funeral, including Malcolm and Caroline. Elise and her husband Mark survived, and Elise always remembered her brother fondly.

The Right Honourable Philip Deakins MP succumbed to the virus with uncharacteristic efficiency while he was out to lunch with his new secretary.

After his former secretary, Jayne, resigned, he had advertised for a replacement, casting only a cursory glance over the candidates' CVs. Oddly, all of the shortlisted applicants were female. Deakins was more diligent when it came to appraising their physical appearance, although it was, presumably, a coincidence that he happened to select the one who wore the shortest skirt to the interview.

He insisted on taking his new assistant out for a working lunch once a week, which she didn't mind at all. On his last day as Secretary of State for the Environment — it being his last day as a living member of the human race — he had woken up feeling 'a bit iffy', as he described it to his wife.

At lunchtime, Deakins still felt rather off-colour, but that didn't stop him conquering both a substantial starter and a daunting main course. He attributed his rising temperature to the stuffiness of the restaurant and the low-cut top that his companion was wearing. He ordered dessert and — while his secretary was visiting the ladies' room — collapsed face-first into a generous bowlful of spotted dick and custard.

Deonar Dumping Ground, Mumbai, India

Kamya did not survive the pandemic. She was seven years old, which was a very young age to die, even for a ragpicker.

In the early mornings, beams of hazy sunlight still reach out to touch the towering dunes of rubbish as if they are something beautiful, and you can even pretend they are real mountains. That's when you often see the bright yellow butterflies.

10:59:59

Author's Note

I wrote Louis's story two years *before* the COVID-19 pandemic. I wrote it to stimulate debate, to raise awareness, to present some uncomfortable truths in an accessible and entertaining way to a new generation, and to encourage readers to make informed choices about the future of their world. I make no claim to be an expert. And of course I would never advocate or condone the murder of billions of people, or even one person, come to that.

Researching for this book was fascinating, depressing, encouraging, infuriating and terrifying. It is, I hope, sobering to think that the facts and figures I've used are all based on truth, and that some are already out of date. Even so, it isn't too late for Plan A.

The issue of overpopulation is more than an elephant in the room. It's a tidal wave. Within my own lifetime, it has changed from being a looming shadow on some distant future horizon, to an imminent threat towering over all of us. Yet *still* we studiously pretend it isn't there. It's a problem that was being frantically flagged many decades ago using words like 'urgency', 'desperate', and 'cataclysm', yet *still* too few of us are talking about it. We must break the taboo of discussing population control and remove the blinkers of economic growth, short-term priorities and misplaced political correctness. None of those will be worth a damn in a world on the far side of ecological collapse, and we are closer to that than most people realise.

Many choose to see discussions about population control as some kind of personal attack and they respond defensively by pointing fingers, apportioning blame, and labelling those who try to raise the topic as elitist scaremongers. The human race is in denial. We're not *in* traffic, we *are* traffic. It takes longer to get medical treatment not because health services are getting worse, but because they have to serve rapidly increasing numbers of people. There is evidence like this all around us, every day.

Some readers might hate me for writing this book. Some will conveniently dismiss and ignore everything in it. Some will call me a snob and a doom-merchant and assume that I'm a pessimistic misanthrope when, actually, that couldn't be further from the truth. I'm an optimist and a romantic. I believe in magic. I am awed by the beauty and potential of the human mind and spirit. And I think that, if you truly want to, creating new life and raising a child is one of the most wonderful things you can do during your time on Earth. The love and laughter I share with my own child, with my parents and with my extended family are precious to me beyond describing; they are the fair winds and gentle currents that have helped me navigate this far on my journey through life.

I also have a deep love for this world. The natural treasures that remain must be cherished and guarded. I know I'm not the only person who can see that humans are destroying our planet. I know I'm not the only person who yearns for wild untamed places, and who knows from seeking them out that they are undeniably becoming harder to find.

There's a saying that the Earth is not ours, we merely borrow it from our children. I want them to be able to swim in clear seas that are teeming with life and not clogged with waste plastic. I want them to be able to breathe clean air and drink fresh water. I want them to experience the thrill of seeing wild animals thriving in their natural habitats. I want them to know what it is to feel humbled by nature's scale and splendour. I want to leave them a world that hasn't been stripped of its beauty and diversity and resources. And I want them, in their turn, to appreciate and safeguard these precious gifts while they borrow them from their own children.

Driving Change

Overpopulation is not someone else's problem. It's *everyone's* problem. Things will not change until we all drive change.

As I said, I'm no expert, but here are just a few things most of us can do:

Challenge societal expectations. Think for yourself. If you decide to start (or increase) a family, do it because you've made an informed choice and it's what you really want to do, not just because it's what everyone else does.

Reduce. Re-use. Recycle. Repair. Refurbish. Repurpose. Re-home. Refill. Just 'Re' the hell out of things to minimise waste. Eat less meat. Don't drop litter.

Learn. Find out for yourself what's really happening in the world. Follow organisations like Population Matters and World Population Balance on social media. There are some useful links on my website: nrbakerwriter.com

Make your voice heard. Help to raise awareness. Lobby politicians to take action. Urge manufacturers to use less plastic packaging. Lend your support to campaigns for climate action, environment protection, sustainability, re-wilding initiatives, access to birth control and education. We all share one planet.

The challenges we've created for ourselves aren't completely insurmountable — not quite yet — but they become ever harder to address as the number of humans increases.

Instead of thinking that none of us can make a big enough difference to such massive problems, we need to recognise that the only way to solve them is if we all make small differences. The cumulative effect of seven and a half billion people making small differences… well, wouldn't that be something?

Did You Enjoy This Book?

If so, there are a couple of small things you can do that will make a huge difference.

The best way you can thank an author for writing a book you've enjoyed is to leave an honest review about it on your favourite bookish website or online store page. It's simple, it's free, and it needn't take you more than a few minutes, but you will have my sincerest gratitude and I love reading your comments.

Authors and independent publishers don't have the financial muscle to pay for high-profile advertisements. We rely on you, our readers, to spread the word. Reviews and ratings are enormously important in helping us to get our books noticed.

Please tell your friends and social media contacts if you enjoyed reading *10:59*. (Or, if you didn't enjoy it, maybe you wouldn't mind recommending it to people you don't like…)

Thank you SO much!

Warm regards,
Niki

Acknowledgements

Writing a book is a long, slow and solitary endeavour but, when your dreams of being published are finally coming true, you realise that you were part of a team, all along.

First and foremost, I am lucky enough to have the constant support and encouragement of my soulmate, Martin. Words are never enough.

I'm also immensely grateful to the family and friends who believed in me, especially those who were my guinea pigs for early versions of the book: Connor Bentham, Sharon Daly, Jen Haken, Cheryl Palframan and Lisa Wilkinson.

Thank you to my test readers for their unbiased reviews and valuable feedback. These included members of Judith Bovington's reading group at Chipping Norton School in Oxfordshire: Cadence James, Tristan Peissel and Morgan Wollerton.

Thank you to my beta readers: Alison, Andreas, Andrew, Cynthia, David, Fi, Joyce and Richard.

And of course, you wouldn't be reading this without my wonderful publishers, Simon Finnie and Pete Oxley at Burning Chair, whose enthusiasm and professionalism have made the long road to publication such a pleasure to travel.

Last — and by no means least — thank YOU. Thank you for buying my book and reading my words. Thank you for sharing Louis's journey. And thank you in advance for not just going right back to munching grass as if nothing ever happened.

About the Author

Niki Baker is an explorer. She doesn't have Sherpas or a frozen moustache, she's just got incurable wanderlust. Whether it's the mountains of Albania, the islands of Indonesia or the jungles of Guatemala, she has always been happiest when she's far off the beaten track.

Niki also loves exploring the power of words and spent much of her childhood up a tree in Somerset with her head in a book, either lost in the worlds created by authors like C.S. Lewis, or writing truly awful tales of her own.

Since then she has earned recognition for her travel writing, poetry, lyrics, flash fiction and short stories. *10:59* is her first full-length novel.

Niki lives in rural France with her soulmate, who is also a writer.

Follow N R Baker
Web: NRBakerWriter.com
Twitter: @NRBakerWriter
Facebook: @NRBakerWriter

About Burning Chair

Burning Chair is an independent publishing company based in the UK, but covering readers and authors around the globe. We are passionate about both writing and reading books and, at our core, we just want to get great books out to the world.

Our aim is to offer something exciting; something innovative; something that puts the author and their book first. From first class editing to cutting edge marketing and promotion, we provide the care and attention that makes sure every book fulfils its potential.

We are:

Different

Passionate

Nimble and cutting edge

Invested in our authors' success

If you're an author and would like to know more about our submissions requirements and receive our free guide to book publishing, visit:

www.burningchairpublishing.com

If you're a reader and are interested in hearing more about our books, being the first to hear about our new releases or great offers, or becoming a beta reader for us, please visit:

www.burningchairpublishing.com

Other Books by Burning Chair Publishing

10:59

10:59

Printed in Great Britain
by Amazon